ELLEN

FINDING A ROOM CAN BE MURDER

JECA CAMPION

Created with Vellum

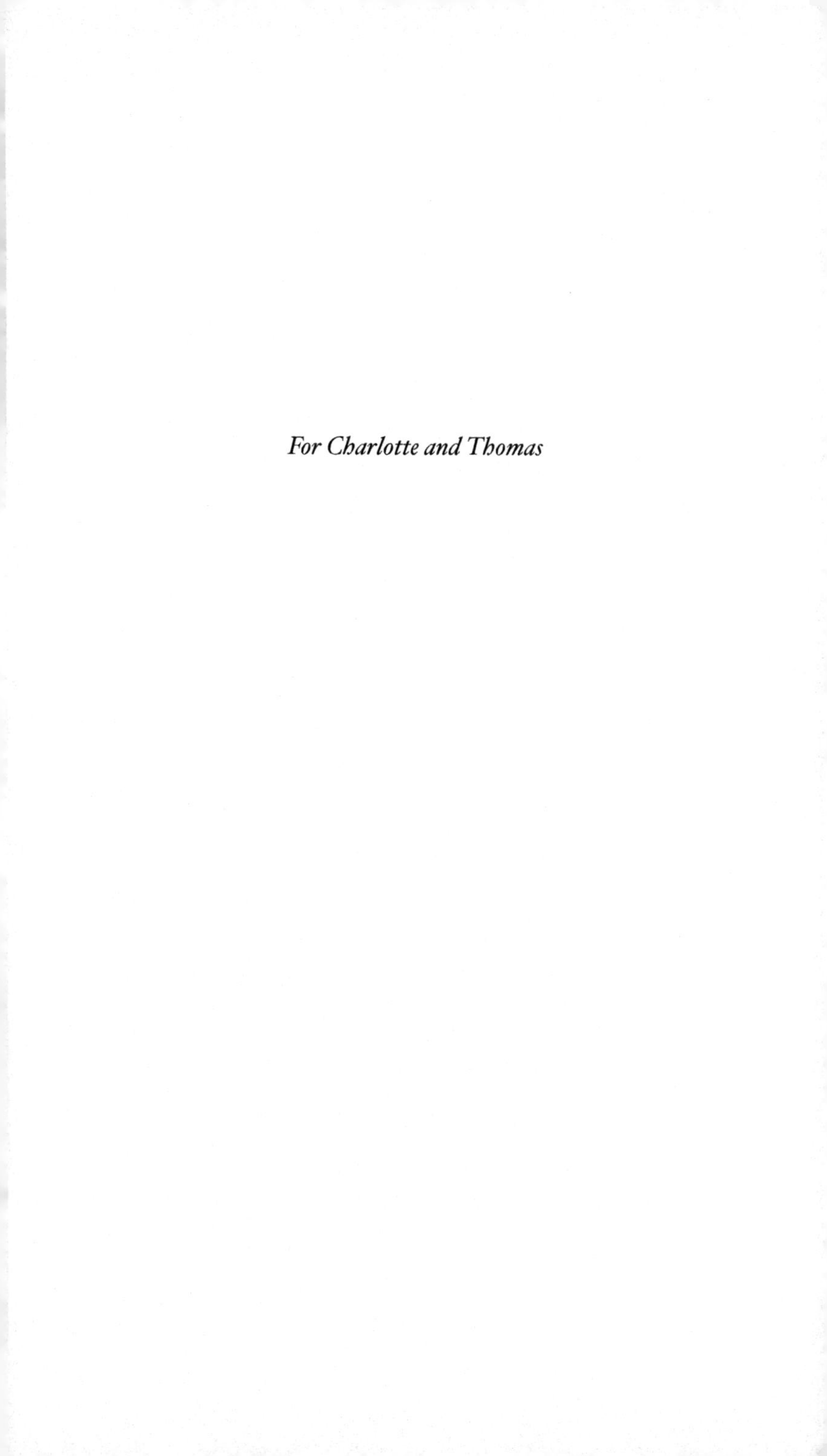

For Charlotte and Thomas

The soul that has conceived one wickedness can nurse no good thereafter - Sophocles

PREFACE

When Steven Finn takes a room in Blanche Hunt's Chiswick mausoleum, his presence soon ignites a simmering obsession in Ellen, Blanche's damaged daughter. A rivalry for his affections between the two women results in deadly consequences for Blanche - and this is just the beginning.

In a devastating illustration of, 'If I can't have him, no one will', Ellen systematically destroys all perceived competition and Steven's life in the process.

PROLOGUE

THE DULL, repetitive thud that brought her up the warped, narrow staircase has stopped. Only the half-hearted buzz of a wasp breaks the silence now, but the little girl remains in the doorway, thumb wedged in her mouth, heart skittering in her chest.

It was a room whose secret she had long been curious to discover but it was a room that had always been locked - until today.

Today, the large brass knob turns easily beneath her small hand and when she gives a push, the door swings inwards revealing a low, cracked ceiling and sunlight filtering in through two grimy windows.

No one here.

But still, she hesitates on the threshold, eyes searching the shadowy eaves where afternoon heat gathers and swells.

No one here at all, silly, she murmurs and finally reassured, she steps inside.

Crossing dusty boards, she winds her way amongst the clutter. Negotiating broken chairs, cracked mirrors, leather packing cases, sagging armchairs, ancient TVs and an old bath overflowing with business files and yellowing invoices.

Perspiration beads her upper lip as she peers -inside boxes stuffed with faded paperbacks, old thermos flasks and dusty tubes of tennis balls. Good places to hide a secret - if you have one.

Feeling a nervous guilt, ears attuned for the sound of footsteps coming up the stairs, she rummages more quickly now but as she reaches the last box, disappointment as dry as dust, lodges in her throat. *There's no secret here* she whispers. *The only thing kept locked in this room is junk!*

And then she feels more anger than disappointment and swiping at the hair sticking to her damp face she stamps back along the furrowed strips of bare board and it's *because* she is so angry that she doesn't hear it - not at first - the gurgling sound. The second time it comes, she *does* hear. The sound is coming from *inside* the wardrobe she realises, the one standing against the far wall but instead of bolting for the door, she freezes, and the shriek never leaves her lips. because suddenly she knows the dry gurgling sound *is* the secret, and she also knows that should she scream or run, whatever dark, frightful thing hiding there, will leap out and spring after her.

Turning slowly, eyes wide and staring she watches the wardrobe door shudder slowly open and even though in these last moments her interest in all things *secret* has been lost forever and she really, *really* doesn't want to see – it's too late, the door is hanging open like a mouth and inside...*inside* is a man.

He swings slowly on a belt, bent knees grazing the wardrobe floor. But the rest of what she sees can make no sense to a little girl of six. She doesn't understand why there is plastic stuff wrapped around his face or rope winding around his thighs and ...*there*.

And it is only then, when she sees his flattened features

struggling for air, mouth feebly sucking in and out, in and out, that a scream finally rips from her throat and as the slumped figure gives its last choking gasp, she claws her nails into the soft flesh of her cheeks and whispers in a terrified voice; *'Daddy?'*

1

Blanche Hunt heaved her bulk into the rear of the Mercedes, bringing with her the stink of cigarettes and booze. Steven glanced into the rear-view mirror, patient while she fastened her seatbelt and crossed short legs.

'Where to, madam?'

Blanche gave her destination. 'Long time since anyone called me, Madam,' she added, dimples winking. It was a coquettish smile and together with the heavy-handed blusher the overall effect was of a grotesque, elderly doll.

'All part of the service,' Steven replied, his features quickly settling into their customary business-like mask. *The woman was sixty if she was a day.*

'Well, that's very nice to know,' Blanche replied. 'Service is something I don't seem to get much of these days.'

Steven glanced into the mirror again, saw the amused eyes bright with meaning and resigned himself to double-entendres all the way to Chiswick.

. . .

LIGHT WAS FADING as they cruised slowly down Briarwood Road. It was a wide street, tree-lined and flanked on either side by large, detached properties. Quiet. Just a few parked cars drifted with fallen leaves.

'It's this one.' Blanche said suddenly, pointing to a large pale brick mansion set back behind weary rhododendrons.

Steven pulled into the kerb and stared up at the house. It loomed impressively against a darkening sky, and he was just able to make out shallow steps leading up to a wide, solid looking front door and an elaborately carved entrance porch.

On the second floor above the large bay, ran a crenulated parapet, bringing to mind a fortress or medieval castle. The architect's intention no doubt. It was a whimsical addition, but Steven liked it. He liked the whole house. It was the kind of house he intended to own one day. 'These grand old Victorian properties should be listed,' he said. 'Protected in some way.'

Blanche smiled. 'It was a picture once. Painted inside and out every other year. Gardener twice a week. My husband insisted upon it, while he was alive. Still,' Blanche continued brightly, pressing the exact fare into Stephen's hand 'you've got to push on haven't you? I started letting rooms after Stan passed away - just to fill the place up a bit. But of course, it helps on the financial side, too.'

Steven turned around. 'I'm looking for a room.'

A flush crept up Blanche's throat at her first clear view of her driver's face. 'Oh?'

'Yeah. I'm staying with a friend at the moment. Not exactly ideal.'

'Well, no, I don't suppose it is ... but you see we have this rule -' Blanche broke off, thought for a moment, then said quickly; 'as it happens my German student is leaving at the end of the month. She's got the ground floor front with the bay. Lovely room. Big. South-facing. No harm you taking a peek, if you have the time.'

Steven followed Blanche's clicking heels up the short pathway and waited as she dug around in her bag for her keys. A cold wind greeted him, rushing around the side of the house and bringing with it the smell of damp leaves. Jamming his hands into his pockets he glanced around. Light was spilling out from the bay, illuminating the garden where a large tree hulked in one corner, its gnarled branches thrown up to the sky. Also, visible now was a general neglect not obvious from the road. But undeterred by rotting windowsills and sagging gutters, Steven stepped into the cavernous hallway.

Crossing an impressive black and white chequered floor, Blanche knocked on a door to their left. As they waited beneath the wan light of a chandelier, Steven took in a curved grand staircase sweeping up into darkness then turned to see a tall thin girl with a pallid complexion standing in her doorway.

'Someone to see your room, Anke,' Blanche announced, barging past.

Anke fixed her eyes upon Steven. 'It's okay,' she said, 'you can come.'

Giving her an apologetic smile, he stepped inside what he guessed was once the grandest room in the house. Even the behemoth antique bed with its bulging contours was rendered insignificant in so much space. He decided not to play it cool; pretend he wasn't smitten. Feeling a dull thud of excitement, he admired the original architrave and the ornate marble fireplace that dominated one wall.

Blanche, quick to pick up on his enthusiasm, led him to the bay and pointed out delicate pastoral scenes adorning the top panes. 'Done by hand, those paintings. Someone famous. There's a signature in the right-hand corner, see?'

Steven dutifully leant forward and peered, but it was when he gazed up at the ridiculously high ceiling, where cherubs peeped amongst mouldings of fruit and trailing vines that he was completely sold. Yes, the room was, in estate agents speak, 'tired', he could live with that, but he was under no illusions, faded grandeur came at a price.

'Take your time, dear,' Blanche invited.

'The name's Finn.'

'Sit down, Finn. Get a feel of the place. Take in the ambience. Anke! Stop gawking and move that tennis bat.'

'It's *Steven* Finn and if the room's available, I'll take it,' he said.

BACK IN THE HALLWAY, Steven handed Blanche his card. Dipping into her crepey décolletage Blanche retrieved glasses attached to a dainty chain. '*Executive Limousines*,' she read aloud. '*Contract and private hire. Airport specialists. Twenty-four-hour service*. Well, that pretty much covers every aspect!' She gave him a playful nudge. 'I see you're an entrepreneur, Steve, like me.'

Steven nodded. 'Business is good despite the downturn. Perhaps you could leave the card on your hall table; it may be useful for the other tenants.'

'Good idea! I'm not one to miss a trick myself. My Stan was in business too, you know. *Plastics*. There was a lot of money to be made in plastics in the eighties. Now then, Steve, I'm not a stickler where it comes to rules, I prefer to run a happy ship, but I may as well mention the few we do have in place.'

'Go ahead.'

'*No* electric fires. Not since the council stuck their oar in, and anyway the central heating is perfectly adequate. Music only to be played at a level that does not disturb other residents. Miss King oversteps the mark on occasions but she's deaf – or pretends to be when it suits her. Oh, and rent paid on the button, no exceptions.' She cut him a sideways glance. 'Does that all sound okay to you, Steve?'

'Fine.'

'Good. Now, such a lovely room does come at a premium of course…' Blanche was all business now and Steven caught a glint of avarice in her eyes as she named the figure. He winced inwardly. It was almost three times what he was paying to flat-share above a phone shop in Ealing, but it was too late now. Already in love with the room he was determined to have it.

'Inclusive of bills of course,' Blanche added quickly. 'I'm Blanche Hunt. Let me give you my number in case you change your mind.'

'There's no chance of that, Mrs Hunt,' Steven replied but he typed the number into his phone anyway.

'*Blanche*, please.'

As they shook hands Steven caught a flash of movement at the top of the stairs. Blanche continued to smile as heavy footfall crossed the landing followed by the violent banging of a door. Still smiling, Blanche said, 'That'll be Ellen.'

2

'SUCH FINESSE.' Blanche sighed as Ellen banged the breakfast tray down beside her and glared at her mother from beneath a lank fringe. 'Oh, Lord help me,' Blanche muttered, 'crack of dawn and she's got a cob on already. Got this to look forward to all day, have I?'

'You've broken the rule! '*NO MEN*'. It's what we said.'

'I know,' Blanche said, buttering her toast. 'So, shoot me.'

Ellen dug her hands into her cardigan pockets. 'So why *him?* What's so bloody special?'

Blanche grinned mischievously and licked her knife. 'I think you'll work that out for yourself. Film star looks, our Mr Finn, Ellen, and that's what they were in *my* day, Proper stars. With charisma. Not like that short one with the big nose, or the rest of the boring non-entities you get nowadays. Plus, Mr Finn has agreed to pay well over the odds and I'm not one to look a gift horse in the mouth. I can't afford to. Not with you to clothe and feed, year in, year out.'

~

IN A GROUND FLOOR flat in Acton, winter sunshine streamed into the small kitchen and eleven-month-old Luke sat in his highchair dribbling Weetabix and warm milk. Dust motes swirled in the sun's rays, and he grabbed at them with a dimpled fist.

'Come on, Lukey,' Caroline Shaw pleaded, scraping the cereal from his chin with a Tommee Tippee teaspoon and forcing it back into his mouth. Luke gave his mother a gummy grin and the Weetabix reappeared.

'Right, my boy, you've had your chance.' Caroline swept him up out of the chair and onto the draining board.

'Mmmf,' Luke said, twisting his face away as Caroline attempted a quick wipe with a warm flannel. A few minutes later, his one and only tooth brushed, they were ready. Except the keys were not in the bowl by the door. A panic-stricken search ensued; Luke bumping up and down on Caroline's hip as she ran from the kitchen to sitting room and back into the kitchen again. Finally, she found them - in the cutlery drawer. Dumped there last night when her sleep deprived brain had temporarily short-circuited. Grasping the keys and her bag she made for the door once more, hoping and praying the elderly Fiat would start first time. Recently It had developed an ominous wheeze that was beginning to sound terminal and if it died on her now - well, that was something it was best not think about.

Strapping Luke into his seat she slid behind the wheel. Mercifully the Fiat fired first time and they set off for the Little Angels Day Nursery. Caroline was blessed with a contented child. As she drove Luke burbled to himself and drummed his heels to Bruce Springsteen. She checked him in the mirror and despite being late - second time that week - and despite the road works - that she hadn't allowed for, she beamed him an adoring smile.

Ten minutes later they pulled into the nursery's parking

bay and Caroline delivered her son into the arms of a waiting nursery attendant. Behind the wheel once more she raced on to her destination, a small primary school in Little Ealing. Keeping her eyes on the road, she fished into her bag and as her fingers closed over a business card her stomach flipped. Seeing Steven again was not a prospect she relished, but pride, she had finally been forced to accept, was a luxury she could no longer afford. He would be less than ecstatic at seeing her, too, of course. Particularly once she dropped the megaton bombshell, she'd naively hoped would remain her secret forever.

3

STEVEN MOVED into Briarwood Road at the end of the month. Once he'd hung his clothes, he rooted around in various black bags for bedding then unpacked his weights and emptied a box of books into the bookcase. Finally, he hunted down the aerial and began tuning his small, flat-screen.

Blanche hovered in the hallway. 'Give me a shout if you need more hangers, Steve. Miss King opposite's got more than her fair share.'

Steven thanked her, then softly closed his door. Turning around he surveyed his worldly possessions and at thirty-four years found it mildly depressing their entirety consisted of only one carload. But until now he'd led an itinerant life, moving from one crappy furnished flat to another, and the need to accumulate *stuff* just hadn't been there. The exception was clothes. His one indulgence. He liked good and he liked expensive, gravitating towards the few designers whose clothes complimented his athletic build.

Going to the chest he pulled out the top drawer and checked inside. It was clean enough. After transferring socks and underwear from his sports bag, he then glanced around the room, acknowledging that for the moment, he was content enough. This house was somewhere he intended to put down some roots, until the business was really established, then, in a few years time he'd get a place of his own. That was the plan.

Gazing out of the window he checked the weather, something cabbies did all the time. Light was already draining from a colourless sky and the wind had picked up to a faint moan. The sudden tap of a skeletal branch against the glass, made him start and it was then he realised he was cold. Not just cold, *chilled.*

He moved the curtains aside, expecting to see an open window, but each catch was fastened. The room must have been cold all along, he decided; he'd just been too pre-occupied to notice.

Setting the alarm on his mobile, he pulled on a sweater and got into bed. Another thing cabbies always did, seize any opportunity to catch up on lost sleep. Bunching a pillow beneath his head he gazed up at the absurdly fanciful ceiling. Finally, his luck had taken a turn for the better and his last conscious thought as he drifted off to sleep was, *about fucking time.*

~

HE WAS on his way to the bathroom several hours later when an elderly woman in the hallway gave him a welcoming smile and introduced herself.

'Cecily King. You must be Steven? Blanche has told me all about you. I do hope you settle quickly and that your stay will be a happy one.'

'Thanks.'

'I've been here so long I've become a permanent fixture but—' The old lady broke off as a dark-haired girl came thumping down the stairs. 'Oh, this is Ellen, Blanche's daughter. 'Ellen! This is our new tenant, Steven...'

Steven stuck out his hand.

Ellen ignored it. 'I *know* who he is,' the girl snapped and shouldering her way between them she dashed for the front door and slammed it behind her.

Steven turned to Miss King eyebrows raised.

Miss King smiled. 'I can only assume that's not the effect you normally have on women,' she said buttoning her coat, 'but social graces are not exactly Ellen's strong point I'm afraid. But you'll get used to her.'

'Got your keys, Miss King?' Blanche's voice came from the top of the staircase.

The old lady fished in her pocket, drew them out and held them up in a thin, papery hand.

'Just checking, dear,' Blanche said.

Cecily King rolled her eyes at Steven and continued on her way out.

'I have to keep my eye on Miss King, Steve,' Blanche said, coming down the stairs. 'I hope she wasn't bothering you.'

'No.'

'Good! Best not to encourage her though. She can be a nuisance if you allow it.'

'I'll bear that in mind.'

'Coming to your room all hours, wanting a bit of company, that sort of thing.'

'Right.'

'Just thought I ought to warn you.'

'Yes. Thanks.'

'Have you met Alison yet?'

'No.'

Blanche nodded towards the door directly opposite his own. 'Lovely girl. Irish. Trainee nurse. You probably won't see much of her though; she works such long hours, poor dear.'

Drawing nearer, Blanche squeezed Steven's arm. 'Glad I caught you,' she said, breathing whisky fumes into his face (it was just past breakfast) 'what say you come up for a drink tonight? I make a point of getting to know all my tenants. You're more than just paying guests here.'

'That's nice to know.'

Blanche smoothed coiffed hair that through some chemical intervention had achieved the toxic shade of lemon curd. 'Shall we say eight-thirty then?'

Steven nodded. 'But I'll only have time for one. I'm working at nine.'

Blanche's made-up mouth puckered like a pug's bottom. 'Oh, well, we'll just have to get to know each other ever so quick then, won't we?'

~

STEVEN WAS in a magnanimous mood as he drove to his gym. Briarwood Road was working out well. No complaints so far. His shower had been long and satisfyingly hot and he'd eaten a late breakfast at the kitchen table in blissful solitude. Perhaps none of the other tenants used the communal kitchen during the morning. That would suit him just fine. Pushing an old Muddy Waters CD into the player he turned up the volume until the thudding bass notes shook the windows.

It was when he reached the top of Dukes Avenue that he saw Ellen again. She was walking on the opposite side of the road, laden down with carrier bags. Long hair obscured her face, but he recognised the cuboid, 4X4 build and it was unlikely there could be two girls in this affluent, fashionable area of London wearing the same tragic Mac.

Slowing, he performed a U-turn and pulled into the kerb ahead of her. Engine running, he waited. When she was abreast of him, he lowered the passenger window. 'Hey, I thought it was you. Jump in. I'll run you home.'

Ellen's head whipped round and she stared at him with palpable hostility. Rather than annoying him, he almost found it funny. He nodded towards the cloud-laden horizon. 'It's going to piss down any minute.'

'I can manage,' Ellen said, hectic spots of colour burning in her cheeks.

'I don't doubt it,' Steven replied pleasantly enough, 'but there's no point getting drenched is there?' The engine idled. 'Are you getting in?'

Ellen remained where she was like a like a wilful child.

The thought she might have mental problems went through Steven's mind. *A*utistic possibly, which would explain her weird behaviour earlier. But now he no longer cared. He'd broken his journey for her and was now wasting valuable gym time. Getting out of the car he walked towards her and reached for the bags. She hung on to them as large rain spots bounced off the pavement. Past irritated he said, 'I don't intend to get soaked, Ellen.' Seconds later the heavens opened. Defeated, Ellen surrendered the shopping and got into the car.

'Bloody climate,' Steven muttered as rain lashed the windscreen. '*Still*, good for business.'

Staring straight ahead, Ellen said nothing.

Steven glanced at her stony profile. *Should have let the silly cow walk* he thought and turned up Capital FM to drown out the chilly silence.

AT BRIARWOOD ROAD, Ellen was scrambling out of the car and running up the path before Steven had time to switch off the engine. Removing the shopping from the boot he joined her under the dripping porch. Scraping rain-plastered hair from her cheeks, Ellen took the bags and as she did so, their hands briefly touched. For reasons Steven could not articulate, the dry brush of her skin against his felt repellent.

In the first-floor kitchen Ellen stood at the sink, every nerve ending in her body tingling with unfamiliar expectancy. Her mother was right; *Steven did have film star looks.* Except that was a stupid old-fashioned term; these days they were called *Movie Stars.*

A man with movie star looks had stopped his car and given her a lift. And he'd touched her. Just the briefest touch, but enough to send lightning burning through her veins.

On trembling legs, she went into her bedroom and to the CD player on the windowsill. Some tenant - she couldn't remember which one, had left it behind years ago, along with a pile of old CDs. Pushing a CD into the player she closed her eyes and waited for Sting's voice to fill the room. *Every Breath You Take.*

That evening with Sting's voice still inside her head, Ellen came out of her room and almost collided with Steven on the landing. For the briefest moment her head swam with delightful possibility as to why he should be there. She gazed up at him expectantly.

'I'm looking for Blanche,' he said.

The smile on her lips died as Blanche, fully made up, opened her door and as Steven went inside, the smile Blanche flashed her daughter was one of triumph.

4

CAROLINE SHAW PICKED her way across ice-filled potholes to reach the Portakabin of A2B Car Hire Company. At the entrance, she paused to read a notice blue-tacked to the door informing, '*Valued Customers*' that the firm would soon be moving to permanent premises nearby. A good sign. Steven was on the up. She went inside.

Squeezed behind a desk, shielded by a plexiglass screen sat a balding anthropoid with a huge beer gut.

'Any fucker clear yet?' he yelled into his headset, 'Heathrow pick-up's still waiting!'

Swinging in his chair he saw Caroline. '*Shit.* Lady present. Take a pew love, be wiv you in a minute.' He waved towards a cigarette-scarred plastic bench. Caroline gave it a glance and remained standing.

The fat man dragged his eyes from her breasts. 'Where you wanna go, love?'

'I don't want a cab, actually.' She pushed a strand of hair behind her ears. 'I'd like to speak to Steven Finn. Is he around?'

The controller shook his head setting his chins in motion. 'Fraid not, love. Just missed him.'

'Are you expecting him back today?'

'Doubt it. I can pass on a message though, if you want.'

'Erm...actually, it would help enormously if I could have his mobile number and home address. We're supposed to be arranging a hook up you see, but we keep missing each other. Maybe I ought to just turn up on his doorstep and give him a surprise, what you think?' Caroline gave Ron a mischievous smile. 'We go way back.'

Caught in late afternoon gridlock, Steven sat watching snowflakes the size of goose feathers whisper down upon Embankment.

Fat Ron's voice wheezed over the PDA system. 'Nothing for you, mate.'

'Just as well, I'm not going anywhere. Any problems?' The Merc crawled forward a few feet.

'Nah, sweet. Wevver's taken a turn for the worse though, innit?'

Steven glanced up at the achromatic sky. 'Plenty more on its way by the look of it.'

'Great. It's bleeding nobblin' in 'ere.'

Steven's gaze shifted to the river where, perched on a barge, three cormorants with outstretched wings created an eerie crucifixion scene. He looked away. 'This kind of weather pays your wages,' he said moodily. 'Don't complain.'

'Yeah, ta, mate. Meanwhile I'll just sit 'ere and freeze me bollocks off.'

That Ron could detect any climatic change through all those rolls of insulating blubber was a mystery. 'Look, if it'll stop you whining, go and get another of those Calor heaters.'

'Yeah, I'll do that. 'Ere. Some posh bit with red hair and a great pair of tits called in to see you earlier. What was 'er name now? I wrote it down. Hang on...' there was a rustle of paper.

Steven stared at the little drift of snow settling between his wipers.

'Ah, 'ere it is. Caroline.'

A slow dark flush crept across Steven's cheekbones, for a moment he was too surprised to speak. He found his voice. 'What the hell did she want?'

'She wants to meet up, you lucky jammy bastard.'

'Meet?. *Where?*'

'Your place I imagine. For Chrissake, what's up? She's fucking gorgeous, you moron.'

'You gave her my address?

'Difficult not to, mate, I was putty in 'er hands.'

Steven snapped off his handset, swallowed a string of expletives and stared at the black, racing river.

5

BLANCHE LIFTED her eye mask and peered at the morning's offering with one bloodshot eye. 'Oh, *God.* Not eggs again. Just give me some tea.'

'Not feeling too good, then?'

'What does it look like?'

'Like you have a hangover.'

'I was just being sociable. Something quite alien to you of course.'

Ellen poured tea and handed her mother a cup. 'He didn't stay long, did he?'

Blanche flashed her daughter a withering look. 'I saw you, creeping about the landing, spying. Any way, he wasn't much fun. Wouldn't drink anything stronger than a diet coke. What a bore.'

Hardly surprising her mother looked so rough then. Ellen thought of the two empty wine bottles she'd found hidden on the floor of the larder that morning, Blanche must have polished them both off alone. Resisting the urge to mention them, she decided to bait her mother with something else instead.

'He gave me a lift the other day – when it was raining.'

Blanche sipped her tea. 'He mentioned it.'

Ellen's pulse quickened. '*Did he?*'

'Yes. Said you hardly uttered a word all the way home. Probably thinks you're soft in the head. Take those bloody eggs away. If I manage to keep some toast down, it'll be a miracle. Oh, *here*,' she shoved a piece of paper at Ellen. 'It's my Bridge Day in case you've forgotten. That's a list of things I'll need.'

Ellen glanced at the window. 'It's snowing.'

'Put your wellies on then.' Grimacing, Blanche settled back against her pillows and yanked down her eye mask.

On her way out, Ellen went to retrieve the wine bottles. As she reached for them a container on the bottom shelf caught her attention. She pulled it out and read the label:

Drain Cleaner

This product contains 91% Sulphuric Acid

She stared at the warning triangle. It was strange she had never noticed the container before, but maybe that was because it was only recently, she'd discovered exactly what sulphuric acid could do. The November issue of *Femme* magazine had run a story about an Indian girl who days after her wedding, had been blinded and horribly scarred by the stuff. Her jealous husband had flown into a rage after suspecting she was sleeping with his brother.

The article showed two contrasting images. The first of the girl in traditional bridal dress with the caption; '*I felt so beautiful on my wedding day*'. The second image, the one that had shown her staring out sightlessly with all her features burned away, had a caption that ran; '*Now, I feel like the Bride of Frankenstein.*' That had made Ellen laugh, but it was with a degree of thoughtfulness that she pushed the container to the back of the shelf and shut the cupboard door.

THE PARADE of shops was almost deserted, all but the most intrepid shoppers having elected to stay home in the warm. In the newsagents Ellen consulted her list. Cigarettes, salted peanuts, two bottles of *cheap* sherry. Blanche had underlined the word cheap. Ellen looked around. A middle-aged assistant was creating a seasonal display in a large window already bedecked with flashing Christmas lights. A second assistant, young, pretty, with white-blond hair and a nose stud, was handing her large boxes of gaudily packaged chocolates. 'What's it look, like, Rache?' The older woman asked.

'Dunno. It's hard to tell from here. I'd have to go outside to get a proper idea.'

'Well! Go on then.'

'What! Do I *have* to? It's bloody freezing.' The girl looked around, saw Ellen. 'Customer waiting.'

'Rachel!'

'Okay, okay!' Clad only in a micro skirt and a thin, clingy top, the girl scooted outside. A few seconds later she bounded back inside. 'Blimey, it's cold!'

'We know that. What's the sodding window look like?'

'It looks *fantastic*. Honest.' She made towards Ellen, breasts perky beneath the thin sweater. Ellen found herself considering them. Her own breasts only ever looked shapeless and lumpy beneath her clothes no matter how new her bra. Like *two ferrets fighting in a sack,* Blanche had once said and the burst of coarse laughter that accompanied the remark had brought on that awful hacking, smoker's cough that Ellen loathed.

As the blonde totalled Ellen's purchases on an old-fashioned till the other assistant in the window stepped back to appraise her display. 'I think I need to position a few more boxes in the front. Y'know, make more of an impact.'

'Yeah. Like I keep telling my bloke,' the blonde said, 'position's everything, innit?' The two females giggled and the blonde smiled at Ellen as she handed her the change.

Ellen felt peeved. She didn't get the joke. A growing awareness told her she needed to understand such things. Pocketing the coins, she noticed that the shop girl had a chipped front tooth that marred her overall prettiness. Cheered, Ellen left the shop and headed for the Off Licence.

Back home, Eva Sugar, one of Blanche's Bridge playing cronies was already ensconced on the sofa. Eva had the irritating habit of being early for everything. Ellen gave her a surreptitious glance as she emptied her shopping. The woman was old, in her fifties at least. How did someone that age still manage to look nice? Well, better than nice really. And then she wondered if it might be to do with Eva having owned a chain of boutiques in the past. Maybe you had to *understand* clothes in the way you had to understand most things. She made a point of studying what Eva was wearing today, a light grey dress that clung softly to her slim figure and around her shoulders a pale blue scarf, or maybe it was one of those pashmina things, but what Ellen really couldn't get was how something so simple could look so ... well, *elegant* she guessed was the right word. She was gazing down at her own drab ensemble when Blanche spotted her.

'There you are! I told you not to dawdle. Here, fill this.' She pushed a silver cigarette box across the table just as the doorbell rang. 'Oh, leave that. *Door*!' she commanded.

Outside Graham and Siddique huddled in the porch,

looking frozen. Graham was swathed in his usual colourful scarf. Today's offering was purple. Ellen trailed up the stairs behind them looking forward to Blanche's displeasure when she set eyes on Siddie, Graham's latest squeeze.

Three-quarters of an hour later the group remained determinedly agreeable despite the late appearance of their fourth player, Joan.

'If the worst comes to the worst,' Graham said refilling his sherry glass, 'Siddie can sit in.'

Siddie groaned. 'I don't know nothin' 'bout cards except they're crap.'

'Why you drag him here is beyond me,' Blanche muttered.

'Because, *dear* Blanche, the alternative of leaving him alone with the family silver is *far* worse.'

'That's nice,' Siddie protested.

'Come on, Siddie, you know we can't start without a fourth,' Graham cajoled.

'Ask *her* then.' Siddie jerked his head towards Ellen, who now sat bent over a jigsaw puzzle, furthest from the fire.

'Ellen's never grasped the essentials,' Blanche said quickly, removing a bowl of peanuts from Siddie's reach.

'Oi, Ellen,' Siddie called, 'why was the Essex girl pleased to finish her jigsaw in eighteen months?'

Ellen felt expectant eyes turn upon her. Keeping her eyes fixed on her puzzle she said, 'answer your own stupid joke, Siddie, I'm not going to.'

''Cos it said,' Siddie continued, giggling, '*from two to four years* on the box.'

Laughter broke out around the table but fearing a volley of Essex jokes, Graham deftly intervened. 'Siddie, show Blanche and Eva our happy pics of Tenerife whilst we're waiting.'

Rolling his eyes Siddle pulled out his phone slouched over

to Eva. Rifling through he selected a flattering, bare-chested photograph of himself. 'That's me on the balcony. I must 'av been a bit pissed.'

'Oh,' Eva's softly accented voice sounded surprised. 'I thought someone of your... persuasion, wasn't allowed to drink.'

Siddie's doe eyes narrowed. 'What you mean - *persuasion?*'

'Oh, um...Hindu.' Eva said quickly. 'You are Hindu, aren't you? I've never seen you drink Blanche's sherry anyway.' Eva glanced at Graham for help.

'Sherry's for old people.' Siddie said stretching across the table to reach the peanuts. 'If you got a few beers in I'd down them alright. All we did on holiday was laze around and get pissed, weren't it Grah?'

'Well, no, Siddie ... that's not all we did, now was it?'

Siddie gave a snort of laughter and tossing a nut into the air, caught it in his mouth.

Blanche broke in quickly. 'I think I'll ring Joanie. See what's keeping her.'

Just as she got to her feet the doorbell rang.

'Oh, *this* will be her,' Eva said, relieved.

'Siddie, be a gentleman,' Graham cajoled.

'Piss off, you go.' Siddie said, screwing in wireless earphones.

With a sigh Graham got up and left the room. He returned a few moments later, eyes flashing excitedly. '*Someone* beat me to it. *Blanche*, you dark horse. You've been keeping secrets!'

Blanche blew a jet of smoke from the corner of her mouth. 'Whatever do you mean, Graham?'

Before he could elaborate, Joan, a small woman with washed-out eyes darted in behind him.

'Oh, what a journey!' she announced breathlessly. 'All this

snow. The 272 had to be re-routed. A nasty accident in Bromyard Avenue we were told. But I'm here now thank goodness.' She glanced at the bowl of peanuts on the table and immediately felt cast down. She had been hoping for something sustaining after her awful journey. A ham sandwich would have been nice and would have kept her going until supper. Struggling out of her coat she sank down on the sofa next to Eva.

'Anyway *Blanche...*' she demanded, 'who on *earth* is that young man downstairs?'

'That's what *I'm* agog to know, but Blanche is being deliberately tantalising,' Graham exclaimed.

Blanche gave a sly smile. 'Look, let's get started, shall we? We've wasted enough time already.'

With everyone arrived, Ellen swept up the coats. Going out onto the landing she threw them across the banister and went quickly through the pockets. Joan's only ever yielded mints and crumpled tissues. Eva's never held anything but loose change, but once she'd found a twenty-pound note in Graham's. With it she had purchased a takeaway from The Hot Wok on the parade and eaten it secretly in her room.

A COUPLE OF RUBBERS LATER, Siddie lay fast asleep on the sofa, his girlish lashes curling on his cheeks and at the rear of the room, furthest from the fire, Ellen battled on with Turner's, 'Calais Pier.'

Intermittent conversation among the group had begun to liven up. With three of the four players' female, and Graham with them in spirit, Eva had no qualms about bringing up the subject of her unsatisfactory love life. It was another conversation that Ellen hovered at the edges of with no expectation of her taking part.

'I mean it. I've really had it with men.' Eva declared.

'He'll ring, be patient.' Graham leant over and gave her hand a reassuring pat.

Eva shook her head. 'No. He was just another *shit* that passed in the night.'

'Why you get involved in the first place beats me,' Joan cut in. 'It always ends up like this. What about that other chap? The furniture designer? He was a wash-out too.'

'Ah,' Eva said reflectively, 'never trust a man who back-combs his hair.'

'Never trust *any* man,' Joan muttered, her eyes on Blanche.

'For God's sake, a girl has to live in hope,' Graham said, refilling Blanche's glass. 'If all women were pessimists like you Joan, the human race would have died out years ago.'

'And if all men were like *you*, Graham, the human race wouldn't have got started in the first place,' Joan retorted, which was quick for her.

'Pffft,' Graham waved a dismissive hand.

Blanche flicked ash into her empty glass and frowned at her cards. 'Let's be honest. None of this sex stuff's all it's cracked up to be, is it? I warned Ellen off it years ago. I told her; don't go putting too much store in all that lovey-dovey nonsense, didn't I Ellen?'

'Explains a multitude,' Graham muttered under his breath.

Ellen remained mute, her shuttered gaze upon her puzzle.

'I mean, no man's ever done me any favours in that department,' Blanche continued, 'not even my Stan. A lot of sweaty fumblings, all to no avail. Sooner have a fresh cream meringue and a glass of Madeira any day of the week,' she finished brightly.

Graham's eyebrows rose sceptically. Eva and Joan remained tactfully silent.

'This new tenant -' broke in Joan, returning to what was

worrying her most, 'are you sure you're doing the right thing? From a safety point of view, I mean? I always thought your *no males* rule very sensible.'

'He's a big bugger,' Graham couldn't resist adding. 'Wouldn't be able to fight him off if he decided to ravish you witless one dark night.' He shivered in mock ecstasy

Blanche smiled innocently, painted talons curled beneath her chin. 'Let's get on with our game, shall we?'

As no one was paying Ellen any attention, the hectic rush of colour to her cheeks had gone unnoticed. She shot a look at the sherry decanter on the table. She knew now what sulphuric acid did to the skin, but what, she wondered, would it do to someone's insides - if they *swallowed* it? Bending her head to her puzzle she rammed a piece of storm-whipped sea into place.

THE COMMUNAL KITCHEN was badly in need of an update. Stirring his coffee Steven stared with distaste at cracked white tiles and a mustard-coloured wall. When he'd opened a cupboard earlier, silverfish had darted amongst the crockery. A sight which spurred him into making a mental note to give the cupboards a thorough clean when he had the chance and perhaps give the room a coat of paint if Blanche was agreeable.

'Hi, settled in yet?' A blonde, bare-legged girl in an oversized tee shirt padded into the kitchen.

He turned to look at her. 'I'm getting there.'

'You can only be Steven.' Candid blue eyes appraised him for a moment. 'I'm Alison. Welcome to Blanche's Mausoleum. Don't you just love it?' Going over to the fridge she rummaged inside.

'Yeah, I do actually,' Steven found himself staring at

smooth, slender thighs and his mood lifted. *Maybe he was about to love it a whole lot more.* 'Blanche said you were a nurse. Working nights?'

'Yep. Eleven to seven. The puke and piss patrol. A scenario you must be very familiar with in your own line of work.'

'Yeah, but at least I can charge my customers when they chuck up all over me.'

Alison grinned and swigged from a carton of orange juice. 'Let me know when you next have a night off. I'll introduce you to some of my mates. We all get together in the Three Bells, and I'm ashamed to admit, get totally shit-faced.'

Steven managed a casual reply even though his gut had clenched with sudden sharp longing. If he could settle for a can of coke at home, he could just as easily settle for one in a pub. *Yeah, right*, said a derisive little voice in his head.

Alison replaced the carton and slammed the fridge door. 'Ah, sure, you might as well,' she smiled playfully. 'Better than sitting in your room basket weaving or whatever it is you do on your nights off.'

Steven puffed out his cheeks as though faced with a tough decision and Alison giggled.

'Good! I see you two are getting along.' Blanche was in the doorway, her eyes cutting from one to the other.

'Oh, we're all one big happy family here, aren't we, Mrs Hunt?' Alison said innocently.

'I try to run a happy ship.'

Alison stuck a finger into her mouth behind Blanche's back and mimed a retch. 'See ya,' she called and padded back to her room.

'Glad I've caught you, Steve,' Blanche continued. 'I'm just off for a late appointment at the chiropodist.' She nodded towards the half-filled saucepan of potatoes and the waiting salmon fillet on the draining board. 'Can't say I had you down as the domestic type.'

'I try to eat healthily. Not easy in my kind of work but there's no point putting time in at the gym otherwise.'

Blanche's eyes flicked over his muscular frame. 'Well, I wish you'd enlighten Ellen on that score. Straight from the McDonalds and Burger King school of thought, that one.'

Steven managed a smile. *Having a word with Ellen on any subject was a sobering prospect.*

'I must say, you made a big impression on my friends this afternoon. They were all agog.'

Steven rinsed the potatoes and turned off the cold tap. 'Really? What did you tell them?'

'Absolutely nothing. Got them going a treat!'

'AN ATTITUDE ADJUSTMENT, that's what you need, my girl.' Blanche was seated in front of her dressing table mirror attempting to remove her makeup. Her eyes were bloodshot, and she was slurring her words. Half a bottle of Glenfiddich stood at her elbow. 'I'd much prefer you to stay in your room if you're going to sit there all afternoon with a face like a smacked arse. Can't you even pretend to be pleasant sometimes?'

Ellen sank onto the bed watching as Blanche shakily poured herself another shot. Just how many had she got through so far? 'Why should I bother to be nice to them?' she demanded.

'Because they're my friends!' Blanche snapped.

'No, they're not. The only reason they come here is because you give them free booze and fags and *their* homes are too small. I can't stand any of them.'

'*You* can't stand anybody. You're not normal. Sometimes I wonder what the hell I've done to deserve you.'

Ellen laughed. It had the harsh, dry sound of a laugh rarely exercised. 'So, who would have done all the running around if you hadn't had me?' she demanded. 'You'd have to pay someone and that would kill you. All I am to you is a slave.'

'A slave!' Blanche shrieked. 'Oh, poor you. My heart breaks. Brought up in this place, a virtual palace! Christ, when I was a kid, we had an outside lav. You don't know you're fucking born and all I get from you is this ... this ...crapola. Do you want to know the difference between you and me, Ellen? I've aspired to *this*,' she gave an expansive wave of her arm, 'and you've aspired to ... nothing. You're nobody. Just a bloody waste of space.'

A nerve pulsed beneath Ellen's eye. 'And whose fault's that?'

'Spoilt, ungrateful cow!' Blanche flung her heavy crystal glass in Ellen's direction. Sober, Blanche's aim was deadly but drunk it was unpredictable and the missile merely skimmed Ellen's cheek and shattered against the wall behind her. Shooting her mother, a look of pure loathing, Ellen felt her face for damage.

'Sometimes,' Blanche added viciously, 'I wish you'd *never* been born.'

'*Sometimes*,' Ellen yelled back, 'I'd rather be dead than spend another day in this bloody horrible house with you.'

Blanche fixed Ellen with a bleary stare. 'So; what's stopping you?' she asked. 'Do us all a favour. But run me a fucking bath before you go.' Collapsing onto a stool, Blanche sat there swaying for a moment, all interest in the argument lost. She put a hand to her head. 'Christ. Don't just sit there, get me some painkillers. *Quick!*'

Ellen stalked off to the bathroom temper writhing beneath her skin. She opened the cabinet above the sink.

Amongst the myriad bottles of Ambian, Diazepam, Valium, hangover cures and Milk of Magnesia were a stash of Nurofen. Fetching a packet, she threw it down on the glass-topped surface of the dressing table and reached for the whisky bottle.

Blanche slapped her hand away. 'Leave it!'

Ellen sighed. 'Let's get you undressed, shall we?'

'Fuck off!'

Staring at her mother's drink-ravaged face in the mirror, something inside Ellen shifted. 'Right, I'll go and run the water then.'

IN THE STEAMY atmosphere Blanche prepared to ease herself into the water. Not only was her head spinning but her back was giving her hell too. As she stepped into the bath a monstrous bolt of pain exploded down her thigh. Biting back a cry, she eased herself into the water. Sweat broke out on her forehead. It trickled down her chin and disappeared into the folds of her fat neck. She took a sip from her glass, lay back and closed her eyes. Drifting between sleep and consciousness she began to dream.

She was in a tropical garden, lying beside a marble swimming pool. Overhead the sun burned down from a lapis lazuli sky and from the surrounding palms came the whirr of humming-bird wings. Intense colour flashed in and out of the foliage; gold, scarlet, metallic green, but then a huge cloud slipped across the sun and in the sudden darkness, something seized her ankles and dragged her towards the pool.

Blanche's eyes snapped open like a ventriloquist's dummy as her booze-fuddled brain grasped that this was no longer a dream. She felt a sudden upward yank on her ankles, just before her head cracked hard against the iron roll-top bath and she slipped beneath the surface with a raw guttural sound. As water rushed into her nose and throat her fat hands flailed, grabbing for the edges of the bath. Mounds of white bucking flesh sent water cascading over the sides as she thrashed helplessly, but finally, when it was over Blanche's body bobbed to the surface like some obscenely bloated pupa.

6

UNDER A MONOCHROME DAWN SKY, the city was coming back to life with a cacophony of street cleaners, hissing HGV brakes and the clatter of fruit-stall traders.

Groggy after a thirteen-hour shift, Steven was glad to leave it all behind for the relative peace of Briarwood Road. But arriving home (and that was how he was beginning to think of it these days), two women met him in the hallway. Eva Sugar introduced herself and Joan, and then went on to explain in hushed tones what had happened.

'Possibly a heart attack. Or she could have fallen in the bath. No one knows yet. There'll be a pathologist's report. The police have been, of course, and a family liaison officer will be contacting Ellen at some point today.'

Steven nodded. 'Christ,' he said numbly, glancing at Joan standing silently at Eva's side. The woman's face was ashen and her red-rimmed eyes, glassy with shock.

'Ellen needn't worry about a thing,' Eva continued. 'We'll be seeing to all the arrangements, there isn't anyone else you see. Here, Joan, put on your mittens.'

Joan took them and fixed her watery gaze on Steven. 'There'll be a post-mortem,' she whispered.

'I've just told Steven that,' Eva said gently. 'Button your coat, dear.' She addressed Steven again. 'We've left Ellen in her room. Blanche's GP has given her something. I couldn't persuade her to come and stay with me, so I brought a casserole over. It'll save her having to cook something tonight. She only has to heat it through. Perhaps you could remind her later? She's quite likely to forget.'

'Er... yeah, sure,' he said struggling to digest this unexpected and unwelcome turn of events.

'*Shit!*' he said slamming his door after the two women left. He was *settled* here for Christ-sake, no *more* than settled, he was *happy*, and how about this for irony? His resident's parking permit had arrived only yesterday morning, giving him a pleasing, but as it had turned out, false sense of permanency.

So, okay, he was a selfish bastard he told himself as he undressed, and, *yes*, he should be more concerned about the feelings of the weird girl upstairs, but despite acknowledging this fact, his last uncharitable thought as he finally closed his eyes was, *Blanche, you inconsiderate old cow.*

ELLEN SAT in the wicker chair by her window. She was staring out at the garden, her head feeling pleasantly muzzy. 'Just a mild sedative,' the doctor had said, but despite it, she was forcing herself to go over what had happened the previous night. Things were already beginning to blur but for some reason she felt it important she remember exactly what had happened - the correct sequence of events.

The ambulance men were first to arrive. One was small with sticking-up hair and a moustache and the other one was tall and thin with a big nose. She'd had to hide a smile when she opened the door because they looked just like the Chuckle Brothers from that tv programme she used to watch as kid.

She waited on the landing while they hurried into the bathroom and did things to Blanche with the door closed. When they came out again the tall one said, 'I'm very sorry, Miss, your mother has passed.'

'I know that,' she'd replied calmly enough, but the little one with the moustache kept darting looks at her, as though expecting her to have an outbreak of hysteria at any moment. Then one of them, she couldn't remember which one, told her that the police were on their way. It's what she'd been expecting. She'd nodded and gone into the sitting room to wait.

Once she'd sat down though she began to wonder how they would get Blanche out of the bath. And then she couldn't help giggling and had to put a hand over her mouth as she imagined the Chuckle Brothers going, 'from me, to you,' as they struggled to haul her out.

Two police officers arrived some time later, radios crackling. They also went into the bathroom to look at Blanche. When they came out, she could hear them all talking quietly on the landing. The tall Chuckle Brother then stuck his head round the door to explain that they would be leaving Blanche 'peacefully' in situ as a police doctor was on his way. The little one avoided her and remained on the landing, packing up the equipment.

When they had left, one of the officers, the one with deep brown eyes and a lisp, came in to explain that his colleague was going to take some photographs and then 'check out' the premises in general.' *He*, meanwhile, would like her to answer a couple of questions, but first of all, he said; 'I'll make a cup of tea, shall I?'

While he was gone, Ellen wondered how he'd manage in

the kitchen. She hadn't cleared up for days and she doubted he'd find any clean cups. But manage he did. Perhaps it was part of police training? When he came back, he handed her a mug of Earl Grey. She recognised the smell immediately. *Her mother's tea.* But Blanche had always taken it black with a slice of lemon. And in a cup, never a mug. What he'd given her was sweet and milky.

Sitting down the officer then asked if there was anyone else in the house he should speak to regarding the incident. When she shook her head he then requested her to go over exactly what had happened, so she went through the whole bloody thing again. Repeating everything she had already told the ambulance men plus the woman who had answered the 999 call.

She couldn't help staring at his ears while she spoke; the tips were pressed hard against his head as though they'd been pinned. She enjoyed noticing little things like that about people.

Just as she got to the end of this third account, the other officer joined them to tell them that there was a detective and a police doctor waiting downstairs. *It was exactly how she remembered last time.*

'Oh, and sorry, but you can't use the bathroom for the time being,' he'd added.

She nodded, listening to the heavy thumps of the two men coming up the stairs.

Detective somebody-or-other from Hounslow CID introduced himself to her. The doctor didn't bother he just went straight into the bathroom and closed the door. After a few moments he called the detective in. They were in there for some time, muttering on the other side of the door. One of them had metal things on his heels and she could hear them clicking across the tiles as drawers and cupboards were opened. And then she heard the creak of the medicine cabinet door above the sink. What would they make of that little lot, she wondered?

The detective finally came out, leaving the doctor to it. He stood while he questioned her, sometimes interrupting if he needed her to repeat something. All the while tapping a pen against his notebook, waiting for her to say something interesting enough to write down. Occasionally he stopped tapping and ran a hand through his thatch of shaggy grey hair.

Asked to describe exactly what Blanche had been doing during the course of the day, she gave a one-word answer: '*drinking.*'

He did seem to find *that* interesting at least, because finally he flipped open his notebook and scribbled something. He glanced up at her then; 'And had anything happened today that might have made her drink more than usual?'

She'd looked down at her hands, knowing this was a question she should answer carefully. After a few moments she explained that nothing *bad* had happened; only that it had been one of Blanche's *bad* drinking days. That she had started before lunch and hadn't stopped.

His face had taken on a sympathetic, almost sad expression. 'So ... do you think it likely that your mother was inebriated when she got into the bath?'

Ellen nodded emphatically. 'Yes.'

'The doctor says there's an injury to the back of her head.'

Ellen looked at him. 'Perhaps she slipped and banged it? Or maybe,' she added, trying to be as helpful as possible, 'she was just overcome by the heat and fainted? I was always telling her not to have the water so hot.'

'It's possible of course that she suffered some kind of trauma. Heart attack maybe.'

Ellen nodded. 'Yes. But my mother was always having falls. When she'd had too much, I mean.' Then she told him about the broken wrist last Christmas and the time Blanche had tripped over the stool in the kitchen and sprained her ankle.

The detective scratched an eyebrow with his pen and then wrote something else in his book. Ellen took the opportunity to study his deeply seamed face. The tan just served to emphasise all the creases. For someone who had just returned from a holiday abroad, he looked very tired.

'I'll need a list of every key holder,' he said, closing his notebook with a snap. 'And also, the contact number of your mother's GP.'

Ellen wrote the information down, and as she handed it to him, the doctor came in to announce an ambulance was waiting outside. The detective nodded, then explained to Ellen that Blanche's body would now be removed and taken to Uxbridge mortuary and in a couple of days' time she would be able to 'view her'.

Ellen repressed a shudder. She couldn't think of anything worse. Looking at Blanche in life had been bad enough. Getting up she'd gone to the window expecting it to be the same ambulance that was there earlier. But this one was small and looked just like an ordinary van. No flashing blue lights. Apparently, a dead person was not an emergency.

As she watched the stretcher being wheeled in, the detective explained about the post-mortem and she'd nodded attentively, knowing they wouldn't find any marks on her legs. She'd made sure of that by wrapping towels around her hands. There was the injury to her mother's head of course, where it had struck the edge of the bath - well, she would just have to wait and see what they made of that.

ELLEN GLANCED AROUND THE ROOM, it was almost in darkness even though it was only three o'clock. She got up and switched on the lamp. Wasn't someone coming to see her this afternoon? Some Family Officer. The detective had said so. 'Won't you be lonely in a big old house like this?' he'd asked as he was leaving, and she'd been stuck for a reply because what had actually changed? Whether Blanche was in the house or not, she had always been alone. The only difference was now, she was *free.* Elation flooded through her at that thought. Moving to the window she pressed her forehead against the cold glass. At the base of her throat a pulse throbbed and throughout the narrow tributaries of her body she could feel her blood drumming hot and fast.

STANDING in front of the steam-streaked bathroom mirror Steven made a decision. Towelling off the remaining shaving soap, he went back to his room and slipped on a clean shirt and jeans. His contract had been with Blanche, not Ellen, so where did that leave him now exactly? Deep in shit no doubt.

Going upstairs and by a process of elimination he found Ellen's room. He knocked gently. When there was no response, he knocked again and called, 'Ellen? It's Steven.'

The door opened abruptly, almost as though she'd been standing on the other side. She stared up at him.

'I'm really sorry - about what's happened,' he began, awkwardly.

Ellen seemed almost frozen in the doorway.

He cursed inwardly. This *really* wasn't the best time to broach the subject. Resolve gone, he felt compelled to offer some sort of unspecified help. 'Look ... Ellen, do you want me to do anything? Get you anything.?'

She shook her head, and then to his dismay, burst into tears. Pushing open the door he took her arm and led her to a small, scruffy chair. She sat slumped over like an old pillow while he searched for the right platitude. 'This must be really tough for you,' he began lamely.

Ellen mumbled something and continued sobbing into a tissue. He glanced around the room, there wasn't a single item here he wouldn't throw into a skip, and it hadn't been decorated in years. Not since before he'd been born, he was guessing, judging by the orange and brown swirly wallpaper. He chose not to speculate on exactly how old the gravy-coloured carpet was. A single bed was pushed against the wall, its faded covers pulled back and lumped together in the middle and on the window sill was a KFC carton and several plates growing penicillin. Unconsciously he wiped his hands on the back of his jeans.

'Your mother's friends were here when I got back this morning. He talked down to the top of her head; her parting was greasy and flaked with dandruff. 'They seem to be rallying round.'

'They've finally had their uses then.' Ellen searched her tissue for a dry corner.

'You'll probably be glad of them. Eva's left you something to eat. She said you just need to heat it up. Don't you have any relatives that could come and stay with you?'

Silence.

'Well... as I said,' he repeated, feeling at a loss, 'If you need me to do anything, just ask.'

Ellen gazed up at him then, her dark eyes fixing upon his face. A loud knock at the front door startled them both.

'I'll go,' he said and took off, running down the stairs, grateful to escape the scuzzy little room and its oppressive occupant.

THE FAMILY LIAISON Officer had springy brown hair and chandelier-like earrings.

'*Please,* call me Linda,' she said, holding out a bony hand. Ellen shook it reluctantly. Then without being asked, Linda sat on the sofa, opened her briefcase and placed her two mobile phones within reach. 'It must have been the most awful shock for you, Ellen,' she began.

Ellen shook her head. 'Something like this was bound to have happened sooner or later.'

Linda smiled uncertainly, revealing crooked, jostling teeth. 'Why do you say that?'

'The drinking.'

'Oh. I see.' Linda smoothed her skirt. 'This is going to be a very difficult time for you, but I'll help as much as I can. Isn't there anyone I can call? A friend? Someone who could come and stay with you for a few days?' Linda looked at her expectantly.

'No.'

'Oh. Well – I'll leave my card. You can ring me any time. You may be feeling strong now, but that can quickly change, my dear. You shouldn't have to go through this alone. And...' Linda rummaged in her briefcase and pulled out some leaflets, 'these are all the various help-lines you can call, bereavement counsellors, that kind of thing and I'll leave you a guide as to what exactly the procedures are in such cases.'

Ellen stared at her. 'What do you mean - such cases?'

'Erm...when a sudden, unexpected death occurs.'

'Oh.' How could she get rid of this woman?

He had come to her room. To her bedroom. She could still feel the warm pressure of his hand on her shoulder.

'Part of my job is to liaise with the coroner,' Linda prattled, 'which means it'll be me who'll contact you with the results of the post-mortem.'

Ellen stood up abruptly and snatched the leaflets from the arm of the sofa. 'I'm sure everything I need is here.'

Linda looked startled behind her thick glasses. 'I really can help if you'd let me,' she said.

'Yes, *thank you*,' Ellen said, 'but I think I ought to lie down for a bit.' She put a hand to her forehead and swayed for dramatic effect.

Linda lurched to her feet clutching her briefcase. 'Oh dear. Yes, of course. The best thing you can do is rest. I'll call in again when I have some news from the coroner. We should hear within the next few days.'

Ellen's fists clenched. She felt like punching her. 'Can't you just ring?'

'With the results?'

'*Yes*. You could leave a message.'

'Oh.' Linda suddenly looked flustered. 'We generally prefer to give this information personally, but if you'd rather... you will of course receive a written report in the post. What line of work are you in?'

Why did people *always* ask that question? What business was it of this frizzy haired, do-gooder what *she* did?

'I *was* my mother's carer,' Ellen said as patiently as she could manage. 'She couldn't do much for herself. She had arthritis of the spine and bad lungs. I'd help her to get dressed, that kind of thing.'

In reality of course, Blanche's alcoholism was by far her most incapacitating condition. On her worst days she would drink herself into a stupor by late afternoon and it was *her* job to prevent the house from burning down by a dropped cigarette end or gas ring left burning on the stove. A job every bit as demanding as the one this stupid woman did, as it was around the clock with never a day off. But of course, it wasn't ever appreciated as such, either by Blanche or anyone else. 'I do volunteer stuff as well,' she suddenly found herself adding. 'The Oxfam shop. That kind of thing.'

Linda nodded enthusiastically, dangly earrings a jingle. 'There is such a need in the community for -'

'- I'll show you out, shall I?'

THAT EVENING ELLEN stood in her mother's bedroom, queen of all she surveyed. Stifling a burst of laughter that even to her own ears sounded unseemly, she went to the large kidney-shaped dressing table that stood in the bay. Displayed on its surface were the familiar items so highly prized by Blanche. Things Ellen had grown up with but had never been allowed to touch. Now, she could touch them as much as she liked – and smash them all to pieces if she so chose.

She ran her fingers over the delicate glass perfume bottles. They were worth a fortune Blanche had told her once. Ellen frowned, trying hard to remember the name of the glass-maker, it was someone French, but the name escaped her. No matter. Now they were *hers*, along with every other single item in the house.

She had lost the stingy payment Blanche would make to her each month, but that didn't matter because over the years her mother had alluded to large amounts stashed away or invested so there was no need for her to fear the future.

She glanced around. After a decent interval she would ferry anything she fancied to her own room. Or maybe give up that shitty little shoebox she'd slept in for the past twenty-seven years and move into this room instead.

Sliding back the wardrobe door she stared at the rail of colour-clashing clothes. She would have a great big bonfire in the garden and burn the lot. Her gaze shifted to the shelf above. Amongst the piles of scarves and gloves and an assortment of hatboxes was the Christian Dior evening bag with the sparkly diamante clasp she had always coveted. And there, at the bottom of the wardrobe, nestling amongst the size seven Van-Dals, was something she had long forgotten, a crocodile skin handbag that had held a morbid fascination for her as a child. She picked it up, ran a thumb across the cracked reptilian hide, but any magic it once held was now gone. She dropped it on the floor and went back to the dressing table. Pulling open a drawer she took out a box. Inside lay a coil of amber beads, glowing like warm honey. Ellen fastened them around her neck and then rummaged through an assortment of smaller boxes, looking for one in particular. Finding it, she pressed the tiny catch. Inside, fiery against black velvet, were the diamond earrings that had been Blanche's favourites. 'Carat and a half each, these, Ellen,' her mother had told her countless times. 'A present from your dad just after we married. I could wrap him around my little finger a treat in those days.'

With a tremor of excitement Ellen took one out of the box. But then she frowned. She had forgotten one small detail; Blanche's ears were pierced. Pushing her hair behind her ears Ellen held an earring against each lobe and gazed at her reflection. The diamonds flashed so seductively against her dark hair she resolved to have her own pierced too. It would be worth it, she told herself. But then came the question – when exactly would she get the opportunity to wear them? She stared back at the shining eyes in the mirror and the answer followed immediately. *On her wedding day of course!* With clumsy jubilation Ellen danced around the room, coming to a breathless halt when the front door below slammed. Switching off the light she went quickly to the window and saw Steven pulling away from the kerb. She watched as the red taillights burned along the empty street. Whispering his name into the darkness she drew a heart on the misted window and inside it, wrote: '*MINE.*'

7

'NOT BLACK DARLING, not with your complexion. Perhaps navy. What do you think, Joan?' Eva turned to Joan. The old woman sat on the sofa looking frail and shrunken.

'I shall be wearing black,' Joan replied. '*Black* shows a proper respect as far as I'm concerned.'

'Oh, ignore her, Ellen,' Eva whispered. 'I'd go for a plain navy wool coat. Cashmere even better if you can stretch to it.'

Ellen stared up from the official letter in her lap, a look of panic on her face. Two days before the funeral and the question of what she was going to wear hadn't occurred to her. Before, she would have considered her old fawn Mac suitable enough. But Steven would be there. How could she wear that old thing? She had to look nice.

'And shoes, you'll need some new shoes,' Eva was saying. 'Do you have a decent bag? Oh, don't worry about a bag; you can borrow one of mine.'

Normally Ellen found Eva's ramblings tiresome but for once the woman was making a sensible point. Ellen's spirits sank. Clothes shopping was an activity she avoided, all those mirrors in the changing rooms. 'Steven has offered to provide the cars,' she stated.

Eva broke off from her dusting. 'Well...' she glanced at Joan, 'I'm sure that's a practical solution.'

'And I've invited him back to have a drink with us afterwards.'

Eva put down the cloth. 'Is it wise to get so friendly, Ellen? I know he's gorgeous but ... actually, it's not just that, is it?' Eva stared out of the window. 'He's handsome, of course, but he has something else too, a kind of raw sexuality. Rare in young men these days, what with all this metrosexual nonsense.' Catching Joan's iced-over expression, Eva picked up the duster again.

A bubble of laughter escaped from Ellen before she had a chance to stifle it. Mistaking it for a sob, Eva crossed the room and gave Ellen a hug. 'That's right, it's about time you had a good cry.'

The phone rang. Eva picked it up. 'Hello?' She glanced at the other two women and raised her eyebrows. 'Hello!' she demanded again. She placed a hand over the receiver and whispered. 'There's someone there, I can hear them breathing ... Oh, charming! The lines gone dead.'

'Crank calls. That's all we need,' muttered Joan.

Ellen stared down at the document again.

'Is it anything I can help you with?' Eva asked kindly.

Ellen waved the Pathologist's report. 'You can read it if you like,' and dropping it on the sofa she got up and left the room. Eva retrieved it and scanned the contents, her expression sobering while Joan's eyes bore into her.

'Well?' demanded Joan impatiently.

'*Cause of death: Asphyxiation*,' Eva read.

Joan looked stricken. 'But she *drowned*.'

'It's the same thing,' Eva said gently. 'It states that very little water was found in her lungs...which means apparently, she couldn't have been under the water for very long. It also says there were contusions on the back of her head.'

'Contusions? What are they?' Joan asked looking stricken.

'Injuries that indicate a fall.' Eva looked over at Joan. 'She fell, struck her head and it says here; 'in all probability went into shock.' Eva chose not to read out the paragraph about how much alcohol had been found in the dead woman's blood stream.

Joan jammed her hands between her knees. 'Do you think she suffered?'

Eva shook her head. 'No, my dear, I'm sure it was quick.'

Taking Eva's advice, Ellen caught a bus to Oxford Street and spent the afternoon wandering from one department store to another, her desperation increasing until she almost wished she had taken up Eva's offer to accompany her. Eva was ancient but she knew about clothes. In Selfridges she plucked up the courage to speak to an assistant. The assistant went off and returned almost immediately with a coat she described as elegant and sophisticated. Ellen stroked its soft velvet collar and then nervously tried it on. Admittedly it no longer looked quite as elegant as it had on its hanger with no lumps and bumps stretching the fabric, but it still looked smart and according to the assistant, was 'ideal' for the occasion. Ellen's stomach churned at the price tag, however. She had never owned anything expensive before and not having any money of her own she had been forced to use one of Blanche's bank cards. She knew the pin number by heart luckily, because it was the one her mother gave her to do the weekly shop. But buying the coat had felt different somehow, wrong. She'd held her breath when she passed the machine back to the sales assistant, expecting the transaction to be rejected, but it went through without a hitch. Afterwards she'd felt a warm rush of something heady, it was similar to how she felt when she finished off one of Blanche's discarded bottles of wine.

GETTING into bed that night she switched on her bedside lamp and opening a battered old copy of the Karma Sutra she turned its yellowing pages. She had almost forgotten the existence of the book but a certain train of thought over the past few days had jogged her memory. She'd retrieved it from behind the wardrobe where she had managed to keep it hidden from Blanche for the past sixteen years.

Ironically, on the very afternoon that Ellen had found the paperback stuffed down the back seat on the bus, Blanche had swooped on her satchel in one of her erratic and infrequent raids. She had been drinking all afternoon, her complexion steadily darkening to puce. A shade Ellen had grown to fear.

She sat silent and frozen, intent only on self-preservation, watching her mother by moving only her eyes and keeping her head and everything else perfectly still.

'Where's a kid your age getting filth like this?' Blanche shoved the book into her face.

'It's not m-mine,' she'd stammered. 'I just f-found it.'

Blanche yanked Ellen's head back by her ponytail, making her yelp.

'*Nasty* little girl, reading *nasty* books. IN THE BIN! That's where trash like this belongs!'

Wrapping the book in a plastic bag, Ellen scurried out to the dustbin. The next morning, she retrieved it before setting off for school. Now, Ellen reminded herself, there really was no need to hide anything. Settling down under the duvet she found it hard to take the old-fashioned drawings of little oriental men with large protuberances seriously. She had only seen one, *real* naked man before. Her father. Did that count? She wasn't sure. But at least she did understand what sex was. It was what you did if you wanted your daddy to love you.

Tiny beads of sweat broke out on her upper lip as she remembered the first of those little *run outs* with Daddy in the car. He had taken her to a place he called, 'the countryside' and found a stretch of unmade track in a secluded spot, shrouded with trees. Then when he asked her if she would like to drive, she had nodded excitedly, and he had pulled her onto his lap and shown her how to steer. She had gripped the wheel and they had wobbled along the track, her normally taciturn father applauding her efforts as he bounced her harder and harder against his groin. That had been her first initiation and there were many more little *run outs* after that. Small and silent she had waited, a growing dread in her stomach for what she knew would follow, when Stanley Hunt eventually found a suitably deserted place. A secret place where he could give her what he called his '*special love*'.

All these years later, memories of those afternoons were still vivid. Daddy's sunburnt, freckled scalp, the oily smell of his rough wool jacket, the sweet smell of toffees on his breath and his old man's skin rubbing against hers as sunlight dappled through the leaves and warmed her bare shoulders.

She wouldn't think of that now.

Sometimes his friends came.

She *really did not want to think* of those things now

Once, she remembered, she was sick on some man's shoes. He'd made her lick it off.

'Am I pretty?' she had asked Daddy once, while he was smoothing down her dress and pulling up her socks.

He'd laughed. 'As pretty as my backside,' he'd said and strolled off back to the ca and his reply had confused her because there was nothing pretty about his backside at all.

Back home, Blanche's sly, knowing eyes would follow her for days...

Why was she thinking of all this now?

Steven would want sex, an urgent, inner voice reminded her.

Yes, ***all right***. She *knew* that she wasn't an idiot. *Somehow* it would be different with him. Pushing the Karma Sutra away, she reached for the latest edition of FEMME magazine and scanned the cover: She had begun buying magazines recently, wanting to learn what life had to offer if you weren't her. If you weren't Ellen Hunt.

'LEST WE FORGET Woman's greatest power is sexual.'

'REAR ADMIRABLE Why men are so turned on by bottoms.'

And another feature that seemed more to the point, 'HOW TO KEEP HIM HOT AND HAPPY IN BED.'

Turning nervously to page 82 she began to read.

STEVEN KILLED the engine and got out of the car. Zapping the lock his eyes shifted quickly up and down the street, checking out all the other parked cars. Someone had followed him home from the gym yesterday and this morning he had been followed again after leaving his AA meeting. Exactly *why* someone should be bothering to tail a West London cabbie with no life other than the one spent behind the wheel of his Merc was a mystery. And one he was too tired to try and solve at half past midnight.

As he walked towards the house there was a clatter nearby followed by a high-pitched bark. A looting fox emerged from around the side of the property and zigzagged across the frozen lawn before sloping off into the shadows.

Steven's eyes moved to Alison's window. Either she was asleep, or on some ward somewhere, ministering to the sick. He felt in dire need of some ministering himself. His mind conjured up images. Alison's slim form walking briskly along a tiled corridor, the skirt of her uniform swishing against her legs.

Letting himself into his room he dropped keys onto the nightstand, threw off his clothes and slipped naked beneath the duvet. Rolling onto his side he thought of the moment he had first met her. She had come into the kitchen, her cheeks still pink from the warmth of her bed, her blonde hair tousled, falling free. He imagined a nocturnal hospital ward not so very far away. A desk, an angle-poise lamp and Alison, head bent over some paperwork, legs crossed, unconsciously protecting what lay between slender thighs.

Far too young, his tired brain reminded him as he turned onto his back and closed his eyes. But then to be fair he reasoned, just before drifting off, she was more than capable of making her own mind up about that.

ABOVE POSH PAWS grooming parlour in a Hammersmith side street, Graham Pearce took a swig of mouthwash and gargled. Through the bathroom mirror he glared at Siddie who stood urinating with the toilet seat down.

'Eight months and still not house trained,' he grumbled reaching for the Dettox spray.

Sid patted his partner's bald patch and went into the bedroom.

'Joan said a strange thing today,' Graham called from the bathroom. 'Set me thinking a bit.' He came into the bedroom and removed his dressing gown.

'Yeah?' Sid slid down under the duvet and yawned expansively.

'I've no wish to inspect your adenoids! Put a hand over your mouth.'

'Sorry!'

Graham moved to his side of the bed. 'I haven't been able to get it out of my mind.'

'*What?*'

'This strange thing Joan said.'

Siddie grunted.

'As though she suspects something.'

'Suspects what?'

'Well ... something untoward.'

'What you on about?'

'Blanche's death! Joan seems convinced it was no accident, and I said ... '

'Oh, Jesus.' Siddie turned over and pulled the duvet over his ears.

Graham sighed, got into bed and picked up a paperback. 'Metaphysical Poets,' he read aloud.

There was a muffled groan followed by; 'For fuck's sake turn the light off.'

'I can see what drives people to it,' Graham muttered.

'To what?'

'*Murder*,' Graham replied, snapping off the lamp.

8

Ellen studied the silhouette through the glass pane of the front door. It wasn't one she recognised. The bell rang again, loud and insistent. Ellen hesitated then pulled open the door.

Standing in the porch was a girl roughly her own age and height, but there was a striking, tragic difference. This girl was beautiful. A Burne-Jones muse, with delicate bone structure and skin as smooth as cream.

'I believe Steven Finn lives here?' the girl said.

Ellen waited up for him, sitting in the dark. As soon as he arrived home, she ran downstairs. His door was ajar, she tapped and not waiting for a response, went in. He turned, surprised.

'Someone came here earlier, looking for you,' she said breathlessly.

'Oh? Who?'

'A girl.' Ellen's hands twisted into a knot behind her back.

Steven broke off emptying change from his pocket and looked up at her. 'Did she give a name?'

Ellen swallowed. '*Caroline.*' She searched his face for the remotest sign, but his expression remained infuriatingly neutral.

'I didn't let on you *were* living here,' she continued quickly. 'I made up a story. I said I'd only just moved in and didn't know the names of anyone else living here yet. Um ... was that okay?'

Steven rubbed the back of his neck. 'Erm...yeah. I guess so.'

Relief swept through Ellen, washing away the fear. The girl meant nothing to him. *Nothing.* Why had she been so scared? She turned to go.

'Did she leave a message?'

Ellen turned back. 'No. She did say she'd rung here a few times. I told her we never answer the landline.'

'Why bother having one then?'

'What?'

'A landline. If you don't use it.'

Ellen gazed around his room wearing what felt like a rictus smile while digging her nails into the palm of her hand. It was moments like this that made her realise how hopeless she was at holding conversations or even just making small talk. Unless she had a specific point to make, she was usually at a loss. People like Eva could prattle on for hours given half a chance. She must learn from Eva. But anyway, the last thing she wanted to discuss right now was the bloody phone.

'Right, about tomorrow. Everything's set up. You don't have to worry.'

Ellen stared blankly at him.

'The funeral, Ellen.'

'*Oh*. Yes. *Of course*. Thank you.'

As soon as Ellen backed out of the door, Steven closed it with a decisive click. Walking slowly upstairs Ellen realised that a hundred times more disturbing than the aspect of her mother's funeral tomorrow was the image *Caroline* had left behind. One that featured a wide, full-lipped, sarcastic mouth and mass of auburn hair.

STEVEN LAY in bed waiting for the antiquated heating system to wheeze itself to a standstill. It was almost one o'clock, but from Miss King's room across the hall, a string quartet was still fiddling its way to a crescendo. It was okay for the old girl, she could sleep in for as long as she liked every morning for the rest of her life.

Twenty minutes later, sleep still eluded him. Getting out of bed Steven pulled a chair into the bay window and looked out across the front garden and deserted street beyond.

Not entirely deserted. A shadow crossed the road. A fox. Perhaps the same fox he'd seen the previous night. It leapt the low wall, broke through the shrubbery and then trotted across the grass, tracking an invisible trail. Coming close to the window it lifted its head and saw Steven. With one lithe movement it scaled the five-foot fence separating number fifty-six from its neighbour and was gone.

Steven stared out into the dark beyond his window and as the string quartet's final climatic strains died away, something finally slipped into place. Now he *knew* why someone had been following him for the past week. Because *Caroline* had paid them to. What he now needed to discover was why? And as much as he wanted an answer to that question, what he wanted even more, was a drink.

9

'Wow, you look great.' Alison greeted Steven as he came into the kitchen. 'What's with the suit?'

'It's the funeral today.'

Alison clapped a hand to her forehead. 'I'd completely forgotten, how awful. Hey, how come you get an invite?'

'I'm providing the cars.'

'Oh ... right. Should I get flowers do you think?'

'I shouldn't worry. From what I've heard, there'll be quite a turnout.'

'Really? For that old cow? Hard to imagine.'

Steven went to the sink and washed his hands after removing an annoying last minute bird splat from the roof of the Merc. He could have gone to the bathroom of course, but when he heard someone moving around in the kitchen, he'd hoped to find Alison.

'I'm about to make some coffee, would you like one?' Alison held up a jar as a warning, 'Funds only run to instant shit at this point in the month, sorry.'

'Black no sugar.' Drying his hands, he turned to watch her move around the kitchen. Her long hair was swept up this time, held in place with what looked like a pencil. He found the unorthodox accessory endearing.

As Alison spooned coffee into mugs, there was a knock at the front door. Steven went out into the hall, but Ellen was already thundering down the stairs, calling; '*I'll get it.*'

The familiar trio, Eva, Graham and Joan filed into the hallway, bringing with them a respectful gravity of mood and also the cold, damp air, which clung to their clothes. They spoke in muted voices to Ellen and then followed her upstairs.

Steven came back into the kitchen. 'Chief mourners,' he whispered.

Alison pulled a face. 'I'm going to make myself scarce. You can bring your coffee into my room if you like.'

He picked up his mug, both pleased and surprised by the spontaneity of her invitation. For a moment he wondered if he should feign hesitation, but the effect would have been lost, as she had already scooted out of the door.

'GOD, I SO HATE ENGLISH FUNERALS.' Alison settled into her armchair, tucking her bare feet under her. 'After the last one, I swore I'd never go to another – too upsetting.'

Steven sat on the edge of the neatly made bed because there was no where

else. 'I think that what they're meant to be.'

'Not in Ireland. We give them a freaking great send off there.'

Steven glanced at the computer perched on top of a cheap, self-assembly desk. Half a page of text was visible on screen. 'Am I interrupting your studies?'.

'Ah, you're okay,' Alison grinned. 'I was desperate for an interruption of some kind.'

'Tough going?'

'You've got that right. My mother back home imagines I'm full of drugs and having sex with every consultant at the hospital. Ha! If only.' She took a sip of coffee. 'Ugh, this is the one without sugar.' She leant forward to switch mugs.

Steven nodded at her bare toes. 'Interesting colour choice.'

Alison laughed and clamped a cushion over iridescent green toenails. 'Gross, isn't it? I keep meaning to take it off.'

Leaning back Steven rested his head against the wall. 'This room's much smaller than mine. You've made it look nice though, sort of homely with the rugs and posters.'

'Homely! God, how can you equate that word with this place? It gave me the creeps even before the Lipstick Rottweiler snuffed it.'

Steven laughed. 'That's a bit harsh!'

'Don't you get the vibes? Something's just not right here.'

He took a sip of coffee, narrowing his eyes as the scalding liquid reached his throat. 'The 'vibes' feel just fine to me.'

Alison rolled her eyes. 'Men are such crap when it comes to intuition.'

'Yeah, but we're good for unblocking drains and opening jars.'

Alison grinned. 'I'll let you off the hook, as you haven't been here as long as me. Actually, I'm really grateful for a friendly face at last. It's been awful with just loopy Ellen and a coffin dodger for company.' Alison grimaced, 'I shouldn't call Miss King that, should I? She's a sweet old thing.'

'Didn't Blanche talk to you?'

'Are you serious? She only spoke when the rent was due.'

Steven remembered the drinks invitation he'd received when he'd just moved in but decided to keep quiet about that.

Alison gazed up at the ceiling. 'Her dying upstairs – it's really spooked me out'.

'I doubt Blanche is the only person to have died in this house, bearing in mind its age,' he reasoned.

Alison looked at him. 'And that's supposed to make me feel better, is it?'

Steven smiled. 'I thought you nurses were tough, taking death in your professional stride and all that.'

'*This* one doesn't.'

It didn't surprise him. There was nothing about Alison that suggested she spent her working life dealing with human suffering at the sharp end.

'Well, let's look on the bright side,' he said, 'you've only got Ellen to deal with now.'

She nodded. 'We've gone from tyrant to mentaller. Great.'

'What do you think she's going to do with this place now? It's far too big for her to manage on her own. I'm not sure if I should be looking for somewhere else to live.'

Alison shrugged. 'I'm the very last person to ask. I haven't had a single conversation with Ellen since the day I moved in here. I tried speaking to her yesterday, just to give her my condolences but she just barged straight past me as though I was invisible. She seems to have taken a shine to *you* though. She's always skulking around down here these days. All puppy dog eyes at the sight of you.'

'What? Whenever our paths cross she goes scuttling off in the opposite direction as fast as she can, almost as though she's afraid of me.'

'More like a schoolgirl crush she can't handle.' Alison laughed. 'See what I mean about male intuition. Hey, let's have some music.'

She was immediately on her feet and going to her computer started searching some streaming service. When something that he thought *might* be Dubstep, but he wasn't sure, (and he certainly wasn't about to ask) burst through the speakers, it came as another uncomfortable reminder of the age difference.

'Oops,' Alison adjusted the volume. 'Better keep it down, don't want to disturb Blanche's little coven upstairs.'

Steven sipped his coffee, his eyes on Alison's mouth. It was soft and swollen looking - like a piece of ripe fruit. He forced himself to stop staring. 'Those people upstairs seem to be Ellen's only friends. Don't you think that's weird?'

'Given her dazzling personality? Nope.'

'But she doesn't seem to do anything, go anywhere. I feel sorry for her in a way.'

Alison nodded thoughtfully. 'Yeah, me too. Just imagine what a fuck-off big house like this could fetch. Plus, she's inherited a load of other investments worth thousands. What a bummer.'

'Who told you that?'

'Miss King and she should know. She's been here three hundred years at least.'

Steven ran his thumb around the rim of his mug. 'Yeah, but even so, her mother's just died, that's bound to be tough for her.'

Alison arched blonde eyebrows, the expression on her heart-shaped face mischievous. 'You could really fall on your feet if you've a mind to. Mad Martha must be worth a fortune.'

Steven shifted in his seat. 'I'm going to make my own money.'

Alison nodded. 'Good for you. Marrying for money is gross. "A wise man should hold money in his head, but not in his heart."'

'Who said that?'

Alison grinned. 'A wise Irishman. My dad.'

. . .

UPSTAIRS the little group were getting ready to depart for the service. Eva, her auburn hair swept up into a chignon, was elegant in Jean Muir. Even Ellen for once looked groomed. Yesterday she had gone to a new hair salon in the High Road and at a cost that shocked her, had her hair cut, styled, and then coloured in a shade the stylist called, 'deep mahogany'. Self-consciously she stood in the corner of the room wearing her new Selfridge coat and with her shiny hair tied back in a ribbon.

'Oh, you look very smart, darling. You've done Blanche proud!' Eva exclaimed. 'Hasn't she Joan?'

Unsure whether it was proper protocol to compliment someone on their appearance at a funeral, Joan remained silent. *She* was enveloped in the black military style coat that appeared at every formal occasion. Faded, with worn cuffs it had to suffice, she couldn't afford a replacement. Graham looked suitably solemn in a dark overcoat, the usual colourful scarf missing. They stood sipping sherry as they waited for Steven.

When he came into the room, Ellen stared at him with shy awe. She had never seen him in anything other than casual clothes, but today he was wearing a dark suit, black tie and shirt, its whiteness contrasting against his fading summer tan. She had never seen him look so heart-stoppingly handsome and she had to turn away quickly and fumble with her buttons to hide a brick-red flush, so fierce it reached her temples.

Across the room Graham was also ogling Steven appreciatively. 'Ding dong,' he muttered under his breath.

Steven addressed them all. 'The cars are here. Ellen, you and Joan are in the first car with me. Eva and Graham will follow on.'

Ellen's stomach fluttered excitedly. Grabbing the bag Eva

had lent her she followed Steven downstairs. 'Do I look ...um, okay?' she said to his back. 'Eva said I look nice.'

Steven turned around and his gaze swept over her. 'Eva's right, Ellen, you do look very nice,' he said.

ELLEN COULDN'T COUNT how many people had turned out. How Blanche would have loved to have been here, at her own funeral, lapping up the attention Sitting on various committees over the years meant she had become a well-known figure in the community. All the pews were crammed with mourners, leaving standing room only at the back. An impressive quantity of white lilies, Eva's and Graham's contribution, concealed much of the ivory casket and the air was thick with their scent.

Ellen sat alone in the first row directly behind the coffin. Aware that all eyes would be upon her she kept her own downcast, only occasionally sneaking the odd surreptitious glance at the other mourners.

In the pew behind, Joan sat sobbing, mashing a wet handkerchief between bony fingers. Eva and Graham sat either side of her, concerned at how frail she looked.

As hymn number two, *Abide With Me*, droned to a close, the vicar stepped forward to launch a eulogy about 'the spirited, community-minded lady he'd had the pleasure of knowing for a number years. A woman who during her lifetime had bravely faced adversity.'

A few of the older mourners, familiar with Blanche's family history, shifted uncomfortably in their seats.

'We brought nothing into this world,' the vicar declared in his sonorous voice, 'and it is certain we can take nothing out.'

Bored, Ellen stared straight ahead, keeping her eyes averted from the casket.

As the service finally ended there was a clatter. Ellen turned as Steven bent to retrieve his hymnbook. Awkwardly she had invited him to join them for the church service simply because it didn't seem right that he should wait outside in the car. As he straightened up, she noticed the dark smudges of fatigue beneath his eyes. He worked far too hard which was silly. Mr Pryce, Blanche's solicitor, had made it quite clear that she, as main beneficiary, would soon be, 'a very wealthy young woman, once everything has been finalised.'

As the congregation shuffled towards the exit, sunlight filtered through the stained-glass window and Ellen stood in its fragmented rays, seeing a bright spring day and a radiant bride walking down the red-carpeted aisle. And then she had to bite the inside of her cheek to stop herself from smiling.

10

ONLY A SMALL GROUP of mourners returned to Briarwood Road. Ellen poured tea and Eva offered canapés and the delicate sandwiches she had prepared early that morning.

The short December day was almost over. Eva and Graham sank onto the sofa as the final guests left. The atmosphere was gloomy and the sitting room felt lifeless with Blanche, its vital component, missing.

Graham frowned and glanced around at the heavy drapes with their tasselled tiebacks and the heavy graceless furniture, a legacy from Ellen's paternal grandmother. On the sideboard, blooms reflected in its speckled mirror were already drooping from their vase and shedding petals on the dusty surface. Rousing himself, Graham got up to light the fire in an attempt to cheer everyone up.

Spirits began to revive, mainly due to some excellent brandy Ellen had discovered hidden behind towels in the airing cupboard. She took pleasure in pouring out large measures into her mother's best crystal. Only Steven declined. He sat in the high-backed wing chair, sipping from a can of Coke, while Eva and Graham gossiped in a desultory way about the guests who had just departed.

Joan sat on a hard dining room chair nursing a cold cup of tea, staring into her lap. Eva took it from her and handed her a brandy. Joan raised the glass to colourless lips and from beneath a worn cuff, her wrist bone jutted.

Sparks flew as a log shifted in the grate.

'Strange, what a mesmerising quality a real fire has,' Graham said gazing into the flames.

Ellen remained silent. Steven could feel her heavy gaze upon him but when he glanced up her eyes immediately skittered away.

'So;' Graham said, attempting to draw Ellen into a conversation. 'Any plans for this place now? Wouldn't hurt to modernise it a bit. Even a fresh coat of paint would make a difference.'

Joan raised her head and glared at Graham. I'm sure Ellen has far more important things on her mind than planning a refurbishment,' she snapped.

'Yes, yes of course,' Graham muttered.

Eva, stultified by alcohol and the warmth of the fire, yawned. 'Goodness me. Sorry. Have to get back on the HRT, it works wonders. Mind you, a spot of shoplifting has the same energising effect.'

Graham glanced over at Steven. 'I've hidden the knives, we're perfectly safe,' he stage whispered.

On a large platter, a few sandwiches and canapés remained. Graham leant forward and held up the plate. 'Any one for anymore?'

No one spoke up. 'Well in that case, I don't mind if *I* do. They are quite delicious.'

'I'm so glad the trivial matter of Blanche's funeral has done nothing to affect your appetite,' Joan said, her eyes glittering in the firelight.

Graham bridled. 'For heaven's sake, Joan. As Eva has gone to considerable trouble on our behalf, it would be rather churlish not to show some appreciation now, wouldn't it?'

Steven caught Ellen's eye and raised an eyebrow. Ellen hid a smile beneath her hand and Joan catching the exchange, shot Steven a look of loathing. Through narrowed eyes, Steven returned the compliment. Joan turned away and with a shaking hand, rummaged in her bag for a tissue.

Of the three friends it was obvious that Joan was hardest hit, but he felt little sympathy for the old woman who snapped like a Jack Russell at every opportunity. Eva and Graham he liked, and he could understand why they would be friends, they were of a similar age and seemed to enjoy the same things, but what they had in common with Joan or even Blanche for that matter was beyond him. He glanced across at Ellen again. She was staring into the fire now, absorbed by the flames. Self-contained and remote, there was nevertheless an intensity in her expression that surprised him. Perhaps there was more going on under the surface than he'd given her credit for.

Eva rose and went to the window. 'Heavens, it's started snowing, quite heavily too. I think we'd better make a move. Don't want to get snowed in, do we?'

'I can think of *worse* things,' Graham said, his eyes on Steven.

Eva went over to Ellen and kissed her cheek. 'Now, please, *don't* be afraid to ring if you have any problems.'

'She knows all that.' Joan said, buttoning her coat, 'Blanche will be depending upon us.'

Graham stood up. 'Turned out to be a good thing after all, this decision of Blanche's to relax the *no men* rule. We can rest assured that Ellen is entirely safe while Steven is around to keep an eye on her.'

'Yes, and it was very kind of you to give up so much of your time today,' Eva added.

Steven shrugged, slightly embarrassed with all eyes upon him. 'Least I could do,' he said glancing again at Ellen, who when she turned to look at him reminded him of his one and only visit to Italy where he'd seen the same rapt expression on the faces of the crowds herding silently outside the Vatican one cold, rainy Sunday, waiting for the Pope to appear. Alison's words came back to him; '*More like a schoolgirl crush she can't handle.*' Feeling a jolt of compassion, he decided he would try very hard to be nicer to her in future.

AFTER THE THREESOME left Ellen got quickly to her feet and began collecting up the dirty plates to cover her awkwardness.

Steven had been about to head for the door himself, instead he draped his jacket back over the chair. 'I'll give you a hand with those,' he said, taking plates from her and carrying them to the little kitchen across the landing.

Ellen remained where she was for a moment. This wasn't one of her warm daydreams – this was *real.* Overwhelmed by a mixture of terror and euphoria she could feel her mind jamming up, freezing. She would have to think of things to say. Things that made her sound clever and interesting. *Not boring. 'Send a glass eye to sleep, that one,'* her mother had said once during a particularly dismal Sunday lunch with Joan. A jibe at her daughter's expense that had Blanche spluttering her wine and laughing like a drain, her eyes shiny with malevolence.

Ellen shook off the memory and lifting a heavy tray of glasses, followed Steven into the kitchen.

'I noticed you didn't drink anything,' she managed, her voice quavery with nerves. 'I did mean to get some beer, but I didn't know which type you liked ... you *do* like beer, I suppose? I looked and looked but there were just so many different types, rows and rows and I just didn't know ...' she broke off, slightly breathless, fearing an incoherent ramble was imminent. Steven was here, *in her kitchen*. It was so surreal and unexpected she needed to pinch herself to make sure it was really happening.

Stacking plates on the draining board Steven loosened his tie. 'In answer to your question, there isn't a beer I can think of I *don't* like.'

'Oh. Stupid. I should have just chosen *something*.'

'Just as well you didn't. I've given up.'

'Beer?'

'Drink in general.'

'Why?'

Steven ran the hot water tap and rolled up his sleeves. 'I just feel better without it,' he said smoothly, 'and with the kind of job I do, it makes sense. Which reminds me --' he checked his watch.

Ellen looked out of the window. The snow was falling thickly now and settling on neighbouring rooftops. 'You're not going to drive in that?'

'Can't afford to lose a whole night's business. We'll keep going for as long as we can.' He fitted the plug into the sink and began to wash the plates.

'*Please.* You don't have to do this!'

'It's okay. You can wipe,' he nodded towards a teacloth and slotted a wet plate into the rack. 'Hey, there's something I can't help wondering.'

Ellen looked up. 'What?'

'Why does Joan dislike me so much?'

'Erm...what makes you think she does?'

'The subtle way she looks at me, like I'm dog shit on her shoe.'

'*Oh*, she looks at everyone like that. My mother was probably the only person she liked or cared about.'

Steven rinsed off another plate. 'Were they friends for a long?'

Ellen nodded. 'Since they were children.'

'She must be missing her then. How are you coping? I mean not having Blanche around anymore. I was fifteen when my mother died, and I didn't have a dad either. It was tough.' He ran the hot tap again and dumped some glasses into the sink.

Ellen considered how to answer this question. Water pipes running down the wall gurgled in the silence. 'I suppose it hasn't really sunken in yet,' she said finally.

Steven nodded. 'These things take time. Changing the subject,' he said lightly, 'and I know this is not the perfect time to bring this up, but I really need to know what your plans are.'

She turned to him, looking blank.

'With the house I mean. Have you decided if you're going to sell up? I'd prefer to know now if I should be looking for somewhere else.'

Ellen looked up at him, her face draining of colour. '*No!* I'm not changing anything. Why would I?'

'It's such a big house. You don't need all this space.'

'But it's not just me, is it?. There's Miss King and Alison and ... you.'

'Well ...yes, but...'

'I don't *want* you to move out,' she gabbled, 'you're not going to, are you?'

Steven gave her a quick glance. 'Not if I don't have to. I'm sorry to have mentioned it, but I prefer knowing where I stand.'

Ellen picked up a glass and swiped at it with the teacloth, her hands shaking. 'Can I ask you something?'

Steven nodded. 'Ask away.'

'Who's this Caroline?'

There was a small silence. The sash rattled. A strong wind had risen, and fast-falling snow swirled past the window.

Steven rubbed his nose with his sleeve. 'Someone I was with for a while.'

'Were you married?'

He handed her a plate. 'No. She wouldn't have me.'

Ellen laughed, he was teasing her. No woman would turn him down.

'It's true,' Steven said, running the tap again.

'Look, honestly, there really is no need for you

to be doing this,' she said suddenly. 'I can finish it tomorrow.'

Steven flicked some bubbles in her direction. 'Shut up and keep wiping.'

Ellen laughed and blushed, and then laughed again.

'Do you have someone sorting out all the financial stuff for you?'

She nodded, 'my mother's solicitor. I'm seeing him tomorrow.'

'Okay. Look, I hope you don't mind me saying this, Blanche's friends are fine, and they mean well, but shouldn't you have some friends of your own age?'

Ellen was thrown by this question. She'd never had friends of her own. Why would she need them? Especially now. *He* was here, wasn't he?

'Maybe you could get a job?'

Ellen picked up a glass. 'My *job* was looking after Blanche and this house. That was enough.'

'So, you've never had one? A proper job I mean, outside in the real world.'

Ellen brushed strands of hair from her face, feeling suddenly hot. 'I left school early, 'cos Blanche needed me here.' *Left, wasn't exactly accurate. She'd been expelled after the ruler incident. But looking back, Ellen had always regretted not getting Amy Carstairs in the other eye too. Then there was the small fire at the back of the tennis courts that she of course got blamed for followed by the bigger fire in the boiler room which, 'had put the entire school and all its pupils in jeopardy' according to Miss Savage, her headmistress. Ellen had liked the word jeopardy. She'd looked it up in her dictionary as soon as she got home. Miss Savage had proved surprisingly co-operative though, promising no involvement of the authorities providing her removal was immediate, stating optimistically; 'Ellen may well become more settled in another school'. But by the time Blanche had calmed down enough to consider a rational alternative, Ellen had passed her sixteenth birthday and the necessity was over.*

'I had no choice but to leave early school too,' Steven was saying. 'Once my mum died, I had to support myself.' He handed her the final glass and pulled the plug. 'Not having the chance to go to university has always rankled a bit.'

'What would you have studied?'

Steven dried his hands. 'I like buildings and

design, so maybe architecture. My mum loved history and old houses. She was always taking me to see stately homes when I was a kid; I suppose that's what started it. We only ever saw them from outside though; the entry fee into the gardens was all we could afford.' He glanced at his watch, 'right, it's time I made a move. Know what I *really* think, Ellen?'

She shook her head.

'I think it's time you got yourself a boyfriend.'

ELLEN STARED UP AT HIM, hardly daring to breath. Across the landing the phone began its shrill ring.

He glanced at her expectantly. 'Aren't you going

to answer that?'

She did move then, although it felt more like she was airborne, floating, but as soon as she reached the phone, the ringing stopped.

Miss King waylaid Steven just as he was about to go into his room. 'How was the funeral, my dear?'

'It went well. I expected to see you there.' Miss King gave a thin smile. '*I* wasn't invited. Certain people have short memories.'

She turned away but not before Steven saw that she was upset. Odd that Ellen hadn't invited her. Why the hell not? She must have known the old lady would feel snubbed. He glanced at his watch again he really did need to get a move on.

The phone extension in the hall started up again just as he'd changed out of his suit. A few moments later Ellen tapped on his door, her face wearing an odd, frozen expression.

'What's wrong. Who is it?'

'It's her again. That Caroline girl. I'll tell her you're not here, shall I?'

Hesitating, Steven pulled on his jacket and then said, 'no, it's okay. I'll speak to her.'

Ellen retreated to the curve in the staircase and sat. Steven spoke quietly but emphatically. It was obvious he was angry. Ellen strained to catch the words but then he fell silent, listening to the voice at the other end.

'Okay, okay,' she heard him say finally. 'Give me your address.'

Ellen crept down a few steps and heard Steven repeat it as he committed it to memory.

Replacing the receiver, Steven went into his room and slammed the door.

Ellen remained where she was, her earlier euphoria dissipated, overtaken by an icy shaft of fear. Miss King came out into the hallway again and saw Ellen sitting on the stairs. She was about to speak, but there was something in Ellen's eyes that made her go back into her room and quickly shut the door.

THE HEAVY SNOWFALL had eased off into light flurries. Steven cut across Heathfield Terrace and then turned off Chiswick High Road into Acton Lane South. The gritting lorries had already been out on the main routes, transforming the snow into a thick, grey milkshake of slush.

He kept his speed down, which wasn't easy.

Caroline's voice had triggered off a whole series of emotions. *And* memories. In the beginning that same voice had held enough power to set his heart pounding hard against his ribs and the blood rushing to his groin. But the sharp tongue that came with it, held the power to inflict some nasty wounds too. He drove on, wondering what could have gone wrong in the gilded world of Caroline Shaw, because that tense, nervous voice on the end of the phone told him something had.

'Fun, fun, fun, 'til her daddy took her T-bird

away.' That line came back to him from an old Beach Boys song. He used to enjoy teasing her with whenever he wanted to evoke a rise from her. It didn't strike him as funny now. Just unkind and juvenile. No wonder they'd had rows. But the final row had been justified. He saw her face now contorted with fury as she hurled his belongings out of a second-floor window. He'd punched a hole in the front door after that little display and the consequences, a night in a police cell, had rounded off the evening nicely. But how the hell was he supposed to react when one minute she's telling him she's pregnant and in the next breath she's informing him that arrangements were already in place to have *his* child sucked out of her and flushed away like something diseased and dangerous?

Un-dipped headlights dazzled him for a moment bringing him back to the present. He swore softly. In her typical Caroline way, she had managed to get him to agree to see her without providing one logical reason why he should. *It was urgent.* That's all she'd said. How the hell could anything be urgent after nearly fourteen months?

The left-hand turn he needed suddenly flashed by. He'd missed it. *Shit.* Now he'd have to continue on the one-way system and double back.

Twenty minutes later he arrived in Ridgeworth Street. It was narrow and badly lit with a line of parked cars that were just vague, white humps in the dark. Here the snow lay thick and undisturbed. Slowing, he checked how the numbers ran. Caroline's flat he discovered was on the ground floor of a converted end of terrace. When he finally squeezed into parking space, he got out of the car and looked around. This mean little street was hardly Caroline's style.

Timberlands crunching loudly in the muffled stillness, he crossed the road, rang the doorbell and waited in the tiny front garden.

Caroline's smile was cool rather than welcoming. She led him down the hallway into a small kitchen at the end. As he followed her his eyes automatically fixed on her backside. It had been a very nice backside, small but enticing. You didn't forget things like that. At that moment a pair of tight-fitting jeans enhanced it and he felt an immediate and unwelcome stirring below his belt buckle. She already had the upper hand.

'Coffee?' She switched on the kettle.

'Is this going to take long, then?'

Caroline slid onto a stool and looked at him. 'Please don't be hostile, Steve.'

He leant against the cooker, arms folded. 'You've got ten minutes, I'm due in work.'

Caroline spooned ground coffee into a cafetiere. Her hair lay on one shoulder like a silky copper rope. In her white open-necked shirt she achieved a classy stylishness that he had once found irresistible. He struggled to mask his thoughts.

The kettle boiled. 'You sure you don't want some coffee?'

Steven looked pointedly at the wall clock and ignored the question. Had he been in a different frame of mind he would have admired her coolness. Instead, it was beginning to grate on him.

Caroline took a deep breath. 'Okay, I see you're in no mood for small talk, so I'll try and get to the point, but this isn't exactly easy for me.' She busied herself pouring boiling water into the glass jug. I'm in a situation that I hoped and prayed would never arise, but I have no choice – I need to ask you for money.'

Steven stared at her. It was the last thing in the world he'd been expecting. Apart from the tic-tic of the cooling kettle, a silence fell. His eyes shifted to the base of her white throat. He'd always found the whiteness of her skin exciting. Her nakedness had seemed a secret thing, reserved purely for him. He remembered how easily her delicate skin bruised. How easily he could leave his mark.

He shifted his weight slightly. 'Go on.' His voice was guarded, but it had lost its hard edge.

Caroline got up from the stool. 'It's probably better if I just show you.'

She led him back into the hall and opened the first door they came to. The room was dark and had the warm stuffiness of a bedroom. The smell of jasmine, her favourite perfume hung in the air. She switched on a lamp. Next to the bed was a cot. The baby lay on his back, arms flung wide, plump, furled lips making sucking motions in his sleep. Steven moved closer. Staring down at the dark silky curls he felt a jolt of recognition.

Caroline broke the tension, 'Well?'

Dragging his gaze from the sleeping child, his eyes met hers. 'He's mine, isn't he?' he said softly.

11

Ellen had long ago absorbed the geography of the area she lived in and was well equipped with her own internal map. Finding Ridgeworth Street would be easy.

Snowfall from the previous evening had all but melted away under the pale winter sun but she battled head down into a raw gusting wind that sliced down the street like a knife. Eyes tearing, she passed an Afro Caribbean hair salon, a rundown launderette and a boarded-up betting shop. Then she took a right turn into Baron Road and finally a left into Ridgeworth Street.

She slowed her pace when she neared number twenty-three, taking in the neat privet hedge, clean paintwork and a window box filled with colourful winter flowers. Her fingers played over the metalwork of the wrought iron gate and on an impulse too strong to resist, she pushed it open.

On the doorstep of 23A, she listened for any internal sounds. The flat was silent. With a quick glance up and down the street, she lifted the letterbox and peered inside. Her restricted vision revealed only a doormat and an expanse of cream floor tiles.

Above her head a window opened. She stepped back quickly, and the letterbox sprang shut on her fingers.

A brown face smiled down at her. 'Can I help?'

Ellen shook her head. 'No ... it's all right. No one's in. I'll call back.' She was already moving quickly down the path.

'The young lady is usually here in the evenings,' the man called out helpfully and closed the window.

ELLEN RETURNED to Briarwood Road in a feverish state. Grabbing the post from the mat, she tossed it onto the hall table. Going upstairs she was struck by how silent and hushed the house seemed. As though it were holding its breath. No sounds of running water, no TV lunchtime news booming from Miss King's room, no dull throbbing from Alison's hi-fi. Just silence, thick and smooth.

No pulse other than her own.

She was about to switch on the TV, just to fill the room with noise when she heard Steven's car pull up outside. She went to the bay window. He looked up and gave her a wave.

Hurrying, she went back downstairs and grabbed the mail addressed to him. 'There's post for you,' she announced as he came through the door. She held the letters out.

Steven grimaced. 'I hate the brown ones.'

Ellen's smile wavered. Steven brushed past her and went into his room, leaving the door open. She followed him and stood in the doorway while he sank onto the bed and attempted to untie his bootlaces. He swayed as he leant forward, almost losing his balance.

'You're drunk,' she said.

'Thanks for that, Sherlock.'

Wincing at his tone she carried on anyway, desperate for the answer to the question that had gnawed at her since last night's phone call. 'That girl. *Caroline.* Why did she want to see you? What does she want?'

Steven's head jerked up. 'Ha. What does she want?' He gazed around the room as though searching for the answer. 'What *she* wants I guess, in simple terms is what she's always wanted. Her own fucking way. What I want simply doesn't come in to it - so no change there!'

Ellen twisted the envelopes she still held, not pretending to understand any of this.

'It's all so fucking stupid,' he went on. 'We were really good together in the beginning. It could be like that again if we both made the effort.' He gave up on his boots. 'I'll make her see sense eventually, though. She'll come round.'

Colour drained from Ellen cheeks. *Come round to what?*

Steven rubbed his eyes. 'I'm too tired and pissed to think about it all now.'

Ellen stared at him, her mind filling with a terrible new fear. Throwing his mail onto the bed she turned abruptly and left.

That evening as the TV blabbed to itself in the corner, Ellen picked up the magazine she had bought a couple of days before. It fell open at the page she had been returning to all day and once again she re-read Agony Aunt Harriet Hope's reply to the Star Letter of the month. *Her letter.*

Dear Ellen,

I think it was Oscar Wilde who said; 'It is only shallow people who do not judge by appearance alone.' Wilde was of course being facetious and none of us are immune to beauty but I do implore you to take a step back and take the time to actually get to know Steven before you lose your heart to him. Finding him as physically attractive as you do could easily prevent you from viewing him objectively as a suitable partner.

You mention that this would be your first relationship.

Therefore, I think you need to enhance the chances of this becoming a positive experience rather than a disappointment. Encourage him to talk about his background, his family and his hobbies. Most men enjoy talking about themselves, so this shouldn't prove difficult. Once you have established some rapport, you may then begin to encourage him to see you as something other than his landlady. In the meantime, cast a critical eye over yourself in the mirror. Be totally honest. Is it time for a new image? A change of hairstyle, an updated wardrobe? Such changes will help boost your confidence and a confident person is an attractive person.

Happy hunting!

Harriet Hope

Ellen closed the magazine and placed it under a cushion. Harriet Hope would help her she was sure. She had already taken Harriet's advice where her appearance was concerned and spent all that money on her hair. Going to the mirror she stared at it now and her bottom lip began to quiver. *Why hadn't Steven noticed?*

At the funeral it had been tied back, she reminded herself. *That* was why.

But today it hadn't been tied back and he *still* hadn't noticed. *Today* he had been *drunk* and he --

Drunk my arse cut in a familiar, taunting voice inside her head. *Blanche's voice. All he's got on his mind drunk or sober is Caroline, you daft bitch.*

~

That evening, just three miles distant from Briarwood Road, Caroline placed her son on his Beatrix Potter changing mat and struggled to manoeuvre a bulky nappy between his kicking legs.

Steven laughed. 'Christ, he's having none of that, his legs are going like pistons.'

Caroline straightened up, her cheeks flushed. She blew the fringe out of her eyes and smiled sweetly at him. 'Okay, *your* turn.'

Steven took the nappy and tried to slide it beneath the kicking child.

'Grab his ankles.' Caroline offered advice over the rim of her glass. 'That way you can lift his bottom and slide the nappy at the same time.'

'That's what I'm *trying* to do.' Steven leant over him and that precise moment Luke stopped wriggling and shot a fountain of pee skywards. Steven recoiled just in time.

Caroline grinned. 'His favourite party trick. You need quick reflexes with this little guy. I should have warned you.'

Putting down her glass, she went to Steven's rescue. Gratefully he stepped back and allowed her to take over.

'I'll get the hang of all this stuff, eventually,' he said.

Caroline raised an eyebrow. 'That's quite an assumption you've just made.' She drew Luke protectively towards her and her voice was cool, 'Give me a top up, would you? I'll go and lay him down.'

Steven picked up the bottle of Chablis he'd brought with him. One he'd taken time and effort to find because it was Caroline's favourite. He refilled her glass wondering exactly what that 'assumption' crack had meant. He could so easily give her a hard time, insisting on tests to prove or disprove his paternity, but what would be the point? On some weird subliminal level, he had just *known* that Luke was his son the moment he set eyes on him. But even if he hadn't *felt* that immediate bond, the physical resemblance alone would have convinced him.

The hangover from his lunchtime drinking session still lingered. Recent abstinence meant his tolerance level was now down to zero. Going to the fridge he found a pack of diet coke. He took one, ripped off the ring pull and downed the contents.

CAROLINE SANK onto the bed and unbuttoned her shirt. Luke fastened on to her left breast and in the warm darkness she rocked him gently. The last thing she should be doing was drinking wine. She hadn't drunk alcohol for such a long time, not since the day she'd tested positive in a Boots over-the-counter pregnancy kit in fact, and half a glass wine had gone straight to her head. But on the positive side it had taken the edge of her nerves too. Seeing Steven again had given her a jolt, stirring up the kind of feelings that had been so dormant she had suspected they'd become extinct. But, she'd discovered this evening with disquiet and a miserable sense of relief; that wasn't entirely true, and if she wasn't really careful ...

Luke's blue eyes were watching her intently as he suckled, as though reading her thoughts, his small fingers clasping a button on her shirt. She smiled as she rocked him, humming softly until his eyelids drooped and his lips parted. Gently she wiped away a milky bubble at the corner of his mouth and considered Steven's comment about 'getting used to all this stuff.' Letting him down gently from whatever hopeful expectations he was harbouring was not going to be easy. All she needed was his financial help, anything thing else on offer would only lead to complications she could do without.

'Don't let your wine get warm,' Steven stood in the doorway holding her glass. Caroline put a finger to her lips and as he moved towards her she quickly buttoned her shirt. Taking the sleeping child from her arms, Steven laid him in his cot.

'He's out for the count,' he whispered.

Caroline nodded. 'For the moment at least.'

Steven gazed down at him. 'Great looking kid, isn't he?'

'I think so.'

'Can't be easy, working all day and then having to come home and take care of him.' Steven sat down on the bed beside her.

Caroline was instantly on her feet. 'Let's go into the sitting room,' she said.

Steven followed, not knowing whether to be amused or dismayed at how she had leapt up off the bed the moment he'd sat down. *What the hell did she think he was about to do?*

As Caroline drew the curtains and lit the gas fire he glanced around and amongst the mainly functional furniture a few familiar pieces stood out. The navy and cream striped sofa they had argued over in Habitat. The rattan coffee table Caroline had always been meaning to throw out and the Victorian buttoned back chair they'd rescued from Camden Market one rainy afternoon.

They'd had sex innumerable times on that sofa; perhaps on the very occasion Luke had been conceived. The button-backed chair had seen some action too, until treated to an expensive makeover, after which it was ruled out of bounds.

Caroline retrieved her glass and they both stood awkwardly in the middle of the chilly room. Struggling to find a neutral topic, Steven nodded towards cans of paint stacked in the corner. 'You planning to decorate?'

'When I get the chance.' She took a sip of her wine and gave him a direct look. 'I seem to be drinking alone.'

'Yeah.'

'You've really given up?'

He walked over to the mantle-piece, picked up a photograph of Luke and stared at it. 'One day at a time and all that.' He set the picture frame down and went off to get a refill for Caroline and another coke for himself.

When he returned, Caroline was sitting on the sofa, hands clasped tightly her lap. She looked paler and thinner than he remembered, and the harsh central light made a good job of revealing the deep exhausted circles beneath her eyes. Exactly where was her mother in all of this? Margaret Shaw didn't work. Had never worked in fact and no doubt had nothing more pressing in her diary than spa and lunch dates with other similarly privileged wives. Surely, she could take Luke off her daughter's hands occasionally so that she could catch up on some sleep? For the moment though, he kept these thoughts to himself. 'Right,' he said, taking the uncomfortably low, button-back rather than the space next to her on the sofa. *He could do without her reacting like he was Hannibal Lecter again.* 'At your request I'm here to talk, so let's get down to it.'

Caroline lent forward, hunching her shoulders protectively. 'I know you deserve an explanation,' she said quietly.

Steven let the understatement go.

'It sounds such a cliché, I know, but when it came to it, I just couldn't go through with a termination. Catholic brainwashing. I suppose.'

Steven gave an impatient nod. 'But didn't you feel an obligation to inform me? All this time I've thought -'

'Yes, I know what you thought,' she cut in, 'and it must have been horrible. But time passed and the longer I left it the more daunting the thought of telling you became. I knew how angry you'd be and to be honest, I just didn't have the energy to deal with it. Then I just kind of persuaded myself it might be better if you never knew.'

Steven stared at her. 'Christ, Caroline.'

'I know you, Steve. At heart you're a good man and you would have wanted to do the right thing, but there's absolutely no way I would want you, or any other man, coming back to me out of a sense of duty.'

Steven gave an exasperated sigh. 'I would have come back, yes. But not out of any sense of *duty.* I would have *wanted* to.'

Caroline's eyes flashed him a look that held a warning. 'Let's be honest with each other, Steve. Things hadn't been working between us for some time, you know that.'

'Because of my drinking. Like I said, I've stopped.'

'It wasn't *just* your drinking. We're too different. You and I could never work. If you remember, we clashed on just about everything and our whole relationship was exhausting.'

'Yeah, but fun too ... at times.'

'Yes. At times. But all that aside, Luke is safe, well and thriving. And we *are* managing. Just. But I feel as though I'm walking a tightrope. At any time, I might slip and there's no safety net. That's what scares me.' She looked at him and her eyes filled with sudden tears. 'I don't want to fail him, Steve.'

'You won't fail,' he said. 'Together we ...'

'*Don't,*' Caroline interrupted.

'Don't what?'

'Start imagining some kind of cosy future. I'm doing this on my own.'

He felt a sudden flash of anger again and waved his hand around the room. 'Here? In this shitty little place? What the hell are you and your parents thinking?'

'*They're* not thinking anything.'

'What does that mean?'

'They don't know they have a grandson.'

Steven looked at her, speechless, and her eyes broke away.

'I just couldn't face it, Steve. The endless recriminations that I was pregnant with *your* child. My mother's disappointment that I am never going to become the kind of hot-shot career woman she dreamt I'd become after all that expensive education. Believe me, Steve it just seemed easier this way.'

Steven shook his head. 'They would have got used to the idea. Your father dotes on you, he'd forgive you anything.'

Caroline's lips tightened as she stared into her glass. 'The truth is, I *have* been in touch with him recently, without my mother knowing, and he did help.'

'Finding me?'

She nodded. 'But I didn't tell him *why* I needed to find you.'

Steven took a sip of his coke wishing he had a shot of JD to go with it. 'I really need to be clear here, Caroline. Exactly *what* is it you want from me?'

Caroline swept her fringe from her eyes. 'I would have thought that was obvious. I need you to help support him. I'm working full time, but I have nursery fees to pay, and you wouldn't believe just how expensive '

'I get the picture,' he broke in. '*You* need money. What about what *I* need?'

Caroline frowned as though she didn't understand.

Steven spelt it out. 'Access. I'd expect to see him on a regular basis. I'll give you whatever help and support you need but you can't expect me not to want something in return.'

Caroline folded her arms across her chest. 'You want me to strike some kind of deal?'

'Damn right. He's my child too. I'd expect to play a part in his life.'

Caroline smiled. 'Provide a role model you mean? I can just see you buying one of those self-improvement books you're so fond of. "Remote Fatherhood for Dummies.'

The smile was sarcastic and briefly Steven's hand itched with the desire to remove it. Instead, he said as patiently as he could; 'There's no way I'm going to allow a child of mine to grow up not knowing who his father is.'

'Like you, you mean?'

'Yeah. Like me. Look, I have no objection to paying

nursery fees.' *It would mean ditching the plan to be in his own home in a couple of years' time he realised, but his son's welfare was the priority now.* 'The business, as your father no doubt shelled out good money to discover, is beginning to do well. Before too long ...'

Caroline threw her head back and laughed. 'Same aspirational Steve.'

He stared at her slender throat, his anger rising again. 'And that's wrong, is it? We don't all get everything handed to us on a silver platter like you.'

Caroline ignored the jibe.

'I've grown up, Caroline. I'm sorting my life out. *This* business is going to be a success.'

'Your other business was doing well too,' she said coldly, 'until you started to drink the profits.'

She had a point. 'An online booze delivery company wasn't the wisest venture for someone who likes drink as much as I do,' he admitted, 'but now I'm doing something that encourages me to stay *on* the wagon, and it's working. Most of the time.'

Caroline gave him a penetrating look. 'And for how *long* do you intend being this role model?'

'What's that supposed to mean?'

'Well ... until you get bored? Until you get into another relationship and have more kids? I'm not having him hurt, Steve. It's no good you being around him just long enough for him to depend upon you and then have you walk right out of his life when the novelty wears off. I'm not prepared to take that risk. I won't allow you to screw him up too.' Her eyes filled with tears.

Whatever anger was left in Steven evaporated. 'Caroline,' he said wearily, 'something good, something worthwhile came out of our time together. Don't try to cut me out. It's not fair, either for him or for me.'

'Do you think that's what I *want*?' she asked incredulously.

'We're in agreement about something then.'

'No, we're not! In a perfect world Luke would be entitled to two responsible, loving parents, but the world isn't perfect, is it? And I'm forced to operate a damage limitation policy. Silver platter, eh?' she laughed and glanced around at her surroundings. 'Well, things certainly have changed. 'But,' she added, 'in case you wonder, I have never, ever, for one single second, regretted keeping him.'

Steven gazed at her. 'No. I can see that.'

Caroline was still for a moment watching him and then something inside her broke. When she came towards him, he got to his feet and pulled her into his arms, where she stayed for some time, sobbing quietly into his shoulder.

'It's been so hard, Steve,' she said in a muffled voice.

He held her tighter and stroked her hair, hardly able to believe what was happening. 'It's going to be alright from now on,' he said softly. 'I'm going to make fucking sure of it.'

Caroline pulled away slightly and her tear-filled eyes met his. 'Promise?'

'Promise,' he said.

ELLEN COULDN'T REST. Hatred twisted inside her like hot wire. What right did Caroline have to be beautiful? Beauty like hers could get her anything she wanted - it could get her Steven.

Listlessly she channel hopped with the remote and then snapped the TV off. Getting up she began to pace the room. Caroline thought she could worm her way back into Steven's life but that wasn't going to happen. *She* wouldn't allow it. Steven was *hers* and no one was going to take him from her.

She remembered the things he'd said about Caroline when

he'd returned from the pub at lunch time. The angry, nasty things he'd said, just before he'd fallen into a dead sleep. He'd called her a cow at first and then he'd called her a far worse name. He'd called her a *cunt*. He'd said it quietly under his breath, but she'd heard him. And then, just as he closed his eyes, he'd said quietly - so quietly she almost didn't hear; something that had made her heart stop dead in her chest.

'It's so stupid. She needs me now, more than ever. I just have to make her realise that.'

Ellen continued with her pacing, white-hot rage boiling inside her. Her breathing becoming more and more rapid until she was almost hyperventilating. Suddenly, she *knew* what she had to do. She knew *exac*tly. *And it was what she had wanted to do right from the start.* From the first uneasy moment she'd set eyes on that white, luminous skin and sarcastic, red-lipped mouth.

Rushing into her bedroom she yanked her coat from the wardrobe and pulled a woollen hat down over her hair. Ten minutes later she was heading towards Ridgeworth Street.

12

Ellen ploughed through the heavy rain, shoes squelching as she negotiated the streaming pavements.

It took her just thirty minutes to reach Caroline's street, but as she turned the corner, something brought her to an abrupt halt. She reeled back into a doorway, breath puffing out in frozen plumes. Right outside the house was Steven's Mercedes.

The bitch. The cunting bitch! Her mind fizzed with rage as rivulets of icy rain ran off her sodden hat and down inside her collar. For over an hour she waited, pressing herself into the shadows.

When Steven finally emerged, she watched him walk quickly to the car, speak into his handset and then pull away. As rain slashed through the beam of his headlights, Ellen turned her burning eyes back to Caroline's door.

Caroline was at the sink when the doorbell rang. *Steven again*. Drying wet hands on her jeans she went out into hall, glancing at the small table as she passed. What had he forgotten? Keys? Mobile? She was smiling as she opened the door, until she saw the rain-soaked apparition.

'Yes?'

The figure moved into the light and Caroline now saw that this person was female.

'Remember me?'

Caroline scanned the girl's heavy features and shook her head. 'Sorry.'

'You came to my house. Looking for Steven.'

Caroline frowned. 'Oh. Yes. I do remember now.'

'It's about him.'

'Steven?'

'Yes.' Ellen moved closer and had Caroline looked down she would have seen Ellen place a foot in the doorway. 'I'd prefer to say what I've got to say inside. It's personal.'

Ellen stood awkwardly, looking out of place in the small room.

'So; you are ...?' Caroline's eyes flicked over her.

'Ellen.'

'Okay, Ellen. Would you'd like to sit down?'

It was a reluctant invitation, Ellen sensed, issued purely out of good manners. She glanced at the expensive looking sofa. 'It's alright, I'll stand.'

Caroline looked pointedly at her watch. 'Perhaps you could say what you have to say, then?'

Ellen said nothing. Instead, her eyes darted around the room seeking clues. *Just what had they been doing all the time she'd been standing outside in the rain?* When she saw the opened bottle of wine on the mantelpiece and the cushions in disarray on the sofa, anger surged inside her like a tsunami about to break. She knew now she had been kidding herself, a warning would not be enough. She had to put a stop to it. To her. To this skinny bitch who had only to flick her hair in *his* direction to make him come running. Her eyes shifted back to Caroline. 'You won't want to hear this,' she said.

'But you're going to tell me, anyway.'

Ellen moved closer. 'Steven is with *me* now. He doesn't want you – he never did. Stop chasing him. Stop ringing my house. *Leave him alone!*'

Caroline stared at lumpy Ellen with her thick legs and cow-like face for a few shocked moments and then she did something she really shouldn't have - she laughed. 'You? Steven? Together? *As in, an item?* She made another spluttering sound, pressed a hand to her mouth.

The room fell silent. Water dripped from the ends of Ellen's hair and sank into the sand-coloured carpet. *'What's so funny?'*

'I'm sorry, I didn't mean to be so -' Caroline had no time to finish. Ellen shot forward and grabbed her plait. Yanking Caroline's head back, Ellen breathed into Caroline's face. '*He's mine*! Do you understand that, you skinny-arsed bitch?'

Astonishment and tears of pain sprang into Caroline's eyes. She clawed at Ellen's fist, stared at the distorted face with its disconnected expression that was now just inches from her own. '*Yes, yes* - I understand,' she babbled. 'You can have him! *Please. Just get out,*' she pleaded.

Ellen loosened her grip and in that moment, Caroline kicked out with her booted foot, catching Ellen's shin. Ellen yowled and Caroline catapulted herself towards the door. Ellen sprang after her and brought her down hard.

Winded, Caroline could only stare up with terrified eyes as Ellen now on top of her, grabbed her around the neck and dug strong fingers into her flesh. Writhing beneath her, Caroline managed to bring up one knee and smash it into Ellen's jaw.

With an 'Ooof! Ellen recoiled as blood burst from her lip and ran down her chin. Caroline had just enough time to draw a lung-full of air and scream an ear-splitting scream before Ellen punched her hard in the face. There was a crunching sound and Caroline fell back with a gasp where she lay dazed and whimpering, blood gushing from her nose.

Ellen pinned her down again, hair sticking to her sweat-streaked face. With no fight left, Caroline begged in a croaky whisper; '*Please*, no more.' Teardrops sparkled on the tips of her eyelashes and the dusting of freckles across the bridge of her ruined nose stood out in stark relief against the whiteness of her skin. And now, *(providing you didn't dwell too much on the blood or the livid bruises blooming on the delicate throat)* even now, Caroline looked lovely and the outrageous unfairness of it all enraged Ellen to the point where she was incandescent - because someone with Caroline's looks could get anyone - someone with Caroline's looks could get *Steven*. Grabbing her throat again, Ellen choked her with all her strength.

'*Get off me, you mad woman,' Caroline gasped. 'You ugly grotesque cow.*'

And now of course it became just like the other times; when once she'd started, she just couldn't stop. Spittle stringing from her swollen mouth, Ellen dug her fingers into Caroline's throat again.

Clawing desperately at Ellen's hands, Caroline's legs thrashed wildly, until in the next room, Luke began to cry. Abruptly Caroline froze; her eyes widening with an awful new terror.

Ellen's head snapped around to this new sound.

Oh, God, no! Caroline writhed beneath Ellen's weight as Ellen tightened her grip, her mouth opening and closing as she gasped and sucked air, in, out, in, out, and it was just like *that* sound... the sound daddy had made and somehow Ellen had to stop it. *STOP IT!*

Lunging forward she grabbed a metal object that lay next to stacked tins of paint. The cans toppled and rolled as she raised her arm and plunged the chisel deep into the base of Caroline's throat. A jet of warm blood spurted, and Caroline gurgled softly.

Luke's fretful cries continued but now his mother could no longer hear them. Her dulled, opaque eyes were staring at some point beyond Ellen's right shoulder, her lips slightly twisted. To Ellen it looked like the beginnings of a smile. A smug, Caroline smile.

Luke's cries became more desperate, but they hardly registered with Ellen now. She got to her feet, slowly and stiffly and seeing the chisel in her blood-slicked hand she dropped it.

Something else in the corner of the room caught her attention now. Something that looked like a small hairdryer. Curious, Ellen located a socket, plugged it in and pressed the trigger. At once it began to whirr.

Ellen glanced at the amount of blood surrounding Caroline's body. It was satisfying but it wasn't enough. Kneeling, she got to work and was soon absorbed in her task. Undaunted by the smell of burning flesh, she continued until the face that had been Caroline's, blistered and blackened under the intense heat of the blowtorch.

Sweat broke out on Ellen's forehead and her lip began to throb, but she carried on. Not until she was entirely satisfied, did she stop. Not until the fine-boned face and delicate features had been reduced to a charred unrecognisable mass did she finally stop.

Next door, Luke's unheeded cries had ceased some time

ago. Wiping her hands on her coat, Ellen went out into the hall and pushed open the bedroom door.

Red-faced, exhausted by his efforts, Luke had almost cried himself back to sleep. Thumb in mouth, he hitched a few shuddering breaths as Ellen's blood-spattered face peered over his cot.

13

Joan Armstrong got out of bed and shuffled along the landing to the bathroom. She fumbled for the switch and light rebounded off white tiles. Waiting in the bath was Blanche. She was wearing her cream wool suit with the navy trim and gilt buttons. Her hair was perfectly coiffed, and her cheeks and lips were bright with colour.

Joyfully, Joan rushed to her and hugged her. 'I knew you wouldn't leave me. I knew you wouldn't go!'

Blanche's eyelids flickered open, revealing two rotting seeping holes. With a shriek of terror Joan reeled back and watched as Blanche gripped the sides of the dry bath and began to rise.

'I'll never leave you old friend. Not me. You can count on that.' Blanche was pulling herself up; she was pulling herself out, onto the yellow bathmat with the daisy design. 'How sharper than a serpent's tooth, Joanie,' she whispered in her dead rasping voice.

'Oh s-s-sweet Jesus,' Joan cried, warm urine running down her legs.

Beneath an embroidered sampler that read; 'ACCEP-

TANCE IS PEACE', Joan screamed herself awake, her heart pounding through her ribs. Sitting bolt upright she felt her faded winceyette nightie clinging damply to her legs, while the sheet beneath them was warm and shamefully wet. Clutching Eddy, her torn-eared, pugilistic tabby in her arms, she stared wild-eyed into the darkness.

~

ELLEN WATCHED from an upstairs window as two men got out of the car. The older man was tall, burly, and bald, the younger one, short and sleek, with sandy-blonde hair. She watched them glance around quickly and then walk up her pathway.

'Good morning, Miss.' The big one spoke first. 'I'm Detective Chief Inspector Hopkins.' He held up a card with his photograph on it. 'This is my colleague, Detective Sergeant Fraser.'

Despite the Inspectors benign smile, Ellen's heart stopped.

'We believe a Mr Steven Finn is living at this address?'

Ellen stared at the men as her heart picked up to a slow gallop. Seconds ago, she had been terrified for herself. Now her fear was for Steven.

'We know he lives here, Miss,' the younger man said. 'We need to speak to him urgently.'

'I ... I don't know if he is here at the moment,' Ellen stalled.

'That's his car parked out on the road isn't it, Miss?' the Inspector said. 'Bit of a clue, wouldn't you say?'

Ellen made a show of peering out of the door at the Merc. 'He must be in his room sleeping then,' she said quickly. 'I haven't seen him all morning. Can't you come back later?'

'We'd appreciate it if you were to wake him, Miss. We'll wait inside if you don't mind.'

Ellen stepped back just a little and the two men were forced to squeeze past her. Going to Steven's door she knocked gently. There was no response.

'Knock harder, Miss,' Fraser prompted.

Ellen knocked again and tried the handle. The door was unlocked. She pushed it open and went in. With the heavy curtains drawn it was dark, but Ellen could just make out Steven's sleeping form. She stood looking down at him and then touched the short curls on the nape of his neck.

'Give him a shake.'

Ellen started guiltily and spun around at the sergeant's voice. The two policemen were standing in the doorway. Putting her hand on Steven's shoulder she shook him. He stirred, mumbled, and then opened his eyes.

'It's the police, Mr Finn. We need to speak to you,' the Inspector said.

'Can't you wait outside? Let him get dressed at least,' Ellen intervened.

Steven pulled himself up to a sitting position, rubbed his face and stared at the two men. 'Okay, what's this about?'

Ellen turned to go.

'That's a nasty cut you've got there, Miss,' Inspector Hopkins commented as she passed him.

Ellen's hand went to her lip. Ducking her head, she slipped out of the room.

A FEW MINUTES later Steven sat on the edge of the bed, as the room rocked and swayed beneath him. 'Jesus Christ,' he said, 'Oh, Jesus fucking Christ.'

Hopkins and Fraser exchanged glances. Feeling in his overcoat pocket, Hopkins pulled out a packet of cigarettes and lit one. He handed it to Steven. Despite having given up five years before, Steven put it in his mouth with a shaking hand and took a long drag.

Going over to the window, Fraser opened the curtains and grey wintry light filtered in. Taking the wing chair, he unbuttoned his overcoat.

Hopkins remained standing, his eyes shifting around the room. 'Do you know if Caroline had any enemies, Mr Finn?' he asked, leaning his considerable weight against the chest of drawers. 'Is there someone you're aware of who may have wished her harm?'

Exhaling a plume of smoke Steven shook his head slowly, trying to clear it.

'No,' he said at last. 'Why the fuck would anyone want to. *Why?*'

Fraser and Hopkins allowed a small silence to fall. Fraser cracked his knuckles. 'So, how was she when you left her Thursday night?' he asked.

'Umm.' Steven frowned, struggling to think clearly. 'How do you mean?'

'Well... was she still breathing for example?'

Steven's head jerked up. 'Of course she was still fucking breathing. She -' he broke off and shot a look at Hopkins. 'How the hell do you know I was at her flat on Thursday?'

'We didn't know for *sure,* Mr Finn. You've just confirmed it. *Thank* you. Caroline had sent a text to a friend on Friday morning, telling her she was arranging a meeting with you that evening; 'to talk things through' as she put it. What exactly needed to be talked through, Mr Finn? She also told her friend that things between you two had got complicated, that things 'needed sorting.'

Steven nodded warily. 'Yeah. Personal stuff. *Christ.*' Steven rubbed his face, he felt sick.

'Such as?' Fraser asked.

'Look. Let me explain a few things. Caroline and me, we were together for three years, right? and then Caroline told me she was pregnant. She was upset about it. Said she didn't want a baby. It wasn't the *right time* and all that stuff. She told me she'd already been to some clinic to arrange a termination and that whatever I said wouldn't make any difference. I made it clear I wanted no part of an abortion that I wanted her to have the baby, but she absolutely refused and, well, we broke up over it. Turns out she cancelled that appointment, and I didn't know - until Thursday.'

'That must have made you angry,' Hopkins's said gently.

Steven drew on his cigarette and focused on its burning tip. 'I think *anyone* would have been angry.'

Then realisation dawned and Steven lifted his head.

'Am I a suspect?'

Fraser with the aesthetic face of a poet and a mouth like a sewer, said; '*Fucking* angry I'd have thought. Even the best of blokes would probably have lost it. I know I would.'

'It was a shock, yes,' Steven said quickly. But then, when I saw him... all that - '

'What time did you leave her?' Hopkins cut in.

'Getting on for nine. I had to get to work.'

'And what time did you arrive at your place of work?'

'About twenty past nine.'

'Presumably you have work colleagues that can corroborate this?'

'Yes.'

'Did Caroline mention she was expecting any other caller that night, other than yourself?'

'No.'

Hopkins tugged a pendulous earlobe. 'There weren't any signs you picked up on that might suggest she was?'

Steven shook his head.

'Was she dressed nicely? Hair done? Make-up? That kind of thing.'

Steven hesitated, thinking, He remembered what she'd been wearing, a plain blue t-shirt and jeans. No clues there. They were the kind of clothes she always wore, whatever the occasion. She liked simplicity, clean lines, minimal makeup. He shook his head again. 'She's always the same ... immaculate.'

Hopkins smiled sadly. 'She must have been a very lovely young lady once.'

Before Steven could grasp the full implication of these words, the Inspector added; 'The fact that you were one of the last persons to see her alive makes you a significant witness, Mr Finn. As such we will require a statement. Get dressed pleased.' Hopkins moved towards the door with Fraser in his wake, pilot fish and shark.

'Look,' Steven said, 'I was there purely to find some sort of workable solution for the sake of our son. That's the only reason. I ... oh, Christ! Luke!' He lurched to his feet.

'It's all right Mr Finn. The child is quite safe and being taken good care of. We'll wait outside.'

'*Where* is he?'

The door closed behind them.

ELLEN SAT motionless watching the local lunchtime news. Her lip throbbed and there was an incessant pounding in her head. She stared at the screen. No report of the murder so far. She'd felt sure there would be. Maybe even some CCTV footage of her quietly leaving Caroline's flat and making her blood-stained way down Ridgeworth Street.

Steven becoming a suspect was something she hadn't bargained for. But she *should* have. Her mother was right, she was *stupid*. The police were known for accusing people of crimes they didn't commit, and now because of her, Steven was in danger. Digging her nails into her wrist she shut her eyes tight in an effort to hold on to her chaotic thoughts, but it did no good. All she knew was that *somehow,* she must protect him.

Something warm and wet trickled into the palm of her hand and as she glanced down at the blood she was suddenly struck by the thought, that not everything had gone wrong, because Caroline really was no more, and a wave of euphoria flooded through her at the thought.

14

ELLEN ANSWERED the phone as winter twilight crept into the hallway of Briarwood Road, safe in the assumption it wouldn't be Caroline.

'Is Steve around, luv?'

Immediately on her guard. Ellen said, 'who is this?'

'Ron. A work mate of 'is.'

'He isn't here.'

'Any idea where the hell he is, then? It's important.'

Ellen tutted. '*No.*'

'Do me a favour, will yer? Tell him the filth have been here, poking around and I thought he needed to know, like.'

STEVEN WAS SITTING in interview room two, a small, featureless space, sipping black coffee. Across the desk, Sergeant Fraser regarded him beneath gingery eyebrows. 'I can't imagine you have to try very hard.'

Steven glanced up. '*Sorry?*' He shifted in his seat and tried to focus.

'Women. I bet they love you.'

Steven frowned. That his looks antagonised other men, was not his fault. It had taken a while, but experience taught him it was better to diffuse such a situation when it occurred rather than rise to it. *Normally.* But today wasn't normal and consideration of this little prick's fragile ego was the last thing on his mind. The door opened and DCI Hopkins joined them.

Hopkins's smile was almost jovial. 'We're nearly through, Mr Finn. You just need to bear with us a little longer.' Hopkins dragged a plastic contour chair across the floor and sat down heavily. Leaning forward he switched on the tape machine that perched on the desk. 'Now; you were with Caroline for approximately two hours last night –'

'One and a half. Approximately.'

Hopkins regarded him beneath bushy eyebrows. 'And at no time did you suspect she may have been involved with someone else?'

'No.'

'Or that she was anxious or frightened?'

'The only thing she said she was anxious about was her situation. About Luke.' He fought to keep the irritation out of his voice. They'd been over this several times. 'She just seemed focussed on getting things sorted out between us.'

Hopkins nodded in an understanding way, opened his drawer, and threw some photographs on the desk.

For a moment Steven couldn't comprehend what he was looking at. When realisation finally did filter through, he closed his eyes and felt the world spin. 'Christ,' he croaked.

'I've stopped the tape.' Hopkins's voice sounded as though it was coming from somewhere far away. 'Would you some water, Mr Finn?'

Steven nodded. Fraser bounced to his feet and darted out of the room while Hopkins sat gazing benevolently at him. Steven dropped his hand and stared at Hopkins. 'You *bastard*.'

Hopkins's expression hardened. 'Not the kind of thing anyone should have to see in their lifetime, are they, Steven? But in an investigation like this, brutal tactics are sometimes necessary.'

Steven pressed fingers against his temple, trying to slow the pulse racing beneath his skin. 'How could anybody...' he couldn't finish.

'Do that, to another living being?'

Unable to speak, Steven slumped forward and put his head in his hands.

Hopkins sighed. Getting to his feet, he turned off the tape and sat down, again folding his arms across his expansive chest. 'You know, Steven, I've been in this game a long time and you can't imagine how many times I've asked myself that question, without once getting an insightful reply.'

Fraser returned with a paper cup and slid it across the desk to Steven while Hopkins pulled out a large white handkerchief and blew his nose with a decisive honk. 'Excuse me,' he muttered and tucked the hanky back out of sight. 'I've stopped the tape, Fraser,' he said. 'we're taking a short break. Mr Finn has seen the photographs and needs a breather.'

Fraser darted a venomous look at Steven, deciding to go in hard once they reconvened.

'A LOT of men would have been extremely angry about Caroline's deceit regarding the baby,' Hopkins said smoothly, twenty minutes later. 'I know I would. Or did you perhaps hope there might have been a reconciliation between you? We know that Caroline was quite determined *that* was not going to happen though because she had been confiding her thoughts to this friend.'

But it did happen. Steven sipped water and wiped his mouth with the back of his hand. *Would explaining what had happened between them last night help eliminate him from the inquiry or implicate him further?* His head was reeling. He couldn't think clearly enough to decide.

Hopkins made an impatient sound. 'Some insight into Caroline's character would be helpful. You were with her for some time and we both know now that if she wanted to keep a secret, she could. We do have to consider the possibility there was someone else. A relationship she'd decided to keep entirely to herself, not even confiding in this close friend.'

Steven took another sip of water. 'That's possible,' he agreed finally, 'but not likely. From what I saw, she seemed to have enough on her hands, what with her job and Luke. It was all taking a toll. I wouldn't have thought she'd have had the time or the energy.'

'So, if it wasn't you who killed her, who was it?'

Fraser cut in. 'The nature of the attack suggests it was fuelled by hatred or revenge. Someone with a strong connection to Caroline. Someone like you.'

'Facial mutilation,' chimed in Hopkins, 'isn't that more likely to be the action of some jilted lover?'

Steven shook his head. 'I can't help you anymore.'

'So far you haven't helped us at all,' Fraser snapped, leaning forward in his seat. 'That lovely girl is dead, and you just sit there staring at the floor!'

Steven's eyes fixed on Fraser's. '*Because* you fucking moron, I don't know anymore than you do!'

'*Okay*. *Okay*, let's leave it there,' Hopkins cut in. 'Please read through your statement, Steven, sign it where indicated and then you're free to go. Fraser, a pen.'

Fraser pulled a ballpoint out of his pocket and threw it across the desk. Steven scribbled his signature on the document without checking it. There was no point. His mind was incapable of absorbing anything right now. 'How do I go about making arrangements to see my son?' he said, dully.

'I'll make enquiries,' Hopkins replied. 'That's the best I can do.'

Steven stood up. "Best you can do is not good enough.'

Hopkins regarded him coolly. 'Patience, please.'

'I've a right to see him.'

'And you will. Once this mess has been cleared up.'

'Once I'm no longer a suspect, you mean?'

'*Exactly.*' A fleeting smile lit Hopkins features.

The door slammed behind Steven. Hopkins leant back in his chair, pushed his glasses up onto his forehead, where they often sat, and rubbed his eyes.

Fraser nodded at the statement. 'I don't believe a fucking word of this. I know it's him, one hundred percent.'

'I've checked with his cab company. His controller backed up his statement. Said he arrived just before nine thirty last night and appeared his normal self. No obvious signs he had spent the earlier part of the evening barbecuing his ex with a blowtorch.'

Fraser gave an irritated shrug. 'When are we getting the post-mortem results?'

'Preliminary by tomorrow afternoon, hopefully.'

'No chance of sooner?'

'They're already making it a priority.' Hopkins got up, went to the window and stared out. Somewhere in the west, thunder rolled. 'So far we have nothing,' he muttered and then scrunching up his face, he sneezed explosively into his hand.

Fraser looked up in alarm, his hand creeping to his jacket pocket. Grasping the ever-present antibacterial pump, he tried to remember if he'd used the phone or keyboard or touched anything else his superior may have contaminated this morning? The tape machine? No, thank fuck, he hadn't touched that.

'Finn could have got awkward about providing the DNA

sample, but he didn't,' Hopkins said whipping out the handkerchief again.

'He was at the flat,' Fraser added, surreptitiously squirting some gel into his palms under the desk, 'and he's only admitted that because he knows it's pointless denying it.'

'No doubt.' Hopkins honked then stuffed the hanky away again. 'Can't say I'm putting too much store in the pathologists report. The room was like an oven when the neighbour, Mr Malik broke in and found the body. That gas fire had been burning for something like fourteen hours. Exact time of death is probably going to be almost impossible to determine. Forensics are still in situ though. Oh, Mr Malik should be arriving around five by the way to give his statement. He's our only lead at present.'

There was a polite knock at the door and PC Walker came in with a file that she placed on the desk.

'That's all so far, Sir. Tanner and Doyle will be running more checks later this afternoon.'

'Thanks.'

Walker went to the door,

'Oh, before you go Walker. Caroline Shaw's father will be officially identifying the body tomorrow morning at ten. Arrange for a family liaison officer to be present, would you?'

'Yes, Sir.' Walker threw a glance at Fraser and then closed the door quietly after her.

Fraser opened Steven's file. 'Let's see what we've got?'

Hopkins slipped his glasses on and lent over Fraser's shoulder, immediately wrinkling his nose, whatever goo Fraser used on his hair to make it tuft up like a baby owl's had the sickly scent of bubblegum.

'Spot of joy riding when he was a kid and he's done a bit of time,' Fraser read. 'Charge of GBH brought against him in 2007. Broke some bloke's collarbone. Claimed it was self-defence, but the judge didn't wear it. Couple of breaches of the peace for being drunk and disorderly, but then look at this; two years ago, he was charged with causing a disturbance and criminal damage.'

'What sort of damage?'

'A door got in his way.'

'Door? What door?'

'The door to the apartment where he and Caroline were living! Proof it was a sparky relationship!'

Hopkins raised an eyebrow. 'Volatile relationships aren't exactly rare, but most couples don't end up murdering each other.'

Fraser couldn't argue with that. Since Becky his ex had dumped him like nuclear waste, he'd spent many an enjoyable evening sitting in the pub with a pint of beer in front of him, fantasising about how he would kill *her* and the knob she had left him for, devising ingenious methods that would outwit the best forensic teams. But had he done it? *Had he fuck*. Six months on, Becky was still shacked up with the gas engineer in a semi-detached in Croydon. A shit-hole if ever there was one, with only a Waitrose to commend it. 'Whoever murdered Caroline, *knew* her,' he stated, focussing his thoughts on the job again, 'which leads us straight back to Finn.'

'How can we be sure she knew him?'

'She let them in.'

'Proves nothing. We're all guilty of letting people into our homes every day that we don't know. Delivery man. Bloke to read the meter, that kind of thing.'

Yeah and fix the boiler. 'Maybe the killer had a key?'

'That's a possibility to be explored.'

'Yeah. But what we know for sure is that Finn *was* there *and* that he's got a motive. His ex goes ahead and has the kid without telling him and then demands maintenance.'

Hopkins went back to the window and gazed thoughtfully

at a huge dark cloud that was spreading across the sky like a bruise. 'He did appear genuinely shocked by the photographs though don't you think? And concerned for the child.'

'Yeah,' Fraser admitted grudgingly. 'But he could be a fucking great actor.'

'He's certainly handsome enough to be one, wouldn't you say?'

Fraser scowled. *The gas engineer looked just like Johnny Depp he'd been told. Good looking types - all predatory bastards. Preying on other men's bored, stupid wives.*

'But a man that good looking,' Hopkins's continued, 'will never have trouble finding a woman. Is it likely he would have become so incensed that this one in particular, wanted nothing more to do with him? I'm not so sure.'

'Yeah, well, look at it another way. A bloke like him isn't used to getting knock-backs, is he? That factor alone could have driven him psycho.'

Hopkins took off his glasses and rubbed his eyes. Heavy rain was falling now upon the emptying car park below. Car doors slammed as staff called it a day and headed off home. He listened to the sound of their tyres on the wet tarmac and briefly thought of Janet. Pictured her at home performing her daily tasks, walking the dog, preparing supper, glancing at the clock occasionally, anticipating his return. Oh, Lord, he remembered suddenly, she wouldn't be doing any of those things. She'd left home early this morning, before him, and driven to Heathrow to pick up her sister, Rowena and the obnoxious Afrikaans brother-in law, Pietie. And as he remembered, the joy drained out of his day.

EVA AND GRAHAM had just returned to her apartment in Swiss Cottage for after-theatre drinks. A night at the theatre usually had a sanguine effect upon Graham. Normally he would bask in the afterglow for several hours. This evening he sensed he was not going to get the chance.

Going to the drinks cabinet Eva poured a whisky for herself and a brandy for him. Placing the glasses on a coffee table she kicked off her small evening shoes and returned to the subject she had begun in the theatre foyer, her earlier phone conversation with Ellen. 'What on earth is going on over there I have no idea. Firstly, Ellen tells me that Steven has been questioned by the police about that awful murder in Ridgeworth Street. Then in the next breath she's telling me she's cooking supper for him. Don't you think it's odd? *I* think it's odd. Why on earth would Ellen be cooking supper for Steven?'

'I can't imagine. I'm just glad I don't have to eat it.'

'Is something funny going on do you think?'

Graham glanced up from his programme. 'What exactly do you mean by 'funny'?'

'Well ... like ... some kind of relationship.'

'What? For heaven's sake! Ellen is hardly going to be his type, is she?'

'She might now that Blanche has died and left Ellen her only beneficiary.'

Graham was silent for a moment. 'Yes, but she's hardly his type, is she? Let's be honest, she's hardly anyone's type and she'd have to be as rich as Croesus before I'd give her a poke.'

Eva gave him a pointed look. 'She *is* as rich as Croesus. That house - the investments.'

'You're right. I'm an idiot.' Graham picked up his glass and studied it for a moment. 'So, what *exactly* did she say when you rang, remind me?

Eva sighed. 'I knew you weren't listening. *Ellen said,* 'I can't stay on the phone, I'm cooking something for Steven's dinner and then she rang off.'

'I don't think we can deduce purely from that there *is* something going on.'

'But it was the *way* she said it, as though she was gloating somehow. I don't know, perhaps I imagined it. But anyway, there was certainly no need for her to cut me off like that. I was only ringing to check she was okay. She is alone in that house with a man we barely know, after all.'

'Of course, darling, but listen, Steven strikes me as perfectly decent sort. He was very kind to Ellen at the funeral, don't you think? He provided those cars and didn't charge her a penny, hardly the actions of a gold digger.'

Eva sipped her whisky. 'Maybe not, but Joan's never trusted him from the outset. She isn't dazzled by his looks like the rest of us. How was she by the way when you called in yesterday?'

'Not good. I think she's getting worse. The house was a mess and she had been crying. I checked the fridge and her cupboards when she when into the other room, just cat food and the barest of essentials. The place was freezing too, she'd only got one electric bar burning.'

'We ought to do something.'

'I did leave twenty pounds by the kettle but --'

'She's missing Blanche in more ways than one,' Eva cut in, tapping a manicured nail against her glass. She must have left Joan *something* surely?'

Graham shrugged. The strange co-dependant relationship that had existed between Joan and Blanche was an uncomfortable subject and one both he and Eva usually skirted around. 'One can only hope.' He glanced at his watch. 'Look, I'll have to be making tracks, darling, I told Siddie I'd be home around now.' Finishing his drink he reached for his overcoat.

'Oh, did Joan tell you about the dreams she's been having?' Eva asked.

'She mentioned something but then went off on some tangent.'

'Well, she told me about one in great detail. A gruesome one she'd had about Blanche. She's convinced Blanche was trying to impart some sort of message to her.'

Graham shrugged into his coat. 'What kind of message?'

Eva waved her hand. 'Some garbled nonsense. Something about a serpent's tooth being sharper than something or other.'

Graham wound his scarf around his neck, thinking. 'It's Lear,' he said. 'How sharper than a serpent's tooth it is, to have a thankless child.'

It was almost midnight and Steven sat at the kitchen table, his elbows resting on the Formica surface, a mug of coffee in front of him.

Ellen ran downstairs when she heard him arrive home. 'You were gone so long! Were you with the police all that time?'

He lifted eyes red-rimmed with fatigue. 'No. Once I left those morons, I just drove around for a bit.'

'You look awful, Steven. What's wrong?'

'Do you remember Caroline... the girl who called here. My ex?'

Ellen nodded.

'Someone's killed her.'

'Is that why they came this morning. To tell you that?'

Steven nodded and rubbed his eyes with the heels of his hands. 'I can't believe it. I just can't get my head around the fact she's dead.'

'I've made you something to eat,' Ellen announced, changing the subject abruptly. Going to the stove she lifted a pan lid and peered nervously inside at was now a congealing brown mess. 'I just need to heat it up. You'll feel better if you...'

'I'm not hungry.'

'But you have to eat something –'

'I said, I'm not hungry!'

Ellen slammed down the lid. She'd spent almost two hours preparing this bloody stew, what with all the peeling and chopping and he couldn't give a shit. She swung around, eyes ablaze, but immediately the fire went out of them. Steven was sitting with his head in his hands, looking tired and beaten. Picking up a dishcloth she took it to the table and began rubbing at a stain. 'They don't think *you* had anything to do with it?'

'Yeah, they do.'

Ellen's face clouded and then brightened into a smile. 'I could give you an alibi. I could say you were here all night with me.'

'I don't need an *alibi,* Ellen. They already know I was at Caroline's flat, but they also know what time I left and where I went after that.'

'Yes, but what I meant was --'

'Ellen, for Christ, sake.'

'*I* know you didn't do it. But even if you had,' she rubbed harder at the stain, avoiding his eyes, 'I wouldn't care. *I'd* stand by you, whatever you'd done.'

He dropped his hands. 'Ellen, *I haven't killed anyone!'*

'Of course not.' She said quickly.

'They're going to stop me seeing my son if they can, but I'll get a lawyer. I'll sue any fucker who stands in my way.'

Ellen stared at him as her mind digested this new piece of information. That baby in the cot was *his?* It simply hadn't occurred to her.

Blindly, Steven pushed aside his mug. It toppled off the edge of the table and shattered on the floor.

'I'll see to that,' Ellen said darted forward again with her cloth.

Scraping back his chair Steven stood up. 'Thanks. I'm going to get some sleep.'

Ellen watched him go, scrunching the dishcloth into a tight ball, a panicky new fear moving inside her. Steven becoming a suspect had not been part of the plan.

Plan? What plan? Who was she kidding? There had been no plan. There never was. She'd operated on impulse. As usual. An impulse stemming from that old dark urge, lying deep beneath her psychological fault-line, and because of it, Steven might now end up in prison. She stared down at the remains of the mug and then moving slowly, went to fetch the pan and brush.

IN HER ROOM, lips moving soundlessly to the lyrics, of '*Every Breath You Take,*' Ellen fixed her famished eyes upon a photograph. She'd attempted to take it without his knowledge but of course she had been clumsy and the camera lens had clinked against the glass just before she pressed the button. He had heard and glanced up at the last moment, surprise on his face.

Closing her eyes, pressing his face to her lips, she whispered into his heart.

15

STEVEN SPOTTED Fraser in the unmarked police car as soon as he'd stepped outside the house that morning and it took him barely ten minutes to lose the moron. The 'tail' Caroline's father had hired to track him down had been infinitely slicker.

Now he was sitting in the Merc carrying out his own surveillance and noting that changes had been made. A gravel driveway had replaced the grass and cherry trees he remembered, but the house itself was unchanged. He had a good memory for detail and the chimneystacks that twisted and turned like barley sugar had stuck in his mind. He was parked too far away to see the brass name plate on the gate pillar, but he knew it would read, 'Doughty House'. He had never actually *been* here before, but Caroline had shown him enough photographs of the place. One in particular stuck in his mind. A gangly twelve-year-old Caroline, playing with a puppy on what had then been an expanse of lawn.

The sun shouldered through clouds as his grief gathered tight within itself. A postman wearing shorts, despite the frost on the ground, delivered mail, and on the other side of the green a girl walked her dog. Life carried on, even though Caroline's life had been extinguished. It was a thought that filled him with impotent rage. But rage was good. It would get him through this. Help deal with his obsessive thoughts of her final terror-struck moments and...the images. Those morgue photographs showing clotted blood in her beautiful hair. Bruises shockingly livid against her pale skin, and far worse, her face, no longer recognisably human, just charred strips of biltong-like flesh. Even her eyes, gone. But when it came to an image of the killer, his mind offered up nothing. He couldn't give the killer a face any more than he could give him a name. What did a sick, crazy fuck capable of doing that, look like? Just *like everybody else,* came the unsettling reply.

Picking up his phone he accessed The Mail Online. All the nationals were running the story now, the public's appetite whetted by the gory details.

Under the Mail's front-page headline, 'SINGLE MUM SLAIN', was a photograph of the crime scene. A police officer stood at the gate, guarding the taped off property. Close to the constable's feet, propped against the wall, was a bouquet of flowers and a single rose. He'd stared at the rose. Had there had been someone else after all?

At the bottom of three columns of print was a second photograph. A graduation day portrait of her, taken in cap and gown. It was one he'd never seen before but it was the kind of photograph newspapers loved to use as click bait. Nevertheless, his face clenched in pain when he saw it. A young girl smiling confidently out at the world assured of a bright and fulfilling future. In Caroline's case it was one never to be realised.

A third photograph was of Caroline's father, taken at a press conference he was sitting behind a bank of microphones looking drawn and distraught, imploring 'anyone who knows anything to come forward.'

But the reason Steven was sitting here now outside Doughty House was due to the caption beneath that third photograph. It stated that a baby found at the scene of the crime unharmed was now being cared for by its grieving grandparents. He was grateful for that. *Of course* he was. But he still needed to see Luke *and* establish his rights as his father. If that meant going to court, so be it. His gut clenched when he thought of Luke, deprived of his mother, in a strange place with grandparents he doesn't know. The poor kid must be bewildered.

Getting out of the car he walked through the open double gates and across the gravel. On the driveway was a silver BMW left at a haphazard angle, looking like it had been abandoned rather than parked. Ringing the doorbell he waited.

It was a while before the door was opened and then he was looking at a tall woman with the delicate features of her daughter. Margaret Shaw had been pretty once, but her neat, blonde hair, coordinating sweater and skirt were in sharp contrast to the ghostly face, devoid of makeup. She peered at him suspiciously through puffy eyelids.

'Mrs. Shaw?'

'Yes. Who are you?' she asked sharply. 'The Press? I've been advised not to speak to the press.'

'I'm nothing to do with the newspapers, Mrs. Shaw. I'm Steven Finn.'

Caroline's mother recoiled as though she'd been stung. *'How dare you,'* she whispered. 'How dare you come here.'

It was the kind of welcome he'd expected. Grasping the door tightly, he prevented her from slamming it in his face.

'I don't know what you've been told by the police, Mrs.

Shaw, but I can guess. I had nothing to do with Caroline's death, I swear to you.'

'You, vile bastard,' she hissed. A white fist struck out at him.

'Mrs. Shaw, calm down.'

'The police,' she gasped. 'I'm calling the police.' She made for the telephone table. Shoving the door aside he grabbed the phone and prised it out of her hand.

Margaret Shaw shrank against the wall, hatred and terror in her eyes.

'I just want to see my son.' He kept his voice calm. 'You can understand that, surely?'

'Get out! 'You killed my daughter and you've

almost killed me. I won't let you anywhere near that child.'

'Mrs. Shaw...'

'Get out!' she screamed, launching herself at him.

Rocking back on his heels he grabbed her flailing arms. 'As his father, I have rights and I'll fight you for custody. Next time I see Luke it'll be legal and there'll be nothing you can do to stop me.'

'Never!' she screamed, hysteria in her voice. 'Not while there's breath in my body!'

Pushing her away, Steven left Margaret Shaw sobbing in her immaculate hallway, aware that as bad as the situation was, he'd just made it a whole lot worse.

Half an hour to closing time Steven sat alone in the Three Bells at a table near to the door. Several double whiskies had been enough to ignite the aggression in him and he glared around looking for a target.

In the corner, above the din of a full and lively pub, a pianist was attempting, 'The Sting' with gusto but very little expertise. He was grating on Steven's nerves, winding them tighter than a duck's proverbial. Fixing the piano player in his sights he glowered threateningly, just as the pub door swung open and along with a blast of freezing air, a group of noisy students piled in and pushed their way to the bar.

'Look out, the Intelligentsia's arrived,' he growled to a startled couple at the next table. Keeping his eyes on the high-spirited group, he watched their antics.

A dark-haired guy with an angular face was fondling a girl who suddenly held Steven's attention. As the couple waited to be served the young guy clasped the girl's buttocks and pulled her against him.

Steven's eyes shifted away and the satisfying thought of smashing the lid down on the pianist's knuckles was going through his mind when he became aware of someone standing at his table.

'Steve! How you doing?'

He lifted his head. Alison smiled down at him.

'*Wonderful*. Couldn't be better.'

'For someone feeling wonderful, you don't look so great.'

'Can't think why that is. I'd get you a drink, but I don't think I'll make it to the bar.' He took a handful of crumpled notes from his pocket and dumped them on the table. 'Buy yourself a drink and one for me while you're at it.'

'I already have one,' she held up a glass. 'I'm with some friends.' She waved towards the group Steven had been watching. 'We're celebrating. Adam has passed his finals at last.'

'Well, that's fantastic news. Clever old Adam.'

Alison touched his shoulder. 'Don't you think it's time you got yourself home?'

The pianist was calling for requests.

'I've got one,' he shouted. 'Shut the fuck up'!'

There was a burst of laughter from somewhere.

'Come on,' Alison said, gathering up the notes. 'It's really stuffy in here. Why don't we get some fresh air?'

'What about Adrian? Won't he be a bit put out if I bugger off with his girl?'

'Shut up and it's *Adam*. We have to make allowances, he's totally shit-faced - *and* I'm *not* his girl.'

'Does he know that? He's had his hands all over your backside for the last ten minutes.'

'I'm not *his* or anyone else's girl.'

'What a waste.'

'What is?'

'He looked up at her and focused. 'You. Not having a boyfriend.'

'Stop it.'

'Stop what?'

'Staring.' Alison was blushing under the intensity of his gaze. 'You're making me uncomfortable.'

He staggered to his feet, knocking his glass over. She took his elbow and guided him.

Outside, Alison kept a firm hold. When Steven made a move towards his car, she guided him away with a hearty, 'come on, the walk will do us good.'

He swayed slightly. 'Not sure I can make it.'

''Course you can. Put your arm around me.'

'You can't imagine how much I've wanted to hear you say that,' he said with a lop-sided grin.

'Ah, now you're being silly. We've only known each other five minutes.'

'Long enough.' Steven came to a halt on the pavement.

'Are you going to throw up?'

He shook his head and looked at her. 'I really like you, Alison. Come out with me sometime?'

'Is this the drink talking?'

'Nope,' he staggered again, and she grabbed him.

'Ask me again when you're sober.'

'I'm asking you now.'

'Steve ...' she looked up into his eyes, saw determination and something else and then he was pulling her roughly into his arms and in the middle of the wet, glistening street, he kissed her.

'Put her down, mate,' quipped a passerby.

Alison broke off, breathless, taken by surprise that a drunken kiss could have such potency.

Steven grinned and leant against a lamppost. 'Mine or yours?'

Alison raised an eyebrow. 'You really think you're up to it?'

He nodded. 'I am at the moment.'

'TMI!'

'By the time we get home, I'll be as sober as, er ... whatever it is, and I can honestly say,' he took her hand again, 'I've never yet ... you know ... disappointed a lady.'

'Such bravado! Tell you what,' she said smoothly, both to appease him and get him to cooperate, 'if we actually do manage to get home, I'll appraise the situation then.'

ELLEN HAD JUST FINISHED WRITING another letter to Harriet Hope. There was no one else she could turn to. Putting on her coat she set off to the Maplethorpe Road post box. When she reached it she stood hesitating. Why not deliver it personally? *Femme's* offices were also in Chiswick (a coincidence she had taken as some kind of sign) Posting would mean it would take days to get there, what with all the Christmas mail. She glanced down at the address on the envelope. She knew where it was, it was in one of those narrow, mainly residential streets just off Chiswick High Street. She'd find it easily enough.

. . .

RETURNING HOME FORTY MINUTES LATER, Ellen came behind two familiar figures, the shorter one supporting the taller. Increasing her pace, she caught up with the pair at the gate.

'What's wrong with him?' she demanded of Alison.

'He's fine, Ellen. Just a bit worse for wear, that's all.'

Steven muttered something unintelligible and grinned.

Together they propelled Steven through the

front door and into the hallway 'It's okay. I'll take care of him now,' Ellen said. 'Where's the key to your room, Steven?

Steven frowned, shook his head and fell against Alison. Alison giggled and tried to steady him.

'Leave him!' Ellen snapped. 'Let me manage him on my own.' Elbowing Alison out of the way she took Steven's weight.

'Sure.' Alison held up her hands in defeat and backed off. 'Night, night, Steve.' She went towards her room.

'Hey, I thought we were on a promise,' he called.

'Stand still,' Ellen demanded, searching through his pockets.'

Alison looked back and Steven blew her a

drunken kiss above Ellen's head.

Slipping into her room, Alison closed the door and leant against it for a moment analyzing her thoughts. Ellen's intervention had been timely, saving her from what might be viewed in the austerity of morning light as an embarrassing mistake for both of them. But, she realized, with a wry smile, whatever she *was* feeling right now certainly didn't feel like gratitude.

16

JOAN SLIPPED her feet into her tartan slippers and pulled on her faded dressing gown. In the cold living room, she took a black silk cloth from the bureau under the window and sat down at a small table. Unfolding the cloth, she took out her Tarot cards. Taking eleven cards from the top of the pack she spread them out in a Celtic cross and turned them over, one by one, until all the symbols were revealed. As her eyes darted from card to card, a feeling of faintness washed through her and gripping the edges of the table, she uttered a mewl of distress.

GEORGIA GOLDSMITH'S mood was as black as her espresso. Julie, her secretary, had phoned in sick for the fourth day running. Two subbing editors were also absent, one on vacation and the other recovering from a skiing accident, Georgia had been making frantic phone calls to various freelancers all morning hoping one might be able to help out. No luck so far and she was facing yet another day with back-to-back editorial meetings and no Julie to field her phone calls or drip-feed her caffeine. Whooping cough? *Only bloody kids got whooping cough*. Running a hand through her luxuriant hair, she gazed through the glass partition at the new work experience boy. Eyeing him as a hyena might a gentle impala her mood lifted. He was cute and *very* young. Sometimes that's just how she liked them.

STEVEN DRAGGED himself out of bed, opened his curtains and stood wincing in bright winter sunlight. His head pounded like a jackhammer and his mouth was dry as sand. Events of the previous day began to slowly come back to him. The visit to Caroline's mother had been breath-takingly stupid. How was a stunt like that going to be perceived by the courts? And then last night. *Alison*. What exactly had happened there? That he was still fully dressed meant it can't have gone far but he did have a vague memory of something. A kiss? Something more? His hand rasped over the stubble on his jaw, and he groaned. Hadn't he enough shit going on without getting involved with Alison? Only two days ago he'd been happily contemplating a new life with Caroline. What was wrong with him? Grabbing a towel and his shaving gear he was heading for the bathroom when he noticed the jacket, he'd worn the night before was hanging neatly on a hanger behind the door. It struck an odd note, given his drunken state. Had someone been in his room, tidying up after him? *Alison?* Maybe something had happened between them after all, and he just couldn't remember.

ELLEN WAS WAITING for him when he came out of the bathroom with only a towel wrapped around his waist. Her eyes feasted on his muscular shoulders. On his chest and legs where the hair lay dark and wet against his skin. Emotion and something else surged through her veins like molten liquid. She could smell his warm, clean flesh and the lingering tang of his shower gel. The expensive French stuff. When she had discovered there was a L'Occitane store in the high street she'd gone inside and bought some for herself. Now she could smell his scent whenever she wanted.

Steven stopped at the door to his room and turned to her. 'Sorry about last night, it won't happen again. As from today, I'm back on the wagon, *promise*.'

Ellen trailed inside his room after him. 'It's okay. Really. Letting off steam, I image, what with Caroline and the police and everything.'

'Yeah.' Steven went to his wardrobe and pulled a clean shirt of its hanger. He turned. 'Ellen. 'I need to get dressed.'

Ellen's fists dug into her cardigan pockets; she was being dismissed as though she was some kind of servant. Biting back a retort, she backed towards the door.

'Oh, wait a minute,' Steven called. 'Was anyone in my room last night?'

She looked at him. 'Who do you mean?'

'Well, it can only have been Alison or you. In here last night ... tidying up.'

'Oh ... yes,' she nodded vigorously. 'It was me. You needed some help.'

'It wasn't your problem.' He turned away from her again, his voice cold.

Ellen stared at his naked back. 'You were sick, Steven. Someone had to clean up the mess.'

He pulled a pair of clean socks out of a drawer and slammed it shut. 'Oh, Christ. Was I?'

'It's okay, I didn't mind,' she said quickly, relieved his tone had softened. 'I'll get you some breakfast, shall I? It's no trouble. I'm going to cook something for myself.'

'No,' he said abruptly, 'but coffee would be great.'

With a sense of purpose, Ellen was about to hurry off.

'Ellen?'

She stopped.

'I know I'm being an arse. I'm dealing with a lot right now, but that's no excuse for being shitty.'

Ellen smiled. He wanted coffee, she would make coffee. She would *always* do whatever he wanted; he just didn't seem to realise that yet.

Spooning instant coffee into a mug, she thought about all pressure he must be under. That was why he'd been irritable of course. That, and the fact she'd just stood there with her hands in her pockets, *'looking gormless.'* That was how Blanche described it. *'Like chips waiting for bloody vinegar.'*

She gave the coffee a vicious stir but then cheered up at the thought she would never have to listen to Blanche's cruel taunts ever again.

When Steven came into the kitchen and sat at the table, her mood had lifted. 'I've been thinking,' she began cautiously, handing him the coffee. 'If the worst comes to the worst, I could hire a really good lawyer for you. Once my mother's estate is settled, I'll have more than enough money.'

Steven gave her a bleary-eyed stare. 'Why the hell would you do that?'

'Um...I just thought that –'

'So, you think *I've* got something to do with Caroline's death?'

'No. Of course not! Ellen chewed her bottom lip. 'It's just that the police car is outside again. It's been here since early morning. They're obviously watching your every move.'

'I'm well aware they're watching me, Ellen, I'm not a fucking idiot!'

Ellen winced. 'There's no need to shout. I'm the only one on your side.'

Pushing the coffee aside, he got up from the table and left, slamming the front door with enough force to shake the entire house.

Adrenaline pumping, Steven strode towards Fraser's unmarked BMW. Although he had nothing to hide, Steven was determined not to fall into any more traps, like unwittingly admitting he'd been in Caroline's flat the night of the murder. If they wanted to question to him further, it would be with a lawyer present.

The DS lowered his window cautiously as Steven approached.

'Isn't there a zebra carcass somewhere you should be hovering over?' Steven demanded.

'What a comedian,' Fraser snarled. 'Listen up you cunt. Go anywhere near Caroline's family again and we'll fucking have you.'

Steven gazed up at the hard blue sky, snapped open his sunglasses and slipped them on. 'You need to sharpen up, mate. Embarrassing how easily I lost you yesterday. But keep at it,' he said walking off, 'busy hands are happy hands.'

Fraser leant out of the window. 'And keep away from the funeral,' he yelled. 'You've been warned!'

''BOUT SODDIN' time!' Fat Ron's belligerent greeting was hurled from the doorway of the Portakabin.

Steven squeezed past his partner and Ron followed him inside.

'Christ, you look like crap,' he said. 'I'll get the kettle on, shall I?'

Steven grunted and Ron went behind the partition into a small area the drivers laughingly referred to as the VIP Lounge. It contained a couple of beat-up old armchairs, a microwave, a fridge, and a small, stained table. But at least it provided a place where the cabbies could rest up between shifts and eat their KFC take-out in peace. Even so, Steven thought slumping into a chair, the sooner they were out of this dump the better.

Ron threw a couple of tea bags into mugs. 'Get my message about Old Bill?'

Steven massaged his forehead. 'What message?'

'I left it with that girl you live with. Told her to tell you they'd 'bin sniffing around and asking questions about last Thursday night. They asked me what time you arrived for work, stuff like that. They've bin here again today. What the fuck you been up to?'

'Nothing.'

Ron poured boiling water into polystyrene cups. 'Come on, mate, what's going on?'

Steven nodded towards a copy of the Daily Star lying on the table. 'The front page.'

'What?'

'The murder in Ridgeworth Street.'

'Yeah? What the hell you got to do with that?'

'Do you remember the red-headed girl who called in here a couple of weeks back, asking to see me?'

''Course. You don't forget a looker like 'er ...' He broke off, '*fuck*. Is it her?'

Steven looked up from the scarred linoleum. Ron was the one person who deserved an explanation. 'I swear to God, Ron, it wasn't me who harmed her.'

'Why would you, mate? Lovely girl like that.' Ron came from behind the table and handed Steven his tea.

'I just want you to know that. It's important to me you know the truth.'

Ron nodded solemnly. 'Your word's good with me, Steve – always has been, always will.'

'Yeah.' Steven stared into his tea.

'Says it was a fucking blood bath.'

Steven nodded. And they'd withheld the worst parts.'

'*Christ*. So why does the filth think you did it? Sounded like it was some kind of nutter off his head on crack. Or maybe it was one of them serial killers.'

Steven shook his head. 'They seem convinced she was killed by someone who knew her. Look, I don't want to talk about it anymore, Ron, except to say I was with her the night she died, which puts me right in the fucking frame.'

Ron looked at him. 'That's what I'd call real bad luck.'

'Yeah. Look, keep as much as you can from the other guys, will you?'

'Goes without sayin'. The cops didn't get no change out of me either.'

'I'd be amazed if they did.'

'Spent ages outside. Going through the wheelie bins.'

Steven laughed. 'Must have found all my other victims, then.'

'They giving you a rough time?'

'They're only getting started.' Steven stared down at the insipid looking tea.

'That's why they wanted to know what time you got here that night, stuff like that?'

Steven took a sip of the milky liquid. *You had to hand it to Ron, he was consistent, his tea was always crap.*

'I only told them the bare minimum,' Ron was saying. 'Never went into any details about your private life, nothin' like that.'

'There aren't any details to tell, are there?'

'Yeah, but...'

'Look. Don't worry. If they come back, just answer whatever questions they throw at you.'

Ron was the one person he knew, who would do almost

anything for him, but he didn't want him being deliberately obstructive and getting himself into trouble.

'Okay. Will do. You here to do some work?'

'Do I have a choice?'

'No. It'll take your mind off.' He opened a biscuit tin and helped himself to a handful. 'That biddy Mrs Morgan's been right pissed off you ain't been available for her Tesco run. Keeps saying she wants the ugly one, so she must mean you.'

'That woman could moan for Britain.'

Ron crammed a couple of biscuits into his mouth. 'Yeah, well,' he said through a splutter of crumbs, 'she's a bloody good regular so treat her nice.'

Steven drained his tea, dropped the cup on the floor and crushed it under his boot.

17

A FIVE-HOUR SHIFT was as much as Steven could manage. He was back at Briarwood Road by four, his head still pounding from the inevitable hangover despite six Nurofen. He was woefully out of practice. Once he could have drunk double the amount he drank last night and still been in the gym at six the next morning.

Alison was in the kitchen when he walked in. Better to clear the air now he thought. Less chance of it becoming cringingly awkward between them after last nights encounter.

'No!' she cried when he went to the sink, filled a glass with water and drank it down in one go. 'Hair of the dog. You have to keep going.'

He turned to her. 'Not the advice I'd expect from a nurse.'

Alison smiled. 'Sometimes I doubt my vocational choice.'

'Last night ...' Steven began, 'it's all a bit of a blur. I hope ... well, I hope I didn't make a complete twat of myself? Try to take things too far?'

'You mean you're not going to marry me, give me lots of babies and die in my arms?' she asked solemnly.

Steven caught the glint of amusement in her eyes and laughed.

'Any good with computers?' she asked, deftly changing the subject.

'Fair. Got a problem?'

'Yeah, with Word. My curser's gone AWOL Tried everything to get it back, but no luck.'

Steven poured himself another glass of water.

'Just say if you don't feel up to it.'

'Go get your computer,' he said.

ALISON LET OUT an exaggerated breath as she looked around. 'I'm impressed. Beyond impressed, I'm amazed. No underpants on the floor. No empty beer cans rolling about. No plates with ten-day-old pizza crusts. This is so not like any other guy's room I've ever been in.' She broke off and frowned. 'Christ, you don't colour code your socks and disinfect the soles of your shoes before you put them back in the wardrobe, do you?'

'If I've got time. In between counting in multiples and worrying that I might be the cause of that earthquake in Japan.'

Alison gave an understanding nod. 'I had a roommate at college who hoovered up crumbs from my plate while I was still eating.'

'Sit down. 'It's hard to concentrate with you prowling around.'

Obediently she sank down next to him and watched his hands moving across the keys her mouth suddenly dry. They were nice hands. A man's hands, if that made sense. Last night he'd been so drunk she hadn't really believed the things he'd said, but that didn't mean she hadn't wanted to.

'Look, whatever I said last night, I had no right,' he said as though reading her mind.

Her response to this was obviously too long in coming as the next moment he was on his feet and locating the nearest socket. 'Battery's low.'

'If I tell you something,' she said, 'do you promise not to repeat it to Ellen?'

Steven plugged in the laptop lead. 'What kind of something?'

'You have to promise first.'

He straightened up and swiped a finger across his heart.

'Okay. Now I know you like it here and I really don't want to spoil it for you but remember when we had that conversation about all the people who may have died in this house?'

'Yeah. It's not something that bothers me.'

'Good, as I've found out something since then. Mark, this radiologist at the hospital told me some time back, before he and his wife were married, she used to rent a room here.'

'Go on.'

'Well, he told me that shortly after she moved in, she found out that the house had a bad reputation with local people. Bad as in creepy. There were a couple of deaths here about twenty years ago apparently. He doesn't know all the circumstances, only that the people who died were family members. Look, I really don't want you mentioning any of this stuff to Ellen'

'I've said I won't. I know her father died when she was a child, she told me that herself. That could be one of the deaths this guy's referring to.'

Alison shrugged. 'Maybe. But Mark implied it was the *way* these people died that made it creepy.' She looked around. 'Your room *is* lovely, but even in here I feel them, the *bad vibes*. Can't you feel them too?'

'Nope. Are you thinking of moving out?'

'No. I...'

'Good.' He held her eyes and the message in them was loud and clear. Colour warmed her cheeks and she looked quickly away. A charged silence hung between them.

'Come here,' he said softly.

Without thinking about it, she stood up and walked towards him. He pulled her hard against him, the heat of his body searing through her as his mouth come down hard on her own.

A sharp rap on the door came as they surfaced for air, light-headed from their second kiss. They stood not breathing, staring into each other's eyes like two naughty children caught out in a prank. Steven put a finger to his lips.

'Steven?' Ellen called.

Alison pressed both hands over her mouth to suppress a giggle. Steven swore and tucked his shirt back into his trousers while she smoothed her hair into some semblance of order.

There was another impatient rap. 'Steven?'

He waited a few more seconds before opening the door.

Ellen walked in, saw Alison and stopped in her tracks. 'Oh. I didn't realise *she* was here.'

'No problem. *She* is just leaving,' Alison said, grabbing her computer. 'I'll bring it back later, Steve.'

Ellen's eyes swept from Alison back to Steven.

'What...' Steven began

As Alison ducked out of the door, Ellen made a quick zipping motion across her mouth, warning him to be silent. Coming from Ellen it was such an incongruous gesture he almost laughed.

Head cocked, Ellen waited until she heard Alison's door close across the hallway before she spoke. 'They came again today. Those two officers. The fat one and the small one.

They knew you weren't here. They wanted to search your room, but I wouldn't let them.'

'And they just went away?'

Ellen rubbed her thick lips and nodded.

'They can't have had a warrant.'

'I said they couldn't search it, not without you being here.'

'If they'd had a warrant, they could have come in whatever you s....'

'*I wouldn't have let them!*' Ellen shouted.

Steven stared at her. 'Right... Okay. Well, thanks for ... helping. I'm sorry they keep turning up and being a pain.'

He went to the door and held it open. Again she was being dismissed. She left reluctantly. Looking back at him with wounded animal eyes.

Alison hadn't been able to concentrate on anything since returning to her room. Giggling like a teenager she was searching through her Playlist looking for something that matched her elated mood, when there was a sharp rap. Almost skipping across the room, she opened it and had to hastily re-arrange her features when she saw Ellen standing there with her teeth bared in what the girl no doubt thought passed for a smile.

'I need to speak to you about last night,' Ellen said, walking straight in.

'Last night? What's to explain?' Alison quickly picked up the pile of clothes from the chair and looked around vaguely for somewhere to put them.

'It's the strain. That's why he's drinking.'

'Strain? What are you talking about?'

Ellen went to the window, lifted the curtain and

peered out.

Alison stared at Ellen. She was a tragic sight. Her broad back sheathed in a grubby beige cardigan and her large feet stuffed into fluffy pink slippers.

Ellen's head shot around then, as though she had heard these thoughts and her eyes seemed so large and dark Alison felt she was swimming in them.

'He hasn't told you, has he?' Ellen stated. 'I assumed as you two were so pally, he would have told you everything.' She gave an unpleasant little laugh.

Alison clutched her armful of washing, uneasy now, wondering what kind of Mad Martha nonsense this was. 'Told me *what?*'

'I don't see he can keep it quiet for much longer.'

'Keep *what* quiet, Ellen?' Alison demanded.

'Come here.' Ellen lifted the net at the window again.

Dumping the washing on her desk Alison obeyed.

'See that blue car?' Ellen pointed.

Frowning, Alison scanned the parked vehicles on the other side of the street. 'Yeah, okay, I see it. What about it?'

Ellen plucked at her bottom lip. 'It's a police car. He's under twenty-four-hour surveillance.'

'Steven?'

Ellen dropped the curtain. 'That murder in Ridgeworth Street.'

Alison stared at her.

'Haven't you seen the papers?'

'I've *seen* the headlines, but I haven't read anything about it. The fact it's a local girl makes it doubly horrible.'

'It's been on the news.'

'*Hang on!*' Alison broke in. 'What are you telling me here? That the police think *Steven* has something to do with that?

'The victim was Steven's old girlfriend. He was there in her flat the night she was killed.'

'I don't ...' Alison began, then found she couldn't say anything else at all, as suddenly it felt as though there wasn't enough oxygen in the room.

'I really thought he would have explained everything to

you by now,' Ellen said. 'Oh. Thanks for bringing him home by the way.'

Alison drew a ragged breath and sat down hard on the chair.

'We haven't set a date yet,' Ellen voice was now a monotone, as though reciting something she had memorised. 'We'll have to wait until all this other business is cleared up first. Oh, one other thing. You'll have to move out. We'll want the house to ourselves before long.'

It took Alison a few moments to assimilate Ellen's last words but by then Ellen had left. She remained sitting, despair as heavy as a rockslide weighting her heart. *This* man was someone she had just kissed, someone she'd allowed herself to develop feelings for. And what the hell had Ellen just implied? That they were a couple? Well, thank God Ellen had walked in on them when she did, she thought numbly, because she was under no illusions, she had been every bit as willing as him to take it further. That thought sickened her now. All that crap she'd believed about him being the kind of man who 'made his own money'. Yeah, right. While secretly making plans to get his hands on Ellen's pile. One thing she couldn't blame him for was making a fool of her. She'd done a perfectly good job of that herself. But that was nothing, compared to this other stuff Seven was involved in. Grabbing her phone, she made a call. This was the very last night she would ever spend at Briarwood Road.

18

There was no sign of the blue police car when Alison left the house at a run. Headphones on, soles of her trainers slapping against wet pavement, she soon got a rhythm going and it felt good to be moving, no longer cooped up in that little room in what has turned out to be some kind of madhouse. If she'd managed two hours sleep, she'd be surprised. A couple of times she'd got up in the night to check, and then double-check that her door was locked, afraid Steven might cross the hall with the intention of finishing what they had started just a few hours earlier.The possibility of that happening had sickened her.

It was raining heavily now. Alison sheltered under a shop's awning and scrolled through her phone, reading the front page of the Mail. Details of the murder were scant and the report was little more than a plea for anyone with information to come forward. But then she read the final sentence.

'A thirty-four-year-old local man was taken in for questioning but released later without charge.'

That happened. Likely suspects released through lack of evidence. Some of them going on to murder again. She stared up at the tin-coloured sky, a sense of loss enveloping her. Exactly *what* she was mourning she couldn't say, but that didn't make it any it less painful. Pulling up her hood she ran all the way back to Briarwood Road unlaced her trainers, kicked them off and flung them into the corner of the room. Never before had she fallen for someone so hard and so fast. But *he*, (she refused to say his name, even to herself) had succeeded in stripping away an intrinsic, inner part of herself she defined as trust, and she would never forgive him for it. Wiping away a few hot tears, she blew her nose and marched out of the door. A few minutes later she was sitting in Miss King's room.

Despite her protests, Miss King had insisted on making some tea. 'I rarely get visitors these days,' she'd said, cheerfully enough.

The old lady had what Blanche always referred to grandly as 'The Suite'. Alison was disappointed. All 'The Suite' seemed to comprise of was a small sitting room with a separate bedroom through an adjoining door.

Keeping a kettle in your room was something Blanche had warned Alison was 'strictly against rules' when she'd first arrived at Briarwood Road. She was heartened to see Miss King was a rebel.

As she gazed around at the photographs and mementos that documented the old lady's life, Alison deliberated the best way to approach the subject. The last thing she wanted was scare Miss King into a heart attack.

While Miss King boiled water, spooned tea-leaves into a pot, and set out faded china, Alison made space on the small occasional table in front of her. 'I had a visit from Ellen yesterday,' she began tentatively. 'Did she come and speak to you too?'

'I regret I was not afforded the pleasure.' Miss King replied with a smile.

'Well, you've probably got nothing to worry about then.'

The old lady looked at her.

'Ellen's asked me to leave,' Alison stated.

'Leave? Whatever for?'

'Oh, it's a personal thing. Ellen and I have never hit it off.'

'But that's awful!'

'I'll be fine, don't worry. I've got friends I can stay with.'

'I'd like to see her try and throw me out! I've no intentions of leaving here other than in a box. *Oh*. That was tactless of me, what with recent events. But moving would be *far* too distressing at my age. I'm used to it here. I'm quite content.' She brought the tea on a tray and set it down on the table before lowering herself slowly into an armchair.

Alison felt momentarily chastened by this old woman's acceptance of her lot. Maybe it was a generation thing, an aptitude now lost. She couldn't think of a single person she knew of her own age who would describe themselves as 'content'.

'Let me pour,' she offered, and leaning forward she filled the thin, old-fashioned teacups. 'The thing is, Miss King, I didn't come just to tell you I was leaving. There's stuff going on here that you're probably not aware of and I just wanted to make sure you are in the picture. Have you seen the newspapers recently?'

The old lady waved a dismissive hand. 'I never buy those wretched things, they depress me so.'

Alison nodded. 'I don't either but after what Ellen told me ...' she broke off, wondering if she could justify what she was about to do. She sipped her tea and thought quickly. Leaving Miss King in ignorance, all alone in this house with a psycho and his dysfunctional sidekick was, she decided, the crueller option.

Miss King regarded her with interest. 'What has Ellen told you?'

Alison took a breath and began again. 'I really don't want to frighten you, but Ellen told me today that our neighbour across the hall, *she still couldn't say his name,* is a suspect in that local murder case.'

'You can't mean Steven?'

'Yes.'

'What utter nonsense. I don't believe it for a moment. Ellen's making up stories.'

'The girl, Caroline Shaw, was murdered four days ago, she was Steven's ex.'

'Have the police arrested him?'

'Well ... he's been interviewed.'

'And?'

'They let him go.'

'There you are then, it's just Ellen's nasty imaginings. I've lived in this house for over twenty years. It was never my intention to stay so long of course, but I became settled and I'm not one who craves change for the sake of it. Anyway, Ellen was a very small girl when I first arrived. She was such a sorry little thing then, scurrying around like a little mouse. You could never get a squeak out of her. Hardly surprising as Blanche used to bully her so and the poor girl was forever at her beck and call. I know I am speaking ill of the dead, but Blanche did treat her abominably. It's no wonder Ellen has turned out a little ...'

'Miss King –' Alison cut in, adopting a more emphatic tone. 'Ellen said the police have stationed a car outside the house. They are watching his every move.'

'Really? Have you seen it?'

'Yes...well, I saw *a* car. But Ellen said– '

'I'm beginning to think Ellen talks a lot of dangerous nonsense and I think I preferred her when she didn't say anything at all. Steven was in here yesterday repairing my vacuum cleaner and chatting to me about all the odd characters who work for his company. He didn't need to go out of his way to amuse an old woman, Alison. I just don't believe for a moment that he would be capable of anything awful.'

'He gets aggressive when he's had a drink.'

'Well, that's a shame, but fairly common and it doesn't make him a murderer. From what I see he works very hard trying to make a go of this business of his and I respect him for that. He hides a lot under that tough exterior but I'm sure underneath it all, he's a good man. I pride myself on being a sound judge of character, Alison, it's one of my few remaining faculties.'

'But what about this? Ellen told me Steven was at her flat the night she died.'

'If that's true, it would place him in a delicate situation. But; I'm sorry my dear, I like Steven and it would take more than coincidence or Ellen's hearsay to convince me he was capable of murdering some poor girl.'

Alison sighed. She'd wasted her time. Steven's charm was just as potent to females as ancient as Miss King it seemed. She'd intended informing her of the impending nuptials but found she couldn't stomach mentioning it. Let the old lady find out for herself. Standing up, she gave Miss King a quick hug. 'I really don't like leaving you here alone.'

'Don't you worry! I will be fine. I can handle Ellen and all her silly nonsense.'

Alison turned at the door. 'Don't you ever get lonely?'

Miss King shook her head and waved towards a bookcase filled with worn hardbacks. 'I have my books and my music, it's enough.'

Alison left Miss King sitting in her armchair, ingots of

sunlight playing on the rug at her feet feeling she had done her duty. She could leave with a guilt-free conscience. If the old girl chose to ignore her warning there was nothing more she could do and as she began to pack her belongings, she made a welcome discovery, the only emotion Steven Finn evoked in her now, was revulsion.

AT THE END of a tiresome day Georgia had just finished reading Love-Struck of Chiswick's second desperate appeal for help. The completely wet sounding girl had failed to snare some equally thick sounding clod, despite having been last month's recipient of Harriet Hope's on-page profound pearls of wisdom. What kind of a loser still relied on archaic Royal Mail to deliver letters anyway? Georgia slid the letter into her waste bin and logged out of her desktop.

In the lift she checked her reflection in the mirror. If she *were* to give any final advice to 'Love-Struck,' it would be to '*take the bull by the horns*'. Maybe she should extend that piece of advice to herself. Unclipping a tortoiseshell barrette, she allowed her hair to fall seductively around her shoulders. Patience was getting her nowhere.

Her driver was standing by the car as she walked down the steps of the building. She smiled as he opened the rear door for her. Tonight, he was wearing a tie. Hermes. He kept it in the glove compartment and only wore it for corporate clients. There were a few other facts she had learnt about him too. That he liked his coffee strong, preferably Starbucks double espresso, that he intended to retire to Italy, and he had a weakness for women he assumed were socially out of his league.

Sinking into the back seat Georgia gazed up at him and smiled. As expected, his face remained professionally impassive as he tucked in the hem of her coat and closed her door. But who was he kidding? She'd been aware of the frisson between them for some time and that made the situation all the more frustrating and irresistible at the same time.

Ignoring the, 'No Smoking' sign she lit up. An immediate whine of electric windows followed. She grinned and blew smoke in his direction. If winding him up was the only way to get a reaction so be it. Yawning sleepily, she stretched. Steven's eyes shifted to the rear mirror in time to see just how perfectly the silk material of her shirt emphasised the curve of her breasts.

Georgia had a self-indulgent evening planned. A long soak in the bath with a glass of Chivas Regal for company, followed by a delivered take-away from Good Earth. A roll in her Egyptian cotton sheets would end the evening perfectly of course, but so far, he wasn't playing. She smiled to herself. *Give it time*.

19

REACHING Georgia's riverside apartment Steven drove into the development and pulled up outside the entrance, engine running. Georgia made no attempt to move.

She drew on her cigarette and the tip glowed brightly in the dark. 'What time do you finish?'

'One-ish.'

'How uncivilised.'

'Yeah.'

'Steve?' Ron's East London twang came through the PDA handset.

'POB, Ron.'

'Okay. But get yer arse back here soon as. Charlie's

rung in sick and I've got two Gatwick's waiting. I tell you mate, I'm up shit creek without a spanner.'

Georgia smothered a laugh. 'A colourful if incorrect

turn of phrase,' she whispered.

Steven clicked off and managed a smile. 'He's

got a genius for them.'

Georgia sighed. 'I guess I'd better let you scoot back to your Ron.'

Getting out of the car she leant towards him through the open window and dropped her business card into his lap. Weary and fog-bound his mind may have been, but another part of his anatomy rose gamely at the proximity of her perfumed skin.

'Use it,' she said.

Fixing his eyes upon her legs as she walked away, Steven retrieved the card that nestled against the bulge between his thighs.

ELLEN LAY on the sofa staring moodily at the wall. From the hallway downstairs came the sound of voices. Alison was moving out. Ellen got up and watched her dragging a large suitcase on small wheels down the pathway in the dark and wet. Parked at the kerb was a Van with its rear doors open. A young man was loading stuff into the back. She struggled to make out the man's appearance under the streetlamp. She could discern lank hair and nondescript features. She smiled to herself. *Nothing like my Steven.*

As soon as the van pulled away, Ellen went downstairs. The room seemed much bigger without Alison's stuff cluttering it up.

On top of the mantelpiece Alison had left a folded piece of paper containing her forwarding address and the keys to the house. Ellen scrunched up the paper and slipped it, along with the keys, into her pocket. As she turned to leave, she saw a poster Alison had forgotten to take, tacked to the back of the door.

An athletically built man was pulling on a pair of jeans and gazing over his shoulder with brooding adoration towards a rumpled bed. In the bed lay a sleeping girl, her expression blissful. The caption read: NOW AND FOREVER.

Ellen moved up close to the poster. Only the profile of the man was visible. A well-defined cheekbone, the straight bridge of a nose. Breathing hard she moved closer still and as she studied the sleeping girl, the blonde tresses spread upon the pillow began to turn to red. The girl's eyes, Caroline's eyes, flew open and Steven turned his head

towards Ellen, fixing her with a mocking grin.

Ellen gave a little cry and reeled back. The she lunged at the door and ripping the poster from the door, she shredded it with her hands.

'Ellen! There you are.'

Evelyn King was standing in the doorway watching her. The remnants of the poster slipped from Ellen's hands. Coming out of the room she quickly closed the door behind her.

'Ellen, are you alright? You're shaking,' the old lady

said.

'*Of course,* I'm all right.' Ellen put a hand to her hot forehead.

'I need to speak to you. Is now a bad moment?'

'What do you *want,* Miss King?'

The old lady blinked at her tone. 'Well, it's just that I had some disquieting news this morning. Alison informed me you had asked her to leave. I see now she has already

gone.'

'She was a bad tenant,' Ellen rattled off. 'Not paying her rent on time, that kind of thing. She also told lies so I wouldn't believe anything else she may have told you.'

The old lady stared at Ellen for a few seconds. 'Well, I *am* surprised, I thought her such a nice girl.'

Was there a note of disbelief in Miss King's voice? The

faintest trace of suspicion. Well, Ellen didn't give a *flying fuck (one of Blanche's old favourites)*

She turned and locked the door. 'I'd never ask *you* to leave, Miss King,' she said over her shoulder, 'you know that.'

STEVEN RETURNED AN HOUR LATER. Ellen heard him unlocking his door. Why did he bother locking it in the first place? Was he too stupid to realise she held a master key to every room

in the house?

'Something up?' he asked her as she came downstairs. 'The police been here again?'

She shook her head. 'No. I'd tell you if they had.'

Steven removed his wet jacket and shook it. Throwing the jacket onto his bed he passed her on his way to the kitchen.

Ellen had the still warm garment in her hands and was going through the pockets when he came back.

'I'm making coffee, would you like one?' Steven stood in the doorway.

Ellen froze. *Had he seen what she'd been doing?* 'You should hang this up, it's soaking,' she said quickly.

A knock at the door made them both start. They stared at each other.

'Police?' Ellen whispered.

'Maybe.'

'Wait here.'

'No, I'll ...'

But Ellen was already on her way to the door. Standing in the porch was Graham, rain dripping off his fedora.

'Ellen! Hello!'

'Graham,' Ellen stated flatly.

'Just thought I'd pop round, see how you are, you know. What a filthy night!'

20

GRAHAM CLEARED a space amongst the papers and magazines on the sofa. Removing his hat he dried the brim with his handkerchief and sat down. The last time he'd been in this room was the day of Blanche's funeral. Despite the sombreness of that occasion the room had seemed cosier then. He took in the heap of ashes in the grate, noted the un-vacuumed carpet and the abandoned dirty mugs and plates, but after that conversation with Eva, he was now seeing the house through an estate agent's eyes. Just what would something of this size and period be worth in today's market?

Several million no doubt despite its run-down condition. That such riches were wasted on this semi-educated, half-baked girl was exactly the kind of demeaning sentiment he despised himself for but was powerless to repress.

Ellen returned from the kitchen with two glasses of red wine. She placed one on the small table in front of him.

'Oh! How nice...thank you.' On the silent TV screen was something he thought might be EastEnders, but he couldn't be sure, as not having watched it for years, he couldn't recognise any of the characters.

Leaning forward he clasped his knees. 'So -- how have you been, Ellen? he began brightly. Ellen was perched on the edge of her seat and for an unnerving moment he had

the sudden, fanciful notion she was about to spring at him. Why on earth would he think that? He found himself easing back in his seat anyway.

'I've been fine.' Ellen was eyeing him expectantly.

He took a quick sip of wine. 'Eva insisted I come. She's rather worried about that fellow downstairs.' Which was true of course, but not the main reason he was here. Next time he vowed, Eva could do her own dirty work. The mild pain in his temple that struck up when he'd arrived had now cranked up several notches and the familiar accompanying nausea told him he was in for one of his migraines.

'Why would Eva be worried about Steven?' Ellen asked, her eyes glittering points in the dimly lit room.

'Graham shifted in his seat. 'Well...er... it's hardly reassuring for us to know you could be living under the same roof as a, ... as a suspect in a murder case.'

'Steven hasn't done anything.'

'How do you *know* that?'

'I just do.'

Suddenly Ellen giggled. The sound struck him as incongruous and slightly unnerving. He massaged his right temple. *Lord*, now the girl's attention was wandering, her eyes moving restlessly around the room. That there had always been a shifting quality about Ellen's appearance . occurred to him now. Sometimes she seemed much younger than her years, her movements quick and fluid as a child's. A cunning-eyed child that is. Other times she appeared much older; slow in movement . You just

never knew which Ellen you were going to get. Tonight's version seemed tense and preoccupied. She was watching something in the shadows. Something beyond his left shoulder. It took a strong effort of will resist the urge to turn around and check no one was standing there. Setting his glass down on the table (red wine and a migraine

were not a desirable mix, and the wine was awful anyway) he forced himself to continue. 'Look. Ellen. We really have no wish to interfere, but you must understand, Eva has known you since you were a child and naturally, she feels concern, even though she has more than enough on her plate with Joan.'

Ellen's eyes shifted back to him. 'How is Joan?'

Graham shook his head. 'Not good. Not since the funeral. It's really set her back. Of course she never really got over Diana, and now this... losing Blanche,' he shook

his head. 'She's become terribly frail, you know. Not eating. We are quite concerned.'

'She seen a doctor?'

'Swears blind by all this homeopathic stuff. But from what I can see it's not doing her any good. She's finding it hard to sleep too and when she does manage to drop off,

she says she has these awful, vivid dreams...'

Ellen's attention was wandering again. Her face slackening as her eyes fixed beyond his left shoulder once more. Under his Harris Tweed, goose flesh broke out

out on Graham's arms. There was something about that intense, focussed stare he really didn't like. But, he reminded himself, all he had to do was be Eva's good little messenger boy and then leave. He cleared his throat.

'About your mother, actually.'

'Oh?' Ellen's eyes came back to him.

'It's understandable. They were very close.'

Ellen nodded.

'And of course we all know she fancies herself a bit

psychic and quite frankly she's got herself into a state. She's absolutely convinced that your mother is trying to reach her. Some message from Beyond. You know the kind of thing. Oh, I'm not upsetting you, am I? Don't let me prattle on.' But he saw that he had gained her full attention now. She was watching him over the rim of her glass.

'What kind of message?'

He smoothed his hands down the crease of his trousers. 'Um...it's probably best if -'

'Shouldn't I know? This is *my* mother you're talking about.'

Graham pressed his hand to his temple again. *God this was so awkward and he hadn't even broached the main purpose for the visit yet.* 'Yes, of course. Well ... Joan has this unshakeable belief that your mother's death was not ... look, please don't get upset.'

Ellen shook her head.

'A belief that her death was not an *accident.* Of course, Eva and I don't encourage her in this nonsense, but no matter what we say, she won't be dissuaded.'

Ellen took a sip from her glass.

'You mustn't be cross with her,' Graham continued, hastily. 'She's become terribly confused, and due to all this other nasty business, she's now convinced Steven is implicated somehow. She's even been bothering the police with her silly notions.'

'Poor Joan.'

Graham sighed, 'Yes, indeed.'

Ellen swirled the wine in her glass. 'She probably just needs taking out of herself.'

Graham nodded. 'I think that's exactly what she needs.' He took a deep breath, 'as well as help of a more *practical* nature. This is delicate, Ellen, and I know I've no right to ask, but Eva and I were wondering ... about the will. You must know if Joan is a beneficiary. She seems to believe she is, and I really hate putting you on the spot, but she really is going downhill fast and we're sure the state of her finances is making--'

'The only beneficiary is me,' Ellen cut in.

Graham stared at her. 'I see,' he said finally. 'That's unfortunate. I believe she was depending on receiving *something*, but of course one must respect Blanche's wishes.'

Ellen gazed at him with what he could only describe as an insolent smile.

Why in God's name had Blanche encouraged Joan in this belief? It seemed extraordinarily cruel. And then another more daunting question followed. Who was going to break the news to Joan? *Not him*, he'd make bloody sure of that. He'd done more than his bit by coming here and sounding the girl out. Now, thank Christ he could go. He moved to rise from his chair. 'Oh. Yes. Nearly forgot. *Christmas*.

If you have no plans; (*and I hope to God you have*) Eva insists you come. It'll be a subdued celebration under the circumstances, but Eva can always be relied upon for a first-class lunch.'

Ellen smiled with her lips pressed together. 'Thanks,' 'but I'll be spending it here with Steven.'

ELLEN SAW GRAHAM OUT. On the doorstep he turned and appealed to her. 'Perhaps you would give Eva a ring? She'd love to hear from you, and it would put her mind at rest a little that you are okay.'

'Yes. I'll ring her.'

'Thank you. Then I'll wish you a good ... ' Before Graham could finish, the heavy oak door closed in his face.

21

Restless after Graham's visit, Ellen left the house. Stuffing her hands deep into her pockets she set off at a decisive pace for someone who wasn't sure where they were going. As the rain turned to sleet, she found herself walking along Frampton Street, past the parade of festive, brightly lit shops. Even the hardware store had gone overboard. Pulsating ropes of LED lights chased themselves crazily around a big bay window, while wire reindeer with flashing red noses pranced amongst the Pyrex dishes and turkey-sized roasting trays. But as she passed the estate agent's window, she saw something that made her stop.

On the other side of the glass, a magical miniature village had been created with an icicle-hung church and watermill and pretty snow-clad cottages, from whose lighted windows came a cosy red glow. There was even a village green, complete with frozen duck pond and tiny skaters and a railway station, where passengers dressed warmly in caps and mufflers, stood on the platform awaiting the arrival of the little train that trundled along a circular track. Congregated beneath the station's awning, were a group of carol singers with red painted cheeks, mouths open in little round 'O's' as they sang.

Ellen stood gazing at the nostalgic scene with her fingers pressed against the glass like a child staring into a sweet shop, until the Rotarian outside Waitrose in a Santa suit, spotted her. Lurching towards her, beard askew, he rattled his collection bucket and breathed boozy fumes into her face. Ellen shoved passed him. It was a hard shove. Enough to make him stagger and nearly lose his footing on the wet, slippery pavement.

She crossed the street quickly and kept on walking until she reached the corner of Dukes and Reckitt Road. Here she stood for a few moments while an easterly wind grabbed at her hair and sent leaves dry as old bones skittering along the gutter. Only then did she realise she was just a few minutes' walk from Joan's house.

Had this been intentional? Well, she wasn't really sure, but she carried on along the empty street anyway, turning over in her mind the conversation she'd had with Graham. Joan taking her crackpot theories to the police was irritating enough, but even more irritating was that Blanche *had* bequeathed her some money. Thirty-five thousand to be exact. But the good thing was, Joanie didn't know it yet. The silly old woman *hoped* of course, and Blanche must have said something to raise those hopes over the years. Having spoken to Mr Pryce her solicitor yesterday she now knew that any other beneficiaries would be hearing within the next two weeks.

Two weeks. A lot could happen in that time. Particularly as Joan was working herself up into one of her states. Ellen waited at the pedestrian crossing wondering just what it would take to make the scraggy old bitch crack. Some late-night phone calls, perhaps? Silent and creepy. Or a visit. *Like the one she's about to make now.*

But then as she crossed the road and passed the fire station, her next thought made her come to a sudden halt. Why bother? Once the lie she'd told Graham was passed on, she might not need to do a thing. It might actually finish the daft old bat off once and for all. And with that thought, Ellen turned her face into the wind and set off towards home, lighter of heart.

22

In the distance St Michael's bells rang out, heralding Christmas day. Groggily Ellen pushed hair out of her eyes and forced herself to sit up, regretting the two sleeping pills she'd taken the night before. The effort required was akin to dragging herself up from a very deep well. Through slitted eyes she peered around. The room seemed strangely bright and from beneath the thin curtain light streamed in. Getting out of bed she went to the

widow and saw that there had been a heavy fall of snow during the night. It blanketed the garden, thick and as yet, unsullied. Only yesterday Steven had told her the bookies had slashed the odds for a white Christmas. He always seemed to know these weird little things.

Pulling on a dressing gown she went barefoot into the sitting room and almost tripped over the box of decorations she'd hauled down from the attic. She *had* intended to put them up, but like a lot of things these days, she hadn't got round to it. She'd

also intended to buy the expensive silver tree she'd seen in

John Lewis to replace the tired piece of tat Blanche dragged out each year. The John Lewis one came with its own fairy lights, all you had to do was plug it in. Somehow she hadn't got around to that either. She stared down at the dusty lid of the box. What would have been the point? Steven was far too busy to spend any of his precious time with her. He'd reminded her of the fact only last night when she'd returned from her walk. Rushing off out of the door to fuck knows where, as though he didn't have a second to spare, without even a *glance* at her.

Invisible. That's what she was. What she had become. Some days she almost wished Blanche was back. Being the object of her mother's despair and loathing had at least provided her with the confirmation she existed. Standing in the middle of the room now, she turned a bottle of sleeping pills over and over in her dressing gown pocket while her thoughts drifted off, wandering the bleak terrain of her mind.

When she came back to herself, she went to the window. The Mercedes was there, within a line of vehicles, all wearing plump duvets of snow. Surely, he wouldn't attempt to drive today? She glanced up at the eye-wateringly blue sky hoping there wouldn't be a thaw. For once there was no distant hum of traffic on the by-pass just the raised, excited voices of children playing in a neighbouring garden.

Shuffling into the kitchen, Ellen lit the grill and hovered over it for warmth. From the front of the house came the repetitive sound of metal striking concrete.

He stopped shovelling when he saw her. 'Happy Christmas, Ellen. Why don't you get dressed. It's too beautiful a day to waste.' There was sweat on his brow and exertion had brought warm colour to his cheeks.

Ellen's sour thoughts were suddenly buried under a wave of something so powerful it left her dazed. She turned and floated rather than ran for the stairs but on the landing she stopped dead, because from somewhere came a sound.

Scritch. Scritch.

And then it came again and in the pit of her stomach something oily churned like a mass of roiling eels. She wasn't aware she'd screamed until Steven came bounding up the stairs. 'Ellen – what the hell-'

Ellen pointed. 'There's something's in there, in Blanche's room,' she panted and leant against the wall for support.

Steven stared at the closed bedroom door. 'Ok, stay there. I'll check it out.'

He moved swiftly, grabbing the brass handle and yanking the door open. A blur of colour darted out and snaked itself around Ellen's ankles.

'Get away!' Ellen screamed, lashing out with her foot.

'Fuck, it's only a cat,' Steven said laughing.

'How did it get in there? How did it? I never open that door.'

'Ellen calm down. I'll take a look, okay?'

Going into the room Steven glanced around and then went over to the sash window and examined it. 'Right, okay. Mystery solved. This top pane has slipped down somehow. Christ, he must have jumped from the roof of next door's extension. That's the only way he could manage it. Quite a feat, even for a cat.'

Ellen stood in the doorway, but she no intention of going in that room, now or ever. Her early enthusiasm for moving into it dissipated immediately after the funeral. Removing the clothes from the wardrobe and the trinkets from the dressing table would achieve nothing. Blanche's insidious presence remained. It hung in the air, real and tangible, like stale cooking smells or cigarette smoke.

'The catch is broken,' Steven was saying. 'Look, see here.'

Ellen remained where she was. 'I'll get someone to fix it.'

'You'll be lucky. No one's going to want to come out to do such a small job. I could do it. I'll just need to find a replacement catch. It's a five-minute job.'

Ellen wiped the sweat from her palms on her dressing gown. 'Are you sure? You don't mind?'

'If I minded, I wouldn't offer.'

The cat had followed Steven back into the room and was now making itself comfortable on Blanche's bed. Steven sat down beside it. 'You just wanted to get out of the cold, didn't you,boy?' He ran his hand down the length of the cat's sturdy body, it arched its back and mewed.

Steven grinned at her. 'I'd have thought it would take a lot more than a mog to scare you. Don't you like cats?

'Not that one'.

'Aww. Poor little bugger. It's probably a stray.'

Ellen watched his hands caressing the soft fur. 'No. It belongs to the doctor in the white house at the end. It keeps getting in.'

Steven gently pulled its ears. 'Oh, so you're here on false pretences are you, mate?'

'Can you put it out, *please*.'

'Okay, okay.' He spoke to the cat again. 'Let's get you outside before you give Ellen a heart attack.' He scooped up the reluctant animal. 'I'll finish the path now. I won't be able to get a catch for the window until after Christmas, but if I can find a piece of wood, I'll prop it closed for the time being.'

Ellen gave him a shaky smile.

'You okay, now?' he asked walking past her with the cat squirming in his arms. She nodded and stepped back quickly to avoid its lashing tail. As she was pulling the bedroom door to, she paused for a moment and stared into the room. Then she slammed it shut and hurried off to find the key. From now on she would keep it locked so nothing could get in or more importantly, *get out*.

'She seemed odd. Odder than usual, that is,' Graham told Eva over the phone. 'I was glad to get out of there, I can tell you.' He had already imparted the worst of the news, that Joan's hopeful expectations from Blanche's estate would not be realised.

Eva had been as shocked as he. 'It'll finish her off. She was really counting on it.'

'She's done something to her hair,' Graham said, changing the subject. 'Dark reddish tints. Not the wisest choice when one is so sallow. *And* she was drinking wine. Never seen her do that before. Such a tragedy isn't it, Blanche's entire estate going to a girl who wouldn't know a Chateauneuf du Pape from the cheapest Portuguese plonk?'

Eva sighed. Graham's bombshell had made her thoroughly depressed. She couldn't understand how Blanche could have deliberately misled her old friend into thinking she had been included in her will. But then possibly, Blanche's oversight was because being the younger of the two, she really hadn't believed she'd be the first to go. Joan's feelings for Blanche, the intensity of them, had been something neither she nor Graham had chosen to speculate on too closely over the years, skirting around the subject, or ignoring it altogether. Often, she had felt the two women's co-dependent relationship shared the same charmless quality as that of tick-bird and wildebeest, but she managed to keep this uncharitable thought to herself. 'So, did you invite Ellen to lunch?'

Graham nodded. '

'What did she say?'

'Not in the least bit interested. Just you and me, I'm afraid.'

'What about Siddie?'

Graham's eyes suddenly filled with tears. 'Oh, Eva, we had the most dreadful row last night. He's cleared off, he's left me.'

23

Ellen tore little strips off the message pad as Eva's voice droned on in her ear.

'They pumped him out late last night, so of course he was very sore this morning. Thank goodness Siddie went back to steal more things or he would never been found in time. Found Graham unconscious in bed, the little shit. Hope it gave him the fright of his life.'

'Graham ought to be grateful to him, then,' Ellen said, flatly.

'*What?*' Eva said. 'If it hadn't been for Siddie it wouldn't have happened in the first place! Ellen? – are you there?'

'Yes.'

'Perhaps you could send him a card or some flowers? I hope you didn't mind him coming round for that little chat the other evening? Erm...we were both rather shocked - to hear about the Will.'

'To hear what about the Will?'

'That Joan is to receive nothing.'

'Oh. That.'

'Yes ...well, none of our business of course.'

Blood was beating heavily in Ellen's temples, her internal storm clouds brewed. 'You're right Eva, it's not.' Slamming down the phone she stalked to the window and peered out. The snow-clad Mercedes was still there. He hadn't gone to work, but he had gone somewhere - on foot. She'd heard him come out of the shower and get dressed while listening to his music. Nearly always some old band she'd never heard of. Old bands with stupid names like Pearl Jam.

HE RETURNED A FEW HOURS LATER. Ellen heard him collide with the hall table and swear to himself.

'Drunk again,' she said, speaking slowly, like someone talking in their sleep. As his bedroom door slammed shut she tore another strip from the Chiswick Advertiser and continued shredding. Her lap, the carpet and the sofa were now covered in little heaps of fragmented newsprint.

24

HOPKINS RELEASED his seat belt with a sense of relief as the car finally pulled up on the grass verge outside Doughty House. He was looking forward to getting out and stretching his legs after ninety minutes cooped up in a small saloon not designed for a man of his size, but he waited patiently while Fraser stripped off his gloves and stuffed them into the side pocket of the door. The gloves had electrostatic fabric on the fingertips apparently. Hopkins hadn't been aware that such a glove existed, but his mysophobic sergeant had enlightened him; explaining that these special tips enabled the wearer to still use their mobile, turn the pages of a book, work on a laptop, *or* drive a car. Such apparel was particularly useful while driving the station's pool car because, and was Hopkins was aware of this? There were seven hundred *different* types of germs per square inch on the average steering wheel.

Hopkins hadn't been aware and would have been grateful it if he still wasn't. Fraser was now transferring his antibacterial gel from his overcoat to his jacket pocket and Hopkins continued to sit patiently while his sergeant deep-breathed and patted the pump in his pocket several times. The two had worked together for four years and Hopkins knew better than to interrupt one of Fraser's little rituals. If he did, they would be here until Lent.

Today, Hopkins was keen to get home to his family and enjoy what would be left of the Boxing Day festivities, even if meant another evening of his brother-in-law cracking walnuts with his teeth and spitting the shells into the fruit bowl. Hauling himself out of the car he waited for Fraser and then the two men walked up the drive.

Hopkins cleared his throat as the door opened. 'Mrs Shaw? Chief Inspector Hopkins and this is Detective Sergeant Fraser. We spoke earlier?'

'Of course. Come in please.'

She stood back and they entered an entrance hall large enough to accommodate a small orchestra. Unsurprisingly, there was no Christmas Tree to greet them, or any other outward sign that Christmas was being celebrated.

On auto pilot, Margaret Shaw waved vaguely at the door mat. 'Would you please?'

They obediently wiped their feet.

'Perhaps you would go through to the drawing room?'

They stood hesitantly, looking around.

'Through there.' Margaret Shaw indicated a door to their left. 'I'll just go into the kitchen and arrange for some tea to be brought.'

'*Drawing room*? What the fuck's that,' muttered Fraser following Hopkins.

'Not up on your Austen, Fraser?' he replied, leading the way into a large, traditionally furnished room with wide, floor length windows, overlooking an expanse of a neat rather featureless garden.

They sat on a cream linen sofa and waited. The room was chilly, despite a gas fire burning. It had fake logs so unrealistic Hopkins found it mildly depressing. If they couldn't make them look more convincing than that, why bother, he wondered. A petite young blonde came in carrying a tea-laden tray and placed it on a table in front of them.

Mrs Shaw introduced her. 'This is Renata,' she said formally. 'She helps out with the house and my grandson.'

Hopkins smiled at the girl, hoping Fraser wasn't leering. Margaret Shaw sat on a matching sofa and poured tea, her thin legs tucked to one side. Without a scrap of makeup, the soft black sweater she wore was draining, the pearls at her neck failing to soften its effect. Hopkins could recall corpses he had seen with more colour than this woman. Taking the dainty china offered, he held it carefully in his large hands. 'We would like to thank you for seeing us today, Mrs Shaw,' he began.

She sat back in her chair and gazed at him, her eyes so raw and red-rimmed, they looked as though every drop of moisture had been squeezed from them. 'It feels like any other day, Chief Inspector,' she replied. We have nothing to celebrate.'

Hopkins nodded. 'I can understand that. We were hoping to speak with your husband too. Is he here?'

'He's on his way. He's been visiting his mother. She's in a nursing home nearby.' She offered a plate of shortbread biscuits. Hopkins shook his head and patted his straining stomach. His lithe sergeant leant forward, grabbed two and tucked them into his saucer.

'Sergeant Fraser here,' Hopkins continued, 'may make some notes while we talk. I hope you won't find that off-putting?'

Margaret Shaw shook her head. A small gesture that seemed to require effort.

'So, how are you managing? With your grandson I mean. Can't be easy having a small child in the house again.'

'No, it isn't. But I think we're coping well. It was

extremely difficult at first. We were total strangers to Luke, after all. It's taken a while but he's settling down now and he's such a good little boy.'

'No doubt a considerable source of comfort to you both.'

Margaret Shaw looked down at her hands. 'He's a gift from God, and all that's left of our daughter.'

'Mrs Shaw, you need to be aware, there will be a police presence at the funeral next Wednesday, but there is no need for concern, it will be a discreet presence, I promise.'

She put a hand to her throat. 'Is that absolutely necessary?'

'In cases like this, yes.'

Hopkins sipped his tea and then placed his cup and saucer on the table. 'Mrs Shaw, do you know if your daughter had any intentions of trying to reignite her relationships with Steven Finn. Did she discuss the matter with you?

'No. But had she chosen to, then naturally I would have tried to persuade her against it.'

'Oh? Why was that?'

Margaret Shaw's lips narrowed to a thin line. 'You know why. I've already explained to the other office that came to ... to break the news. Steven Finn was not the type of person we thought suitable for our daughter.'

'I see. But you hadn't actually met him, had you? Not until he came here, three days ago.'

Margaret Shaw's expression became defensive. 'It's silly to ask questions you already know the answer to.'

'I'm sorry. I imagine Caroline prevented you from meeting him because she guessed you wouldn't approve?'

'That's the conclusion we came to. Yes.'

'But she must have talked about him? They were together for quite a while.'

'A bit. In the beginning. She seemed quite besotted with him. But he's a person with no background, no education. He had a business that was failing for heaven's sake. Well, if you can call selling alcohol after hours a legitimate business. What could a man like that offer my daughter? And we've been proven right, haven't we? All he did was make her unhappy and then he made her pregnant and then ... he killed her, in the most horrible...' Margaret Shaw turned her head away, a hand pressed against her mouth.

Hopkins and Fraser shifted in their seat. 'We have absolutely no evidence, yet that Finn *is* the murderer, Mrs Shaw,' Hopkins said. At the moment it's purely circumstantial. He happened to be with her the night she was killed. *But,* he insists she was still very much alive when he left.'

'And you believe him?' she snapped.

'If he *is* guilty, forensics will do for him, Mrs Shaw. Once we get all the results back, we'll know whether he's our man.'

'Why is it taking so long?'

Hopkins sighed. 'I'm sorry. We're doing the best we can. The amount of data collected in an investigation of this type is enormous. All Christmas leave has been suspended and we have several forensic teams at Caroline's flat as we speak.' When he'd stopped off there last night to check on progress he'd watched the white, Tyvek-clad teams, crawling and swarming, like maggots on a corpse. 'They'll be there for some days,' he finished.

'I'm sure you're doing your best, Inspector Hopkins But can you imagine what it is like for us, thinking of her lying in some awful morgue?' Margaret Shaw's face crumpled for a moment.

Hopkins made a sympathetic sound. 'Can I ask you, Mrs Shaw, did Caroline ever talk much about what her relationship with Finn was like? Do you know if he was ever violent towards her for example?'

'They were *always* having rows. She'd finish with him, or

he'd leave her, but then within days they'd be back together again.'

'Did you ever see bruises on her? Signs of physical abuse?'

'No, but that in itself meant nothing. She would have kept anything like that hidden from me. Too much pride.'

'Did you know that she was in financial difficulties?'

Surprise registered in her eyes. 'No.'

'Was it another type of issue she would have kept to herself?'

'Probably. Look, Inspector, we did our bit. She was given a generous allowance from her father while she retrained to become a teacher, which of course we continued even after she qualified. It's such a poorly paid profession, one we tried really hard to discourage her from pursuing. We wanted her to do something lucrative, respectable. No one has any respect for teachers these days, do they? She had a law degree for heaven's sake. She was such a bright girl, she could have done anything, but she was adamant she wanted to teach. And once Caroline had made up her mind, that was it.'

'So, even with her teaching salary and your allowance, she still couldn't manage.'

Margaret Shaw suddenly looked uncomfortable. 'We put a stop to the allowance eventually,' she said.

'I see. When was this?'

'When she moved in. With *him*.'

'How did you and your husband feel when Caroline confided in you that she was pregnant?'

Margaret Shaw's parched looking eyes blinked at him and for a moment and the only sound in the room was the rasp of Fraser's pencil as he scribbled in his notebook.

'We didn't know about the baby,' Margaret Shaw continued. 'Caroline broke off all contact with us around that time. You can't imagine how painful that was.'

Hopkins regarded the woman for a moment. Her intense

antipathy towards Steven Finn was becoming clearer. He provided somewhere else to lay the blame. Had she been a genuinely supportive mother who loved her daughter unconditionally, she might, just might, have saved Caroline's life. Instead, when things got tough for Caroline, she had only Finn to turn to, the man who quite possibly murdered her.

There was the sound of tyres on gravel. Margaret Shaw got to her feet and brushed something from her skirt. 'This will be my husband.'

Roger Shaw was a stocky Scot. Red-headed like his daughter, with a russet, wind-burned complexion. A golfer Hopkins fancied.

Greeting the two policemen he glanced at their empty cups. 'I see only tea has been on offer, would you gentlemen prefer something stronger?' He walked over to the drink's cabinet. There was an easy geniality about him. Deep creases around the eyes. He looked like the kind of man who enjoyed a laugh and being married to Caroline's mother, probably meant he needed one. Hopkins could just picture him at the bar of his club, guffawing loudly to some mildly off-colour joke with his golfing buddies.

'They're on duty,' Margaret reprimanded.

'Ah, yes, of course. But *I'm* not.'

'Mr Shaw,' Hopkins began. 'From what I understand, you and your daughter were particularly close? Is that correct?'

Margaret's sharp laugh cut in. 'She was always Daddy's girl.'

Roger Shaw splashed Scotch into a heavy looking tumbler and chose an armchair, which Hopkins noted, was some distance from his wife.

He and Fraser waited expectantly.

'This must very difficult for you, sir,' Fraser nudged.

Shaw nodded, and suddenly unable to speak, covered his eyes with a hand. Recovering after a few moments he stared down into his glass and began. 'Caroline came to me roughly six weeks ago. She told me that she needed to find Finn. I asked her why, but she wouldn't say. Apparently, she'd been looking for him for a while but hadn't been able to trace him. She asked me if I would hire a private detective on her behalf. As I was not in the habit of denying her anything, Inspector. I did as she asked.'

Margaret gasped. 'What in God's name –'

'Shut up, Margaret! I hired this guy and he tracked Finn down. Found out where he worked and where he was living and then I passed that information on to Caroline. So, you see, Inspector – indirectly, I'm responsible for my daughter's death.'

'THAT WAS A FRIGGIN' bombshell that was.'

Hopkins and Fraser were crunching their way back down the drive, towards the car.

'Wouldn't want to be in the poor sod's shoes tonight,' mused Hopkins.

'*Tonight*? For the rest of the poor fucker's life, I reckon.' Fraser zapped the lock. 'Did you see the look she gave him? Christ.'

Hopkins grunted as he buckled up. 'You know, I still don't feel I'm getting a clear picture of Finn at all. I think we should go and have a talk with that young woman he rents his room from. I got the impression they were quite pally.'

'That dark-haired bird?' Fraser retrieved his gloves and slipped them on. Can't imagine we'll get much out of her.' Fraser started the engine. There was a clang of exhaust against kerb as they tore off the grass verge and set off back to Barnes.

25

THREE ENVELOPES with familiar scripts lay on the hall table. Today was Ellen's twenty-seventh birthday. Taking the cards upstairs she waited until she had eaten her breakfast before opening them. There was no pleasure of anticipation. She knew exactly who the cards were from.

Graham's offering this year depicted a French girl in old-fashioned dress, exercising a small, fluffy dog in some place called the Place de la Concorde. Inside he had signed it in uncharacteristically shaky handwriting, executed no doubt from his hospital bed.

Eva's card was a copy of an old painting. Ellen quite liked it. The fruit sitting in the bowl was so life-like she could almost taste it. Inside was the familiar scrawl but this year no X's skittered across the page.

And then there was Joan's card. Cheap looking. Yellow roses in a blue vase. Ellen opened it and read the message printed in an erratic hand beneath the salutation.

THe momENt ofTruth has aN edge as SHarp aS aNY SwOrd

Ellen stared at the message. What was the old bat on

about? The jumble of words meant nothing to Ellen. Getting up from her chair she went over to the dresser, opened a drawer and shoved it inside amongst the chaos of broken biros, balls of twine and leaking batteries. The other two cards she put in the bin.

There was one card missing this year of course. The usual hurriedly purchased, garish token from her mother.

Ellen stared listlessly around the small kitchen. Steven had left the house around six and she didn't expect him back until late afternoon.

She wandered downstairs. On the hall table lay a small pile of his unopened mail; she was going through it when she heard his key in the lock. Hurriedly she replaced the letters and stepped away.

'Ellen. Good. I wanted to speak to you,' he said. *No smile or greeting.* He stood at his door. 'Can you come in for a minute?'

It was the first time he had ever actually invited her inside, but she was in no mood to be grateful for any crumbs he might drop. Following him she stood gazing at him reproachfully while he loosened his tie, threw his keys and wallet on the bed, and took off his jacket.

He didn't even know it was her birthday.

'I heard Alison's moved out,' he turned and looked at her. 'That you asked her to leave.'

Miss King. Ellen brushed hair from her face. It hung in unwashed clumps and there was a cold sore clinging to the corner of her mouth. 'People come and go.'

'So... you didn't throw her out?'

Ellen shrugged. *Why the fuck was he so interested?*

'Do you know where she's gone?'

'No.'

'So, she didn't she leave a forwarding address for her mail?'

Ellen's eyes shifted to his. 'She left owing rent. She wouldn't want me to know where she is, would she?'

Steven held her gaze for a few moments, his lips tightening, and then he turned away. She was dismissed.

An hour and a half later, Steven walked through the reception area of Ealing hospital. The main desk was unstaffed but seated at a trestle table was an elderly woman with sparse purple hair and a 'Volunteer' lanyard around her neck. Steven approached her. 'I'm looking for a nurse who works here. Her name is Alison Doyle.'

The woman looked up at him timidly. 'Erm...I'm afraid we're not allowed to give out information about staff members. Would you like one?' She pointed to various leaflets laid out on her table. 'You can take them away,' she added helpfully. He glanced at them, saw that one was for an alcohol dependant help group. 'Could I leave her a message?'

The old lady looked up at him. 'Pardon?'

Steven repeated the question, exaggerating his enunciation.

The woman fiddled nervously with her hearing aid. A muscle clenched in Steven's jaw. Jamming his hands in his pockets he walked away.

Outside the sprawling building he was crossing the car park when he spotted a group of young nurses threading their way through the parked cars. He changed direction and walked towards them.

They watched him approach, tucking stray wisps of hair under their caps. He concentrated his efforts on the dark-haired one. She exuded a cheeky confidence, and her wide smile was almost a come-on. The others stood around eyeing Steven while he spun the brunette a line. Five minutes later he was back inside the main entrance. He passed a Costa Coffee and made his way to the bank of lifts.

The sluice room was on Level 2 of the new surgical centre. He negotiated the featureless maze of corridors leading to it, his boots squeaking on the linoleum. No one attempted to stop him or question why he was there. He waited while a porter pushing a patient on a gurney trundled past and then when the corridor was clear, he pushed open the heavy rubber doors. They swung back behind him with a sucking sound.

In the brightly lit room smelling of disinfectant, Alison leant over a huge sink surrounded by white tiled walls and stainless-steel counter tops. She turned to him her eyes widening. 'How the hell did you get in here?'

He moved towards her. 'I'd imagined a warmer welcome.'

She backed away, anger and something else, (*fear?*) registering in her eyes.

He stopped, puzzled. 'What's wrong?'

'You're a piece of work, you are!'

Steven looked at her. 'I think I must be missing something here.'

'Don't play the innocent. Ellen, your bride-to-be, has explained everything. Where is the mouth-breather by the way? Choosing a venue and the bridesmaid's dresses?'

He stared at her. 'Have you been at the drugs cabinet?'

'You're a bastard liar! Pretending you weren't interested in her and all the time you were...you were....' She found it too painful to convert the images in her head to words. 'But then that's nothing compared to the rest of the shite you're involved in, is it?'

He reached for her arm. She wrenched it away.

'I swear Caroline's death has nothing to do with me'

'Fuck off. I'm calling security.'

'*Listen* for a moment.'

She tried darting past him and there was a clatter as she collided with a zinc bucket. He caught her just before she reached the door and clamped a hand over her mouth before she screamed.

A rustling uniform passed the door. Steven held onto her tightly, her eyes blazed above his hand. In the brief silence all they could hear was the wind outside and rain splattering against the window.

The footsteps faded away. 'This Ellen stuff,' Steven said, 'I've no idea why she'd make up this kind of crap or why the hell you would believe her. Promise not to scream if I take my hand away?'

She glared at him.

'I'm going to have to trust you.' He released her.

Alison rubbed at her mouth and put distance between them.

'What has Ellen told you about Caroline?'

'Enough. But I'm capable of reading newspapers.'

'But you wouldn't have made the connection on your own, would you? I would have explained it all to you – at the right time. You leaving like that –'

'I left because big-thick Ellen kicked me out. Don't flatter yourself it had anything to do with you. But I would have gone anyway. Do you really think I could stay under the same roof as someone who killed that girl and left a child motherless? Christ, only a monster could do that.'

'You think I'm capable of being a monster?' he asked quietly.

'I don't know. I don't *want* to know. Look, *you're* not *getting it, are you?* I just want you to leave me alone!'

Steven held up a hand. 'Okay. Message loud and clear.'

Alison made for the doors, then turned and gave him a searing look. 'Don't *ever* come here again.'

. . .

FINDING his way back to the main entrance, Steven passed through the automatic exit doors so distracted he didn't see the slight figure sheltering in the lobby.

'Steve?'

He turned. 'Siddie. What are you doing here?'

'Visiting. You?'

'Sort of.'

'Graham?'

'No. Is he here?'

'Yeah. Ward Eleven. Didn't Ellen tell you?'

Steven shook his head. Rain clattered on the Perspex roof above their heads. 'What happened?'

'Tried to top hisself.'

'Christ.'

'We had a row the stupid old git. Such a drama queen.'

'How is he?'

'All right. They had to pump him out, though. Precaution they said. He didn't take *that* many. 'Hey, can you give me a lift? I had to get the bus here and it was a bloody nightmare.'

Steven nodded and moved through the sliding exit door and headed for the car park with Siddie following.

'Ere – ,' Siddie asked breathlessly, running alongside Steven to keep up, 'what did the bloke who'd fallen out of the top window of a tower block say as he passed each floor?'

'I don't know,' Steven grunted.

Siddie grinned. 'So far so good, so far, so good.'

Steven shot him a look. 'Siddie, I don't mind giving you a lift, but cut the jokes, will you? I'm not in the mood. And take that thing off your head.'

'What this?' Siddie plucked at his hood.

'Yeah.'

'Why?'

'I don't like them that's why and if you've got a problem with that, get the fucking bus back.'

. . .

Hopkins slapped Caroline's autopsy report on his desk and began relaying the information to Fraser.

'Time of death clarified?' Fraser cut in.

Hopkins shook his head. 'Anywhere between nine pm and five am is the best they could do.'

'Bollocks. Are we going to keep up the pressure on Finn?'

'For the moment, I think so. He's all we've got.'

26

THE MUSIC HAD BEEN GOING on for some time. Ellen heard it in her sleep, echoing up from some dark and empty corridor of her mind.

Blanche was launching into her favourites. Pounding away on the keys of the Baby Grand.

Ellen woke with a jerk, cold and trembling. Willing herself, she turned her head on the pillow until she could just make out the shape of the doorknob. She fixed upon it, straining her ears and her eyes in the darkness. Just in case that doorknob should slowly begin to turn. Just in case the shadow of a small child should dart or start up its bitter crying somewhere within the walls.

Stop it!

Ellen sat up abruptly and fumbled for the lamp switch. Something fell off the bedside table and she groped for it, her fingers closing on the birthday card from Joan. Why had she had taken it from the drawer last night?

Who was she kidding? She knew why.

~

'Just ringing to thank you for my card.'

Silence, apart from Joan's soft breathing.

'Didn't understand the message though. I suppose you were trying to tell me something in your own mental way, but I didn't get it.'

The line went dead.

Ellen replaced the receiver and giggled.

Later, in the dusk-filled cemetery, Joan stood alone except for the clamorous rooks in the branches above her head. Oblivious to the bone-chilling dampness she scraped bird excrement from the small makeshift cross, washed a vase, refilled it with clean water and then arranged the bunch of inexpensive, scentless flowers she had queued in the market for. Bending, she placed a few tired blooms in the vase.

Ellen witnessed all this as she walked along the footpath. *Joan's nervous quick movements*. She never could see the woman without thinking of a mouse. Hearing Ellen's footsteps approach, the little creature jerked up onto her hind legs, quivering, just as a mouse might at the approach of a cat.

Ellen hadn't been able to leave it, of course, despite her earlier intentions. Why allow Graham or Eva to deliver the bad news when it would be so much more fun to deliver it herself? 'Shouldn't you be at home in the warm? Ellen said by way of greeting. 'You'll catch your death here.'

Joan's washed-out eyes regarded her. 'She'd expect me to keep it nice. It's the least I can do for her now.'

Ellen nodded. 'A sort of repayment I suppose. I added up all those old cheque stubs. Came to quite a bit over the years, didn't it?'

Joan's bloodless cheeks flushed as she pulled out a tissue and wiped her lips. 'Your mother was very generous, Ellen. More than I deserved.'

'With what would have been *my* money. How will you manage now? With no more fat cheques coming your way?'

Joan stared down at a wilted bloom in her hand.

'One thing you need to understand, Joan. Whatever my mother told you about leaving you money in her will? It was a lie. She lied to you, Joanie. She's left you nothing. Not a penny.'

Joan's head jerked up, she stared at Ellen and whatever life force she had left, drained out of her.

Ellen smiled. 'It *all* comes to me.' Beneath the dripping yews, falling mist had wreathed the tombstones in ghostly shrouds. 'What's really beginning to piss me off though Joan, is all this trouble you're been stirring up. All this rubbish you've been feeding Graham and Eva, and all these stupid phone calls you've been making to the police.'

Joan's lower lip trembled, her eyes were wet with tears. 'I've bought a plot here too, you know,' she whispered. 'I'll always be with her then, you see'

Ellen stepped closer. 'Perhaps sooner than you think,' her warm breath brushed Joan's hair.

Joan recoiled, and stepping back her foot struck the wicker basket she always carried. She tottered for a moment until Ellen grabbed her elbow.

'Stop making up these stories. I'm warning you and I'm only going to warn you once.

'*The devil takes many forms*,' Joan hissed, struggling to free herself.

Ellen's strong fingers dug deep into the frail flesh. '*See*. That's just the kind of nonsense that's really going to get you into trouble.'

'*I don't care!* You can't hurt me anymore than you already have. I know what you did,' she glared at Ellen now, still trying to extricate her arm. 'I *know*. Blanche has told me. The cards told me. First, I thought it was Steven. Then I thought it was both of you together. But now I'm sure of the truth. It was you, Ellen. You alone. Wicked, wicked girl!'

Ellen gave her a violent shake. 'Shut up you mad old cow. The police said it was an accident. There's legal papers to prove it.'

'I *know* the truth. God knows the truth!' Joan shouted.

'*SHUT UP*!' Ellen glanced around the deserted cemetery. In that moment Joan bolted, coat flapping, skinny legs propelling her forward, towards the muddy bank. Above their heads, roosting rooks exploded noisily into the air as Joan scurried beneath the trees and struggled up the bank, towards tangled undergrowth.

Ellen went after her. Catching her halfway she grabbed at Joan's coat. Joan screamed, her heart taking a wheezy leap in her scrawny chest as she pitched forward and fell heavily.

Ellen seized her by the collar. A few feet to their right lay broken, twisted railings. She dragged Joan towards them. From further up the bank came voices. Two boys in school uniform broke through the screen of bushes. Pushing and shoving each other, they made for the footpath. Releasing Joan, Ellen ducked behind a laurel.

Seeing Joan sprawled on the ground the boys stopped and hung back for a moment, assessing the situation.

'Can't you get up?' One of the boys called to her.

Joan ignored him, managing finally to struggle to her feet. She tried brushing the leaves and mud from her face but a shooting pain in her right arm prevented her. She began to cry.

The two boys pushed each other self-consciously again and then laughing went on their way. Joan limped after them as fast as she could, casting frightened glances over her shoulder.

. . .

'ANOTHER THREE CARS got pulled over last night, this is beginning to get right on my tits,' Ron complained.

Taking the call on Briarwood Road's landline, Steven stood in the draughty hallway trying hard not to conjure up an image of Ron's tits or any other part of his anatomy. He sighed wearily. 'Bastards are determined to pin something on me. Un-roadworthy cabs will do if they can't do me for murder.'

'Yeah, well, we're dealing with a bunch of fuckwits ain't we? That kid's been hanging around again.'

'Siddie?'

'Yeah. He wants a job.'

'Too young.'

'Says he's twenty-one.'

'I doubt he's eighteen.'

'Says he could undercut the Albanians on the valeting – interested?'

'No. They do a good job. The cabs have never been so clean.'

'Yeah. Thought I'd mention it. You sound really down, mate.'

Steven deflected the comment. 'I need you to get those accounts off to the bookkeeper. You said you'd do it last week. She's been on the phone, asking where they are.'

'That's first on me 'to do list' for the morning, stop worrying about it, you've got enough on your plate.'

'Yeah. Okay. See you later.'

'Yeah. Laters.'

The front door opened and in with a blast of icy wind came Miss King. She waved a box set of old-fashioned cassettes at him. 'I'm brushing up on my French, my dear.'

Despite himself, Steven couldn't help but smile. 'Good for you, Miss King. Go for it.'

'Bon nuit,' she said cheerfully and went into her room.

Steven stood in the hallway, his face settling back into hard, angry lines. Despite having suffered enough anguish in the last few weeks to last him several lifetimes, he couldn't shake the feeling that something worse was on its way. He lifted his head. There was a charge in the air and his face felt moist. An approaching storm no doubt. As he mounted the stairs, he heard a distant rumble of thunder.

FOR THE FIRST time since the funeral, Ellen had lit the fire. Now she sat motionless, staring into the flames, her eyes dulling. A sharp rap at the door and someone's far off voice broke through her deepening fugue and in those first confused moments she had no idea where she was.

'Ellen!' The voice called again.

Getting to her feet she walked slowly to the door. Opening it she was only half aware of something streaking past her, as her eyes were on Steven. The angry set of his jaw made her instantly alert and wary.

Walking straight in he went over to the fire and stood warming his hands, staring down at the shoes she had placed on the hearth to dry. The pair still caked in cemetery mud. The cat joined him. Steven ruffled his ears. 'How *do* you keep managing to get in, you bad cat?' he said quietly.

Ellen blinked nervously in the firelight, *waiting*.

Finally, he turned and looked at her. 'What are you playing at?' His voice was low and utterly furious.

'What?' a slow blush crept up her neck.

He moved to the sofa and sat on the arm. 'All this crap you've been feeding Alison. All this shit about us getting married. The *stuff* about Caroline.'

Ellen's heart beat quickened. *He had spoken to* Alison? *How?*

How had he contacted her? 'I did say some things,' she muttered, fixing her eyes on the little polo-playing figure on the breast pocket of his shirt. 'But it was only because she kept going on and on about some stupid boyfriend she had, and ... and,'

'And what?'

'I didn't want her to think that I didn't have a boyfriend too. I just made it up, Steven. It was stupid. I didn't mean any harm. It just came into my head, and I said it.'

He gave her a hard look. 'Boyfriend? She's never mentioned any boyfriend.'

'Well, she has one. I saw him. He came here to pick up her things in a van.'

She got up and moved towards him, her eyes pleading. 'I *did* tell her that we care about each other, because we do, don't we?'

Steven got abruptly to his feet. 'Stop it, Ellen! All this shit stops now, understand?

'Yes...yes. We don't need to talk about it now,' and without thinking she reached out with fluttering fingers to touch his cheek.

Steven's head jerked back. '*Don't,*' he said and brushing her aside he walked to the door.

'*Steven!*' she called as the door slammed behind him. She moaned then, clutching herself, stricken by his rage.

Coal hissed in the grate, blue flames licked and danced prettily but Ellen didn't see them. All she saw was a dark place, where dank flowers bloomed and all she felt was a monstrous pounding in her head and thick, sick misery slowly filling her throat.

Clasping her hands to her head she waited for her vision to clear. When it did, a pair of feverish eyes burned back at her from the mirror above the fireplace. Lightning cracked then, ripping open the sky above Briarwood Road. Snatching up the heavy ashtray from the mantelpiece, Ellen smashed it into the glass. Shards flew, landing in her hair and on her clothes. She whirled around shaking them off like harmless confetti; and then she saw the cat. It had darted beneath the sofa and crouched there, trembling. Eyes blazing, Ellen lunged towards it.

27

Siddie stood on the doorstep, shivering in a thin jacket. Behind him the front garden was silvered with frost and early morning light. 'Eva told me to come.'

Ellen's expression was glazed.

'Can I come in? I got bad news and it's freezing out here.'

Huddled in her dressing gown, Ellen turned and trudged off towards kitchen, her slippers loosely slapping against the tiled floor. Siddie stepped quickly inside and shut the door, glad to be out of the cold. He trailed after her, the crotch of his jeans hanging level with his knees. His eyes darted towards Steven's room as they passed it. 'Is *he* in?'

'The fuck should I know?' Ellen muttered.

'It's just I might want a word with him... after,' he said.

In the kitchen Siddie slid onto a kitchen stool and stared

and stared around. 'This room could do with tarting up, innit? I know a bloke in Ealing who sells these well cool kitchens. I could get you a banging discount if you slipped the business his way.'

Ellen stared at him. Siddie coughed delicately. 'Yeah. Um...anyway, it's Joan. She's dead.'

Ellen's hand went quickly to her mouth, not as a gesture of shock, but to hide the birth of a smile.

'Some neighbour found her lying the garden. She'd been out there all night. Must have froze to death. Horrible innit?'

'Horrible,' Ellen agreed mechanically, a mixture of expressions shifting across her face, unsure of which one to wear.

'Eva reckons she was probably out looking for that cat of 'ers. Maybe slipped over on some ice or somethin'. Anyway, that's what I was told to come and tell you.'

The front door opened. Grateful for a diversion, Siddie slid off his stool, hoisted his jeans and went out into the hall. Ellen slipped out after him, going straight upstairs without a single glance at Steven.

'*Steve*, my man! I got this bloke who owns a car lot in Streatham. He can get your drivers good clean motors at knock down prices 'case you're interested.' Let Graham and Eva get their knickers in a twist over Steven, but Siddie was not one to put their vague concerns before his own self-interest.

'Yeah? I'll bear it in mind.'

'Here's me number, bro.' Siddie handed him a scrap of paper. 'I wouldn't mind doing a bit of driving myself, if ever you're short.'

'Yeah, Ron did mention it. Again, I'll bear it in mind.'

'Cool. Better shoot. I'm supposed to be opening up the shop today. Graham's getting all antsy about losing trade. Can't risk him going off on one again.' Giving Steven's bicep a punch in an affable manly gesture, Siddie scurried off.

IN THE KITCHEN Steven whisked eggs in a bowl, relieved that Ellen was keeping out of his way. Going to the fridge he pulled out half a loaf of bread and stuck two slices under the grill. It wasn't until he was turning them over that he spotted the mould. 'Shit,' he muttered and grabbing the toast and the rest of the loaf, he made for the back door.

A wheelie bin stood right outside. He pulled up the lid, was about to throw the bread inside, but instead he froze. An explosion of bloodied ginger fur and spilled guts greeted him. The creature's head was missing, but even without it, Steven recognised the corpse. Slamming down the lid, he dry retched, suddenly very grateful his stomach was empty.

Ellen was sitting on the sofa, feet tucked up under her, watching morning T.V. He didn't bother to knock this time, just walked straight in. 'For fuck's sake, Ellen!'

Ellen muted the TV but kept her eyes on the screen.

'Did *you* put that cat in the wheelie bin?'

'I meant to warn you. What do you think happened to it?'

'Christ knows.'

'A fox, maybe, we get lots-'

'You could have least wrapped it in something, covered it up!'

'I didn't want to touch it more than I had to. And in case you hadn't noticed,' she suddenly yelled, '*I'm* the one that does everything around here, with no help from anyone!'

Steven stared at her. 'You could have asked me to bury it.'

'Oh, says the person who never has time for anything! The ground's frozen fucking solid anyway.' She turned her head away. 'Anyway, I'm sorry it's dead. You really liked it, didn't you?'

28

BARNES. Southwest London. Seven thirty am: No discernible dawn, just a gradual, milky paling of the overcast night sky. DCI Hopkins sat beneath a buzzing florescent strip, rolled back shirt-cuffs revealing thick hairy wrists. Laid out before him were the crime scene photographs. A career in the Met spanning thirty-five years had taught him the world is a place full of cruelty and hideous surprises and despite this grim acceptance, the images before him still managed to twist his heart.

The vaginal swabs had come back negative. There was no internal bruising and no seminal fluids found either outside the body or at the scene. No signs someone had forced entry into the flat. It hadn't been turned over and with thirty pounds still inside Caroline's purse, they could rule out a robbery gone bad. The injuries inflicted post-mortem, like the burning of the face, implied a rage-fuelled attack. Something personal. The fact Caroline hadn't been attacked sexually could also imply the killer was someone who had been in a relationship with her. Familiarity lessening the urge to rape.

It was a line of thought that brought him straight back to Steven Finn.

Taking off his glasses, Hopkins rubbed the bridge of his nose. Fraser was probably right. The kind of pressure Caroline was exerting made Finn crack. He'd killed her quickly with the screwdriver and then desecrated her body perhaps to provide a smoke screen.

Frustratingly, Finn had an alibi. But at this stage it was far from watertight. Finn's controller could be lying through his teeth and entries made into the logbook stating his time of arrival that night could have been falsified. DS Winter had designated a team of three officers to track down the four passengers Finn claimed to have carried after his nine pm arrival. So far, they had not had any success.

Hopkins was still shifting through the photographs when Fraser arrived, clutching his half-consumed breakfast.

'Don't get any prettier, do they?' he muttered, sliding the remainder of his Bacon and Egg McMuffin into the bin.

Hopkins opened the file and took out a different photograph. He held it up and looked at it closely.

'What's that?' Fraser asked.

Hopkins passed it to him. It was a picture taken of Caroline in life and the poignant comparison was not lost on Fraser. An ordinary holiday snap, it showed Caroline perched on a sun-bleached rock against a Mediterranean backdrop. She was laughing into the camera, one slender arm stretched out, pointing to something beyond the camera's range.

'Such a beautiful girl,' Hopkins stated.

Fraser nodded. 'Yeah. She was.'

Hopkins leant back in his chair and loosened his tie. 'Start a thorough check on her sexual history. We need to unearth every boyfriend she's ever had, right from when she first became sexually active. Means going back to speak to her mother again. You can arrange that.'

Fraser groaned. Visiting Mrs Shaw again was not an attractive prospect.

'Also, I really think we should go and have another chat with that girl at Briarwood Road. Maybe she has some enlightening insight that would help us get to know Mr Finn a lot better.'

Fraser sat at his desk and scrabbled around in a drawer for a pen. 'Somehow I doubt it,' he said.

'No stone, unturned Fraser.'

'From what I remember, she looks like she's just crawled out from under one,' Fraser muttered.

Ellen was ensconced on the sofa again spooning Ben and Jerry's Phish Food into her mouth and watching a daytime quiz show. She particularly liked this show and had the volume turned up. The contestant had just won twenty-three thousand pounds.

'What will you spend it on?' asked the host, flashing blindingly white teeth at the camera.

'A conservatory!' yelled the female contestant. 'I've *always* wanted a conservatory.'

Ellen nodded in agreement. She didn't know exactly what sort of function a conservatory provided, but that didn't matter. 'Conservatory' sounded nice. It sounded like the sort of thing a person *should* have. Like an electric toothbrush. She had one of those at least. The same one that Steven had. She'd had to go to John Lewis to get the exact same make. These days she spent a lot of time in his room while he was working, going through his drawers, checking the pockets of his clothes for receipts and other clues of his outside existence – his life away from her. This way she had gleaned all kinds of information about him. His mobile phone number for example. His National Insurance number and the exact amount in his current account, and that very morning, another search had unearthed something interesting. A gold bracelet, each heavy link hallmarked. At first, she thought it was a man's. That it was Steven's. Until she read the inscription.

'Georgia my darling.'

The heavy weight of it on her wrist, took her out of the show. Now as she sat twisting the cold metal links round and round, a strange, disconnected sensation overtook her, like the one she experienced whenever she'd ducked her head under water, that temporary, sensory loss. She was trying to hold onto her thoughts, but they kept darting away from her, like little fish.

A heavy knock at the front door brought her back with a faint start. When she got up to look out of the window, two familiar policemen were standing in the front garden, squinting up at her.

If they hadn't seen her, she wouldn't have opened the door. What did they want to talk to her about this time? *What if it was Blanche? What if they suspected something even though the postmortem said it was an accidental death?* She sat on a kitchen stool and waited, a queasy feeling in her stomach. The old one pulled out another stool and sat down too, although it was much too small for his fat backside, and it hung over the sides. The other one remained standing, looking like there was a bad smell under his long, thin nose.

'I'm sure you remember our names by now.' Hopkins began.

Ellen nodded and regarding him from the corner of her eyes with unease.

'I hope you don't mind us just dropping in like this, but we'd like to have a little chat if that's okay?'

The fear in Ellen's stomach sharpened.

'Big old house this,' Hopkins said folding his arms and glancing around. 'Can I ask who else lives here with you, aside from your tenants?'

'No one.'

'So much space to yourself, eh? A luxury these days, eh, Fraser. having so much space.'

'Yeah, wouldn't know myself.'

'Particularly in London, where a percentage of the population live in just one room. My Sergeant used to be one of them,' he confided to Ellen, 'rents being what they are.'

Fraser gave a grunt. 'Yeah, well. Some time back.'

'So where do your parents live? This must have been their house once.'

'They're not anywhere. They're both dead.' *Why were they interested in this stuff?*

Hopkins raised an eyebrow. 'Both? That's a real shame. A long time ago?'

'My mother died recently.'

'How recently?'

'Eight weeks.'

'As recent as that? Difficult time for you, then.' He turned to Fraser, 'Didn't Finn tell us he's been living here for roughly the same amount of time?'

Fraser nodded. 'Yeah, he did.'

'Long illness, was it? Your mother I mean.'

Ellen's hand crept to the bracelet, she turned the links slowly. 'No. She died suddenly. An accident.'

'An accident?' 'Hopkins tutted sympathetically. 'How did that happen?'

'She fell. In the bath. She drowned.'

'A terrible shock. Miss Hunt. I'm sorry. Going back to Steven Finn. Do you know if your mother carried out checks, prior to him moving in. References, that sort of thing?'

Ellen relaxed. *It was Steven they were still interested in, not Blanch at all. She* answered the question. 'Sometimes she did, sometimes she didn't. I don't know what she did in Steven's case.'

'So how have *you* found Mr Finn, since he's been living here? Does he mix, talk to the other tenants?'

'There's only one other tenant now. She's an old lady. He talks to her and fixes things for her.' She was beginning to find it hard taking this man's questions seriously. He looked nothing like a policeman with his fat red cheeks and fluffy white hair. All he needed was a beard and he'd make a perfect department store Santa.

'What about girlfriends? Does he bring any here?'

Ellen twisted the bracelet and looked him in the eyes. *'I'm* his girlfriend.'

Hopkins regarded her over the rim of his bifocals. 'I see. I didn't realise that.'

Ellen flicked hair from her face, allowing a smile to light her features. 'We're getting married, once all this stuff is over.'

'Eight weeks!' Hopkins bushy eyebrows shot up into his high, pink forehead. 'You're getting married after eight weeks! I don't understand you young people. Why are you all in such a rush? 'In my day you had a long courtship, several years in most cases. People had to save up for things, you see. No credit cards back then.'

'Can I say something?' Ellen cut in.

'Of course,' Hopkins smiled.

'Whoever killed that girl – it wasn't him.'

'How can you be sure of that?'

'Because somebody bad must have done that and Steven isn't bad.'

. . .

FRASER COULD HARDLY CONTAIN his glee on the drive back to the station. 'Finn's screwing that! Christ, I'd sooner stick it in a bacon slicer.'

Hopkins grunted. The girl had seemed very tense when they arrived and a little odd. The remark about 'bad people' had seemed odd too. Out of place. He gazed out of the window, the frown lines between his eyes, deepening. Everything about this case was strange and he could feel it slipping through his fingers like water. But he was a patient man. Some cases took years to crack, but good usually vanquished evil in the end, and if that sounded old-fashioned, he didn't care. It was this simple belief that had kept him in the job for thirty-five years.

'What the fuck did we learn?' Fraser was asking. 'Diddlysquat that's what. Oh, yeah, Finn helps out the old biddy in the next room. But I'm still in shock. I mean why the fuck would he be interested in that munter?'

Hopkins turned his head. 'A cynical person might say it was more likely the property he was interested in Fraser.'

His sergeant fell silent, staring at the road ahead, and then he scowled. 'If that bastard fell in pig shit he'd come up smelling of Paco fucking Rabanne'

PROPPED up in his hospital bed, Graham's face was grey and drawn against the white sheets. Eva fussed a little and plumped his pillows. Siddie, forgiven and reconciled, was tapping the toe of an expensive trainer in time to a tune in his head and attempting to remove a splinter from his finger with Eva's nail file.

'What time do they bring the food round?' he whined.

'I neither know nor care. It's truly awful.' Graham's voice was still weak.

'You should have gone private. You'd have had better grub

and your own room. He waved at the other beds in the room. 'This is really depressing, innit, being surrounded by all these coffin dodgers.'

'I can't afford both private health care and you!' Graham snapped.

'Yeah, yeah, all right. Christ I'm thirsty. Can I get a coke from somewhere?'

'Don't tire him Siddie.' Eva said sharply.

Graham patted Eva's hand. 'There's some change in my drawer there and I think there's a vending machine in the next corridor.'

'I'll have a coffee,' Eva decided rummaging in her bag for her purse. 'Would you like one too, Graham?'

'Heaven forbid. That's diabolical as well.'

'Come along Siddie.'

Siddie followed Eva and as soon as Graham was out of earshot, she rounded on him. 'I hope you're proud of yourself. It's your fault he is in here. Goodness knows why he's taken you back.'

Siddie's lustrous eyes widened. 'How is it my fault? He's neurotic. We had a row that's all and he just went off on one. Bloody diva.'

'You'd better take good care of him when they send him out, Siddie, if you don't ...'

'Yeah, yeah.'

They had reached the vending machine at the end of a long corridor.

'Another thing, Siddie, don't you dare mention Joan.'

'He's gonna hear about it sooner or later.'

'Siddie!'

'All right. I won't say nothin'. But he'll wonder why she ain't coming to see him.'

'*I'll* tell him when he's a bit stronger.'

Siddie shrugged. 'Whatevers.'

. . .

Eva and Siddie had gone, Graham lay with just his thoughts for company. He was touched by Eva's attempt to keep him ignorant of Joan's demise, but he already knew. He'd glanced at the evening paper the night before and seen the few column inches dedicated to it.

Poor Joan. But she had been a very silly creature. He could see her so clearly, glued to Blanche's side, nodding dutifully at each bigoted outburst. He sank back on his pillows then, ashamed of such uncharitable thoughts. Whether Joan's death *had* been an accident, or something else, coming so soon after the crushing news about the will, was something they'd never know and it was pointless, speculating. Poor, poor Joan. Still, at least she was out of it all now and closing his eyes, he couldn't help feeling just the smallest pang of envy.

29

THINGS WERE GETTING LIVELY in the Three Bells. An hour to closing time and a small group of medical staff from Ealing Hospital was being particularly raucous. It was Sophie Ellery's leaving party. Having recently qualified in Obstetrics she was taking up a position in Wrexham Hospital. Alison hadn't yet hardened herself to losing her best pal, but the Tequila Slammers lined up on the bar were making it temporarily less painful.

Moving on from the giggling stage, the two girls had their arms wrapped around each other and Adam Westbrook, the young intern with a weakness for Alison, was trying to insinuate himself between the pair. The girls were frustrating his attempts and as the pub door opened and four suited business types came in and pushed their way to the bar. Behind them was a lone individual and his presence had an immediate sobering effect upon Alison. She turned her back quickly and gave Sophie a sharp dig to get her attention.

'*Oh, my God*, it's him.'

'What? Who?'

'It's Steven, you big thick. Look. *No*, don't look, *he'll see us*.'

Ignoring instructions Sophie scanned the newcomers, her eyes settling on the slightly dishevelled, dark-haired guy who was now leaning on the bar for support. She stared at him openly, with more than a touch of morbid curiosity. After Steven's unwelcome visit, Alison had wasted no time in singling out her friend and telling her all about it.

'I can't believe the police haven't locked him up. And I can't believe I was so stupid as to direct him straight to you in the sluice room.'

Alison darted a glance in Steven's direction. 'You weren't to know.'

Sophie's lower lip trembled. 'He could have killed you, Al. He could have done to you what he did to that poor girl.'

'*Hush.* Has he seen me?' Alison whispered, even though no-one less than a half a metre away was going to hear her above the racket.

'Don't think he can *see* anyone. He's completely hammered.'

'What's he doing?'

'Buying a pint. Now he's looking for somewhere to sit. Surprised they served him, he can hardly stand up. Can't see him now, he's disappeared over the far side.'

'What are you two on about?' Adam had returned from the bar with more drinks.

'Nothing. Allie's just spotted an old acquaintance, that's all,' Sophie said.

'Here, hold my drink.' Alison handed her friend her glass.

'What are you doing?'

'Stay here. I'll only be a minute.' Alison set off, fighting her way through the crowd. Steven was sitting on a long bench against the far wall, his back against a huge floor to ceiling mirror, staring into his untouched beer.

Emotion pulsed through her at the sight of him. Jumbled feelings she couldn't quite get a handle on. Gut instinct told her he'd been telling the truth about Ellen, but then she fretted, was that her damaged ego trying to convince her of something she wanted to believe? And as for all that other dark stuff he was involved in? The truth was, how could she possibly know? She'd read numerous times that wives of serial killer often have no idea of their husbands' little hobby, despite having lived with them for years.

She circumnavigated the pub and arrived back at Sophie's side feeling depressed.

'Come on girl, get this down, you look like you need it.' Sophie pressed a glass into her hand.

Alison knocked the Slammer back in two gulps. Adam passed her a replacement and as she downed that too, a cheer went up from the other three nurses. She turned to Sophie, eyes flashing. 'Let's have some fun!' Rifling through her bag she brought out her phone.

'Who you calling?' Sophie asked excitedly, up for whatever Alison had in mind.

'His little puppy. I'm going to ring Briarwood Road just for the crack and tell her he's here, pissed and helpless as a child, and just see how long it takes her to gallop to his rescue.' She grinned and swivelled her wrist to check her watch. 'In fact, I'm going to *time* the stupid bitch!'

Sophie giggled. 'Okay, but...'

Alison held up a silencing finger. 'Hello. Ellen?' she shouted above the din of the pub. 'This is Alison Doyle. Thought you might be wondering where your fiancé is?' Alison strained to listen to Ellen's wary response and almost choked with laughter. Staring at Sophie she tapped the side of her head miming, 'loony'. Sophie snorted loudly and Alison flapped a hand at her.

'No, nothing's happened to him. Not yet anyway. He's here in the Three Bells. Only problem is, he's absolutely *wasted*. Can't put one foot in front of the other. Think he'll probably need some help to get home in one piece. Sorry to disturb your evening, but I know how you worry so.'

Alison listened for a second and then cut the call. 'God, the sad cow, she's on her way.'

THIRTEEN MINUTES later Ellen pushed her way into the pub. Alison dissolved into giggles at the sight of her. Digging Sophie in the ribs she raised her arm and called. 'Hey, Ellen, over here!'

Sophie cast an appraising glance at the approaching woman. 'Lord, it's Shrek,' she muttered under her breath.

Ellen elbowed her way through the drinkers and came up to the two nurses.

'Ellen!' Alison greeted her like a long lost acquaintance. 'How's it hanging?'

'I can't see him,' Ellen snapped, her head swivelling round.

'Nice to see you too, Ellen,' Alison admonished. 'Let me introduce you to my colleague and best friend, Sophie.' Sophie raised her glass in a salute.

'Ellen's my ex landlady, Sophie,' Alison explained unnecessarily in a loud voice. 'God, we had some fun at Briarwood Road, though didn't we, Ellen?'

Ellen's expression shifted to one of mild incomprehension.

'Well, no, we didn't actually, did we, now I come to think of it. But, what the hell, never mind, that's all in the past. *Ellen* is engaged to *Steven*, Sophie. You remember me telling you *all* about *him*, don't you?'

Ellen's eyes darted to Sophie, who nodded, playing along. 'Oh, yeah. Cheek-bones I'd kill my grandmother for.'

'So, have you set the date, Ellen?' Alison asked.

Ellen's eyes searched over Alison's right shoulder. 'That's none of your business. Where is he? You said he was here.'

Alison was determined to prolong Ellen's agony a little longer. 'Must be hard trying to plan a wedding with the cops on your back, don't you think, Sophie?'

'Bloody off putting, I'd say,' Sophie agreed.

'You must have started looking for a dress at least, in preparation for your big day? A piece of advice. Choose something cut on the bias, very slimming.'

Sophie made a choking sound.

Ellen moved up close to Alison so that only she could hear. 'I'd shut my mouth if I were you,' she said quietly. 'Unless you want a glass in it.'

Alison took a few steps back. 'I can see you're desperate to go and rescue your poor man, Ellen,' she said with forced bravado. 'You really should keep him on a tighter leash. He was over there, last time I saw him.' She jerked her thumb towards the rear of the pub. 'Probably unconscious by now though.'

Ellen backed away into the crowd; cold, furious eyes still fixed upon Alison. Sophie exploded with laughter but then she hadn't heard Ellen's last words and Alison was too shaken to join in.

Adam came over to them, slid his arms around the two girl's waists and addressed the rest of the group. 'So, who's up for a curry?'

'Yey!' An enthusiastic shout went up from the other nurses but for Alison the fun had gone out of the evening.

STEVEN COLLAPSED on his bed still fully clothed. Ellen had managed to remove his boots, but that was all so far.

'Steven. Sit up so I can get your jacket off.'

'I'm trying!' He struggled up to a sitting position but then keeled over on his side. Ellen attempted to pull him up, but he was too heavy and she sank down on the bed next to him.

Unable to help herself, she stretched out a tentative hand and touched his shoulder. He muttered something into the pillow. It didn't sound like a reproach. Emboldened she touched the soft curls on the nape of his neck. 'Steven,' she whispered.

He grunted.

'I do love you Steven,' she said, gathering all her courage, 'so very much, I'd do *anything* for you. *Anything*.'

What felt like an endless silence followed and then she heard a muffled sound coming from the pillow. *He was crying!* Alarmed, she leant over him.

'Steven, please, don't,' she begged. 'It's all going to be all right.'

But then, when he turned his face to the light, she saw there were no tears – *he was laughing*.

'Forfucksake, Ellen,' he said and he was laughing uproariously now. 'Don't you think I've got enough crap to be going on with?'

Ellen recoiled like a whipped puppy. Dragging herself from his room and back upstairs she paced up and down, arms tightly wrapped around herself. He had laughed at her. *She had finally told him she loved him and he had laughed.*

How dare he! After everything she'd done for him – or would do, if only he'd allow her.

She hated him now! *Hated* him. And she hoped he was satisfied, because now he had no one. No one who believed in him. No one who would protect him from the police. She stormed up and down, up and down, legs pumping, tears of rage coursing down her cheeks.

You won't like me when I'm angry.

That phrase from a kid's TV programme fired through her mind. It was a character she'd always identified with because sometimes when *she* got angry, that same consuming rage she had no control over would sweep out of the recesses of her mind and –

She stopped in her tracks. Fearful of what she was capable of in this state. She took a long shuddering breath, wiped her face on her sleeve and admitted with a choking sense of defeat that she could never hate Steven. He was in her blood, in the very core of her, like some deadly disease. Some cancer that could never be cut out. But then she punched herself hard, in the side of her head. *She was so stupid.* Why did she choose to tell him something so important when he was blind drunk? Had she told him his bed was on fire he would have laughed his head off at that too. *That's* how drunk he was. She had just chosen the *wrong moment* that was all.

Staring out of the window filled with night she felt her mood pass, like some violent thunderstorm that had erupted out of nowhere.

Creeping back to Steven's room, she stood over him as he slept. He lay on his side, on the extreme edge of the bed. She watched the rhythmic rise and fall of his shoulders for a while and then, cautiously, she lay down next to him and after a moment moved closer, breathing in the citrus scent of his skin. Now she was so close she could press her lips against his shoulder – but she didn't dare.

Outside, a driving rain began to fall. It lashed the window and a high wind sloughed through the branches of the old tree. Ellen drew closer, hungry for his warmth and so many other things. But Steven had '*enough 'shit'* to deal with right now and he'd expect her to understand that.

Her hand slid beneath her sweater, caressed a breast, imagining it was his hand, his touch, his warm skin upon hers and in the moonlight her eyes burned like embers.

30

FEMME MAGAZINE'S offices were situated half-way down a long narrow street in a white three-storey building. It was midday and snow as fine and dry as sugar-dust had begun to fall.

Ellen stood outside the building, hands thrust deep into her pockets, chin tucked into the collar of her coat, feeling her earlier confidence trickle away. Standing on the pavement blocking the path of rushing, lunch-hour workers, panic engulfed her. She had taken Harriet's advice, done exactly what she had advised her to do, but Steven was either

too tired or too drunk these days to notice *anything*. Harriet had to tell her how to *make* him notice. She stared up at the building. There was no one else she could turn to. And *yes*, the agony aunt was no doubt a very busy woman, what with all the letters she received, she did *understand* that. But what Harriet had to *understand* was that she *had* to speak to her *now,* face to face, and she'd wait all day if necessary.

The foyer was suffocatingly warm. Beyond a wide expanse of tiled floor was a huge curved reception desk. A black man in a uniform was seated behind it. He regarded Ellen over his newspaper as she approached.

'Can I help, Miss?' He had a Jamaican lilt and was perspiring slightly.

'I'd like to speak to Harriet Hope please.'

The man looked confused momentarily then he grinned and a gold tooth flashed.

'Harriet Hope?'

'Yes.'

'You mean Miss Goldsmith?'

'No. I mean Harriet Hope.'

'That isn't possible, Miss.' The man's mouth twitched as though he was trying not to laugh.

Ellen's eyes drilled into him. 'Harriet Hope works in this building. Look.'From her coat pocket she pulled out the page she had carefully torn out of Femme Magazine. The page which featured her letter and Harriet's reply. She pointed to Harriet's signature at the bottom of the page.

The black man didn't even glance at it. 'Let me explain to you, Miss,' he said, with underlined deliberation. 'Harriet Hope is a *pseudonym.* She don't really exist.'

'Of course, she does. She wrote to me. This is one of her letters.' Ellen held it up again.

'It was *Georgia* who wrote to you. *Harriet Hope* is her *pen* name.'

The man's eyes were alight with amusement.

Ellen stared at him for a moment and then moved the letter close to his face.

'I need to speak to the person who wrote this letter.'

'*Georgia*.'

Ellen's eyes locked with his. 'Yes.'

'Then you need an appointment, Missy. You got one?'

Ellen hesitated, then shook her head.

The receptionist kissed his teeth and his gaze became insolent. 'Without an appointment she don't see no one.'

Ellen gripped the edge of his desk. 'I won't keep her long, it's important.'

The man's eyes cut across the foyer. Ellen turned and saw another man leaning against the wall, next to the lifts. He was watching her with mild interest and the word 'Security' was emblazoned on his pocket. Ellen stepped away from the desk and the receptionist picked up his newspaper again.

WANDERING DOWN A SIDE STREET, Ellen found a small café. Going inside to get out of the cold, she ordered a coffee and a teacake. The coffee when it arrived, looked like grey sludge. She hunched over her mug. Why would the person who called herself Harriet Hope only pretend to be Harriet Hope and all the time be someone else? She sat brooding,

picking currants out of the teacake, creating a little pile on her plate.

Around five o'clock she headed back to the Femme building. Positioning herself outside, she waited, confident that she would recognise Harriet/Georgia from the photograph that accompanied her column. The staff began to emerge after six. Lights from inside the building flooded the steps and Ellen could see the face of each person clearly as they came out, bundled up in their winter coats and scarves. Most were in small groups, animated by the fresh fall of snow.

Georgia emerged at twenty past six. Ellen recognised her, despite the magazine photograph being just another lie. The living version of Harriet was younger, prettier. Perhaps 'glamorous' was a better description, Ellen decided. The image in the magazine showed a caring looking woman, wearing glasses. This woman wasn't wearing glasses and didn't look in the least bit caring. Her hair was different too. In the picture it was pulled back from her face, not falling in soft bouncing waves as it was now.

Ellen moved into the pool of light. Georgia came down the steps towards her, high heels clicking and Ellen moved into her path.

'Excuse me.' Georgia's voice was sharp with irritation as the two collided. Ellen stumbled out of her way and Georgia swept past her.

Ellen turned at the sound of churning slush. Saw the car pulling into the kerb and Georgia step inside it. A glimpse was all she caught of the driver, but she'd know that profile anywhere. His image was burned into the retina of her eyes. A small seismic shock ran through Ellen as Steven drove Georgia away, leaving her transfixed on the narrow pavement, white noise rushing in her head.

And then the paralysis broke and taking a gasping breath, she leant into the biting wind and lurched across the street.

She had no memory of how she got home. But that wasn't important. What *was* important was what she was going to do now. Using the master key she went into Steven's room and pulled open the top drawer of the chest. Her fingers closed on the gold bracelet she had returned the day before.

When she had been killing time in the café earlier she had been filled with a growing anxiety. Why had Harriet Hope's real name struck her as familiar?

The answer to that now lay in the palm of her hand. She turned the bracelet over and re-read the inscription; 'Georgia my darling.'

It's staring you right in the face my girl.

The familiar loathsome voice rose up inside her head.

'No!' Ellen said, locking Steven's room and going back upstairs. 'He was just doing his job that's all. He picked her up because that's what he's paid to do.'

Blanche snickered. *You fool. All that twaddle you've been*

lapping up. She's been giving you the wrong advice on purpose. She's wanted him for herself all along. Never heard of playing hard to get, Ellie. That's the way to nail them, you ninny.

'And how the fuck would you know?' Ellen snarled.

They're playing Park the Car in the Garage as we speak. She's beaten you to it my girl and all you can say is: He's only doing his job! Jesus Christ on a bike. The bracelet Ellen, the bracelet! Blanche's dead voice shook with laughter.

'It's not true.' Ellen whimpered as she walked unsteadily into the kitchen. Going to the sink she turned on the cold tap. Reaching for a glass her sleeve brushed a milk bottle on the draining board and sent it crashing to the floor where it exploded on impact. Picking up a cloth Ellen bent to clear up the mess.

He's cruising up her cul-de-sac right this minute, Ellie. Blanche whispered in her ear. *He's giving her a slow, hard ride, the best she's ever had...*

'Shut your filthy mouth!' Ellen screamed. Sinking to her knees she grabbed a shard of glass and sliced through the palm of her left hand. Bright beads of blood burst through the skin.

Well, I can't hang around here all day, Blanche said cheerily. *I've got other fish to fry.*

With her mother's sly grin dancing before her eyes, Ellen slashed and slashed at her hand.

31

GEORGIA SLAMMED DOWN THE PHONE. 'FUCK!' Her voice was shaky and incredulous. Snatching up the phone again, she rang 999.

PC EMMA WALKER and PC Bradley Beaumont arrived almost an hour later. Beaumont, pink-cheeked and fresh from Hendon, was happy for Walker to take the lead. They seated themselves in the two ergonomic visitor's chairs on the other side of Georgia's desk. PC Walker regarded Georgia expectantly, while Beaumont produced a notebook and pen from his Met vest.

'Before we start,' Georgia said twisting the cap of her Montblanc and looking PC Walker squarely in the eyes, 'I need you to understand exactly what sort of person I am. You can ask *anyone* who works in this building to describe me, and I know exactly what they'll say. They'll say I'm a ruthless cow. A bitch-with-balls to be precise. Does that sound to you like the kind of person who scares easily?'

The officers' heads shook in unison.

'So, when I take time out from an impossible work schedule to speak to people like you, it's because I've got a very good reason.'

PC Walker's gamine features settled into a detached, professional expression, while Beaumont, scrutinising Georgia from beneath thick black eyebrows, swallowed nervously.

'Tell us exactly what's happened, Miss Goldsmith?' Walker asked calmly.

'This ... *lunatic,*' Georgia continued, ignoring Walker, 'doesn't sound like the kind of person who wastes her time either. I believe she meant every word she said, and you'd better make damn sure she doesn't get the chance to carry out her promise.'

'We take *any* kind of threat seriously, Miss Goldsmith, I can assure you. What exactly did this woman say?'

Georgia exhaled. 'What this woman *said* was that one night she'll be waiting for me and in her pocket would be a small container...'

'Waiting where?' asked Walker. 'Outside here? Your office?'

Georgia shot her an annoyed look. 'She didn't specify *where* exactly, officer. It could be outside here or outside my home. If she knows where I work, it's quite likely she knows where I live too.'

Walker nodded for her to continue. Georgia uncapped and re-capped her pen. 'This *person* then informed me in graphic detail, exactly what this container of liquid would do to my face. She told me I would feel my features literally melting away and my eyes being burned out of their sockets. She told me that after she'd finished with me, a man wouldn't be able to look at me without being sick. Then she said; "I'll make fucking sure Steven never smiles at you in that way again."

'Steven? Who's Steven?' Walker asked.

'That's what I said. I asked her which particular *Steven* she was referring to as I've known quite a few in my time and *she* replied, "*you know* who I'm talking about, you bitch, *Steven Finn*."'

Walker held Georgia's gaze for a few moments. 'Steven Finn?' she asked.

'He's a driver. Our magazine has an account with his company. Sometimes he drives me home.'

'So, your relationship is not a personal one?'

Georgia tossed back her hair, irritated. 'No. I'd say if it were, wouldn't I?'

Walker's eyes flicked sideways to the scribbling Beaumont, checking he was getting it all down and then flicked back to Georgia.

'So, where would this person have seen you together?'

'In his bloody cab I imagine. That's the *only* place she could have seen us together.' Sliding out a bottom drawer, Georgia produced a bottle of Chivas Regal and poured herself a shot. 'There's a non-smoking policy in this shit-hole, but not a non-drinking one, not yet anyway, thank Christ.'

Walker and Beaumont shifted in their seats.

'This person has got it totally wrong, then,' Walker continued.

'But *something* has set this person off, 'Beaumont offered shyly, glancing quickly at Walker. 'You don't ring people up you don't know and threaten them for no reason.'

Georgia chose to ignore this blindingly obvious comment. Under different circumstances she might have had some fun with this fresh-faced infant, but she was hardly in the mood.

'Tell me about the voice.' Walker asked.

Georgia took a sip from her glass and was silent for a moment, thinking. 'It was youngish I think. Quite deep really.'

'Deep? Could it have been a man trying to sound like a female?'

Georgia sighed and rubbed her forehead. 'I'm pretty sure it was female.'

'What kind of accent?'

'Not one I picked up on. Classless I suppose, in the way that so many are these days.'

'Did you get the feeling you'd heard it before?'

'No.'

'Did she ring your direct line or come through the switchboard?'

Georgia frowned. 'Erm...switchboard, I think. Yes, that's right. I remember Jasmine putting her through. *That's a point!* Could you check the phone records?'

'It's almost certain she withheld her number, but we will check.'

'Okay. Right. So now I need to know exactly what you're going to do. What sort of protection I can expect?'

'There's not a lot we can do at this point,' Walker replied apologetically. 'You need to take all sensible precautions for the time being. Make sure security and your secretaries are aware and have all your calls screened. It might be an idea to make a list of any women you know who may hold a grudge against you?'

'Christ. That would take from now to *next* Christmas.'

Walker couldn't help a small smile. 'Perhaps we should have a word with Mr Finn. He might be able to shed some light on who it might be.'

Georgia's head jerked up. 'Do you know him?'

Walker nodded. 'He's helping us with another line of enquiry.'

'Really?' Georgia took another sip of single malt.

'Who ever this warped person is,' Walker continued she probably gets her kicks from just scaring people.'

'She's succeeded.'

'Hopefully, she has no intention of taking it any further.'

'Hopefully? I expect you to do more than just hope.'

'We'll check the phone records like I said, but if it was a withheld number there is nothing more we can do... until she rings again, and even then it could be a slow process tracking...'

'Well, *thank you* officer. I can't tell you how much safer I feel after your visit. Now, if you don't mind, I'm the kind of person who actually puts some effort into their working day and I've got a shit-load of subbing to get through.'

Georgia downed the rest of her drink as the door closed behind the two officers. Swivelling her chair, she stared out of the window into the street below. This person, whoever she was, could be down there now right now, moving invisibly in and out of the crowds, watching and waiting. The pity of it was that the only sexual encounters that had taken place between Steven Finn and herself had been in her mind. For once in her life, she was an innocent party. But that was not going to protect her. That hateful voice, spitting venom down the phone line had been enough to convince her of that.

Margaret Shaw stood at the kitchen window. The sun shuttered in and out of the clouds sending shadows scudding across the lawn.

Roger Shaw stood in the doorway. 'We have to believe she's in a much better place, Marg.'

His wife turned from the window her tear-streaked face twisted with raw grief. 'But I want her *here,* with me *now*.'

Roger moved towards her.

'Get away!' she spat. 'It's your fault. Your fault!'

From the first floor came a lusty yell. Renata the au pair was transporting Luke across the landing for his afternoon nap. Margaret Shaw stared at her husband with loathing in her eyes. 'Please – just *go*,' she said.

After ringing the A2B's cab office and leaving a message for Steven to ring her urgently, Georgia spent the rest of the afternoon immersed in her work, refusing to dwell upon the caller. But every time her phone rang, she stared at it nervously as though it were a cobra about to strike, before picking it up.

It was late in the day when Steven finally received Georgia's message. Ron had passed it to Lenny and Lenny had left it with Stan, the sprightly seventy-year-old who was manning the office for the early evening shift. Pulling a crumpled piece of paper out of his jacket pocket, he'd handed it to Steven as soon as he arrived.

Steven made a point of smoothing out the note before reading it. Stepping outside the office, he rang the number. Georgia's husky, sixty-a-day voice answered after several rings.

'It's Steven.'

'You took your time. I said it was urgent.'

He ignored her aggressive tone. 'What can I do for you?'

'We need to talk.'

'We are.'

'I mean face-to-face, smart arse. Somewhere private.'

Steven picked up on the nervous edge to her voice. 'Something wrong?'

'Yes. Could we meet somewhere? About six thirty?'

He glanced at his watch. 'I'm about to do a Heathrow job. That'll be cutting it too fine.'

'When will you be finished?'

'About seven. Then I'll take a break and be in again around ten.

'I need to speak to you *tonight*.'

'And you're not going to tell me what this is about?'

'Can I meet you around eight?'

'Where? The cab office?'

'No, not there. It can't be anywhere public and I certainly don't want you coming to my place.' She was silent for a moment. 'Look, I'll come to yours. Where do you live?'

Steven hesitated, realising he didn't entirely trust her motives. Georgia was the kind of woman who was used to getting what she wanted and she'd flirted with him on numerous occasions. Was this just a ruse or some kind of game?

He glanced up at the bank of heavy clouds building in the west; business would be good tonight if they fulfilled their promise. 'Okay,' he heard himself saying and against his better judgment he reeled off his address.

GEORGIA RAN up the path of Briarwood Road, a hood covering her distinctive hair. No one seemed to be following her, she had checked throughout the cab ride, but still, she wasn't taking any chances.

She glanced about her, pressed an antiquated doorbell, realised it didn't work and used the heavy knocker. This huge pile couldn't belong to Steven, surely?

A girl, about a decade younger than herself opened the door.

Removing her hood Georgia faked a smile. 'I've come to see Steven. He's expecting me.'

When the girl didn't react, seemed rooted to the spot, in fact, Georgia wondered if she was some sort of special needs case. 'Would you tell Steven Finn I'm here,' she said slowly.

Behind her, the familiar Merc pulled into the kerb. Both women waited in the doorway as Steven came up the path.

'Sorry I'm late. Crash on the M4. It's okay Ellen, she's a friend of mine.' Taking Georgia's arm, he led her straight into his room and shut the door.

Ellen stood in the hallway an expression of trapped horror on her face. At first, she told herself she was hallucinating. But the joint murmurings coming from Steven's room confirmed that this was very, very real. Fury began to fill her body. It climbed up into her throat, half choking her until she could hardly breathe.

'So, THIS IS YOUR DOMAIN?' Georgia had slipped out of her coat and handed it to Steven. It was a light, silky fabric that almost slipped through his hands. The perfume he had begun to associate with her, wafted up to him.

Georgia stood looking around. 'It really is a nice room. I'm guessing you don't own the rest of the house?'

'Sit down.' He indicated the armchair near the window then squatted to fire the ignition of the old fashioned gas fire. It made a popping sound and flared into life. 'Ellen owns it. I'm just renting here for the time being.'

'And who is Ellen? What is she?'

He ignored her mocking tone. 'The girl you saw when you arrived.'

'*That* fashionably impaired girl owns all this?'

'Yep.'

'Well,' Georgia said opening her large leather bag and taking out a pack of cigarettes. 'When will I learn not to judge by appearances alone?'

'Maybe the day you give up that shit.'

'We all have our *shit,* Steven,' Georgia said, tapping out a cigarette from a pack. 'Oh, I'm sorry. It's horrible for me to smoke in the room you're obviously going to...' she waved towards the bed, '*sleep*' in. But if you'd had the day I've had...' She broke off and lit the cigarette. Drawing deeply, she exhaled and shook out the match.

Steven glanced around the room for a makeshift ashtray. An empty paper clip box was the best he could find. He placed it on the table next to her.

She looked up at him. 'Do you have anything to drink?'

Wondering where this was heading he went to his bedside cabinet and took out a bottle of Famous Grouse. He held it up. 'Acceptable?'

'Wonderful.'

Producing a glass from the same cabinet, he poured a shot of whisky and handed it to her. The seductive smell had him screwing the cap firmly back on the bottle and putting it back in the cupboard. He was driving later.

'The reason I'm here,' Georgia began briskly, 'and I'm sure you're wondering, is because I received a really unpleasant phone call today from some woman. The purpose of which was to warn me 'to leave you alone' and if I didn't, she outlined some pretty horrible things that would happen to me.'

Steven sat on the bed and looked at her. Whatever he'd been expecting, it wasn't this. 'What did she mean? Leave me alone?'

'Well...she's obviously convinced we're having some sort of a relationship.'

'Any idea who this woman is?'

Georgia drew on her cigarette, exhaled. 'Not a clue. I was hoping you would know and if you don't, then basically I'm screwed.'

'Why would *anyone* think we're seeing each other?'

'Christ knows. I certainly don't. The only time they could have seen us together is when you've picked me up from the office. Your car *is* unmarked of course. That could explain her assuming you were a boyfriend I suppose.'

Steven rubbed the stubble on his jaw. It made a harsh, scratching sound in the brief silence. 'I'd have thought even a nut job would need a bit more than that to go on.'

Georgia stabbed out her cigarette impatiently and lit another. 'It doesn't matter what *you* think. What matters is what this woman thinks. She scared me, Steven. Her voice ... it was like dripping venom. She threatened to disfigure me, blind me with acid for God's sake and what if she knows where I live? I'm scared to go home. Really.'

Any assumption he'd made that this visit was merely a ruse was now dispelled, Georgia's fear was palpable.

'Have you had just one call?'

'So far. That was enough.'

'Did you report it to the police?'

'Waste of time. They were useless.' Georgia waved a thin curl of smoke away. 'Look, are you sure you don't have any girlfriends past or present, deranged enough to have done this?'

'Nope. No girlfriends full stop. Deranged or otherwise.' Steven looked down at his hands, preferring not to explain just how impossible it was for his last girlfriend to pose any kind of a threat at all. It was something Georgia really didn't need to hear now, she was freaked out enough as it was.

'How did this woman refer to me?'

'How do you mean?'

'Did she only use my first name for instance? In which case it could be any Steven in the British Isles she was referring to. She could just be some weirdo who simply got the wrong number. A coincidence.'

'She just said Steven to start with. But then she clarified it by saying, Steven Finn.'

'No coincidence then.'

'Absolutely not. Also, when she came through the switchboard, she asked for me by name, I checked. The message was definitely not meant for anyone else. The police have advised me to make a list of any potential enemies. Christ, where do I start? I expected some kind of protection but until they find my dismembered torso on the hard shoulder of the M25, there's not much they can do apparently. What the fuck am I paying taxes for?'

Steven couldn't force himself to trot out platitudes. Tell her things like that only happen in movies. That would be rich coming from someone whose ex had just been slaughtered like an animal. Dull, hollow pain accompanied that thought. 'Why don't you stay here tonight? I'll be working up until three and then I can get some sleep in the office.'

Georgia shook her head. 'Thanks for the offer, but I'm afraid I'm too addicted to my Egyptian cotton.'

'The offer stands if you change your mind later. Oh. I've got something of yours.' He got up and went over to the chest of drawers. Pulling opening the top one he felt inside, amongst the paired socks.

'That's weird. I'm sure I put it in here.'

'What?'

'A bracelet of yours. I found it in on the floor of the Merc.'

'Oh, I wondered what had happened to it.'

'It was *here*.'

Georgia waved a hand. 'Really. Don't worry about it. The sentimental attachment it once held has long since faded.' She finished her drink and her second Marlborough.

Steven took a business card out of his jacket pocket and scribbled his private mobile phone number on the back. 'Ring me if you get any more calls. How are you getting home? I'm assuming you don't want me to drive you?'

Georgia arched a brow. 'No *thank* you. *You've* got me into enough trouble already.' She stood up. 'Oh, the officers that came to see me seemed to know you. Said you were helping them with some other inquiry?'

Steven handed her coat to her. 'Nothing important. One of our drivers was accused of a theft that's all,' he lied smoothly.

ELLEN FINALLY SLUNK upstairs after Georgia's arrival. Pressing her ear to the door to overhear their conversation had been pointless, the door was too thick and their voices muffled. She'd tried peering through the keyhole too, but the key on the other side had blocked her view. Now she paced the sitting room, blood sizzling in her veins.

The sound of a car pulling up outside had her running to the window. A small, sporty looking thing idled at the kerb, a woman at the wheel. She gave a short beep of the horn.

Movement downstairs. Voices in the hallway. Then the Georgia bitch, hood thrown over her head, ran out of the house and down the path towards the waiting car.

Five minutes later the front door banged again and this time it was Steven leaving the house. Rain spattered against glass and an occasional car swished past, its headlights briefly illuminating the room - and the lone figure standing in the window.

32

THE INCIDENT ROOM was large and overly lit by numerous fluorescent strips but despite the brightness, a depressing quality remained. Grey partitioning divided up the space, concealing regulation desks and metal filing cabinets. PC Walker, forced to forgo both shower and makeup due to oversleeping, made her way straight to her desk. For some reason Georgia's story had played on her mind in the night. It was an odd situation. Had the woman really been telling the truth when she'd said she and Finn were not involved? 'Morning, Sarge,' she called as she sat at her desk.

Fraser was attempting to un-jam the photocopier. He glanced around at her. 'You look like shit,' he said. Straightening up he levelled a kick at the machine. 'Fucker,' he muttered.

Walker poked her tongue out at his back and switching on the computer she typed in her password and waited while the system logged her into CRIS, the crime report system. 'Something you'll be interested in came up yesterday,' she said. 'We had a malicious communication complaint from the editor of some woman's magazine.'

'And?' Fraser replied, straightening up and levelling another kick at the machine.

'*And* the point of this nasty call was to tell her to keep her hands off …guess who?'

Fraser turned to look at her again. 'How the fuck should I know?'

'Steven Finn.'

'Really?'

'But the editor swears blind there's nothing going on between them and never has been. But then, why the threat?'

'Let me speak to him,' Fraser said. 'See if he tells the same story. Give him a ring and tell him I'd like a chat. Good excuse to keep up the pressure.'

'Can I be in on it?'

He gave a mean smile. 'Only if you promise not to wet your panties.'

'Sarge!' Walker was affronted.

'Make the call.'

STEVEN WAS LEAVING the gym and on his way back to his car when Walker rang.

'We need to have a chat,' she said.

'I don't have time.'

'It's a matter unrelated to Caroline Shaw. You don't have to come here. I can meet you somewhere convenient.'

Steven glanced around the tightly packed car park. Another member was pulling in who would need his space. 'What's this about?'

'It's about a complaint we received yesterday from Georgia Goldsmith about a threatening phone call.'

'I can't help you.'

'You know her though? She said she was a client.'

'Yeah. She's a client and that's all she is. I've absolutely no idea why anyone would threaten her on my account.'

'Sounds like you know about this already?'

'Yeah. Georgia's spoke to me last night.' He omitted the visit.

'Steven, could we meet? Perhaps in your local? We can have a chat about it over a pint. I promise we won't take up much of your time.'

'Who's we? You and that cretin Fraser?' He gave a thumbs-up thanks to the driver waiting patiently for his space and got into the Merc.

'Would around two be all right?' Walker was pushing. 'The call was a particularly nasty one. We have to take a threat like this seriously and make whatever enquiries we can. Off the record, it'll look bad if you refuse.'

Steven sighed. 'Two o'clock in the Three Bells,' he agreed reluctantly. But you'll be wasting your time -- and mine.'

FRASER WAS DISGRUNTLED that Walker had accorded Finn any degree of civility. 'We should have hauled him into the nick,' he said, elbowing his slight frame through the 'Bell's' lunchtime crowd.

'I didn't see the point of winding him up unnecessarily, Sarge. We may get more out of him this way.'

'You reckon?' He caught the barmaid's attention. 'Pint, love. What you having?'

'Tomato juice, thanks. I'll see if I can grab a table.'

Steven arrived five minutes later. Walker felt herself colour slightly as he took the stool opposite her and nodded in her direction. Fraser he ignored.

The sergeant got to his feet. 'I'll get a refill.' He looked at Steven. 'What you having?'

'A coke.'

'Walker?'

'Same again. And some crisps. Lightly salted if they've got them. I'm starving.'

'Right.' He set off towards the bar with his usual prissy speed.

Steven turned to Walker and spoke quickly, as though wanting to pre-empt the questions and get it over with. 'Georgia Goldsmith is a client of mine, like I said earlier. *Femme* magazine holds an account with us. We provide cars for a few members of their staff, she just happens to be one of them. Why someone would assume there was something going on between us I haven't a clue. We've never met socially.'

'But she's been in touch with you about the call?'

'She spoke to me late yesterday. Naturally she wanted to know if *I* had any idea who may have made the call.'

'And you don't?'

'I've answered that.'

'Perhaps for the time being she should use another firm.'

'She already is.'

'Here.' Fraser dumped two drinks and a bag of crisps he'd clamped under his arm on the table. 'No lightly bloody salted,' he said and went back to the bar for Walker's tomato juice.

Feeling it prudent to postpone any more questions until Fraser joined them, Walker opened the crisps, wrinkling her nose as a pungent aroma of cheese and onion was released, her least favourite flavour. She offered one to Steven. He shook his head.

'Oh, sorry. I guess someone with your physique is into low carb diets and all that.'

'Pays to make the effort.'

Walker straightened up from her slouched position and sucked in her stomach.

'A bit more effort than that.'

Walker laughed, a few fine lines fanning out around her eyes. 'How you doing, Steven,' she asked.

'What? Being your one and only suspect and having that retard,' he nodded in Fraser's direction, 'tailing me day and night?'

'What I really meant was with your kid.'

Steven shifted his gaze to the window deciding just how much or how little to impart. Walker noted that he'd dropped a few pounds since she'd seen him last. He looked a little gaunt, with hollows in his cheeks and exhausted circles beneath his eyes.

He turned back to her and kept his reply brief. 'His grandparents are taking care of him. As far as I know he's fine.'

'You haven't seen him?'

'No. They're refusing me access.'

Walker's expression softened. 'Hopefully this will all be cleared up soon.'

Fraser slammed down the coke. 'Having a nice little tete a tete, are we? Don't mind me, carry on. Perhaps you'd like to get around to your confession, Steve, while we're at it. Save time in the long run.'

Walker raised her eyebrows at Steven and gave an imperceptible shake of her head. Steven looked as though he was fighting the desire to grab Fraser from his stool and pitch him through the delicately- etched pub window.

Fraser lowered his voice, 'We'll nail you for it, eventually.'

Steven stood up, fury contorting his face. He slammed his hands on the table and a cruet set fell to the floor. Bringing his face close to Fraser's, he snarled, 'you stupid, stupid bastard. Whoever did that to Caroline is still out there -- and all you can think of doing is trail around after me like a stray dog.' Shoving the table towards Fraser he stormed out of the pub.

'That went well,' Walker muttered, mopping up her spilt drink with a beer mat. 'Well done, Sarge.'

Fraser flipped back a lank fringe. 'The sooner that psycho is locked away the sooner I'll relax. I *know* he did it. I know he's as guilty as fucking sin.'

Walker leant back in her seat and regarded her superior. 'Gut instinct tells me otherwise, Sarge.'

'Really?' Fraser turned towards her. 'Well, don't lose any sleep over it,' he said nastily. 'As of tomorrow, you're back on street duties.'

33

Four days passed without any more sinister calls. It was time, Georgia decided, to put it all to the back of her mind and get on with her life.

A message on her answering machine when she returned from lunch lifted

her spirits.

'Just ringing to see if everything's okay.' It was Steven's voice. He'd sounded curt, business-like, but that, she had come to learn, was just his way.

From the rear of her own taxi Ellen watched Georgia walk down the steps of the Femme building and get into a black cab. When it pulled away she instructed her driver to follow.

Pushing through the rain and snarl of evening traffic they reached the riverside apartment twenty minutes later. As Georgia's cab swung into the car park, Ellen's driver followed and parked in a resident's slot. Ellen sat and waited while Georgia paid her fare and walked into the apartment block.

Five minutes later Georgia's silhouette moved against the

light of a third floor window as she closed the blind. And it was as easy as that.

'THANK YOU FOR YOUR MESSAGE. I was touched that you've been worrying about me.' Georgia was back on form and her usual flirtatious self.

'Have there been any more?'

'Thank God, no. It was just a one off. Still, good has come out of it, hasn't it?'

'Has it?'

Georgia switched the BlackBerry to her left hand and poured herself a drink. 'Of course. It's drawn us closer,' she said sweetly.

Steven laughed.

'What are you doing? She asked.

'With my life in general or at this exact moment in time?'

'This very second.'

'Lying on my bed, flicking through the TV channels, trying to find some sport, if I'm honest.'

'A night off then?'

'Yeah. Just wasn't in the mood.'

'Well, I *am* in the mood, so why don't you come over? There's caviar and a nice bottle of Krug on offer. Plus whatever else might take your fancy.'

Steven laughed again, but it was a cautious laugh this time. 'Not the kind of offer I get every day of the week.'

'So you'll come?'

'You think it's okay? Safe I mean?'

'Yes. I think if they knew where I lived, they wouldn't have been able to resist letting me know by now, don't you?. Do me a favour though. Park your car a few streets away, no point in taking chances.'

. . .

THE COMMUNAL AREA of Georgia's red brick mansion block enjoyed the traditional advantages of high ceilings, marble floors and large windows but Georgia's apartment had been totally modernised. Remodelled in a masculine, minimalist style that Steven hadn't been expecting. He voiced his thoughts as Georgia waved him towards a white sofa.

She pursed her lips prettily. 'What were you expecting, Laura Ashley? Hardly my thing at all. Actually, I have to confess, the previous owner was a member of some now defunct boy band. He was responsible for most of it. I've made my own little mark though I like to think.'

Steven raised a hand. 'Hey. I wasn't criticising. I like it.'

'Well, I'm glad.' Taking the champagne from the ice bucket, she leant over him, her black curls falling over her face as she poured. On a low glass table, blinis had been arranged on a Japanese-style white platter. Taking the seat opposite she raised her glass. 'Chin-chin,' she said with a mischievous smile. 'Please - help yourself.'

Steven sipped his champagne and Georgia's eyes locked upon his over the rim of her glass. The message in them quickened his pulse. She nodded towards the food, her eyes still holding his.

'Is there something else you might prefer?'

For an answer Steven put down his glass and moved towards her.

ALISON STOOD in Adam's minuscule kitchen in Acton Green, micro-waving her supper. She was now beginning to realise just how lucky she'd been back at the 'Mausoleum', as far as space went. Adam's entire flat would fit easily inside the kitchen at Briarwood Road with room to spare.

It had been a relief when her flatmate Adam had diverted his amorous attention elsewhere, finally accepting her as a lost cause, but two days ago the flat had been rendered even smaller by the arrival of Tamara. The new girl in Adam's life was an aspiring model and now Alison was forever tripping over shoes, designer bags and hair tongs.

The microwave pinged. Alison removed the 'Asparagus and Ricotta Linguine'. From the photograph on the packaging it had looked promising. Ripping off the scalding layer of film she tipped the contents onto a plate and stared at the reality. Poking it with a fork didn't help. It looked like something, Mimsy, her grandmother's Shih Tzu, might puke up.

Carrying her plate into the lounge she perched on the arm of the sofa bed and gazed around the room. Three adults in a one bedroom flat was not a tenable situation.

Funnily enough, it was not so much the sounds of energetic sex going on behind the thin wall that unsettled her. Much more it was the soft intimate murmurings that followed on, combined with the sudden bursts of hushed laughter at shared jokes that heightened her own sense of aloneness.

Opening the patio doors she stepped out onto the tiny balcony. The view across the road of a sodium-lit bus terminal, grimy tarmac and huddle of glass-sided bus shelters was hardly inspiring. In the street below, an unceasing stream of traffic raced God only knew where.

In the distance, a cacophony of sirens told her of dramas being played out in other parts of this big city she was once so desperate to be a part of. Raising her eyes above the brightly-lit Hammersmith skyline, she stared at the moon. No more than a sliver tonight. Curved and delicate like the manicured tip of a fingernail. Then with a jolt of homesickness, she thought of Ireland. She missed the beauty of Lough Mask silvered with moonlight. She missed the soft, misty hills of County Mayo, and even more she missed her family. Her mother, three sisters and her father, who ran the farm almost single-handedly and who would, she worried, work himself into an early grave.

She sighed, the thoughts made her sad. But at least she was dwelling on something other than Steven.

Below a group of girls were clacking along the street with linked arms and Big Night Out plans, judging by the tortuous heels and stream of exuberant chatter. She leant on the balcony rail and watched them pass beneath her. Suddenly, her throat went dry. There was something creepily familiar about the girl on the extreme left of the group. She couldn't see her face, so it could only be the heavy-footed, slightly lumbering walk. As if through some kind of telepathy, the girl turned her head and looked directly up at her. But instead of the unsettlingly flat gaze Alison was expecting, this girl's expression was animated and friendly. Feeling slightly embarrassed, Alison waved. The girl gave a cheery wave back.

What the hell is wrong with me she wondered? Ellen, going for a night out on the town with a group of friends was about as likely as the Pope getting married. Ellen's nasty threat in the pub must have unsettled her more than she'd realised. That threat hadn't been normal. Ellen wasn't normal.

Alison deep-breathed the freezing night air. It seemed to be clearing her head, unclogging all her confused thoughts. Now, she was beginning to see Mad Martha for what she really was, a lonely, pathetic fantasist.

She shivered. It was too cold to stay outside any longer. Going back into the warmth she closed the doors and took her uneaten meal into the kitchen. As she scraped it into the bin she glanced at the washing machine. Her wet clothes still languished in the drum from the night before because Tamara's damp sweaters and underwear were commandeering the only clothes dryer. She sighed. It was time to get her backside in gear and find a place of her own, as once again, she was in the way.

. . .

ELLEN WAS WATCHING a late-night movie on channel five. Brad Pitt was playing a cop married to Gwyneth Paltrow and they seemed to be in love. Since buying Femme magazine she had become familiar with most of the Hollywood movie stars and TV celebrities. The magazine was lying open on her lap right now, or rather the remains of it. Harriet Hope's page had already been torn out and the photograph dealt with. Harriet/Georgia now smiled sightlessly out at her readers, her eyes blinded by a biro tip, and across her throat ran a jagged rip from which Ellen had drawn teardrops of black, dripping blood.

She gazed up at the screen again, not recognising the black man Gywneth was talking to now. It seemed Gwyneth might be in love with him too as she seemed to be flirting with him, but it was hard to tell. The scene changed and it was Brad again. Ellen studied his features. What *was* there to get so excited about? He was nothing compared to *him*. Nothing compared to Steven. She continued to watch the screen, but she was no longer following the plot as it was becoming increasingly difficult with the volume off, and the only sounds in the room the shredding of paper and the incessant tapping of her foot.

34

On the fourth floor of Harrods, practically hugging the walls in a desire not to be noticed, Ellen circumnavigated, 'Way In', glancing nervously at the rails of clothes. She hesitated where several almost diaphanous garments hung, wondering who on earth would wear this kind of stuff and where. A sales assistant appeared at her elbow.

'Anything you're looking for in particular?' she inquired sharply, glancing at the grubby bandage on Ellen's hand. Ellen shook her head and moved on until she came to some rails with more sensible attire. Jeans, T-shirts, denim jackets. She flicked the price tag of a pair jeans over and stared at the figure. It was six times above what she would normally pay. But she needn't worry. The previous day her mother's solicitor had called her to explain something called a 'Statutory Declaration'. She had only been half listening, until he explained that this meant a large sum of money had been released from one of Blanche's accounts to tide her over until the estate finalised. The prices in this store *were* extortionate but what did that matter if she could afford them?

She moved on to another rail. A black sweater in a light,

fluffy material caught her eye. She felt its soft fabric, glanced around to ensure the prowling assistant had disappeared and quickly took it to a full-length mirror.

Directly facing her now, behind a glass counter sat another sales assistant. Ellen didn't spot her until it was too late.

Unfolding her long legs the girl got up and sauntered over. Ellen lowered the sweater and looked at the girl feeling a bright stab of envy. She was precariously thin and exceptionally pretty. Ellen took in the pouty mouth, made sticky-looking with raspberry-coloured goo and the hipbones, jutting from low-slung jeans.

And then that awful inner voice, Blanche's voice, rose up inside her head and she was laughing that awful bronchial laugh that Ellen had been forced to listen to all her life.

You're doolally you are. Do you really think he cares a fig what new clothes you buy, you pathetic ninny. Look at this girl. ***This*** *is the kind of girl Steven wants.*

'Shut up,' Ellen muttered through clenched teeth.

'Black's not gonna do you any favours.' The assistant said, taking the sweater from her. Bending her gleaming blonde head she riffled through the rail. 'A sixteen?'

Ellen flushed.

'Here, this is better.' The girl had found the exact top, but in emerald green. 'And try these with it.' She pulled out some trousers in an equally soft fabric and then produced another top, wine coloured this time. 'This will be good with your hair colour too. The changing rooms are just over there.'

Christ, you'll look a right dog's breakfast in that little lot, Blanche piped up helpfully.

'*Shut Up*!' Ellen shouted. The assistant's head jerked around.

'Sorry! Not you, someone else.' Ellen apologised.

The assistant wasn't fazed. Half of London walked around

gabbling into earpieces these days, looking like escaped patients from mental hospitals.

Ellen grabbed the garments and almost ran to the changing rooms, banging the cubicle door shut behind her. She was doing this for Steven's sake. Steven liked *pretty* girls in *nice* clothes. *Girls like Caroline*. She ripped off the sweatshirt she was wearing. *Girls like Georgia*. She pulled off her jeans with such force she nearly lost her balance, then snatching the green sweater from its hanger she pulled it over her head. She was breathing fast now and there was a film of moisture on her top lip. Pulling on the new trousers she zipped them up and fished out the scratchy price tag that had got caught in her waistband. *Anything to delay the moment – the moment when she had to look at herself in the mirror and see cruel reality staring back at her.*

'How you doing?' the assistant called and pushed open the cubicle door. Ellen prepared herself for derision.

'Cool,' the girl said, nodding, impressed with her own expertise. 'Yeah, I said that was your colour didn't I?'

Ellen scrutinised the girl's face. No, she didn't look as though she was about to burst into hysterical laughter. The girl's reaction seemed genuine. Ellen turned and stared at herself. 'Oh,' she said and clasping her hands between her breasts. 'I look ... nice.'

'Yeah,' the assistant agreed, smiling. 'You look fantastic. Try the other one now.'

35

Sunlight squeezed through a gap in the curtains and slanted across the bed. Ellen lay on her stomach, listening to the sounds coming from downstairs. Steven had slept late but at last she heard him moving around but a quick lunch and he would be gone for the rest of the day.

Quickly she got out of bed and began to pull on the clothes she had worn the day before, and then she stopped. Going to her wardrobe she pulled out the emerald green top and black trousers. Finding a pair of nail scissors she cut off the price tags and slipped into the clothes. Standing in front of her mirror she brushed her hair and dabbed on a pale lip-gloss she had also bought in Harrods.

When Steven came out of his room she was waiting for him. Talking on his mobile he walked right past her.

Following him into the kitchen she waited until he had finished his call. 'I've bought some new clothes,' she said, talking to his back as he was now busy rummaging inside the freezer compartment of the fridge.

'Good,' he said pulling something out and slamming the door shut.

She nodded and cleared her throat. 'The assistant said this was my colour,' she plucked at the green fabric.

'Yeah, great,' he said, still with his back to her.

'You haven't looked.'

Steven shot her an annoyed look over his shoulder. 'Ellen – I'm in a rush, okay?'

Leaving whatever it was to defrost on a plate, he went back to his room, emerging a few moments later with a towel slung across his shoulder. Ellen heard him locking the bathroom door and then a moment later the mobile phone he had left on the worktop began to vibrate.

She watched it for a few seconds and then picked it up. The message on the illuminated screen said, *'Georgia calling.'*

ELLEN SAT ON HER BED, anger drilling and buzzing somewhere deep inside her while her head was filled with so many thoughts she couldn't keep a grip on them, they just kept slithering away. And then in the empty room, she laughed. It was a hard, merciless laugh and utterly devoid of sanity.

Getting to her feet she stamped across the shredded remains of the new clothes to get to her wardrobe and pull out another new purchase, a long black puffer coat with a hood.

GEORGIA WAS CURLED up on her white sofa under a cream cashmere throw. A gel fire flickered in the hearth and Richard Hawley sang softly in the background. She yawned, fighting to keep her eyes open and continue with her novel. Then, turning on her side she cupped her cheek in the palm of her hand and closed her eyes.

Outside, Ellen stood beneath the trees watching the

lighted window. Between her shoulder blades was a harmless looking rucksack. An unsuspecting passer-by may have taken her for a student had they given her any thought at all, assuming the contents of the blue Nike bag were nothing more sinister than a jumble of text books, a battered old Thesaurus and a crumpled copy of Time Out.

ALISON SENT the text to Steven on her way to work that evening. All afternoon she had fretted whether to send it or not, but once she'd made the decision and sent it, she put it out of her mind. Let him make of it what he will. Now she allowed the patients, the reports and the emergency admissions to squeeze everything else from her mind and only once, during the long, quiet, lonely hours, did she allow her thoughts to return to Steven Finn.

ELLEN WAS BEGINNING to enjoy herself. The initial urgency to leave had dissipated as she began to wander around Georgia's apartment. She had only seen homes like this on television or in magazines and she stood in the kitchen admiring the sleek shininess of it all. She twiddled knobs, opened glossy cupboard doors and examined the contents of the powder-blue fridge-freezer. When she shut the door she frowned, picked up a teacloth and wiped away the bloody fingerprints she'd left. It was a shame to spoil something so pretty. In an absent move, she folded up the cloth neatly and placed it back on the worktop.

Then she went into the bedroom and rifled through the chest of drawers. Georgia's underwear was a mixture of silky fabrics and lace. One particular garment in a delicate pale green with pink ribbons held her attention. The laces at the back made it look like some old-fashioned garment. Ellen pulled it out of the drawer and held it up.

See! I told you. This is what you're up against, Ellie. You don't stand a chance. Not when there's slut's like this dressing up for him, fulfilling his dirty fantasies!

Ellen pushed the basque back and slammed the drawer shut. Going over to the wardrobe that took up one entire wall she slid back the door and gazed at the clothes hanging there. She fingered some of them but could only imagine the softness of the fabrics through the bloody latex gloves.

Back in the main room she crunched across glass and stepped over the sprawled, half-naked body. Georgia had been wearing a towelling robe and nothing else when she had opened the door to her.

It had been so easy getting in. She had simply pressed the button and spoken to Georgia through the intercom.

'Miss Goldsmith? Interflora. I have a bouquet for you,' she'd announced, using a voice she didn't know she had. Lighter, younger. And that had been enough, enough to persuade the daft bitch to buzz her in. By the time she got to the first floor, Georgia was standing at her door with a stupid half-smile on her face.

Ellen glanced around the sitting room now. Since her arrival she'd done a little redecorating of her own, but she couldn't claim it was an improvement.

Broken glass from the coffee table littered the pale wood floor and the once pristine walls were now covered in blood sprays and gobbets of flesh.

The meat cleaver lay in front of the fireplace where it had slipped from her hand, clumps of hair and gore stuck to the blade. She savoured the moment she had flung back her arm and brought it down on Georgia's skull. The editor's expression had changed to one of dull surprise.

'Gahh,' she'd said dropping to her knees.

'Gahhh,' she said again, before finally keeling over from the impact of the second blow.

The glass Georgia had been sipping from a few moments before had fallen from her hand and rolled across the floor. Picking it up, Ellen saw the imprint of her mouth on the rim. And as she looked at that rosy, semi-circle of lipstick, thoughts and images of where that mouth might have been, what that mouth might have done, exploded in her brain and the white hot rage roaring in her head obliterated everything else. Reaching for the cleaver, she abruptly.

36

OK I'LL LISTEN but make it good.

Alison

Steven re-read the text and his throat tightened. It was pathetic how grateful he felt. Storming her place of work had been an act of total stupidity. He felt embarrassed just thinking about it. He'd treat her with the respect and consideration she deserved from now on. If *ever she* gave him the chance.

Setting off in the direction of West Ealing he headed towards the Green Man Lane Community centre. He'd be late. The AA meeting would already be under way but he'd felt compelled to put in an appearance today. If he carried on as he was, he knew the small progress he'd made over the past months would all be for nothing.

AN HOUR and ten minutes later he left the meeting feeling drained but good about himself. The regulars were glad he was back. Members dropping off the radar were unsettling for the group as a whole, highlighting the stark reality of failure.

Sitting in his car he checked his phone. One message awaited him. A picture message. Who would send him one of those? He waited as the photograph downloaded. At first he was unable to comprehend what he was seeing. He stared hard at the screen. Was it a joke? Some sort of sick hoax that Georgia might think amusing?

Saving the image with a less than steady hand he accessed his contacts list.

The receptionist connected him quickly to Georgia's extension, but it was someone else who picked up the phone. A harassed female voice informed him that; 'No,' Georgia is not in yet,' and; '*No*, she hasn't rung in sick either.'

He refused to acknowledge the stirring of unease in his gut. 'Have you tried her mobile?' he persisted.

'No joy. Going to voice mail.'

'Is it unusual,' Steven asked slowly, 'for her not to call in if she's unwell?'

The girl thought for a moment. 'Yeah. Yeah, it is actually. She must be feeling really rough.'

He finished the call, a dull thump started up in his chest.

IN ANNIE'S Tea Rooms just off the high street, Margaret and Roger Shaw sat separated by an expanse of white linen.

Roger sliced a scone in half, buttered it meticulously, smeared a thin layer of jam over the butter and then replaced the scone untouched on his plate. Wiping his fingers on a paper napkin he turned his attention to his tea. Spooning in sugar he stirred it distractedly and with no other displacement activity left to occupy him, he slumped back in his chair and regarded his wife through sad, defeated eyes.

Margaret sat in the window seat, the harsh morning sunlight emphasising each line and blemish on her face. In the past three weeks she seemed to have aged ten years. It was as though the life force had been sucked out of her. Leaning forward Roger reached for her hand. She snatched it away.

'Marg, don't be like this,' he pleaded. 'For God sake, I loved her just as much as you.'

She darted him a venomous look.

'Marg,' he implored, sick of his impersonal room at the Royal Berkshire and longing to be home again.

'I don't want you back. Not ever,' she said. 'I'm sorry but that's how I feel,' and gathering up her gloves and her bag, Margaret Shaw left.

37

Ellen took another two Nurofen and sat at the kitchen table. The wound in her hand, which had begun to heal, had opened up again after her previous night's exertions. It had throbbed all night keeping her awake but as she sat at the kitchen table, a smile lit her features as she imaged the expression on Steven's face when he saw the 'little surprise' she had sent him.

What he really didn't understand, *what he had no real concept of*, was just how angry he had made her. *Or just how angrier she could still become.*

She sat in the quiet kitchen, her heart beating away time.

Steven drove towards home, slow dread growing in the pit of his stomach. Fuck the Twelve Step Program, he had never needed a drink as much as he needed one now.

Turning into the Three Bells car park he squeezed the Merc between a Ford transit and a Toyota, dimly telling himself he would only have one - but he'd make it a double and when it came, the glass felt as comforting as a warm touch from a friend.

He placed his mobile on the bar and kept it under surveillance while the effects of the alcohol took hold. It was running thorough his blood like nitrate when the phone vibrated with an incoming call. He wiped his mouth with the back of his hand and as much as he was loath to touch it, he made himself pick it up.

'Steve?' Alison's voice was the last voice in the world he was expecting to hear.

'Did you get my note?'

'Uh. Yes.'

'I meant it.'

'Thanks.' His voice cracked a little but reigning in his emotions he added; 'I appreciate it.'

'Yes. Well, I've been thinking about it all and I've decided to believe *you* rather than that loop-the-loop, Ellen, and I just hope ... well ... to be honest I hope you don't give me cause to regret my decision.'

'You won't. Listen ... I ...er...'

'What's wrong?'

'It's just...'

'I've called at a bad time, haven't I? I'd better go.'

'Yeah, it's... everything's just gone a bit weird. Can I call you later? What time do you get off?'

'Not until four, but I'll have another break at two, you can ring me then.'

'I'll try.'

'Bye.' Alison's voice sounded flat, disappointed, but he couldn't worry about that now.

He swallowed what was left in his glass, swung himself off the stool and made for the exit.

In the car he rang Femme magazine again. Nothing had changed. Georgia still hadn't arrived at work or returned any calls. The gnawing sensation in his stomach worsened. Instinct and recent experience was telling him to fear the worst.

Lowering the window he sucked in cold air and forced himself to think clearly. Two choices presented themselves.

The first was that he go to the police now, show them the photograph and explain that no one had heard from Georgia since the previous day. He'd run the risk of making a total tool of himself if it turned out Georgia was carrying out some elaborate hoax of course. But if she wasn't and the image was real, he knew what would happen next, he'd be banged up in a police cell on a double murder charge before the day was out.

Option two was that he go to her apartment to check on her himself. No doubt she's fine he reassured himself. Just enjoying her tasteless joke and ignoring all calls...

But it looked so real.

He breathed cold air again and chased the image from his mind. Thinking about it, he decided he preferred option two. Checking on Georgia was the priority but there was another motive for visiting her apartment. It meant he could retrieve the Tag watch he'd inadvertently left there. Removing it when it caught in Georgia's hair he'd left it on her night stand and hopefully it was still there. If it were to fall into the police's hands the serial number would make it instantly traceable to him. Scattering gravel he drove out of the car park towards Barnes.

STEVEN FOUND a parking meter a short walk from Georgia's apartment. Parking the distinctive Merc in one of the resident bay's would not be smart. Pulling a baseball cap down over his eyes, he set off. Clammy, river-damp air settled on his clothes and skin, chilling him as he walked, but beneath the cap his scalp prickled with sweat. He fingered the screwdriver in his pocket. If he had to break in he would, if she was too sick to get out of bed – or worse.

Reaching the main entrance he pressed the intercom buzzer while his heart struck up a slow canter in his chest. He buzzed again. *Open the fucking door, Georgia, he willed*, careful to keep his head down and his back to the wall-mounted CCTV camera.

He tried the buzzers for apartment one and two. No response from them either. *Shit*. When he pressed buzzer number three he finally got a drawled; 'Yes?' from a female voice.

'Delivery for number four. Let me in please.'

A slight pause, then a click and the door opened. Crossing the Yucca filled lobby he ran up the stairs to the first floor. The corridor was deserted. He walked the long, carpeted length of it. Georgia's apartment was the last on the left.

There was only one lock. A Yale. Easy enough to pop out if he had to - but he didn't have to, the front door stood open. He stared at it for a long, immobile moment. *She's here. She's fine,* he reassured himself over the mad thumping of his heart. *We all do this on occasions. When we're pre-occupied, when we've got an arm-full of shopping...*

The reassurances didn't work. He wanted desperately to leave now probably more than anything in the world, but instead he nudged the door with the toe of his boot and as it swung inwards, he stepped inside.

Passing through the small hallway into the living room he found the heavy drapes still drawn and it would have been dark but for the lamp lying on the floor, pooling soft golden light onto the carpet. When he'd seen that lamp last, it had been standing on the low glass coffee table. But that wasn't possible now. The table's surface had been reduced to a million shattered fragments that crunched beneath his feet. He raised his eyes to the wall that had housed the funky, boy-band gel burner. Ripped from its alcove, it too lay in fragments, smashed to fuck.

Dragging his eyes above that piece of handiwork he gazed at the blood-soaked wall. He knew it *was* blood of course. The metallic, butcher-shop smell told him that.

He retraced his steps, groped for the light switch. Everything looked better in

the light, right? But the spiky, modern take on a chandelier only served to reveal the complete horror.

The once pristine white sofa was covered in blood splatters and clots of matter his mind refused to speculate on, while dark chunks of flesh, hair still attached, were pasted to the drapes. Nausea crawled the walls of his stomach.

A bloody trail led behind the sofa. He made himself step forward despite the awful image that rose up in his mind; Georgia, stricken, weeping and terrified, dragging herself along the carpet in slow, futile flight from her attacker. A groan of relief escaped him when he saw that at the end of the trail there was nothing.

He turned, called, 'Georgia?' in a voice that was no more than a hoarse whisper despite hardly expecting a reply. Nerves twanging like wires he moved towards the kitchen. The stench was stronger now. Blood mixed with a sickening undertone.

He stepped inside, his footsteps gritty on the floor and if he'd needed further confirmation that Georgia had indeed met the most awful fate – he had it now.

Her naked body as white as the marble floor was revealed in the muted, under cabinet lighting. She hung head down from a steel beam fixed above the central aisle. Metal hooks had been forced through the tendons of each ankle, her arms pinned to her sides with flex. Blood from a head wound caked her breasts in rust coloured streaks and her matted, bloodied hair cascaded onto the granite counter top where more blood pooled and congealed.

An iron fist slammed into his diaphragm, knocking all the air out of his lungs. 'Jesus fuck,' he whispered gripping the work-top. Looking into her upside down face he knew that what he was seeing would never leave him.

Eyes gone. Stabbed out. Lips gone too. He turned quickly away. The exposed teeth and fleshless mouth seemed to be grinning at him.

Unable to think or breathe, his eyes fell upon a globe-like fish tank where the occupants nibbled at something on the bottom. It took a few seconds to register that the delicacy was Georgia's lips.

He made it back to the hall where the air was sweeter but the ground seemed to be falling away. Leaning against the wall, he deep-breathed for few moments. *The watch!* He *had* to retrieve the Tag. Forcing himself to move he went into Georgia's bedroom.

Everything was tidy, intact, but for a bloody smear on the wardrobe door. He moved over to the nightstand. It wasn't there. He opened the drawer. It wasn't there either. He dragged back the duvet, checked under the bed. The Tag had gone.

To tear the place apart would take an hour or more and all the while Georgia would be hanging from the ceiling like a side of beef in a slaughterhouse. He needed desperately to get outside into clean, fresh air.

Closing the front door behind him he hurried back along the hushed corridor. There was no point worrying about fingerprints, no real point in worrying about the watch. Two nights ago he would have left enough DNA in the apartment to convict him a thousand times over.

. . .

Back at Briarwood Road, Steven threw clothes into a case and stuffed a large holdall with most of his possessions. He flung his toothbrush, shaving gear and the few sentimental items dear to him into a plastic bag and by four thirty was negotiating the Tolworth roundabout and travelling south.

38

ELLEN WOKE from a deep and for once dreamless sleep. Her left hand throbbed and there was a dull ache in her right shoulder. Reaching for some painkillers she found the packet empty.

Thirst drove her out of bed. Throwing on a stained tee-shirt, an old cardigan and some joggers, she went into the kitchen and drank several glasses of water and wondered when was the last time she had eaten. Not that it mattered. Her foggy brain was clearing and a sudden delicious anticipation settled upon her. How had Steven reacted to Georgia's picture? She was desperate to know. He'd deserved a punishment and he'd got one. She went out onto the landing. From the ground floor came the strident strains of music and a woman squawking at the top of her voice. Miss King's music, not Steven's.

Perhaps he was still sleeping. She paced a little, and then unable to contain her impatience any longer, she went downstairs. There was no response to her knock. She knocked again and tried the handle. The door opened. She slipped inside and for a few stunned moments she hardly breathed. *Something was horribly wrong.*

Running to the wardrobe she flung open the door and a bolt of horror ripped through her heart. Spinning around she saw the discarded hangers strewn across the bed. Rushing to the chest of drawers she yanked them out one by one. His possessions had gone. *He had gone!*

'Oh, no,' she moaned. '*Oh, no, no, no.*' Clapping her hands to the sides of her head, she screamed.

ELLEN STARED up at the house. It was early evening and the curtains had not yet been drawn. On the ground floor lamps glowed invitingly behind diamond leaded panes. It was a storybook house. One she could imagine a perfect storybook family living out their perfect storybook lives – and the sight of it enraged her.

That the occupants of this lovely home had already been destroyed by the slaying of their only child was not something that remotely registered with her, but even if it did, it wouldn't stop her doing what she was about to do now.

Following a path that ran alongside the house she came to a back door. The kitchen light was on and there was movement inside. Cupping her hand to the window she peered through the glass. A girl of roughly her own age was loading a dishwasher. She was small and skinny, with blonde hair pulled up on top of her head.

Ellen felt in her pocket for the Christmas card she had taken from Caroline's apartment. 'To Mummy and Dad' was written inside, along with some stuff about meeting in the New Year, and hoping to 'build bridges', whatever that meant, and then Caroline had finished by telling them; 'I have the most wonderful surprise for you both, you really can't imagine!'

Well, they didn't get a chance to imagine anything as it turned out, but no doubt Caroline had still managed to surprise them by getting herself killed. The card had been a real stroke of luck because Caroline had addressed the envelope but not got round to posting. Now Ellen was delivering it personally.

She tapped on the glass. Startled, the girl looked around. Ellen gave a reassuring smile and held up the card. Coming to the back door the girl unlocked it.

'This came to us by mistake,' Ellen said, with a cheery smile. 'We're at number 65,' she nodded in some vague direction. 'I'm sorry it's late, but better late than never.'

'Oh,' the girl said. 'Tank you. Is very kind.' As she reached for the envelope Ellen grabbed her.

IN THE SITTING room Margaret Shaw was staring at the TV screen. A lively discussion was taking place on Question Time regarding new government proposals on how best to deal with the continuing influx of illegal immigrants. Fiona Bruce pointed her pen at an Asian member of the audience who had raised his arm to speak. Margaret concentrated for a few minutes on what the Asian man had to say, before, as was usual these days, her mind began to drift. It was brought back to the screen again by some irritating student types heckling from the rear of the audience. Margaret muted the sound with the remote control and closed her eyes.

The phone ringing at her elbow jerked her out of her doze.

'Sweet little baby,' whispered a singsong voice in her ear.

'What?' Margaret said, groggy from her nap.

'Poor little boy' crooned the voice.

'What on earth...' Margaret was suddenly wide-awake.

'He's sleeping now.'

'*Who* is this?'

'Want to know how I know he's sleeping?' the whispering voice asked. *'Because I'm upstairs holding him.'*

Terror climbed into Margaret Shaw's throat. Dropping the phone, she was out of her chair and sprinting for the stairs, arthritic knee forgotten. She was still running when she entered Luke's bedroom. At the cot, in the dark, she felt frantically for Luke's little body – until a sound made her freeze. The sound of someone breathing. She turned and her bowels loosened as a dark shape moved out of the shadows towards her.

The shape became solid. Something, *someone* was holding Luke. A howl tore from Margaret Shaw's throat and she launched herself at the intruder. But Ellen was faster. She stepped sideways like a matador making a pass and Margaret careered on into the wall. Ellen threw Luke back into his cot as if he were nothing more than a bag of washing and Luke was too shocked to cry. Grabbing Margaret by a fistful of hair her other fist punched Margaret hard in the face. Margaret's head rocked back, she screamed, choked on blood and teeth and screamed again. Ellen released her and watched her slide down the wall. Turning back to the cot, Ellen reached in for the baby, but Margaret was scrambling to her feet and despite her swollen mouth and broken teeth she still managed to scream at the top of her lungs: 'Renata!'

'She can't help you, you dried up old crotch,' Ellen said stooping to pick up a glinting object lying on the floor.

'*Oh, please. Oh, dear God, no,*' Margaret whispered. Rushing for the door she managed to get as far as the stairs, had even began a dignified descent before her knees finally buckled. Then, dropping like a stone, she rolled the rest of the way down the oak staircase with the axe handle sticking out of her back.

. . .

WHEN STEVEN WOKE he was lying face down on a strange bed, in a strange room with a searing headache. He peered around through slitted lids and flinched at the bright morning sunlight. Sparks skittered across his vision and he quickly shut his eyes again. Perhaps he was moments away from an aneurysm. The way he was feeling, it was fine by him. Bring it on. But oblivion failed to materialise and after a few minutes he was unable to withstand the smell of the stale bed linen any longer. As he sat up his foot struck something on the floor. An empty bottle of Johnnie Walker toppled and rolled across the carpet, spilling the remainder of its contents. Whisky fumes filled the room.

Dry-heaving his way to the tiny en-suite, he washed his face with cold water and avoided catching his hung-over reflection in the mirror. As he returned to the bedroom a flashback of the previous night came back to him. He remembered ordering the booze from the downstairs bar. He remembered its arrival and how he had sat on the bed with it in his lap for a long, long time before finally unscrewing the cap.

Picking up the bottle now an image came to him. His mother lying on a vomit and blood-streaked kitchen floor, three empty vodka bottles beside her. There were other equally unwelcome images too, stored away at the back of his mind, like musty old clothes in a trunk

He shoved the bottle into the waste paper basket, making a vow that whatever hell he was about to be subjected to, (and he sensed a truck-load more was on its way) he *would not, would not,* under *any* circumstance allow himself to do that again. Not ever. And it wasn't because of the nauseous rolls his stomach was performing or because of the drilling for oil that was going on inside his skull, but because he never wanted to despise himself again as much as he did right now.

Outside, seagulls quarrelled on rooftops, reminding him

of where he had ended up after a three-hour drive out of London. Hove. Wet, windy and out-of-season desolate. Arriving in the early evening he had searched for the most anonymous looking B & B he could find. The Curlew fitted the bill. Situated in a scruffy side street with nothing to recommend it other than a pub a few doors away.

Checking in, he had given a false name and paid in cash. The gormless boy, who had shoved a register at him to sign, didn't once raise his eyes from his iPhone during the checking-in process. He'd sat texting with one hand and picking at an outbreak of pimples flaring across his cheeks with the other.

Steven hauled a suitcase from the car. It would make him less conspicuous, he'd thought, more like someone with a real reason to be in the arse end of nowhere. But as he carried it up the three flights of stairs to his room he realised how naive that thought had been. It was the kind of dive where a human trafficking ring would go unnoticed.

Going over to the small window he pulled back dusty-smelling lace. A sea mist had now vanquished the early morning sunshine. It crept over wet rooftops bringing with it grey, wintry light, deepening the depression that threatened to overtake him.

Forcing himself to do something constructive, he walked purposefully back into the en-suite, no bigger than a cupboard, no doubt it had once *been* a cupboard, and squeezed himself inside the cubicle. The water that trickled from the shower head was little more than lukewarm and he wasn't in the least surprised.

Ten minutes later he sat on the bed debating if it was too early to call Alison. He looked at his watch. Yes, it probably was. He rang Ron instead and left a message that he had been struck down with flu and felt as though he was dying. He hoped it would keep Ron off his back for a couple of days.

Boiling some water in the small kettle that stood on a scratched melamine tray, he made himself a cup of instant coffee. He drank it quickly and managed to keep it down while considering whether running from the police was really such a smart tactic. How could it be smart if it was making him feel so bad about himself? He checked his watch again. It was still way too early to ring Alison, but he decided to anyway.

39

STEVEN CUT a furrow through the milling crowds of commuters at Richmond Station and made towards the AMT coffee stand where Alison was waiting. No smile greeted him and her expression was wary as he steered her towards the exit and led her to an Irish pub with 'England v Croatia - Live Tonite!' emblazoned across the plate glass window.

The growing crowd of punters at the bar made getting served difficult but the upside was that the over-stretched bar staff would have no time to register the strained -looking couple huddled in the corner.

Alison sat on the edge of her seat, poised for flight, and he could hardly blame her for that, *and* he reminded himself, she hadn't even heard the worst of it yet.

He had come back to London, not only to face the likes of the Dumber and Dumber Met team but also because he needed an ally, someone with a good brain who, if the time came, would be the credible defence witness he so desperately needed. And yet as he looked at the slight, tense body crouched over the bottle of Corona, his justification for drawing her into the hell that was now his world drained away.

She was watching him too, through narrowed, untrusting eyes. 'You've got ...' she consulted her watch, 'exactly five minutes to convince me, that, one: I'm not a complete imbecile for being here and half way to believing your story and, two: you're the kind of person who deserves my trust.'

Steven stared down at his coke and exhaled slowly. 'Okay,' he began. 'You know about Caroline. Ellen told you and you've read the papers. Just before Caroline and I broke up, the *reason* why Caroline and I broke up was that she'd found out she was pregnant. I was pleased – she wasn't. She gave me a lot of crap about it "not being the right time" and said she wanted a termination. I didn't want that. But no matter how I tried, I couldn't persuade her against it. In the end I moved out. I didn't want to be with someone who was capable of doing that and I certainly didn't want to be around when it happened. I didn't see her again until a few weeks ago. That's when I found out about my son, Luke. She hadn't gone ahead with the termination after all.'

'I read about a little boy in the paper. That's quite a stunt to pull on somebody.'

Steven was heartened to see that she had relaxed a little. Shame there was worse to come.

'He's a really lovely little kid and deep down I didn't care that she'd lied. I was just pleased that he's here.'

'So what made her get back in touch? Was she hoping you two could start over again?'

'No. All she wanted was maintenance. I told her I was happy to support her as much as I could, that I'd pay whatever she wanted, on the condition she allowed me access. But she wasn't having that.'

'Why?'

'She had her reasons. We argued about it, but in the end I

know we would have worked something out, had we got the chance.'

Alison picked at the label on her bottle, but kept her eyes on him. 'Do the police still think it was you?'

'Yeah. But they have no evidence. Unsurprising really as I didn't do it.'

'And you've no idea who could have been responsible?'

He shook his head. 'None.'

'What I've read – it sounded so brutal. Someone must have really hated her.'

'Yes.'

'Unless it was totally random. A madman.'

'That's what I thought at first.'

'What do you think now?'

He rubbed the back of his neck. Sighed. 'I don't really know anymore. I've gone over and over it so many times, I've just confused myself.'

The tables either side of them were taken now in readiness for the match. Steven glanced around. A pub suddenly didn't feel the right place to enlighten Alison about the rest of the unfolding horror. If he showed her the picture of Georgia right now she would probably leap up and run screaming to the nearest police station – and who could blame her.

He glanced up at the pub clock with a sinking sense of hopelessness. Once Georgia's body was discovered, (and it was likely it already had), and forensics had discovered his DNA in her apartment, what chance would he stand?

His eyes met Alison's and he made the decision. He just wanted a bit more time with her before he went to the police. 'The match is about to start and it's going to get noisy, let's get out of here.'

Alison glanced around, anxiously. 'I don't know.'

'There are a couple of hotels on the Hill. They're always

quiet. If you don't want to risk getting in the car with me, we can walk.'

She stood up. 'I really hope I'm not going to regret this.'

Outside it was bitingly cold. Alison hurried at his side. 'God, it's freezing! How far is this place?

'Half a mile.'

'Let's get the car.'

Cutting through a quaint little passageway they arrived at Richmond Green where they were forced to negotiate an assembling theatre crowd. The sight of them lit an irrational spark of anger in Steven. Why were these people allowed to go about their uneventful lives and simple pleasures while his own life was spiralling into something resembling an apocalyptic horror film? He shouldered his way through, knowing he wasn't going to get an answer to that particular question any time soon.

The car waited on an avaricious meter. Alison hung back, chin tucked into her collar. 'How do I know you haven't got a bottle of chloroform in the glove compartment?'

Steven zapped the lock. 'You can check before you get in. Check the boot for a rape kit too.'

Alison looked like she wished she were back in the pub.

'Would you feel better if you drove?'

'Haven't passed my test,' she said opening the passenger door and climbing in.

The hotel lounge was quiet. Just two suited business colleagues, a man and a women, engaged in muted conversation over their open laptops.

Alison made for a leather sofa while Steven went to the bar. When he returned he was almost amused to catch her furtively checking out the exits.

He took the space next to her, aware that to any outsider

they would look like an ordinary couple on a date. If only. The gnawing in the pit of his stomach and the cold sheen of sweat on his brow was a constant reminder of the gravity of his situation.

Alison had requested a vodka and cranberry juice. 'Less calories than beer,' she'd muttered.

Steven sipped a mineral water and glanced around. Apart from the murmuring of the other couple, the soft music and the clink of glasses coming from the bar, there was a hushed tranquillity to the place.

Alison leaned across suddenly and took his hand. '*Stop* it.'

He stared down at her small fingers unaware he'd been drumming some nervous tattoo on his thigh. He turned her hand over, exposing a soft vulnerable-looking palm. He rubbed it gently, almost absent-mindedly with his thumb while his mind struggled with formatting cohesive explanations. In the end he just spewed it out.

'All this mess I'm in, it doesn't stop at Caroline. There's a whole lot more.'

Alison pulled her hand away, her forehead creasing into a frown. 'I'm not sure I can deal with more.'

'I have to tell you all of it. Someone else needs to know what's going on. I had a client. She worked on a magazine called Femme.'

Alison nodded. 'One of the expensive glossies.'

'We have a contract with them and some nights I'd drive Georgia home from the office. Two weeks ago she received a threatening phone call from a woman. The woman mentioned my name and warned her off me, made some nasty threats, which was weird because at that time our relationship was nothing other than a business one. Georgia reported the call to the police and asked me if I had any idea who it could be. I didn't and for the time being she decided it was safer if I didn't drive her any more. A sensible precaution and totally fine with me. Almost a week went by and there were no more phone calls. Georgia relaxed and decided whoever it was had lost interest, perhaps found another victim to scare and, well, we got together. She invited me to her place and ...'

'I get the picture.'

He gave her a direct look. 'It was never going to be a relationship. It was just a casual thing - a one-night stand.'

'Good for you.' Alison's voice was small and hard.

Steven ploughed on. 'Then yesterday I received a picture text. Of Georgia.' He lifted his glass, drained its contents then took the phone out of his pocket. A quick glance at the other couple reassured him that they were still suitably engrossed in their spread sheets, graphs or whatever other shit was floating their boat. He placed the phone on the table in front of them.

'At first,' he went on, 'I thought it was a sick joke. Georgia was a bit ...unpredictable, and I thought it might be the kind of thing she would do. But I rang the magazine anyway, just to check she was okay and they told me she hadn't turned up that morning. I rang a few more times but she still hadn't put in an appearance. So then I went to her apartment and I ... I found her.'

Alison stared at him. 'How do you mean? Found her?'

Steven's eyes held hers. 'She was dead, Alison. She'd been butchered.' He went to take her hand again but she pulled it sharply away, her eyes now wide with shock.

'I know what you're thinking,' he said quickly. 'If the situation was reversed, I know I'd be having the same thoughts. But I swear to you on my little boy's life, that I had nothing to do with her death *or* Caroline's. I swear it.'

Alison snatched up the phone and stared at the screen and then with an inarticulate sound she clapped a hand over her mouth. 'Oh, Jesus,' she muttered, her face draining of colour. She reached out blindly for her coat and bag.

Steven grabbed her arm before she could get to her feet.

'Alison. I *am* going to the police but I just wanted to convince you first that I'm not involved in any of this. I'm not even sure I know why it's so important to me that you believe me. All I know is that it is.' Then he released her arm, giving her the freedom to walk if she chose to.

Alison shook her head. Confusion, panic or something else kept her in her seat. And then the phone in her lap beeped. 'Take it,' she ordered.

Steven picked it up, dread bubbling in his gut. He was convinced whoever had sent that picture wasn't done yet, and then he wasn't thinking coherently at all, because what had *all* of his attention now, was the image on his screen. Luke staring back at him with an expression of wide-eyed incomprehension and the accompanying message: *'I'VE GOT HIM'*

He was unaware of the wounded animal sound he made, a sound that made Alison snatch the phone from his hand.

'It's Luke.' His voice was dull with shock.

'But ... I don't... *who's* got him?'

40

STEVEN SAT behind the wheel of the Merc, his jaw set as he rang the unfamiliar number. The call connected immediately but whoever picked up on the other end remained silent.

'Speak to me, you fucking piece of shit. Tell me what you want!'

Silence.

'If you touch him, if you harm him ...'

'Hello, Steven.'

For the next few moments Steven sat staring through the front window, waiting while the slow recognition of that voice struggled to reach the circuits of his brain.

'Ellen?' His tone was incredulous.

There was a soft giggle.

'Ellen?' He repeated, a mixture of incomprehension and bright panic exploding in his mind. 'For Christ sake ... what are you doing?'

A low-pitched laugh was her response. 'I'd have thought I'd made that obvious, Steven, even to you. But it's all in the past now, isn't it? Along with that stupid cunt Caroline. Oh, and the other cunt, Georgia. Did you enjoy the pic I sent you? I don't think she was really looking her best at that point though, do you?'

Steven's horrified eyes locked upon Alison's. '*Ellen* – Luke, he's just a baby. He's never done a thing to hurt you. *Please, please* - don't harm him.'

Ellen sighed. 'What you should be worrying about is not *if* I'm going to harm him – but *how*.'

'*Ellen!*' The line went dead.

Steven punched the steering wheel hard then tried calling the number again. It rang and rang without going to voice mail. But then a beep heralded the arrival of another message.

'IF YOU GO TO THE POLICE I'LL KNOW. IF YOU GO TO THE POLICE I'LL KILL HIM NOW. BUT STEVEN IT WON'T BE QUICK.'

Steven dropped the phone and dived outside as nausea overwhelmed him. Alison pressed herself up against the door, mute and terrified as she read the message.

In the hotel car park Steven took deep lung-fulls of freezing air in an attempt to hold onto the contents of his stomach and whatever scrap of sanity he still retained. Pushing open the passenger door Alison went to him. 'Oh my God, Steven.'

Steven covered his face and turned away from her.

Putting an arm through his, she coaxed him back into the car. Once inside she said in a trembling voice; 'What do we do?'

He shook his head unable to articulate a single sound. Starting the engine he backed out of the space on auto pilot and headed out of the car park.

Alison forced herself to keep quiet. He needed to concentrate on the road but he was driving way too fast - out of Richmond.

'*Steven,* where are we going?'

'Guildford.' He stared straight ahead, a muscle working in his jaw.

'Guildford? Why the hell are we going there?'

'His grandparents live in Guildford. He gripped the wheel tighter. 'I need to find out for myself. I need to know if she's really got him. That this is not just some crazy mind-fuck game of hers. Maybe she's managed to get hold of a photograph of him somehow.'

'You have the pictures on your phone and the text messages. Wouldn't it be best if we go straight to the police?'

'*Alison!* Did you read that warning?'

Alison stared at him. 'Okay,' she said after a few moments thought. 'Say she *has* managed to snatch him, where could she take him? Certainly not back to Briarwood Road and wherever else she went, she would be conspicuous. Children don't exactly disappear into the woodwork, particularly a child as young as Luke. They cry a lot for one thing.'

Alison rubbed a hand over her eyes. 'Can you slow down, I'm feeling sick.' There was a barely perceptible drop in speed. 'Caroline and Georgia; how did she find out about them?'

'It wasn't difficult. They came to Briarwood Road. Ellen saw them both.'

Alison shivered. 'Oh, Christ.'

THEY PICKED UP THE A3. Steven was being careful now to keep his speed just under the limit, anxious not to attract the attention of a traffic cop, but Alison could still feel tension humming off him. She forced herself to remain quiet, to ignore the multitude of questions screaming in her head, they would have to wait.

After a while, Steven gave her a concerned glance and caught her gnawing on a thumbnail. She dropped her hand.

'I have no excuse for involving you in all this,' he said. 'My only justification is to make sure that *someone* knows the truth, just in case something happens to me. But it has to be someone I can really trust. Can I trust you Alison, not to contact the police? Not yet, anyway.'

Alison's head crowded with 'what if's'. What if Ellen was lying? What if Luke was already dead? What if it was Steven all along? Sending messages to himself, pretending it was Ellen? In which case *she* was the one in real danger now.

She kept her eyes fixed ahead. 'You're asking an awful lot of me,' she said finally.

'I know,' he replied, nudging the speedometer up to eighty.

41

Driving though quiet, affluent suburbs they reached the outskirts of Guildford twenty minutes later. Narrow streets, crowded with small cottages gave way to wider roads dotted with mellow stone-built villas. Finally they entered a semi-rural village. When they reached a small green, Steven braked and swerved into the kerb. 'That's Caroline's home!'

Alison pressed a hand to her mouth and they both stared out at a drama that was unfolding. Inside Doughty House lights blazed in every window and parked on the driveway, behind yellow incident tape stood an ambulance and two large police vans. Lining the kerb were squad cars, their blue lights flashing silently into the darkness.

'Fuck. Oh, fuck.' Steven said softly.

'Something terrible has happened,' Alison muttered, with a helpless sinking of her heart.

On the grass in front of the property, a small group of locals had gathered. A nerve jumped in Steven's cheek. 'Go and mingle with that crowd. See what you can find out.'

Alison threw him an anxious look but then pulling up the collar of her jacket, she jumped out of the car and ran across wet grass and singled out a middle-aged couple. The woman clutched a tiny shivering dog wearing a diamante collar. She nodded at Alison. 'We were just on our way to the Crown,' she said, tucking the dog inside her coat. 'You don't expect this kind of carry on around here, do you, Ken?'

Her husband shook his head. 'Two body bags they've brought out. I mean ... bloody hell.'

'Big or small?' Alison forced herself to ask.

The couple looked at her.

'There's a child living there too,' she clarified.

A young woman in front of them turned round. 'It's Mrs Shaw and the girl. Au pair I think she was. I overheard some journalist phoning the story to his paper.'

'No mention of a baby?'

The woman shook her head. 'Not that I heard.'

Alison ran back to the car.

Steven listened, staring out at the scene. When he got his hands on Ellen he would take her by the throat and strangle her – slowly. And then he'd do it again.

Snatching up his phone he tapped out a message. Alison read it over his shoulder.

'Ellen. *Please.* Show me that Luke is alive.'

The pleading, the begging, was unmanning him. But worse than that, Ellen had dehumanised him because never before had he wanted someone dead so much he was prepared to do the job himself.

He leant back against the headrest, the lights of the emergency vehicles sweeping across the bones of his face. Had he believed in a compassionate God he would have prayed then. Instead, he closed his eyes for a moment and longed for oblivion.

The next moment his eyes were snapping open as the phone on the dashboard vibrated with a response. He grabbed it.

Another photograph.

With shaking fingers he accessed it.

Luke was sitting on a bed gazing blearily into the camera as though he had just been woken. Behind him something had been bundled up to support him, a duvet perhaps. Balanced on a pillow next to him was a digital clock. The time showing was 22.17. They both turned to look at the clock on the dash; 22.19.

'He's alive! *Thank Christ*,' Alison said.

Steven couldn't speak at all. His fingers moved over the keys again. 'Please let's talk. Tell me where you are.' He fired it off.

'*Hey!*' Alison said with sudden urgency. 'Let's have another look at that first picture she sent, see if we can tell where it was taken.'

Steven scrolled quickly back and found it. 'There's nothing to see. It's just some room.'

Alison switched on the interior light. 'Just look,' she snapped. 'As hard as you can.'

He stared intently at the screen again and shook his head.

Alison grabbed the phone from him. 'People look but they don't *see*. Right. It's been taken in what I imagine is a sitting room.'

'I'd worked that out.'

'Luke's sitting on a sofa and there's a cushion in the corner there, see? It's got large yellow flowers on it. Perhaps sunflowers and just to the side there's a lamp.'

Steven stared over Alison's shoulder. 'The lamp base,' he said, 'it's a horse's head.'

Alison glanced up at him. 'Have you seen it before?'

He nodded. 'Briarwood Road,' he said slowly. 'Ellen's sitting room.'

Alison stared at him. 'Does she have access to a computer?

'I don't think so, no. I've never seen her using one. Why?'

'Because if she has, she could easily fake a photograph like this, couldn't she?'

Steven shook his head. 'No. She's taken him there. If you think about it, where else would she go?'

He stared across the road. The crime scene tape was being removed to allow the ambulance to back slowly out of the driveway. Switching on the engine he gunned the accelerator. 'One thing is certain. When I find that sick fucking bitch I will kill her and that really is a promise.'

THE HOUSE LOOMED dark and secret against the night sky.

'Maybe she's gone,' Alison stated flatly. Steven remained silent, staring up at the building. Beyond those blank windows, he sensed a malevolent watchfulness and he made a mental note never to dismiss Alison's intuition again, because now, he too had a strong sense of those 'bad vibes'.

'Or she could be at the back of the house,' Alison speculated quietly. 'Or else she could just be sitting in the dark.'

Steven yanked the keys out of the ignition. 'Stay here.' It was an order.

She grabbed the sleeve of his jacket. 'You're not going in there? Are you freaking mad?'

Shaking off her hand he got out of the car.

The house was cold and all he could hear was the thud of his own heart. He passed his old room, hesitated and then went back and opened the door. It looked exactly as it had when he'd dumped a few of his worldly possessions into black bin liner and left.

Back in the hall he took the stairs, every muscle taut. On the landing he kept

close to the wall, avoiding the fragmented moonlight pooling in from the stained-glass window.

Positioning himself outside the sitting room door he listened hard for any sounds, while trying to quell a terrifying image that rose up in his mind. Ellen, standing just the other side of that door with a meat cleaver in her hand. Suddenly he felt very, very stupid. He had nothing to defend himself with.

He could go into the kitchen and search for a knife, but what if he hit a loose board? The element of surprise was the only weapon he had. Grabbing the handle, he shoved the door back as hard and fast as he could, just in case. Just in case that's where she was hiding. But Ellen wasn't there or anywhere else in the room either.

He went to the small table next to the sofa. There was the horse's head lamp and beside it, on the sofa was the sunflower cushion. He picked it up, and then froze at the sound of soft footsteps behind him. Spinning round he saw a white-faced Alison standing in the doorway.

For fuck sake,' he whispered, 'can't you do as you're told?'

'I gave you five minutes. Your five minutes are up,' she whispered back.

He held up the cushion.

She nodded.

Making an emphatic sign to her to stay put, he went outside.

In the kitchen he pulled a knife from the rack, it looked the sharpest and the longest, and then went back into the hall. No light shone from beneath Ellen's bedroom door but that meant nothing. She could still be in there. Planning her next atrocity.

Gripping the knife he pushed open the door. The squalid little room was empty. It had a sour, stale smell. *Odour de Ellen.*

Heart hammering, he checked under the bed, just in case

she'd somehow managed to squeeze herself beneath it but all he found was a stack of dust covered magazines.

Going back outside he checked the other two bedrooms and the bathroom. Then he took the attic stairs.

When he returned to the sitting room a few minutes later, Alison was gone. *Fuck!* He rushed out again and collided with her in the hallway.

'Come and see this,' she said. She grabbed his sleeve and led him back inside Ellen's bedroom. 'Look at these.' She had laid a couple of magazines on the bed. 'Look what she's done.' They stared at the destroyed faces of the models on the cover. Ellen had slashed them to shreds.

'She hates beautiful women. Now, take a look at these.' Alison went over to the wardrobe and pulled open the door. Blu-tacked to the doors were about thirty photographs, all of Steven.

Alison jabbed her finger at them. '*You* shovelling snow from the path. Coming out of the shower. Arriving home after a days work.'

Steven peered at them. 'Christ.' He fought the urge to rip them to pieces but that would be stupid. They were evidence.

'*Oh – my – God.*' Alison had pulled open the drawer of the bedside cabinet and was now sifting through even more photographs. She pulled one out and handed it to him.

Steven's blood chilled. 'She came into my room. When I was sleeping.'

They went back into the sitting room together. Exhausted, Steven sank into an armchair 'Part of this makes no sense,' he muttered. 'One minute she's fantasizing about me, the next she's trying to destroy me.'

Alison sat down on the floor next to him. 'It's just the other side of the coin, She hates you now as obsessively as she loved you.'

'I suppose that makes some kind of twisted sense. But all

I did was try and be nice to her, and by *nice* I just mean civil and friendly.'

'That's all it took. Heard of erotomania?'

He shook his head.

'That's what we're dealing with.'

'Much prefer insanity. More of a ring to it.'

A small smile lit Alison's features. He glanced at her and saw a slight, feisty girl whose worldly attitude didn't quite match the expression in her unclouded blue eyes. But now wasn't the time to examine the strength of his attraction to her or to speculate on any feelings she might have for him. He *had* noted her choice of the word *we* and that lifted his spirits a fraction.

He got to his feet. 'Look for anything that might tell us where she's gone.'

Alison's search of the living room yielded nothing. She moved into the small kitchen.

'Yuck,' she stared at the mess. Work surfaces were hidden under piles of newspapers, drying clothes and discarded food containers. Plates and bowls towered in the sink. Gingerly she opened the fridge. All it held was half a packet of cheese covered in mold and two bottles of beer. She took the beer and shut the door. Searching for a bottle opener she saw the saucepan in the sink.

'Nothing in Ellen's bedroom.' Steven was behind her.

Alison turned to him and held up the saucepan her eyes radiating meaning. 'Before she left she heated some milk.'

He looked at her blankly.

'Babies of Luke's age drink cow's milk. She warmed milk for him.'

'Go through everything in here,' Steven snapped with sudden intensity.

'What am I looking for in here?'

'An address book, phone numbers. I'll check the other two rooms.'

He raced into Blanche's bedroom first. It was still full of her clutter and smelt musty and unused. He doubted Ellen ever came in here. He glanced at the bed. It was still made up, as though Ellen was anticipating her mother's return. With that creepy thought, he went out and closed the door behind him.

The spare room was furnished with a single bed and a chest of drawers. Under the window stood an old trouser press and a ladder-back chair. Perched on top of the chair was a hatbox. Steven lifted its lid. It seemed to be full of what looked like legal documents.

'Look what I found!' Alison was in the doorway flourishing something small and black. 'Blanche's address book. Lots of names and numbers as you might expect.'

'Great. Take it into the sitting room. I'll go through it while you look through the stuff in this box. You never know, We may find a clue as to where she's gone.'

'Okay. Want a beer?'

He hesitated then shook his head and wiping the dust from the lid of the box with his sleeve, he carried it into the sitting room. Together they sat in Ellen's sitting room and by the light of the horse head lamp they sifted quickly through the minutia of Blanche's life. Steven worked his way through the address book in between frequent glances at the phone. He was torn between desperately wanting it to ring and never, ever wanting to hear that hateful voice again.

'Found anything?' he asked after a few minutes.

'Just lots of old legal papers and insurance policies so far. You?'

'Both Eva and Graham's numbers.'

'Oh,' Alison broke in, 'there's a box hidden under all this

stuff.' She took it out and her brow furrowed into a frown. 'It's locked.'

Steven reached over and took it.

Alison delved into the bigger box again and pulled out three files. 'Look these are property deeds. She sifted through them. 'A seafront flat in Bournemouth. A semi-detached in Ealing. And this one, a cottage with an unpronounceable name in Wales. Do you think Blanche owned them all at one point?'

'Maybe she still does Take everything out of the box. See if there are anymore.'

Alison coughed; she could feel dust settling in the back of her throat. Taking a sip of beer she resumed her search. 'No. No more property, but there's an old photo album here.' She lifted it out and photograph fell from between the pages of the first one. She held it up. 'God, the Adams Family or what? Look, Blanche's hair was dark then. She looks like Morticia with shoulder pads.'

Steven glanced at his mobile before moving closer to her.

'*That* can only be Ellen,' Alison was pointing to a thin, dark-haired child seated in front of her mother. 'Christ, she looked psychotic even then. Look at her glaring into the camera, she can't be more than five or six. Who's the baby I wonder? And who's that old guy? Her grandfather do you think?'

'No, that's probably Stanley, Ellen's father. He must have been quite old when Ellen was born.'

Alison's eyes suddenly fixed upon the door. 'Steve. Do you think she's coming back?'

He looked down at her. 'No, that would make it too easy.'

Alison nodded, she couldn't help but feel relieved.

He took the album from her. 'See what else is in the box.'

The room fell eerily quiet. Despite the reassurance he'd just given, Steven had to resist a strong urge to look over his shoulder. Because, truthfully, how the fuck could he possibly know what was going on in Ellen's demented head? He felt for the knife at his side, glanced again at the screen of his mobile, willing her to make contact, even if it was just another heart-stoppingly cruel message, because even that would be better than this awful, ominous silence. He flicked through the photo album then passed it to Alison. 'Take a look. It gets better and better.'

Alison turned the pages, faster and faster until she reached the end, then looked up at him. 'Mother of God.'

The clock on the mantelpiece chimed midnight. Steven grabbed the wooden box. The lock looked flimsy, the little brass hinges flimsier still. He grabbed the knife and worked the tip of the blade beneath one. It lifted. He worked on the other and within a few moments the box was open.

Inside, lying on top was a thick pile of old premium bonds. He pushed them aside and pulled out what appeared to be deeds and underneath those were two white, A4 sized envelopes. One had the word, 'Certificates' printed neatly on the front and just below that was the name,

'Jimmy', printed in the same firm hand. Opening the first, he slid out the contents and found the Hunt's marriage certificate and three birth certificates. Blanche's, Ellen's, and another, belonging to a male. James Stanley Hunt, born May 25th 1997. He paused. He couldn't remember Ellen ever mentioning having a brother. What had happened to him?

The last certificate put a sorry end to that speculation by announcing James Hunt's death. August $3^{rd,}$ 2000, aged three years.

He opened the other envelope. It contained just one item, an old newspaper cutting. Carefully he unfolded it. Halfway down the page of the Chiswick and Acton Times, dated October 20th 2000, was the headline: 'Tragic Drowning of Local Tot'

'An inquest at West London Coroner's Court heard today that the death of James Hunt, three years of age, was a case of misadventure. James was found by his mother, lying face down in a paddling pool at their home in Chiswick earlier this month. He had been in the company of his elder sister, when the tragedy occurred. Attempts were made to revive the little boy but he was pronounced dead on his arrival at Hammersmith Hospital.'

'Look at these,' he passed the certificates and cutting to Alison. Ellen had a brother.' Going back to the photo album he found the family group again. He gazed uneasily at the image of Ellen, cradling her baby brother while staring into the camera with unnatural intensity, and he really didn't want to go where his thoughts were taking him now.

Rain pattered softly on the window pane and downstairs a door opened.

Alison's head shot up while he sat rigid in his seat, hair prickling along his forearms. Then palming the knife he got to his feet, and with a fiercely whispered instruction to Alison stay exactly where she was, he moved silently onto the landing.

The downstairs toilet flushed. *Miss King.*

He hadn't given her a thought since he'd arrived back. When the old lady came out of the bathroom he was waiting for her.

'Steven!' she gasped. 'For goodness sake, you startled me!'

'It's late I know, but I need to speak to you.'

'But I'm about to go to bed. We can talk in the morning, surely?'

Steven took her firmly by the elbow, led her back to her room and sat her in the armchair.

She looked up at him, alarmed. 'Whatever is it, Steven?'

'You've lived here a long time and you must know quite a lot about what's gone on under this roof.'

A wary look came into her eyes. 'What kind of things are you – '

'Ellen told me that Blanche had owned other properties. Lying he decided was better than admitting he'd spent the last hour ransacking the place and going through Blanche's private papers. 'Do you know if she had kept them?'

'Blanche had all kinds of investments I believe, but why ask me when you can so easily ask Ellen?'

'Ellen isn't here. She's gone and I need to find her.'

'What do you mean. Gone?'

'Ellen's snatched Luke, my little boy and run off somewhere, Miss King. That's why I'm asking you and if I don't find her soon, she'll kill him.'

The old lady stared up at him. 'Steven have you gone quite mad?'

'Not yet, but I expect to be fully certifiable by the time she's finished.'

'For heaven's sake, Steven! Why on earth would she want do such a thing?'

'To hurt me. In the only way she can.'

'You don't really believe she's capable...'

'I need to show you something.'

'Steven!' Miss King's exasperated voice followed him as he left the room and took the stairs at a run.

He returned with the photo album and dropped it onto her lap. 'Take a look, Miss King. What would make a mother go through an album and cut her daughter out of every single photo, except this one?' He showed the one that had fallen from the first album, 'the one where Ellen is holding her little brother, James.'

Miss King stared at the photograph. 'Jimmy,' she said at last. 'He was always Jimmy. How have you got hold of that? *Never mind,* I don't want to know.'

'She killed him, didn't she?'

'Steven! *No one was there*. No one *saw* what happened.'

'Blanche knew. Look at the album for Christ sake,' he said with disgust. 'You're still doing it, aren't you? Covering up for her. You. Blanche. Blanche's friends, all in denial. Protecting a monster.'

The old lady plucked at the tie of her dressing gown. 'This is most unpleasant. I refuse to listen to any more.'

'Would Eva know about these properties?'

'It's possible. Ask her. And now if you don't mind, I'm going to have a brandy and go to bed.'

Steven grabbed the album and had reached the door when Miss King said, 'Listen, to me Steven. Just before it happened, Ellen had suffered a very bad trauma, no doubt she was in a disturbed state of mind. In those days things like that were just swept under the carpet. Today, she would have received all kinds of counselling.'

Steven swung around. 'What trauma?'

'Her father,' she muttered. 'She found him in such awful circumstances.'

'Found him? As in dead?'

'Yes.'

'Had she killed him too?'

'Now you're being ridiculous.'

'*Don't you get it?*' Steven demanded angrily. 'Ellen has been doing it for years. Killing people.' He yanked open the door.

'Steven.'

He turned again.

'I really think you've got it wrong. Ellen wouldn't take your little boy – she hates children.'

42

Eva answered her phone on the third ring. Her voice guarded at this the late hour.

Steven paced the sitting room floor as he talked and he had neither the time nor the inclination for pleasantries. 'Ellen has gone missing. Do you have any idea where she might be?'

'Missing? Why on earth would she be missing?

'I can't go into it all now I just need to find her.'

'Well, I'm the last person to know what's going on. Since the funeral she hasn't kept in touch at all. In fact the last time we spoke she implied that you two were very close so I would assume you would know her whereabouts better than I.'

'Disregard all that.'

'Really?' Look, Steven - '

'I'm worried about her state of mind. If she wanted to hide herself away for a while, do you have any idea where she would go?'

'No. Not a clue.'

'You have to think, Eva. She told me once that Blanche owned some properties.'

'Properties?'

'Do you know anything about them? Do you know if she sold them off?'

'No...I'm sorry, Steven, I really can't ...'

'Ellen has my son, Eva. He's eleven months old.'

'What? '

'That's why I need to find her. Take down my number. Just in case you remember anything.'

'Steven, I...'

'*Please,* Eva. Take it down.'

There was a silence followed by a reluctant, 'Yes, alright... I just need to find a pen.'

Steven swore silently, raking through his hair until it stood up in wild tufts while Eva searched. When he finished the call he threw his phone on the arm of the sofa and fighting off a suffocating feeling of hopelessness, he resumed the search through Blanche's papers. Engrossed in their own tasks, both he and Alison jumped when the mobile at his elbow suddenly went off.

Grabbing it, Steven clamped it to his ear. '*Ellen?*'

'No, no. This is Graham.'

'Eva's explained things to you?'

'Yes, she's rather alarmed.'

'Yeah, I ...'

'Listen, sorry to interrupt but this might help you. You mentioned properties to Eva? Blanche did own several rental properties, which now of course belong to Ellen.'

'So she didn't sell them?'

'No. Blanche believed in holding onto her assets. I know more about Blanche's business affairs than Eva. She used to confide in me.'

'Are any of these properties empty?'

'I'm pretty sure they were all tenanted up until Blanche's demise, with the exception of a place she owned in Wales. It used to be their holiday home once upon a time but after Stan died Blanche no longer went there and she rented it out to holiday makers instead, but being so far away made it difficult for her to maintain. In the end she lost interest in it and it's been empty for some time.'

Steven's pulse rate quickened. 'Do you think Ellen might go there?'

'Well, it's possible. I seem to remember she enjoyed it there as a child. Being near the sea and all that, and it is quite remote a remote spot apparently, so the perfect place to hole up for a bit if that's her intention. I can't see her booking into a hotel. I don't think she'd know how.'

'Okay. Thanks.'

'Anyway, I can't pretend to understand what's going on Steven and it's none of my business but you may as well know we intend cutting ties with Ellen from now on. She lied to Joan, you know. Told her Blanche had left her nothing in her will. But when Eva went through Joan's unopened mail yesterday she found a solicitor's letter stating the opposite. I can't comprehend that level of unkindness. Eva and I just wish you luck in your endeavour to find her.'

Steven thanked him, feeling more gratitude than he had time to express but his smile was bitter when he ended the call. Eventually Graham would learn exactly what 'levels of unkindness' Ellen was really capable of.

Alison was staring impatiently at him. 'He knows where she's gone?'

'Probably that place in Wales. If she did, she went by train.'

'Or cab?'

Steven shook his head. 'A journey that long? Too risky. The driver's bound to start a conversation, ask questions. A train journey's more anonymous.' He got to his feet. 'Get all this stuff together,' he indicated Blanche's boxes and papers and then a thought came to him. It was possible she had booked a ticket using her mobile but it was just as likely she had used the landline. Crossing the room he grabbed the phone out of its cradle and dialled 1471. A robotic female voice informed him that a 0845 number had been called at 7.45 pm. He jotted down the rest of the number and rang it. An answering service announced that he had rung First Great Western and apologised that their booking office was now closed.

Ellen, I'm coming to get you.

Alison came back from the kitchen clutching a couple of bin liners. 'What have I missed?'

'She's in Wales. Graham was right!' he said triumphantly. The last number called was Great Western.' He rammed the phone back in its stand.

Alison regarded him warily. '*Okay.* So what do we do now?'

'*I'm* going after her. What *you're* going to do is go home with all the evidence we've collected up.' He strode off to the kitchen. Alison went after him.

'No, Steve! What you're going to do *now* is ring the police.'

He gave an emphatic shake of his head. 'Can't risk it! They've got no one else to nail for Caroline's murder and now there's Luke's grandmother and Georgia in the mix. They'll make a case I killed them all. I'll be questioned for hours and Christ knows what she'll be doing to Luke in the meantime. Ellen wants my undivided attention and she's fucking got it. The only way to keep Luke alive is to play along. Until I can get to her.'

Alison watched him fill two empty Evian bottles with tap water and throw them into a bag. 'And you're going to be able to find her, just like that?'

'Those deeds show the full address. Of course I'm going to find her.' Dumping the bag on the landing he went into

Ellen's bedroom to grab all the photographs she had taken of him. There was no way he was entrusting any of this stuff to the police. He'd read valuable evidence often went 'missing' when forensics started bagging things up.

Alison was behind him again, her face creased with anxiety. 'Right. Okay,' she said, speaking as rationally as she could manage. 'So you find where she's hiding out. You know for *certain* she's there and *that's* when you call the police, right?

'Yes.'

'Promise.'

'I promise.'

Alison looked into his eyes then, her own were very grave. 'You'd better stick to that promise, Steve, because if this goes wrong, *you'll* be the one living with the consequences. If you're still alive that is.'

LEAVING BRIARWOOD ROAD, Steven insisted this was as far as Alison went. He'd extracted a promise from her that she would do nothing, call no one, until he rang her and gave her the go ahead but now she was refusing to co-operate. 'I'm coming,' she'd said, her small chin jutting in defiance, 'or the deal's off.'

They stood in the icy drizzle, arguing.

'If you leave me here I'll go straight to the cops. I mean it. There has to be someone watching your back.'

'That's blackmail,' he growled, hustling her into the car and throwing the bin liners filled with evidence and the water bottles into the boot.

43

On the westbound M4, Steven settled down to a steady speed of seventy, despite the anxiety gnawing at his insides.

By now Georgia would have been found and he was pretty sure the police would be searching for him. Every second counted. He sat hunched over the wheel, eyes flicking constantly to the rear view mirror, anticipating the appearance of a convoy of flashing blue lights.

Alison sat alongside him, forcing herself not to look at the clock on the dashboard, fretting when Ellen would text again.

Unconsciously, Steven's hand kept creeping to the top pocket of his shirt. The place he'd always kept his cigarettes, until the day he'd given up. He put his hand back on the wheel.

Alison turned towards him then her face illuminated by oncoming headlights. 'Hey. Little brother drowns. Blanche drowns. Bit of a coincidence?'

Steven nodded. 'Something else. I found Miss King's contract in one of the

boxes. She's been paying a fraction of the rent she should have be paying for years.' He threw her a look.

Alison didn't like what he was implying. 'She's been there such a long time. Maybe Blanche was just being kind?'

'You think that's likely, knowing Blanche? No. The old girl knew too much.'

Alison sighed. 'Fuck. I really liked Miss King.'

'Her thinking's totally screwed. The one she feels sorry for in all this is Ellen.'

'She must be as crazy as Blanche implied!' Alison allowed herself a glance at the dashboard clock. 'Why is Ellen denying herself the pleasure of torturing you with another text?' she demanded.

Steven shook his head.

Alison suddenly clicked her fingers. 'Mobile phones can be traced. The police could find her that way.'

'She probably bought a pre-paid. Much harder to trace and when I tried calling her back the second time, her phone was switched off, which makes it impossible to locate.'

'Christ, how does she know this stuff?'

Steven shook his head and fixed his eyes on the road. Alison turned her face to the window and her ghostly reflection stared back. She was far too wired to sleep and for a long time they drove in silence.

44

DAWN BROKE EARLIER over the western tip of Pembrokeshire. Ellen stood at the kitchen window of Ty Haven and stared across the isolated stretch of water at a peaceful scene. From the water's edge came the piping call of an oyster catcher and on the other side of the estuary, a herd of dairy cows grazed peacefully, dark sturdy shapes moving through a blanket of mist.

Apart from the derelict boathouse there were no other buildings in sight. Once off the A477, it had taken two miles of country lanes and one mile of unmade track before the cottage was reached. The taxi driver from Carmarthen station had whined all the way, going on about his suspension.

She'd sat in the back of the cab, her hair hidden under her woollen hat, while the baby sat mercifully silent on her lap, dried tear tracks on his cheeks. Occasionally, she had bounced him up and down and loudly called him 'Lucy', for the driver's benefit. The outfit he wore – a denim jacket over a little pink dress with and purple tights she'd managed to grab in Monsoon on Chiswick High Street just before it closed, was meant to be further confirmation that this was a female child. It wouldn't be long before one of those media alert things was underway for a missing Luke Shaw.

The sleeping suit he'd been wearing when she'd snatched him, along with the tiny anorak she'd found hanging in the hall she had dumped in a sanitary towel bin in the 'Baby Changing Room' on Reading concourse. She'd had to hold her breath, as sweating like a pig in that confined space, she'd managed to change his stinking nappy and clean him up a bit, while he thrashed and bawled.

Turning from the window she listened. Upstairs, all was quiet. Silence was something she had come to cherish. After they left Doughty House he had screamed his head off for hours and she had fought the urge to wheel the buggy into a deserted side street, put her hands around his tiny neck and snap it.

But Jimmy was sleeping now and ... She stopped half way across the kitchen – *no*, this baby *isn't* Jimmy. Jimmy's hair was blond and he had big red cheeks and dimples in his squidgy little hands and when she held them too tightly, fat tears rolled down his face and... Ellen stopped. *Best not to think of these things now.*

She went over to the stove, gas hissed as she stood staring at a damp patch on the wall. When she finally came back to herself she lit the burner. There was a loud 'pooff' and a blue flame leapt. Setting the kettle over the flame she turned and saw the carrier bags on the kitchen table. She couldn't remember what was in them. Going over to them now, she tipped out their contents. Basic groceries plus two packets of Huggy Bear sweets, chocolate, disposable nappies, ten jars of baby food and a book on baby care that she seemed to remember purchasing in the W.H. Smith's on the station. It was important that it didn't die just yet.

She had also bought a couple of magazines at the same time and flicked through them on the train as a means of diverting herself from the squalling thing in the buggy. The indulgent expressions of her fellow passengers had become less indulgent by the time they reached Bristol.

'I expect she's teething. She needs some gel for her gums,' one busybody remarked.

Ellen tried jigging him on her lap. It hadn't helped. His eyes had bulged in terror at the sight of her and so she strapped him back into his buggy and jiggled that instead. Eventually he'd fallen asleep, probably through exhaustion.

Exhaustion was making him sleep now she supposed, along with the small piece of temazepam she'd added to his bottle.

IT WAS light by the time they crossed the Severn Bridge. Alison stretched stiff limbs. 'Where are we?'

'About fifty miles from Cardiff.'

Traffic was light and they were making good time but once they'd by-passed Cardiff, Steven allowed the speedometer to creep to ninety.

'You must sleep. You can't just keep going,' Alison said, wondering for how much longer she could keep her own eyes open without a triple espresso. She rubbed her window. It was raining now and a thin mist had fallen.

By the time they passed the Cardiff turn off Alison was asleep. A call came through on Steven's mobile. Thankfully he'd glanced at the display screen before taking it and seen that the number was withheld. The only call he'd taken recently from a withheld number was a call from PC Walker. So they were looking for him already. A development he was going to keep from Alison

Despite being so tightly wound a profound weariness threatened to overtake him and his eyes, locked upon the monotonous stretch of road ahead, burned in their sockets.

He thought of the Evian bottles on the back seat. So far he had resisted the urge to drink, to avoid the necessity of stopping along the way. Dehydrated, with his whole body crying out for rest, he hunched over the wheel, fighting to stay awake. Alison stirred beside him, sat up. 'How much further?'

'Another hundred miles roughly.'

She lifted the lid of the CD compartment between the front seats and rifled through it.

'John Lee Hooker. Moby. Vaughan Williams. Hmm. What am I supposed to make of this eclectic little mix?'

Steven tried a smile but it was a half-hearted affair.

Alison sighed dramatically. 'Now all my preconceived ideas about you are out the window.'

'Such as?' He played along, recognising her strategy to keep him awake.

'Ah, that you were basically a simple soul, pumping iron in the gym, getting smashed in the pub, but now there's your choice of music muddying the waters. Genuine deep-down dirty blues and the bloody Lark Ascending. Must be some hidden depths lurking somewhere.'

'Hidden shallows, more like. I'm a blues man through and through. The Vaughan Williams was a gift.'

'Who from?'

'You don't need to know that.'

'I do. That's the difference between men and women. Women need to know everything, it's how we're wired. *Men* actually prefer not to know. They like being bewildered. It gives them the excuse to go blundering about getting everything wrong, from serious stuff like wars to the kind of flowers their wives prefers.'

He didn't have the energy to argue.

'You still haven't told me who bought you the CD. Is working for MI6 your sideline?'

'Caroline.'

'Ah.' Alison went quiet for a moment. 'Tell me about your childhood – about your parents.'

Steven doubted Alison was really interested but anything was better than falling asleep at the wheel and annihilating them both.

He pushed back into his seat. 'Right. It won't take long. Never knew my old man. He legged-it when my mother got pregnant. She did the best she could with no money and a drink problem. Somehow, and I don't know how, she managed it. I never went hungry. She died five years ago. Cirrhosis of the liver.'

Alison stared ahead. 'Tough and it explains a lot.'

'Yeah? What exactly?'

She glanced at him. 'Why Luke is so important to you. You have no one else.'

His eyes remained fixed on the road.

'I'm sorry I got you so wrong ... you know, in the beginning. You're one of the good guys, Steve Finn.'

He glanced at her then, but now *her* eyes were glued to the road and it was too dark for him to see the faint blush on her cheeks.

THE M4 finally ended near Carmarthen and they were now on the A477.

'I'm really sorry, but I'm desperate for a pee and something to eat.' Alison announced.

'Okay. I'll turn off when I can.'

Ten minutes later Alison pointed to a sign. 'A place called Amroth is coming up. The turning's just ahead. See?'

Steven nodded and took a sharp left. Alison grabbed the door handle.

They continued down a narrow country road.

'Do you think Amroth is a proper town?'

'Doubt it. Some small resort probably.'

'I don't care what it is as long as I can get a bacon sandwich and a hot cup of coffee. *You* need a sleep. Even if it's just half an hour.'

Amroth consisted of just one coastal through road. Cottages and a few shops stocked with seasonal paraphernalia fronted one side of the road and on the other side was the Bristol Channel.

Steven pulled into a parking space in front of a low, rough wall. Beyond it, a heaving expanse of grey water pounded the shore beneath a lightening sky.

'Look, thank the Lord, there's a public loo,' Alison announced. Struggling against a fierce wind, she pushed open her door, yanked up her hood and made a dash for it.

Steven slid back his seat and closed his eyes. Returning, Alison peered in the car window and made the decision to allow him to sleep on. Jumping down from the wall onto the pebbles, she ran head bent into the wind. Above her, seagulls wheeled beneath low scudding clouds, swollen with unspent rain. She stood for a while watching the progress of a liner far out on the horizon, grains of sand stinging her cheeks. When her stomach gave a ferocious growl she realised that if she didn't eat something soon she would faint.

She glanced across the road. Interspersed between the pastel coloured cottages was a gift shop, a café and a fish and chip take-away. She checked her watch, only half past seven. It would be another hour at least before anything opened - *if* they opened at all during winter months. But then to her joy she saw the flicker of a fluorescent strip inside the café.

Ten minutes later she emerged with several slices of hot buttered toast wrapped in paper napkins, (all the proprietor could manage at that hour while he waited for a delivery) and two steaming coffees in Styrofoam cups. She had taken just a few steps towards the car before she realised the engine was gunning and the passenger door was wide open.

'Get in!' Steven yelled.

Alison ran towards the car, scalding coffee splashing her hands. She was hardly in her seat before Steven reversed at frightening speed and tore off in the direction they had come.

'What's happened?'

Steven's face was white, his jaw tightly clenched. Finally, he spoke and his voice cracked. 'She rang me.'

'What did she say?'

'She said ...' Steven shook his head, couldn't finish.

Alison shoved the toast into the glove compartment and wedged the coffee between her feet, her appetite gone.

'She said ...' he began again, 'that she hadn't yet made up her mind ... exactly how she was going to kill him.'

Alison felt colour drain from her face. She couldn't think of a single comforting thing to say and so she stared out of the window. They were now on a stretch of dual carriageway, flanked by of banks of raw, red earth.

On the dash board Steven's mobile vibrated. They stared at each other, mutual dread in their eyes. Trapped in fast moving traffic, Steven nodded to her. 'Answer it, but don't speak.'

Alison held the phone to her ear.

'Is it her?' Steven rasped.

Alison shushed him with her hand, listening intently. 'It's a baby. I can hear a baby in the background. Oh, Steve, he's crying.'

Steven grabbed the phone from her. 'Don't you fucking hurt him!' he yelled. 'Ellen? Do you hear me? Fuck!' he flung the phone down. 'She's gone. What the hell is she doing to him!'

'Probably nothing,' Alison gabbled, trying to sound

convincing. 'Baby's cry all the time. It's what they do. Particularly if they've just woken up.'

She grabbed the phone. 'Hey, this is a different number. She's using some other phone now.'

'Still a mobile?'

'Yeah.'

'Cunning evil bitch. How come she knows all this stuff. How come she knows she can't be traced this way?' Steven wiped the sweat from his forehead with the back of his hand. They had come up hard behind a huge, foreign plated HGV. Indicating, Steven pulled into the middle lane and overtook. He was just pulling back into the left lane when Alison turned around, craning her neck.

'We just missed a sign for Pembroke. That's where we're heading isn't it?

Steven cursed. 'There's another turn-off ahead, I'll take that one.'

They sped into the side road in fourth gear. Alison gripped the bottom of her seat. They were now in what was little more than a lane.

'This doesn't look too promising,' Steven muttered

Alison looked out across the bleak fields they were dissecting.

'It's too narrow to turn. I'll have to keep going.' The next bend Steven took too fast. Cursing he jammed on his brakes in a desperate attempt to avoid what was in his path. Tyres screeched and the car went into a skid. Sheep scattered, leaping up banks, bleating hysterically. Steven struggled to gain control but the wheel jerked from his grip, wrenching his shoulder. Gathering momentum the car careered off the road and ploughed into a ditch.

. . .

In the silent aftermath Alison gingerly checked herself for broken bones whilst thanking God that they were still alive. Steven was leaning back in his seat, a handkerchief soaking up blood gushing from his nose. Retrieving every tissue she possessed from her bag, Alison passed them to him and then fished out the paper napkins from the glove compartment and handed him those too, ignoring the blood trickling down her own cheek.

'Your eye's taken a bashing,' she said.

Steven grunted and then checked her out with his good one. 'Your face is cut.'

Pulling down the vanity mirror, Alison lifted her fringe and traced the source of the blood to a split eyebrow. 'Ouch.'

'Anything else hurt?' Steven eased off his seat belt, pain flared in his chest and shoulder.

'Just my elbow. How come your airbag didn't inflate?'

Steven shook his head and nodded at her cut. 'You'll have a scar.'

Alison sighed. 'Eyebrow scars were so cool a while back. Trust me to be too late.'

Steven lifted his shirt and looked down. Across his chest bright purple welts were forming where he had smashed into the steering wheel. Carefully he prodded his ribs just under his heart and sparks of pain flared. Pulling down his shirt he cursed the God he didn't believe in and tried to straighten his left leg. Excruciating pain exploded in his knee.

Once the nosebleed abated he opened his door and hobbled round to the front of the car – except that the Merc didn't have one anymore. It had crumpled on impact. Alison's worried face peered at him through the cracked windscreen. He shook his head.

Alison tried to open her door but it was wedged tight against the bank. She scrambled across the driver's seat to climb out and surveyed the wreckage.

'Oh crap. What the hell do we do now?'

Steven treated it as a rhetorical question. He glanced up and down the lane. There was nothing. No cars approaching. No houses anywhere. Just a few remaining sheep, which having squeezed back through the hedge, were now rubber-necking through the bars of a gate, like onlookers at a motorway pile up.

Alison climbed back inside the car and rummaged in the glove compartment. She returned with cold toast. 'Eat,' she commanded.

Steven forced himself to take a bite and then devoured two slices in seconds.

Alison attacked hers too and then looked down sadly at her feet. 'The coffee's ruined my new boots.'

'There's water in the back of the car. We can spare some to wash up a bit.'

Alison looked at his swollen blood-streaked face. He attempted a smile, but it was too lop-sided and strange to be reassuring. In that moment something inside her moved and then she was in his arms. They held each other for a comforting while, until the sound of an approaching vehicle pulled them apart.

A black Lexus 4 x 4 rounded the bend and sped towards them. It slowed when Steven stepped out into the road.

Lowering his window a young black guy stuck his corn-rowed head out and surveyed the scene. 'Jesus, bad luck, mate. You both okay?'

'Yeah. Thanks for stopping.'

The guy jumped out of his jeep. 'Car don't look too clever does it? Bloody write off.'

They stared at the crumpled Merc. The guy looked around. 'No one else involved?'

Steven shook his head. 'Just some sheep.'

'Fucking dumb animals. You look pretty smashed up too. You'd better get to a hospital. Get checked over, just in case.'

Steven nodded. 'Yeah. First on my list.' He went to the boot. When he returned he was clutching something wrapped in a white cloth, a long wooden handle protruded. The guy stared at it and then looked at Steven, dismay in his eyes.

'Look,' Steven said quietly, 'I'm sorry to be doing this but we're dealing with a life or death situation. Give me your keys.'

Corn-row's eyes shifted back to the knife. 'Man, I can give you a lift somewhere, y'know, just drop you off.'

Steven withdrew the knife from the cloth.

'Look, I got a gig tonight, man! I gotta get there. It's my living.'

Steven moved towards him. 'I don't think you're listening. ... what's your name?'.

'D...Dwain.'

Steven's left eye was almost swollen shut now but his one good eye glittered with evil intent. The blood down the front of his shirt added to the overall effect.

Dwain's teeth chattered.

'It's just a loan, Dwain. You'll get it back in one piece, I promise.' Steven took another menacing step towards him.'

'Okay, okay, man.' Dwain threw the key fob at his feet.

'And your phone.'

'Aw...man!'

Steven held out his hand. Dwain slipped it out of his shirt pocket and threw it at Steven's feet.

'Get the stuff out of the boot,' Steven instructed Alison. She threw him an incredulous look but obeyed, moving quickly, transferring everything to the back seat of the Lexus.

Steven was already revving the engine. As they sped off, Alison turned and half raised her hand to give Dwain a consoling wave. Standing on the narrow strip of grass verge he had the stricken expression of someone about to cry.

'Now we're fecking car-jackers!' she muttered, yanking at her seat belt.

Steven grunted.

'He'll go straight to the police.'

'He's not going anywhere at the moment.'

He nodded at the recess in the dashboard where the 'Sat Nav screen should be. 'For fuck sake,' he growled, 'we're not having any luck. Look out for signs. Llanmathrey's where we're heading.'

Lowering his window he threw Dwain's phone into a hedgerow. Flooring it, he made up for lost time.

TWENTY-FIVE MINUTES later they were on the outskirts of a small village. Characterless bungalows lined both sides of the road.

Steven scanned them. 'This doesn't look too hopeful,'

'Stop!' Alison instructed. 'There's a corner shop. Good chance they'll know where the cottage is. Steven braked, reversed and pulled onto a piece of rough ground. Grabbing the old faded estate agent details he'd found filed with the deeds he got out of the car and limped to the shop's forecourt, coming to a dead halt at the door where he suddenly flung his arms into the air in exasperation.

'What's wrong?' Alison asked as he climbed back into the Lexus.

'It's closed.'

'Hang on, don't pull away yet. Show the picture to this guy.'

A middle-aged man with a sprightly walk was heading towards them accompanied by a spaniel.

'He doesn't look like a local,' Steven muttered.

'Why?'

'He's too tall.'

Alison gave him a look. 'Not all Welsh men are short.'

As the man drew level Alison lowered the window. 'I wonder if you can help,' she called. The man stopped and smiled politely. She held up the leaflet. 'Do you happen to know where this property is? It's in this village somewhere.'

The man barely glanced at the picture. 'I'm sorry,' he said in a clipped, English accent. 'I'm not terribly familiar with the place. I'm just visiting a relative I'm afraid.'

Alison thanked him anyway and raised her window. 'Okay. Now what?'

Steven pointed towards a row of flat-fronted terraces that tilted up a steep hill.

'That must be the old part of the village. I'm going to knock on a few doors.' He climbed out of the Lexus and made off up the road.

A young woman answered the door of the first property. Alison watched them exchange words on the doorstep, her fingers drumming on the dashboard. The woman shook her head when Steven showed her the picture of the cottage. She looked over her shoulder and seemed to be calling to someone inside. An older woman, probably her mother joined them.

Alison watched the silent tableau play out. The older woman then came outside onto the street and pointed towards the development of new-builds.

Steven limped back in her direction and then veered off towards one of the bungalows on the left. The property was screened behind a high conifer hedge and she lost sight of him once he'd entered the gate.

Six minutes later, (she timed him on the inset clock) Steven was back.

'The old lady living there recognised it! She's lived in the village all her life. We follow this road up the hill and keep going until we cross a cattle grid and then take a sharp right into a lane. I think I scared her shitless to start with.' He took a quick look in the mirror. 'Yeah. I can see why.'

Starting the engine he sped off, spraying loose stones in their wake. They climbed the hill, passing the flat-fronted little houses.

'It's like a ghost town, Alison muttered, unable to detect a flicker of life in any of them.

'Slow down - the cattle grid!' she yelled a few minutes later.

'I see it.' Steven slowed to a sensible speed and they bumped across.

A tense silence settled between them. Steven was sweating again, his shirt sticking to his back, but inside he was icily calm. Just as he approached the right turn, he slowed. Set back behind a yew hedge on their left was a low, plain building, a chapel with the date '1848' carved into the lintel. Pulling up onto a grass verge he manoeuvred the Lexus under the drooping branches of some ancient looking trees. He switched off the engine.

Alison looked at him. 'Now what?'

What he had to do next, he had to do alone and convincing Alison of this was going to be his first major hurdle. 'Listen,' he said. 'According to the old girl, that unmade track there leads to the cottage. I'm going the rest of the way on foot, because if Ellen is there, I can't risk her hearing a car approach. You stay here. Lock the doors when I go and keep yourself warm. There's a duvet in one of bags on the back seat.

As he'd anticipated, Alison was outraged. 'Why can't I come? I can be quiet.'

Steven grabbed her chin and tilted her head so she was

forced to look directly into his eyes. 'I want you to promise me you'll do as I ask.'

She pulled away. 'But what if -'

'I'm just going to do a recce, okay? And then I'll be back.'

'How do I know that? How do I know you're not going to do something stupid, like just rush in there and –'

'I promise I'm not going to do anything crazy, but I need you to stay here where it's safe for the moment, okay?'

Her voice rose a pitch. 'No!'

'Alison, you know how I felt in the beginning about you coming? I realise now I probably can't do this without you. You are the only one who knows that Ellen has got Luke and if something *did* happen to me, you'll be the only one in the world who can help him.'

Alison raised fearful eyes.

'Do you understand that?'

'*Yes*. I'm not a feckin idiot.'

'Is your phone on?'

Alison rooted around in her bag and pulled it out. 'It's on. Promise me you'll ring me – once you get to the cottage?'

'I promise, but I really do need to trust you this time. You have to keep yourself safe, for Luke's sake.'

She lifted a hand, touched his bruised cheek and studied the face that was becoming as familiar as her own, and despite the battering it had taken and all the blood, it was still a face she could *almost* understand someone killing for. There was a flash of silver in the slate-grey eyes. It could have been arousal but it was more likely a warning. She dropped her hand and let him go.

45

He checked his watch and limped off down the narrow lane with a bottle of water and the knife inside his jacket. His progress was slow and if the woman from the village was right he estimated in his present condition, it would take him at least half an hour to reach the remote cottage. As he walked he concentrated on keeping as much weight off his damaged knee as possible and prayed that Alison would not betray her promise.

Twenty minutes later the lane narrowed further to a single track. He stopped and rested his knee for a moment. In the hedge, tiny birds darted issuing shrill warnings and above his head a pair of buzzards wheeled against a monochrome sky. At least the rain had stopped just before the crash. Something he was grateful for. He took a long swig of water. The wind ruffled his hair and brought with it the smell of the sea. He washed his face with what water remained in the bottle. His head hurt and every muscle in his body was crying out for rest - but he and Ellen had a date. A *real* one this time. Not one dreamt up by her diseased brain in that little room that reeked of delusion and loneliness.

Throwing the bottle over the hedge he carried on, following the deeply rutted track until he reached a clearing. On his left was a large paddock. Two rain-sheeted thoroughbreds, a grey and a chestnut, gave him a cursory glance. To his right, a thickly planted pine wood climbed a steep slope. Directly before him a weed choked driveway dropped down towards a dark stretch of water. The cottage was in a dip, the old woman had said, invisible from the track.

He jogged towards the woods as fast as his shrieking knee would allow. Ducking between the sweet-smelling branches he kept going until he'd reached the furthest edge of the trees, breaking cover only when he heard the slap and suck of tidal water.

To his right was the estuary and set back from the water's edge was a dilapidated boathouse. A concrete ramp sloped from the ruin into the water and alongside it was a wooden jetty. But he was only taking in this information on a subliminal level. For there, crouching low, directly in front of him was the stone cottage pictured on the leaflet. And when he saw what was parked inside the porch, his heart gave a sudden leap. It was a child's buggy.

She was here – and so was Luke.

He ducked back under the trees and took out his phone. He might be a liar these days but he still liked to keep his promises.

Alison answered immediately.

'I've found it.'

'*Is she there?*'

'Yeah.'

'How do you know?'

Steven sucked in some air. His heart was pounding. 'There's smoke coming out of the chimney and a faint light in one of the ground floor rooms, *and* there's a buggy in the porch.'

'Oh, God. Steve ... we ring the police now, don't we?'

'I've already done that.'

'You have?'

'They're on their way.'

'Thank God.'

'Alison?'

'I'm here,' her voice sounded small.

'Stay exactly where you are. When the police come they will need to speak to you, okay?'

'Okay. So you're just watching the house until the police come and that's all?

'That's all.'

He switched off his phone and stuck it in his back pocket. Absolutely everything depended on him not screwing up now. The irony that at a time when he faced the biggest battle of his life his body was completely fucked, was not lost on him. The searing pain in his chest was ominous and his busted knee would be a serious handicap. Yet he swore, as God (the one he didn't believe in) was his witness, he would not fail his son.

Pulling out the knife he broke from cover, and low to the ground ran towards the cottage. Avoiding the gravel path he kept close to the rough walls of the cottage where the grass was long and wet. A sudden gust of wind flung sand at the house. It stung his eyes and stuck to his lips. Keeping his head below window level he crawled trying to keep most of his weight on his good knee. Inching forward he found the back door. Pressing his ear against it he listened. No sound at all. An image of a small body wrapped in a bloody sheet rose up in his mind. He closed his eyes, blotted it out and it was immediately replaced by another, albeit irrational fear.

What if this stealthy approach was pointless because she already knew he was here? What if she was on the other side of that wall right now, tuning into the electrical impulses of his pounding heart?

At this stage he was quite prepared to believe Ellen capable of anything.

Sweat dripping from his face reached up and tried the door handle. It was locked. Inching forward he passed beneath another window and it was then that he heard a sound from inside. He froze, heart thudding as he waited. W*aited for the bitch to come rushing around the side of the house with an axe in her hand and insanity in her eyes.*

For long agonising moments he stayed in his crouched position, listening to the dry rasp of breath in his throat. Somewhere in the dark woods something wild shrieked and he was mindful once more that if he blew what he was about to do now both he and Luke were dead. His fingers tightened around the knife.

He glanced up, saw that light was already draining from the sky. It would be dark in twenty minutes. Urged on, he half-crawled and half dragged himself around to the other side of the cottage, where a small extension jutted. A ground floor bathroom, judging from the window. In other circumstances and some other life he might have laughed at the incongruity of that frosted glass. Who the hell would see you taking a leak here, other than an itinerant sheep or the occasional buzzard?

With his free hand he felt around in the grass. His fingers closed on a slate tile. The window was wide rather than deep and he would need to remove his bulky jacket in order to squeeze through it. He unzipped it with numb, clumsy fingers.

The glass was thin and old and broke easily with very little noise. Careful to remove all the loose glass first, he reached inside, grasped the curved metal handle and pushed the window inwards. The old metal frame scraped across the sill, dislodging a piece of glass he'd missed. He cursed silently as it fell and smashed on the bathroom floor. He ducked down, his mind gibbering, *she'll hear, she'll hear*.

Wind from the estuary sliced through his shirt, icing the sweat on his skin. He tried to focus on its steady keen whine and the rhythmic breaking of the waves.

No. The sound of breaking glass had not brought Ellen running. Perhaps she was asleep. Please God, (*the one he still didn't believe in*) let her be asleep. Getting to his feet he stuck the knife between his teeth and hoisted himself up onto the window ledge. He dropped down on the other side into a cramped, musty smelling space. Sticking the knife into his belt and pulling his shirt out of his jeans to cover it, he glanced around. In the gloom he could make out an old bath, a small sink and a toilet with no seat.

Avoiding the broken glass littering the floor, he limped towards the door and caught a movement in the mirror above the sink. His stomach clenched. It was several seconds before he realised he was looking at himself. The reflection staring back had the waxy pallor of a corpse and eyes that had sunken into deep purple pouches of flesh. His nose, split across the bridge was now puffed up like a prize-fighter's and a livid cut zigzagged down one cheek. Dismay overwhelmed him, although he could *almost* see the funny side. If Plan A failed, half-baked Plan B had been to seduce Ellen until her defences were down. A sinking certainty told him now that that particular plan was dead in the water, unless by some remote stroke of luck, she was into Halloween ghouls.

He opened the door as quietly as he could and stepped out into a small, dark hallway. From there he took a right into a room with a low beamed ceiling and an inglenook fireplace. The only light came from a candle on the dining table, its flame casting shadows on the rough, stone walls. Embers burned in the grate and the acrid smell of soot and wood smoke hung in the air. Reality struck. *She's here.* He stood utterly still, expectant while silence sifted down like a snowfall. Yes he could sense her somewhere in this chilly place, in this damp corner of the world where the calcium was licked from your bones.

He felt her before he heard her. Her breath warm on the back of his neck.

'*Steven.*'

He turned slowly.

She was smiling. It was almost a flirtatious smile and at odds with the unlit eyes and what she held in her hand.

His heart slowed to dull thuds. 'This is what we both want, right?' he managed hoarsely, 'you and me together finally.'

A sudden draft whipped the candle flame and it guttered momentarily then flared. In that shadowy room he saw her face darken.

'Steven. Your face!'

'Yeah. A prang in the car. Nothing serious.' He attempted a winning smile. 'I'm not happy you seeing me like this.'

Not that she looked too hot either in her layers of mismatched clothes and her hair hanging down in greasy clumps.

'Can I clean up a bit? Would that be okay?'

She stepped back. 'I think you know where the bathroom is.'

He ignored her knowing look, dismayed that she had already outsmarted him. *Did you really think she was stupid enough to turn around and lead you to the bathroom, Steve? Giving you the opportunity to ram your knife up to its hilt in that fleshy back?*

'Actually, there's no rush,' he said casually. 'I can wash later. Let's just enjoy being together again for the moment.'

Ellen smiled again and the smile frightened him more than the hammer she held because there was something very wrong about it.

'So,' he continued with strained cheeriness. 'Why don't we celebrate being together at last?'

She gave him a sly look. 'How?'

'Well ...let's see. We could have a drink? Bollocks. I'm an idiot, I should have brought champagne shouldn't I?' He took a couple of casual steps towards the stairs.

Why was he so quiet? Babies cry all the time - that's what Alison said.

'Where are you going?'

He turned back to her; saw an axe lying in the grate.

'I'm thirsty, Ellen. Anything will do. Tea, water. I don't mind. While you're getting it I'll just go up shall I, and –'

'No!'

Red sparks flashed in her eyes and he tried not to speculate whether it was a reflection from the dying firelight or something else entirely. 'Ellen, tell me - he's okay isn't he?'

She swung the hammer. 'How the fuck should I know?'

He took a few steps back. 'Don't get angry. I just need to check on him and then we can concentrate on...'

'NEED, NEED! WANT, WANT!' she screamed suddenly, spit bubbling at the corners of her mouth. 'It's all about ***you*** isn't it, Steven? You're just like Blanche. What ***I*** want counts for nothing. It never has.' She swung the hammer again.

His hands gripped the edge of the table behind him. 'Ellen, please stay calm. I've driven over six hours to see you, and here you are yelling at me already. Look, let's sit down, discuss the whole thing properly.'

With a nonchalance worthy of an Oscar he walked around the table and pulled out a chair. He bit his bottom lip to stop himself from crying out as he sat down and the knife handle dug sharply into his back, but none of that mattered. He was waiting - for the perfect moment. And when it came he would strike without mercy. Luke being alive or dead was now immaterial to that decision - he *was* going to *kill* the cunt. As soon as she sat down he would ram the knife through her throat. But first he needed to placate her.

She swung away from him and put a hand to her head. 'I should have put my foot down,' she spat out. Right at the outset. I should have told you what you could and could not do.' She paced to the fireplace and back again. Steven stared up at her face blotched with anger. Spreading his hands on the table he faked an expression of deep concern. 'I'm sorry Ellen. I truly am. I've let you down, no question. But I want you to forget about all that. I want you to forgive me so that I can make it up to you. I want us to have a future together, I really do.'

She stopped pacing and turned towards him. 'You're the *only* person I've ever wanted, do you know that, Steven? Or are you too thick to realise? *You are the only person in this whole shitty world that I ever wanted* for *mine.*'

She was shouting again. He struggled to find words that might diffuse her anger while keeping his eyes on the hammer hanging loosely in her grip, because he knew, it would take just one wrong word, one wrong move, for her to smash his skull like a melon. 'I feel that way too, Ellen. I wouldn't be here otherwise, would I?'

Her nostrils flared, detecting lies, the way forest animals scent fire. 'So why were you seeing all those other woman?'

'Which women? I swear to you I wasn't seeing anyone. I was waiting, for the right moment, Ellen. But things kept happening, getting in the way. Blanche died for one thing. And then ... well, I had some problems of my own, but it was always going to be you and me, Ellen, I swear to you.'

'*You're a liar*!' she shrieked, drawing something from her pocket and throwing it onto the table. It landed with a clunk.

He stared at it. The *Tag*. The one he had failed to find when he went back and discovered Georgia's body.

'I really can't believe a word you say, can I?' Her lips drew back into a sneer and raising the hammer she smashed it down on his hand. With a lightning reflex he had no idea he possessed, he snatched it away with barely a second to spare. The table took the brunt of the blow. The solid oak juddered and the candle, jolted out of its saucer, rolled across the table, casting crazy shadows on the wall.

He stared up at her. 'Ellen, are you breaking up with me already?' he croaked.

She glared at him through a tangle of hair. 'Go ahead, make as many stupid jokes as you like,' she dragged the hammer back.

He wanted to get to his feet but exhaustion and terror overwhelmed him. She leapt towards him. His body tensed, preparing for the second blow but this time she merely grabbed the candle and shoved it back in the saucer of melted wax.

'What are you getting from all this?' he asked, his tongue thick in his mouth.

She pushed the hair from her eyes. 'Haven't you worked that out yet? *You* begging *me*. That's what I'm getting from it. All those texts!' she sniggered. 'Oh, *please*, Ellen, *pretty* please, Ellen. Don't *hurt* him, I *beg* you.'

Steven's jaw worked. His voice cracked when he spoke. 'I understand why you hate me and I'm sorry for the hurt I've caused you. I'm sorry for the hurt the *world* has caused you, Ellen. But Christ, what harm has Luke ever done you?'

She rolled her eyes in a show of boredom and under the table, Steven's fists clenched. He longed to finish it now but she was too far away to use the knife. *Come closer you deranged fuck.*

'You just can't stand the fact he's loved, can you, Ellen?' he taunted. 'And that's why you hated Jimmy, isn't it? He was the favourite, he was the –

'*Liar*!' she screamed. '*I* was *Daddy's* favourite. *ME.*' She swung the hammer again. '*I* was the special one. That's what he always said when he took me out in the car.'

'It wasn't Jimmy's fault, Ellen,' he said quietly, 'he was just a little boy.'

Her lips drew back from her teeth. '*He spoilt it*!' she spat out. 'He wanted to come with us and he screamed and screamed until he got his way. And then because of Jimmy, *I* wasn't special anymore.'

'Of course you were, why wouldn't you have been?'

'*Because*,' she screamed, her eyes filling with quick, bright tears, '*that's* when he started giving Jimmy his special love too! *And what was so fucking special about it then, answer me that!*'

Steven stared up at her as awful clarity dawned. He saw the bald, hollow-cheeked old man in the photograph and his stomach gave a sickening lurch. 'So you drowned Jimmy in the pool,' he said softly. 'You pushed him under the water and held him there until he drowned.'

Ellen swiped at her nose with her sleeve and stared uneasily at the wall behind him. 'Who's been telling you these lies?'

'It doesn't matter now, it's all the past. But *Luke* is not Jimmy, Ellen. Please don't punish him too. Let me take him, I need –'

'*Sometimes,*' she yelled, *her eyes bulging with fury, 'I don't think you listen to a word I say. This is not about you or what you want at all. For once in my life it's about me! My needs. And what I need Steven, what I really need is to hurt you in the worst way possible, because you're a dirty liar, just like daddy was. So do you finally get it? You - you, thickshit!*

Dropping her head like a charging bull she came for him then, hammer raised, hair hanging in her eyes. He was up on his feet without being aware of it. Grabbing a chair with his left hand he swung it up in front of him. The first blow smashed both front legs, driving him back. Jolted from its saucer once more, the candle rolled and spluttered out.

In the sudden darkness he had just enough time to raise the chair again before the hammer smashed down on the seat, almost wrenching his shoulder from its socket. The chair slipped from his grasp, and she charged again, heavy breasts swinging.

He went for the knife pulling it free as an explosion of pain erupted in his left shoulder. There was a crunching of bone. He gave an agonised moan as she came at him once more, arm raised. Pulling himself up he lunged. Something warm and wet splashed onto his hand and with an, 'Ooof,' she fell heavily against him.

They stood for a moment like lovers, her head tucked neatly under his chin - except the feel of her meaty body made his flesh crawl and her filthy reek was almost worse than the excruciating pain in his shoulder.

Had he hurt her enough? Had the knife done enough damage through all that thick clothing?

With all the strength he had left, he pulled out the knife, now slick with blood and shoved her off him. She staggered, lost her footing and fell heavily against the brass fender of the fireplace.

'Ha! You crazy bitch,' he yelled and rushing at her, he grabbed her hair and yanked back her head with every intention of slitting her throat like a sacrificial animal. But then in his peripheral vision he just had time to glimpse the metal blade before it sliced through his left ear. He staggered back, felt blood spurting.

Ellen sprang to her feet and slammed the axe into the side of his head. He grunted, dropped the knife and fell to his knees.

Looming over him, breathing heavily, Ellen felt for the wound in her side. 'Were having so much fun aren't we,

Steven? Let's bring Lukey down! No reason he can't join the party too.' She flashed him a frightful smile and made for the stairs.

Stark terror ripped through him. In each second that passed he heard Luke's piercing scream in his head. Ellen clattered back downstairs clutching something wrapped in a blanket.

He tried to get to his feet, slipped in his own blood.

'Stay back!' she screamed.

And then his vision blurred and darkness overtook him.

HE CAME to with a jerk that made him hurt all over. Panic burst in his mind. *Where was she? Was she still in the room? Standing behind him with the axe poised, ready to split open his skull?*

But then he remembered in his last moments of consciousness he had heard the slam of the back door. She had gone. He thought he recalled something else too, a faint mewing sound coming from the blanket. Or had he imagined that?He prised dry lips apart. He had to get up; he had to go after her. He pushed himself to a sitting position and dizziness washed over him. He waited a moment for his vision to clear.

His ear. Why did it feel as though it were on fire? And then he remembered that too – she had cut it off. Most of it, anyway. He lifted his hand and tentatively touched the side of his head. His fingers came away coated in congealed blood. He glanced down, the front of his shirt was soaked with blood too, it felt stiff and cold against his skin. And then he saw the axe. It lay on the rug, gleaming in the moonlight. He moved towards it, sweat running down his face. Grabbing the handle, he used it like a crutch and pushed himself up onto his feet. Making it to the kitchen door, he staggered outside.

A light burned in the boathouse window. She had to be in there, there was nowhere else. He limped towards it. *You're too late, you're too late, she's killed him* a panicky voice screamed in his head. '*Shut the fuck up,*' he growled and head down, he pushed on into the wind, towards the sagging doors.

In the dim light of the overhead bulb he saw her. She was crouching in a corner behind an old motor boat. Her eyes glittered when she saw him.

'Stay just where you are,' she ordered.

The baby in her arms was silent. One limp arm hung down from the blanket.

He leant against the wall to stop his knees buckling. 'Ellen, give him to me. I swear I am going to rip your fucking head off if you don't.'

Ellen laughed. An arid sound, devoid of humanity. 'You can't have looked in the mirror lately.' Transferring Luke to one arm and keeping her eyes on Steven she leant over the boat and reached inside. When she straightened up, she was holding a can.

He edged towards her. '*Put him down*, you evil cunt,' he snarled.

She grinned, held up the can and shook it. He heard the swish of liquid inside and stopped. This is what she had been planning all along. An evil encore. With him in a front row seat.

'Put the axe on the floor, Steven.'

He dashed sweat and blood from his eyes. '*If* you hand him over.'

'I will - you can have him. *Once* you do as I say.'

Opening his hand he let the axe fall from his grasp.

'Now -step - back.'

He did as she said, and laying Luke on the cold concrete, Ellen darted forward and grabbed it. Then with a flourish, she lifted the can and doused the edges of Luke's blanket.

Steven smelt the petrol fumes. 'Ellen! For God's sake, don't!' he screamed. '*Hurt me,* not him.'

'But I *am* hurting you, Steven. And I'll keep hurting you until you know exactly how it feels to have your heart ripped out and trampled on!'

'You're fucking demented,' he screamed. 'You killed Caroline, you killed Georgia and you've destroyed me. Isn't that's enough?'

'Oh, boo hoo,' she stuck her bottom lip out in a parody of sadness. 'Poor you. You see, it *always* comes back to you, doesn't it? Because what's most important in the whole world? *Steven fucking Finn.*'

He moved towards her.

'Stay back!' she warned and then holding his eyes, she pulled a box of matches from her pocket and lit one. He had never realised what utter terror was until that moment. He could only scream; '*NO*!'

She savoured his reaction and then let the match fall. There was a sickly smell as the edges of Luke's blanket burst into flames and Steven saw Luke's little hand flinch. He lunged forward, just as a shadow darted from the rear of the building where coils of oily rope, outboard motors and other paraphernalia were heaped.

There was a chilling scream, and as Ellen swung around towards the sound she took the full force of a blow from the plank of wood Alison was wielding.

Ellen dropped to her knees. But the next moment she was scrabbling for Luke. Steven got there first, plucking him free from the blazing blanket. With the toe of his boot he flicked the burning material towards Ellen. It fell across her face and she howled pulling it away, but already her hair was alight and as she flailed at her head with her fists, her sleeves caught. There was a whooshing sound as her upper body burst into flames. High-pitched, feral screams pierced the night.

'Get some water!' Alison shrieked.

Steven, with Luke safely in his arms, was not about to run for water - or anything else. He had got to his son in time, although one of Luke's hands was red and the sleeve of his sweater singed. But much more worrying was that his eyes were closed and he wasn't moving at all. Steven frantically searched for a pulse. 'Leave her,' he shouted and pulling Alison towards him, he thrust Luke into her arms. 'Tell me he's okay,' he begged.

Alison cradled Luke while behind her; Ellen crawled in a circle, making low, guttural sounds. And then, somehow she got to her feet, and they both watched her, transfixed, as she marched stiff-legged from the boathouse, blazing arms outstretched heading towards the sea.

And she almost reached it, before collapsing and dragging her burning body the last few yards; until at the water's edge she finally stopped.

In the distance the sound of sirens filled the night. Steven's head jerked up from Luke.

'I called them,' Alison said.

He nodded. 'Why isn't he moving?' he asked, and passed out.

46

AT THREE THIRTY the following afternoon Luke Shaw's condition finally stabilised. It had not been the minor burns that had caused the medical staff most concern. Alison, recognising the symptoms of sedation, had ransacked the cottage to find whatever drugs Ellen had been giving him. Her search revealed a phial of Temazepam and some antihistamines had been stashed in a coffee jar. She handed them to the ambulance crew as soon as they arrived. An action that probably saved Luke's life. A toxicologist was standing by when they arrived at Carmarthen Hospital.

'She was playing Russian Roulette,' the doctor informed them. 'Sedating such a young child with powerful drugs like that, however small the quantity, was potentially lethal.'

'He will pull through, though?' Steven forced himself to ask.

The elderly doctor got to his feet. 'If he gets through tonight, he'll make it. He's a tough little chap.'

. . .

In the dimly lit children's unit, Alison watched the dawn break after her vigil. Luke had made it through the night and despite still being attached to wires and tubes, and despite the burns and severe dehydration, his condition was now stable.

Back in Steven's ward they celebrated with orange juice. 'You realise when this story breaks you'll be hounded by the media?' She grinned. 'Shame you're not so photogenic anymore,' she touched his bandaged ear, mindful of the stitches.

He hadn't thought about the press. He groaned, 'Christ. Not more hell.'

She took his hand. 'County Mayo is the greatest place to bring up kids, particularly on a farm. Dad really does need another man around the place. Maybe once you're fit and all?'

Steven thought it over. That sounded good to him. In fact it sounded just about perfect. There was just one point he needed to clarify, 'Will you be there too?'

For an answer she leant forward and kissed him gently. 'Okay, are you ready?' she asked.

'As I'll ever be.'

She went outside and walked down the long corridor to where Detective Chief Inspector Hopkins and Detective Sergeant Fraser sat waiting for their statements.

The two men got to their feet and followed Alison back down the corridor to Steven's room. Both officers had already made her a promise to withhold a certain piece of information and she would make damn sure they kept it. Both she and Steven knew that Ellen's body hadn't yet been found and assumed it had been dragged out to sea by the tide. What she learned later, while Steven was undergoing surgery on his ear, made that theory unlikely - because the tide was coming in at the time.

It was a piece of information Steven really didn't need right now – if ever.

ENDS

READ on for four complimentary chapters of Jeca's new novel, Little Lamb.

LITTLE LAMB

Prologue

THE EVENING SKY is streaked with violet and gold, the light breeze feeling soft on my

skin. A blackbird's song fills the air. I listen to the pure, tremulous notes, wondering how long I've been standing here – a bottle of Grey Goose in one hand, a Glock 17 in the other.

I don't believe in fate, so when my mobile vibrates in my pocket, just as my finger tightens on the trigger, I need to call it something else. Happenstance. That's as good a word as any.

1

Eight days later

I've been up two hours and it's barely dawn. Breakfast was three cups of Illy espresso. It sloshes around in my stomach, making me nauseous and jittery. Gripping the sides of the basin I stare back at the face in the mirror, a face that looks five years older than I remember.

My hand shakes as I dab concealer on the dark shadows under my eyes. The booze is to blame. Well, the cutting it out to be precise. Deprived of its anaesthetising qualities, I've hardly slept in days. There's a fading bruise on my forehead and it's worrying I can't remember how I got it. But then I can't remember a lot of things, which is the whole point of drinking, isn't it?

With nothing to disguise the hollow scoops at the base of my throat or the jutting cheek bones, I pull on the linen shirt I've so painstakingly ironed. A snug fit once, it now hangs loosely off my frame, swamping me. I button it up. No time to iron another.

Car fob in hand, I open the front door, and shaking, step outside.

The route to Jubilee House is traffic-choked. Fumes already clogging the early morning air. I snap off the Aircon, a sense of dread building inside me.

What the hell was I thinking when I took that call. What possessed me to say *yes?* I wasn't thinking straight. I was pissed, for Christ sake.

On the end of the phone was my boss, DI Patrick Haynes. What was on offer was the kind of career-changing case most detectives only dream about and despite the best part of a bottle of vodka sweating through my pores, I jumped at a lifeline thrown my way.

'See you Monday,' DI Patrick Haynes said finishing up, and I was astounded to hear myself say, 'yes', he would. Then I'd run to the bathroom and thrown up in the sink. Sobered up, doubt consumed me. Who was I kidding? I was nowhere near ready to return to the job. And particularly not ready to take over a case of this magnitude. Nausea crawled the walls of my stomach for days. Countless times I grabbed my phone to ring Patrick, reject his offer. Yet the gut twisting thought of disappointing the one person who still believed in me, when I no longer believed in myself, stopped me every time.

The car crawls forward. I glance in the mirror, practise lifting the corners of my mouth. *Hi! Great to see you all!*

Great to be back.

Everything's good.

All better folks.

But by the time I pull into the staff parking bay and get out of the car, dread grips my insides and won't let go.

All better, folks, I laugh. *Bullshit.* That bitter taste in my mouth is the acid tang of fear. Passing through the familiar sliding doors I cross the threshold, biting my bottom lip so hard it feels like it's going to split.

In the lift, I'm braced rigid on the balls of my feet. Snatching in air I scrabble in my bag and pull out a blister of blue pills. I dry swallow two. That I can convince my colleagues I'm up to this with a fake smile and forced pleasantries seems ludicrous now. The lift jolts to a halt. My pulse throbs in my throat. Wiping sweating palms on my trousers, I step out onto the second floor.

2

My old desk is situated in a coveted spot beneath a high window. That no one has dared steal it allows me a small sense of satisfaction. I slip into my seat, grateful there's no welcoming committee. My team feels awkward, not knowing how best to handle the situation; kid gloves or a breezy pretence nothing has happened.

Glancing up at the framed slice of blue untroubled sky, I make a conscious effort to slow my breathing, grateful my back is to the rest of the room. Waiting for my prehistoric Dell to fire up, I'm only too aware of the hushed conversations going on around me.

DC Sean Snowdon, all pink cheeks and cow eyes, makes a point of stopping by. 'How's it going?' he asks quietly, his concerned frown at odds with the sugar glistening on his top lip and the dab of jam at the corner of his mouth.

'Good!' I say brightly, as my stomach gives a queasy roll. I point my pen at his doughnut. 'You're a walking cliché, Sean.'

'I know.' He grins, licks his fingers. 'Tea?'

Grey Goose over ice is really what I crave but I smile, say; 'tea would be great.'

'Milk. No sugar?'

I nod. 'Nothing's changed.'

Nothing. When I arrived this morning, the 'Make My Day' Dirty Harry mug was already sitting on my desk waiting to greet me. *Fraser*. The little shit. No wonder he's keeping his distance.

'That'll take some wading through,' Sean nods at the three-inch thick file in front of me. 'Patrick given you any help?'

'Dick Dwyer and Dick Henderson,' I reply in a low voice. The Two Dicks. Inseparable jobsworths a year from retirement.

'Those donkeys!' Sean exclaims, rocking back on his size thirteen's.

Heads turn in our direction. Marvellous. Now everyone knows who's assisting me on the case. 'Sean, I'm grateful for anyone. Not that I'm in a position to issue any actions yet. Not until I know exactly where I am with it all.'

Sean's six-foot four frame leans over me blocking light as he studies the images spread out on my desk. 'Poor little kid,' he mutters. 'Listen, we're quiet. I'll give you some hours if you need them.' I look up at him. The pink in his cheeks deepens. 'I mean when you're ready,' he mutters and goes to make the tea.

A black cloud hovers. The presence of Detective Inspector Pullman. Cylindrical in shape, he's buzzing listlessly around the office like a sated blowfly. Pudgy hands paste remaining strands of hair to his scalp as he orbits my desk, and then homes in.

I slide a folder over the photographs.

'*Harriet!* Welcome back!'

His belly is almost in my face, but I manage to slap on a smile for our Family Liaison Co-ordinator. 'Hello Clive.' He fakes a preference for informality by insisting we ditch the 'Sir'.

'I'd heard a whisper!' he proclaims, sucking on a sweet, 'but wasn't told exactly when you'd be returning to the fold.'

'Yep,' I reply brightly, dodging the butterscotch breath. 'Seems like I've surprised quite a few people.'

'Excellent!' Cold case I hear. Interesting.' His eyes scrutinise me. They crawl over my face and hair and settle in the V of my shirt. He creeps me out. *Go away*.

'Let me know if there is anything you need and I'll deal with it personally. You only have to ask.' His palm rests lightly on my shoulder. I feel its moistness through my shirt.

The phone on my desk rings. I snatch it up, for once not caring who's on the other end. I give Clive a pointed look. 'Excuse me.'

'Of course,' he drifts away, giving me a sly backward glance.

It's Patrick. Making the briefest of courtesy calls, checking that I'm at my desk and settling in.

'I just want to quickly reiterate what I touched upon before,' he announces in his rapid-fire way. This is the ten-year anniversary review of the Angel Sorenson Case. It needs a fresh critical eye from someone I can trust to be thorough. But it's a sensitive one due to past publicity and requires the right pair of hands.'

It's a confidence boosting call, I realise, grateful he's taken the time.

'You'll need a fresh strategy,' he races on, 'but begin by forensically reading the investigation as it was left. With any luck new lines of enquiry will surface.'

I'm about to reply, to thank him and make reassuring sounds that I'm up to the job. But as I fumble for the words, pffft - he's gone - and then the panic comes from nowhere, volting through me so fast it makes me dizzy. My throat feels as though it's closing up, my forehead is slick with sweat. It's not just the overwhelming sense of starting at the bottom again, with everything yet to prove, but also the enormity of what I've taken on, *and* being uncomfortably aware that letting down both Patrick and the Sorenson family I have yet to meet, is not an option.

I try to focus on the photographs again. One in particular. A morgue shot of a small head raised on a polypropylene block. I absorb the cascading blonde hair, pillow lips and stare into eyes as blue and empty as the sky beyond my window. A livid ligature mark dissects the neck, violating creamy skin.

Angel Sorenson. Five years old.

Separating crime scene photographs from the rest of the pile, I sift through them. A few are of Angel's bedroom, and the window through which the killer may have entered. Others are of Angel's body as it was found. In bed, tucked up, as though sleeping, in the one place in the world she should have been safe.

I scan the autopsy report, scrub a hand over my face. Clear my throat.

A cup of tea appears at my side. Sean goes quietly away.

I move on to photos depicting Angel in life. Professional shots of a painted, sexualised baby. It's hard to comprehend the false eyelashes, spray tan and candy pink lip gloss. Or parents who would exploit their child in this way and turn them into a performing pet.

Dubbed 'The Baby Beauty Queen Murder' the case inevitably drew comparisons with JonBenét Ramsey's case. Both little girls were pageant pros, primped and prancing their way through competitions with nauseating names like Little Miss Sparkle. Both ended up being murdered in their own homes.

I open the file and begin to familiarise myself with the

facts surrounding a case the TPHQ at Earls Court have decided to reopen. Usually, it coincides with an anniversary. It was ten years ago, that Angel Sorenson was found murdered in her bed. As soon as this story hit the headlines a feeding frenzy broke out in the press. Tailor-made for tabloid exploitation it titillated with all the right elements, set as it was in one of Surrey's most exclusive environs. For months every newspaper was saturated with images of the photogenic Angel. But despite an eighteen-month investigation, the largest Surrey Police had ever undertaken, her killer is still free. A month ago, restricted by tight budgets and lack of manpower, Surrey was only too pleased to cede to the Met ownership of a cold case without a case solid suspect.

Logging into the system, I pull up Angel's full pathologist's report. In a sexually motivated murder of this type, the investigation starts close to home, with all male family members under immediate scrutiny. Should autopsy reports reveal signs of historic or chronic sexual abuse, that's where suspicion remains, but in this instance, injuries inflicted upon on Angel during the attack were so severe, previous molestation could neither be established nor ruled out.

I turn back to the summary of the case and continue reading, zoning out the ringing phones and buzz of office activity.

Paul Sorenson, Angel's father, and her fifteen-year-old brother, Max, were eliminated from the investigation almost immediately. Paul Sorenson could prove he was flying back from Amsterdam on a first-class Lufthansa ticket the night of her death and Dulwich College verified Max was sleeping in his dorm. That both sets of grandparents had died long before Angel was born meant another dead end.

Allegra, Angel's thirteen-year-old sister, was also not at home that night, having stayed at a friend's house, which meant the only family member present on the night Angel was killed, was her mother, Susan Sorenson.

Surrey's Detective Superintendent Savage then focused his team's attention on forty-year-old surgeon Gary, Paul Sorenson's younger brother. Gary Sorenson was a frequent visitor to the house and Savage flagged the high number of attendances he'd made at Angel's pageants. Later, under threat of arrest, Gary reluctantly produced an air-tight alibi for that night, admitting he'd spent it at iCandy, a Gentleman's club in Staines where he purchased the services of twenty-two-year old lap dancer, Lila Sheik, for the night. Cell site analysis, credit card receipts and eventually Lila, confirmed Gary's story and cleared him, but I'll need to talk to him anyway. If anyone knew the dynamics of the Sorenson household at that time it would be him.

Of the six hundred and fifty plus people interviewed over the course of the investigation, only one person of interest remained. Peter Grimes. A known paedophile, who shortly before Angel's death, had been working at a property just a few private roads away from the Sorenson's home on the exclusive Wentworth estate.

Grimes's history makes chilling reading. In 1991, while working as a gardener at a boy's school in Leeds, he snatched an eight-year-old pupil and subjected him to a brutal assault. Arrested and convicted, Grimes spent the next eight years in Wakefield prison. Monster Mansion as it's fondly known, houses Britain's most dangerous high-risk sex offenders. On release he settled in Surrey, a verdant county where he could exploit the gardening skills picked up in prison. Due to his predilection for children and knowledge of the Wentworth area, Grimes was taken into custody and questioned at Staines police station. While being held, his rented room was searched and officers left with three computers containing over 2,000 indecent images of pre-teen boys.

But, for the evening in question, Grimes had an established alibi. CCTV footage confirmed his attendance at a bare-knuckle fight at the rear of the Black Horse Inn in Wraysbury until the fight finished around ten. Grimes's claim that he'd gone home straight afterwards was backed up by his landlady. Esther Bell verified she had heard him come in some time after ten thirty. Eliminated as a suspect for the Sorenson murder, Grimes was sent back to Wakefield for possession of child porn.

One month into his new sentence, Grimes attacked his cell mate, a lifer called Kenneth Dwyer. After gouging out Dwyer's eyes, he chewed his genitals to mush, decapitated him and stuffed his head into a toilet bowl.

When asked to explain his motive for attacking Dwyer, Grimes's recorded response had been; *'I decided to live a little.'*

A diagnosis report from a team of psychiatrists followed, resulting in an immediate transfer to Peak Hill, a high security psychiatric hospital for the criminally insane, where he will remain for the rest of his life.

Curiosity spiked; I slide the DVD footage of Grimes's interview at Staines Police Station into my computer. Fast forwarding the introductions of the officers' present, I stab 'play' as soon as a man with a shaven bullet head, sunken into powerful shoulders, appears. His eyes above a hooked, raptor-like nose are large, and luminous and so intense that when he angles his head and stares directly into the camera, I recoil in an involuntary spasm. The voice is harsh and raspy, a slight asthmatic whine accompanying each out breath. Barely concealing an amused contempt, he offers, 'Yes, Miss, No Miss,' answers to the female DS, even when she applies pressure. But at the end of the interview, when he looks into the camera again, the jovial mask has slipped and it's like glimpsing something prehensile and rapacious sliding beneath murky water.

Yanking off my earbuds, I rake through my hair, nerves crackling. That I don't relish meeting in the flesh someone capable of radiating such evil energy on screen, is an understatement, but Grimes is at the top of the list of people I need to speak to. Alibi or no alibi, the fact he was working close to Angel's home two months before her death is a huge red flag. To get things moving in what could prove to be a lengthy process, I pick up the phone and ring Peak Hill.

My first day back slides past without my noticing and without my hand straying to the diazepam. I'm proud of my small achievement. Locking Angel's files in my drawer, I shove my chair back from my desk and stand up. I do it too quickly and for a moment my head spins. Four pairs of eyes settle on me. One pair, DS Nick Fraser's are lit with amusement. 'Low sugar levels,' I mutter.

Chahna peers at me from beneath her glossy fringe. 'We're all knocking off shortly. Fancy joining us at the Blue Bar for a couple?'

Chahna is new to the team. She's a loud, pretty overweight girl, but from what I've heard, she's good at her job. As a Family Liaison Officer or FLO, she works directly under Pullman, so I can't help but feel sorry for her and her invitation seems genuine enough.

'I'd love to,' I say, 'but maybe another night?'

'Cool,' she says quickly. 'No problem.'

DS Nick Fraser's head jerks up, a sneer flickering across his top lip like an electric current. 'Thought you were laying off the beers?' he throws at her. 'Fucking need to. Any fatter and you'll need harpooning.'

Wow. *Nasty*. Even for Fraser. A shocked silence is followed by a reproving chorus of; 'Sarge!'

Chahna's cheeks flame. She ducks her head and resumes typing at blurry speed. I'm mortified for her. Particularly as I suspect it's my return to duties that's sparked Fraser's spite, triggering all the other irrational, petty issues he has with me. Normally I'd ignore his hostility, but this time it's directed at a lower ranking officer who can't fight back. 'That's low, even for an arsehole like you,' I growl.

Fraser juts his bottom lip. A parody of boo hoo.

'It was a joke, Harry. Lost our sense of humour, have we? I'm just gutted you're not up for a few pints.' He looks pointedly at his watch. 'From what I've heard you must be gagging for one by now.'

The room falls silent. I swallow, glance around at the faces looking up at me, realise, they all know. My face burns. I can't trust myself to speak. *What is there to say anyway?* Throwing Fraser a disgusted look I head for the door.

'Oh, crack a smile, Sarge,' he calls, playing to the room.

I give him the finger behind my back, and he laughs.

'*Harry*. You know you love me really.'

3

ON THE SERVICE stairs I grab the handrail and deep breathe. I've managed to get through my first day. I've also managed to resist an invitation to the pub I and I won't allow Fraser to derail me. I ought to feel like celebrating - but I don't. What I really feel I need to do, is to go home, and sit, in the quiet and the dark.

Ignoring the lift, I'm about to take the stairs when I hear the tattoo of high heels purposefully heading my way and a voice I loathe call, 'Harriet!'

Christ. I can't do this now. Blood pounds in my head. Steel banisters dig into my back.

'Such a co-incidence we should bump into each other on your first day back!' It's Chief Superintendent Ingrid Price, head of DPS, the directorate responsible for investigating internal misconduct and fucked up Met investigations. During the Christopher Marshall review she'd tried her hardest to end my career.

Her eyes sweep over me now, assessing the damage. *Am I coping - or about to fall apart?*

'*Look... Harriet,* Matt and I... well we're sorry for what has happened. Hardly .what either of us had anticipated.' She tucks caramel strands of hair behind her ear. 'Life has a way of throwing some very odd curveballs at times, but as our paths will continue to cross, it's probably a good thing we're getting the chance to clear the air now. Sooner rather than later.'

The lift doors ping behind us and two uniformed officers step out and glance our way. Price pulls me into the shadows of the stairwell. 'That's not to say it won't be difficult, or awkward at times. But I'm hoping we can avoid allowing our personal lives to spill over into our working relationship. Prevent us from behaving professionally. Don't you agree?'

She then follows up this little speech with something outrageous given the circumstances - she gives my arm a little squeeze.

'But it's got to stop, Harriet,' the squeeze tightens. 'All the calls. He's tired of it. Tired of you and the nocturnal drunk dialling. Get a grip, *please*.'

I glance down at her hand and for some reason the manicured perfection of her nails ignites a terrible rage deep inside me. 'It's impressive, I'll give you that,' I spit out, 'the way you manage to fit it all in. The high-pressured job and killer hours, endless salon appointments and all the sweaty hours spent in the gym, desperate to defy gravity, keep everything where it should be. No mean feat at your age. Yet, miraculously, on top of all that, you still found the energy to steal my husband.'

Price looks at me unsparingly and her voice takes on an edge. 'I've apologised. It's your prerogative to accept it or not.'

'Well, I don't,' I say, moving closer, 'and I never will. So, off the record Ma'am and with all due respect – keep the fuck out of my face!'

4

DISTINCTIVE. He recognises it immediately. Metallic green with purple longitudinal stripes down the wing casing. Chrysolina Americana, or Rosemary beetle to give it its common name.

Plucking the beetle from the tip of a blackened shoot he squashes it, wipes his fingers on his dungarees and then checks the rest of the lavender thoroughly (these pests do not confine their devastation exclusively to rosemary) in case it's brought some friends.

The sun beats down on his shaved head, warming pale skin. He scans the sloping lawns where sprinkler droplets sparkle in the grass like jewels. Leaning on the hoe, he lifts his head and breathes the air; lavender mingled with the heady perfume of a Gertrude Jekyll. Gently, he lifts a bloom as though it were the head of a shy child.

'Peter?'

He turns. Staff Nurse Sykes is standing in the long shadow of the greenhouse tapping his watch 'Doc Heun's office, Pete. He's waiting.'

. . .

I've set off for Peak Hill High Security Hospital on what is the hottest day of the year so far. The sun's glare sears my eyeballs and I pull on a pair of Ray-bans that are wedged in the car door's side pocket. Matt's, I realise, when they slide down my nose.

Richmond town centre pulses with young girls showing yards of tanned limbs. By comparison, I feel like some sickly white grub, squirming at the sudden exposure to light. An image of Ingrid Price, sleek and gym honed flashes through my mind. Working out who Fraser's snitch was didn't take long. Even drunk, I could sense her malevolent presence in the background whenever I rang Matt. Not that his guarded tone wasn't enough of a pathetic give-away.

Gripping the wheel, I force myself to bury these thoughts and focus on the man I'm about to meet.

It took Dr Heun, Grimes's psychiatrist, nine days to make a decision about my visit. A period that gave me time to familiarise myself with the case, wade through the majority of statements and locate as many witnesses as possible. A monumental task after a lapse of ten years that saw me working late into the night.

Requesting a visit rather than an interview was less likely to meet with a rejection and as Grimes was discounted as a suspect, I hadn't much choice. But there is something in a witness statement made by Grimes's landlady that I keep returning to. She claimed that she *heard* Grimes return home on the night Angel Sorenson was murdered, not that *she* saw him. It's a point I need to clarify with her.

The whine of the air-con begins to grate. Switching it off I lower my window. The air that streams through is thick and heavy.

Last night, I Googled the 'hospital' I'm about to visit and read up on its history. A grainy photograph, circa 1934, showed a sinister-looking red brick pile. Built in 1888, Peak

Hill's original purpose was, it stated, 'for the incarceration of lunatic paupers. No calling a spade, 'an implement devised for the purpose of digging,' back then. Political correctness these days mean these holding pens for the dangerously deranged are categorised as hospitals, and to further protect the resident's sensibilities, they're referred to as 'patients' rather than prisoners. No doubt it's only a matter of time before they become 'Clients,' or even God forbid, 'Service Users'.

Taking a swig of water, I nudge over into the slow lane where the tarred seams beneath my wheels create a regular rhythm. Once I leave the M25 I'm in deep countryside, negotiating narrow country lanes where the hedgerows are blowsy with wilting cow parsley. Half an hour later a heron flaps across my path, trailing skeletal legs and through the trees I glimpse Peak Hill's infamous tower. Set high upon a clearing it dominates the hazy skyline. A siren replaced its bell in 1998 but the obsolete tower remains, now serving as a distinctive landmark.

I take a blind bend and then the road settles on the straight and begins a gentle climb. Before long the whole of Peak Hill comes into view, looking just as forbidding as it did in the old online photograph. These days the hospital boasts an enlightened stance on rehabilitation. Most of its two hundred and eighty patients, the ones that can be trusted with sharp implements that is, take an active part in the running of the place, working in the kitchens, the laundry and the library.

Two years ago, a new and highly advanced unit was opened to treat the twenty or so patients with Severe Antisocial Personality Disorders - and that's where I'm heading now.

A sign announces I'm approaching a High Security Hospital, upon which is sprayed: 'WARNING: Contains Nuts.'

I crack a smile and some of the tension drains away. Mentally I'm as prepared as I can be for meeting a classified insane individual whose behaviour can only be controlled by anti-psychotic drugs.

A bank of dark cloud building in the west tells me we're in for a storm. Unpeeling my shirt from the back of my seat I keep going until I reach closed gates. Getting out of the car and above a rumble of thunder, I speak into an intercom, announce my name and the purpose of my visit. By the time I get back into the car the gates are already swinging open.

Approach to the hospital is via a long tarmacadam drive, skirted either side by horse chestnuts. Eventually this widens and I enter a walled parameter with neat lawns. I'd been expecting razor wire and visible security devices, but this could be the entrance to some exclusive golf club.

Passing an empty gate lodge, I drive between two stone pillars into a cobbled courtyard and slant park in a space marked for visitors. The main building looms over me now like some huge, red-faced bully but, thankfully, it's the newer administrative block I need.

Heat engulfs me once I step out of the car and consult a multi-armed signpost. Directed to a path that that runs alongside the main building, I follow it with the sun hot and heavy on the back of my neck.

LORRAINE DOWNS, Executive Director of High Secure Services, is waiting for me in Reception. She's in her mid-forties and tall. Taller than me. Five eleven I would guess. Her cheekbones are razor sharp and she has prematurely white hair worn sleek and poker straight. Wearing a severe tailored suit, her only nod to femininity is the floaty scarf draped around her neck. Introducing herself in a two-pack-a day rasp, she shakes my hand then checks my warrant card and day pass. I hand her my business card and she glances at it before slipping it into her pocket. Close up I can just make out the tiny white skull motifs on her scarf. The whimsical accessory seems at odds with her grim persona. Handing back my pass she waves me towards a desk. A staff member in a blue uniform comes from behind it and hands me a tray. I place my watch, mobile phone and car key fob into it then allow my fingerprints to be taken. Afterwards Lorraine asks me to pass through an arched scanner, the kind you get in airports Once through, I'm handed a lanyard.

'Keep it on at all times. Right up until you leave the grounds,' she instructs, 'don't want to get mistaken for an escapee, do we?' I smile on cue and follow her down a brightly lit corridor with colourful abstracts on the walls. I'm a fast walker, but Lorraine is faster, like one of those high stepping horses they use in harness racing. I struggle to keep up. When we reach a set of internal doors, she swipes her badge over an electronic eye.

'These doors are something, aren't they?' she says almost lovingly. 'Seven inches thick, magnetic locks that only the staff can operate. It's rarely ever happened, but if despite our best efforts, a key does go missing, every lock in the entire place has to be changed.' Lorraine snaps her head round to look at me. 'Take a little guess how much that costs the taxpayer?'

'I couldn't.'

'Two and a half million,'

'Wow,' I say, to provide the reaction she's hoping for.

A puff from the air lock, the doors slide open and we're off again. 'Must be extremely challenging working here. Do you enjoy it?' I ask, keeping her on side.

'No Silence of the Lambs jokes? That's what I usually get.'

I shoot her a sideways glance, surprised anyone would crack a joke in her presence. High stepping on she leads me through a gloomy labyrinth of corridors. We must now be moving through an old part of the building. Here the linoleum is cracked and worn, ammonia hangs in the air.

We reach suddenly what appears to be a recreation centre and I tense, but the patients seem peaceful enough, engrossed in jigsaw puzzles or some other gentle activity A few huddle in corners, staring at nothing. We carry on, passing a nursing station and continue through a small glass atrium that links us to the modern block. Patrolling male nurses tell me I've reached my destination, the Severe Personality Disorder Unit.

Lorraine introduces me to the waiting staff members with a small wave of a large, bony hand. 'Nurse Jennings and Nurse Campbell. They will be sitting in with you.'

They nod in unison. Two bulky, tightly muscled guys, the type you'd find on any nightclub door. I'd been warned I'd be chaperoned, and I'd been both irritated and relieved.

Lorraine checks her large steel-faced watch. 'Right, I've got to scoot but I have to warn you, should Peter at any time become upset or disturbed during this visit it will be terminated. You do understand?'

'Of course.' *Heaven forbid the sensibilities of a sick bastard like Grimes should be upset.*

She nods, 'Good.' Then with a slightly unpleasant smile, she's off, cantering back the way we'd come.

'Follow me,' Jennings says.

We turn off into a side corridor and reach a set of double doors. Campbell has gone ahead of us. I hear an electronic buzz and the sound of doors clicking open. Both men stand back, allowing me to enter a medium sized room with a painted concrete floor and bolted down tables and chairs.

Jennings indicates a table nearest the barred window. As I take a seat, they take up their own positions on a moulded bench at the front of the room. Jennings folds arms as thick as railway sleepers. Campbell eases his mobile out of his pocket and taps at the screen.

I glance around while we wait. Note the recessed camera mounted in the ceiling above the door. 'Does Peter get visitors?' I ask.

They look at each other. 'No,' Campbell decides to reply.

'Guess that's hard for some patients?'

Campbell nods. 'It's really hard for someone who loves attention as much as Pete.'

Which probably explains why Grimes agreed to my visit. What about phone calls? I'm about to ask, but don't get the chance, because at that moment the door opens and Grimes walks in.

He doesn't acknowledge my presence; his eyes are on Jennings and Campbell. He's dressed in a dark blue strong suit. It looks like any other overall, but the difference is, it's made from untearable material. No zips. No drawstrings. Nothing that could be fashioned into a weapon.

'Sit here, shall I boys?' he asks benignly enough, indicating the chair opposite me.

Jennings nods. 'Now, be nice, Pete,' he warns.

Grimes sits down and the table shakes. The air crackles around him. He isn't a tall man, five nine at most, but his presence fills the room. Suddenly, I feel reluctant to meet those hypnotic eyes captured in his photograph. He places unfettered hands on the table. They are broad, fingers thick and stubby. The room is silent, apart from the sound of his breathing. The asthmatic rasp I remember from the tape accompanies each out-breath. He waits. A man with all the time in the world

'This is an unofficial visit, Peter,' I state, my tone as friendly as I can muster. He nods, his face impassive and at odds with the hooded intensity of his eyes.

'I'm just going to cover old ground. Try to clarify a few things.'

He leans forward a little and I smell him. Oily skin combined with the sharp smell of cut grass.

'Nice of you, to come all this way... just for a chat,' he says cheerfully enough. His doughy skin has the pallor of the long-term incarcerated and his lips, with their pronounced cupid's bow, are soft and moist. He holds my gaze, his expression inscrutable.

I take a tape recorder out of my pocket and place it on the table between us. He rests his cheek in his hand without comment.

Pressing the 'record' 'button I explain why I've requested this visit. 'We've been given funds to revisit a ten-year-old murder case, that of Angel Sorenson. You were interviewed during the course of the original investigation.'

His stare is unwavering.

'The case has never been solved and the family have never had the closure they deserve.' I listen to myself and feel ridiculous. I'm talking to someone who rapes little boys. Someone who cut off the head of a cell mate with a broken CD case because he had a stutter that Grimes claimed; 'Got right on my tits.'

I push across the table the only other item I was allowed to bring in with me, a transparent folder containing a photograph. 'This is Angel Sorenson.'

He grins at me without glancing at the photo and I glimpse teeth that are small and surprisingly inoffensive-looking. Except for the chipped eye-tooth with its jagged point. In hideous clarity I see Grimes lifting his head from Kenneth Dwyer's genitals, blood dripping from that tooth.

He slides the photograph back. 'You're barking up the wrong lamppost. I like boys, remember?'

I nod. 'That's what you stated when you were interviewed

shortly after Angel was murdered. Can you remember what you told the police you were doing the evening of the first of July, two thousand and nine?'

He frowns, lays a thick, dirt engrained forefinger on his chin and stares up at the ceiling, pantomiming that he's thinking hard. 'First of July, two thousand and nine...' he repeats slowly. 'Let's see. Oh, yeah, that was the night I was cross-cataloguing my porn collection.'

I give him a level look. 'That's not what you told the police at the time, is it?'

He lifts a shoulder.

'You stated that you'd been to watch a fight. Arrived home after eleven and didn't leave the house thereafter.'

He sighs, leans back in his chair, feigning he's already bored with me and this conversation. His shaven head glistens under the strip lighting while he play-acts. I hear one of the guards' yawn and the sound of a phone on vibrate.

'Come on, Peter,' I coax. 'Help me out and we can move on.'

He opens his arms in theatrical appeal. 'This isn't a formal interview? It's beginning to fucking feel like one.'

'All I need you to do is confirm everything contained in your original statement. If there's anything you didn't mention at the time, I'm giving you the chance now. I'm just trying to clear a path so I can focus on other leads.'

He frowns, stares through the barred window. 'Focus away. I got nothin' to add.'

'Okay,' I say after a moment, 'let me put something to you which if you give me an honest answer, will not, I promise, incriminate you in any way. Accepting that you weren't involved, I think it's possible you may know who was. So, okay, Angel wasn't to your taste, but you were working in that area close to the time she was killed and it's feasible you saw her at some point. Knowing a lot more now than we did ten years ago about how paedophiles operate, I believe it's possible you tipped off another paedophile, one you knew who would regard Angel as their textbook fantasy.'

Grimes looks at me, unmoved.

'Any cooperation would go down on your records, that must be good for something.'

He grins and I really wish he wouldn't. A glimpse of those teeth and I'm reminded of Dwyer again.

'Yeah,' he replies. 'Big whoop. Two scoops of ice cream instead of one.' He swivels round to face Jennings and Campbell. 'Not that I'm complaining, lads.' He turns back to me, 'it don't do to complain in a place like this place, Harry... that's what they call you, isn't it? *Dirty Harry?*'

The breath leaves my lungs in a whoop as though he's just stamped on them.

'Oh, I still get to have a little fun on the outside, Harry Vaughn,' he whispers, eyes twinkling with malevolence. 'Right old balls up, weren't it? DPS worse than useless. Negotiators drowned out by the fucking helicopter. Gold and Silver Command having some kind of dick swinging contest. You shouldn't go blaming yourself, Harry. All them tactical errors. Radio's down. All you had was visuals on a kid gone ruthless, firing at fuckers in the street and then about to have a go at Old Bill. 'Course that changes everything don't it? When it's one of your own. Some schizoid Muppet off his head on Kestrel and Special K? Ain't gonna end well is it. And Harry, you made fucking sure of that, didn't you?' He nods at the photograph of Angel and leans back. 'I blame the parents. Dress your kid up like a tart, what you expect?'

'You state you prefer boys,' I say, my voice shaking. 'Does it really matter what gender they are if your preference is to sodomise them? Angel Sorenson was sodomised.'

Grimes's eyes narrow, then he laughs, it's a short bark, totally devoid of humour. 'Oooh!' he says archly and swivels round to appeal to his audience who are now watching us closely. 'And you warned *me* to play nice.' He turns back. 'Listen,' he says, lowering his voice again, 'I know all about you and your shitty career to date, Harry, and it has been shitty, ain't it? But here's a friendly warning. Ambition ain't your friend. Keep this review on the down low, if you don't, you'll be wishing like fuck you had.'

'If you had nothing to do with the case, why the need to threaten me?'

He leans back in his chair. The luminosity has gone from his eyes now, they're dark and impenetrable. 'You're not what I was expecting.'

'Whereas you're *everything* I was, but with bells on.'

Grimes snickers, his hands grip the arms of his chair, and I can only guess at how much he'd prefer them to be around my throat. I stare at the sick deformity for a moment, then ask; 'Out of interest, what were your parents like? Your mother had a sense of humour at least... naming you after an opera.'

He stiffens and fixes me with sudden burning intensity. Can evil actually radiate off a person? I'm three quarters of the way to believing it can and have to shove my hands between my knees to stop them trembling.

'You think you understand me?' he demands.

'Not by a long shot.'

'You think you can manipulate me?'

'Far as I'm concerned, we're just having a conversation.'

'My mother was a beauty. Beautiful inside too. A beautiful person.'

'Does she visit?'

He gets to his feet. 'Haven't seen the cunt in years.' He turns to Campbell and Jennings. 'We're done here.'

. . .

The storm has finally broken. I shelter from hard, vertical rain beneath a dripping chestnut. My name is Harriet. To family and friends, I'm Hals. Or Harry. But it's only amongst work colleagues I'm known as Dirty Harry. A sobriquet earned after my stint as a firearms officer. More specifically, earned after the death of Christopher Marshall. That Grimes should possess in-depth knowledge of the case is worrying enough, even though the case was widely reported in the press at the time, but this, this is something else. Only someone in the know, only someone with links to my murder team could have provided him with that nugget of information.

Oh, I still get to have a little fun on the outside, Harry.

His words resonate in my head as branches thrash above my head and I stare up at the hulking pile that is Peak Hill.

ABOUT THE AUTHOR

Jeca Campion is an author of more than forty published short stories. ELLEN is her first novel. LITTLE LAMB, her second novel, is a police procedural featuring Met Detective Harriet 'Harry' Vaughn. She is currently working on the second in this series while outlining a stand alone novel featuring a psychic detective set in rural South Wales.

Jeca lives in Wiltshire with her criminal lawyer husband, also a writer, and a rescue Birman called Jasper.

If you enjoyed ELLEN it would be greatly appreciated if you could leave a review on Amazon. The link to Amazon is https://read.amazon.co.uk/kp/embed?asin=B09J3V2P8K&preview=newtab&linkCode=kpe&ref_=cm_sw_r_kb_dp_KBF6N90RZ0M2S68S56TR

I'd be pleased to hear from you on jennifercampion@gmail.com

Join my mailing list and I'll let you know when my next books are going to be published.

ALSO BY JECA CAMPION

Little Lamb - to be published in January 2022

Last Laugh - to be published mid 2022